# CHAPTER WAR

THROWN DOWN FROM the Emperor's grace long ago, the Soul Drinkers Chapter, at the behest of their leader Sarpedon, is in search of redemption. Their quest takes them to Vanqualis, an Imperial planet that has been invaded by orks. Desperate to prove their loyalty, the Soul Drinkers go to the aid of the beleaguered citizens, but soon find they are surrounded by foes within and without as the Howling Griffons Chapter arrives to destroy them. Meanwhile, a breakaway faction of Soul Drinkers instigates a rebellion that engulfs the Chapter in a deadly civil war!

*In the same series*

SOUL DRINKER
THE BLEEDING CHALICE
CRIMSON TEARS

*More Warhammer 40,000 from Ben Counter*

GREY KNIGHTS
DARK ADEPTUS
DAEMON WORLD

A WARHAMMER 40,000 NOVEL

# CHAPTER WAR

## Ben Counter

A BLACK LIBRARY PUBLICATION

First published in Great Britain in 2007 by
BL Publishing,
Games Workshop Ltd.,
Willow Road, Nottingham, NG7 2WS, UK.

10 9 8 7 6 5 4 3 2 1

Cover illustration by Leonid Kozienko.

A CIP record for this book is available from the British Library.

ISBN 13: 978-1-84416-458-6
ISBN 10: 1-84416-458-5

Distributed in the US by Simon & Schuster
1230 Avenue of the Americas, New York, NY 10020, US.

See the Black Library on the Internet at
**www.blacklibrary.com**

Find out more about Games Workshop
and the world of Warhammer 40,000 at
**www.games-workshop.com**

IT IS THE 41st millennium. For more than a hundred centuries the Emperor has sat immobile on the Golden Throne of Earth. He is the master of mankind by the will of the gods, and master of a million worlds by the might of his inexhaustible armies. He is a rotting carcass writhing invisibly with power from the Dark Age of Technology. He is the Carrion Lord of the Imperium for whom a thousand souls are sacrificed every day, so that he may never truly die.

YET EVEN IN his deathless state, the Emperor continues his eternal vigilance. Mighty battlefleets cross the daemon-infested miasma of the warp, the only route between distant stars, their way lit by the Astronomican, the psychic manifestation of the Emperor's will. Vast armies give battle in his name on uncounted worlds. Greatest amongst his soldiers are the Adeptus Astartes, the Space Marines, bio-engineered super-warriors. Their comrades in arms are legion: the Imperial Guard and countless planetary defence forces, the ever-vigilant Inquisition and the tech-priests of the Adeptus Mechanicus to name only a few. But for all their multitudes, they are barely enough to hold off the ever-present threat from aliens, heretics, mutants – and worse.

TO BE A man in such times is to be one amongst untold billions. It is to live in the cruellest and most bloody regime imaginable. These are the tales of those times. Forget the power of technology and science, for so much has been forgotten, never to be re-learned. Forget the promise of progress and understanding, for in the grim dark future there is only war. There is no peace amongst the stars, only an eternity of carnage and slaughter, and the laughter of thirsting gods.

# CHAPTER ONE

'What is the greatest failure against
which we must guard?'
'The failure to die when death would
serve the Emperor's purpose.'

    – Daenyathos, *Catechisms Martial*

'PRESENT ARMS!' YELLED Lord Globus Falken, and
thousands of troops drew up their autoguns to
salute the Aristarchical Pavilion. Magnificent in
white bearskins and jackets of midnight blue and
silver brocade, the Warders of the Vanqualian
Republic trooped in perfect formation across the
grand Processional Quarter with the banners of
their ancient regiments flying alongside the top-
most spires of Palatium. They were by far the

7

mightiest fighting force in the Scaephan sector, the primary defenders of the Obsidian system and the proud sons of Vanqualis, and they looked the part. Their officers were resplendent in the heraldry of the Falken family from which they all hailed, and even the casings of their artillery and the hulls of their tanks shone in brass and blue.

'Sloppy this year,' said Count Luchosin Falken, whose uniform was so ornate it looked like his ample frame was swathed in hundreds of clashing flags. In a way it was, for he had to symbolise all the regiments of the Warders. The sun beat down hard on Palatium. The Aristarchical Pavilion, tented in silks and with several valet-servitors trundling around serving drinks, was one of the few places in the Processional Quarter that was not sweltering. Even so, Count Luchosin sweated gently where he sat.

'Globus has got them digging trenches and mucking out the horses,' said Lady Akania Falken-Kaal, standing idly beside Count Luchosin. Lady Akania looked rather more rakish than most of the men, sporting an athlete's frame under her cavalry-woman's uniform and an eye patch thanks to a hunting accident in her youth. 'No damn respect.'

Lord Sovelin Falken, sweating under his bearskin and the heavy crimson sash of the Vanqualian Artillery, looked out across the sea of marching men and their forest of raised autoguns. To him it was still astonishing, a wondrous and powerful statement of Vanqualis's stability and traditions. Far away from the jungles that surrounded Palatium and covered the continent of

Nevermourn, there were towering hives with billions of citizens who lived and died beneath their churning factories. Were it not for the rule of the Falken family, and the traditions such as the Trooping of the Warding Standard, the whole of Vanqualis would be like that. Nevermourn, a continent of magnificent natural beauty, was a miracle. It was far more fashionable to denounce it as dull and crude, but it filled Lord Sovelin's heart with pride.

'Globus wants them ready to fight,' said Lord Sovelin. 'I don't think there's anything wrong with that.'

Lady Akania cocked her one visible eyebrow. 'Fight? This is not an army for fighting, Sovelin! This is an army for reminding those vermin in the cities who is in charge. If it weren't for that the citizens might realise there are more of them than there are of us. The Falkens rule Vanqualis by magnificence, Sovelin, not by the gun! Killing them in the streets is fine for the rest of the Imperium but we do things differently. Do you not agree it is better this way?'

'Of course, Lady Akania,' said Sovelin. Lady Akania was an aunt of his a couple of times removed, though he was not much younger, and he was fairly sure she had seniority over him. Most of the family members on the Pavilion were higher up the ladder than Sovelin, which was probably why he had been palmed off on the artillery.

'Fight!' snorted Lord Luchosin with derision. 'What's there to fight?'

A sharp volley of gunshots rippled across the assembled troops, tens of thousands of autoguns loosed off to salute the sons and daughters of the Falken family. With perfect timing the regimental bands opened up and blared the ancient songs of war and rulership, the rhythm punctuated by volleys of disciplined gunfire. It echoed around the white stone spires of Palatium and the immense jungle trees that crowded up around the city walls, around the regimental banners and the gilded eagles atop the minarets of the Temple of Imperator Ascendant.

'No respect,' spat Lady Akania. She turned and walked off briskly, waving away a regimental underling who tried to get her attention. He was carrying a field vox-unit.

'Not now,' said Lord Globus. 'It's not the time.'

'My lord,' said the officer. 'It is a communication from Fleet Admiral Thalak.'

'Thalak has no idea what we are doing here!' growled Lord Globus. 'The man's a peasant. He can wait.'

Sovelin waved over the officer. The man was sweating and it wasn't just from the heat. He wore the uniform of the Mechanised Cavalry.

'It's the emergency channel, my lord,' said the officer.

'Give it to me,' said Sovelin. He took the vox handset and put it to his ear, wincing at the harsh screech of feedback.

'...the love of the Throne!' shouted a voice, barely distinguishable from the howl of static. 'The

*Starstrider* is down! They've hit the docks! They're killing us up here! They're killing us!'

'KILLING US, YOU hear?'

Fleet Admiral Thalak was thrown off his feet as the *Sanctis Chirosian* rocked again, as if it were afloat in an endless sea and great waves were battering against it. Thalak's head cracked against the deck and the vox handset kicked out of his hand and clattered away.

Hot blood sprayed over him. He coughed, covering his face, trying to wipe it out of his eyes with the sleeve of his black Naval greatcoat. The sound was tremendous, metal screaming – and men screaming, too, screams cut short as steel pounded against steel.

Thalak rolled onto his front and got to his knees. The blood was from Petty Officer van Staelem, who had been impaled through the abdomen by a great shard of metal. Her body was split open and she shuddered as she died, blood running down her chin.

Thalak had to fight to remember where he was. This place, with its dark wood panelling and friezes of silver cherubim, was the Cartographers' Hall where the navigation officers pored over huge map tables or immense orreries suspended from the ceiling alongside the chandeliers. Now half the hall was caved in, huge jagged blades of twisted metal pushing through from the industrial guts of the ship. Lights flared as a display of planets and stars fell free of its mountings and crashed to the floor, enormous metal globes crushing fleeing crewmen as they ran, sections of the silver hoops cutting ratings in half. Greyish liquid sprayed in from a torn fuel line and caught light, flame flowing around the wrecked metal and devouring the injured crewmen crawling away from the destruction.

Thalak spat out a mouthful of van Staelem's blood and ran, stumbling as the deck tilted again. It felt as if some huge hand had grabbed the *Sanctis Chirosian* and was dismembering it, crushing it here and tearing it apart there.

He ran towards the communications helm that budded off from one end of the Cartographers' Hall. A ringed planet rolled by, its thin silver rings slicing through the floor like a blade as it rolled, cutting Senior Navigation Officer Rorkren in two. Fragments of burning star charts fell in flurries. The ship tilted alarmingly again and the mass of twisted metal forced its way in further, crewmen scrabbling away from it and screaming as it crushed them against the far wall.

'Admiral!' yelled someone from the communications helm. Thalak looked up and saw an arm reaching down to drag him into the helm. The helm was set into a large spherical room with its walls covered in monitors, its officers slumped in gravcouches with their faces covered by the heavy interface units through which they communicated with the other ships of Battlefleet Scaephan. Several of the monitors had blown out, like blinded eyes, and the others showed images from throughout the battlefleet's moorings around the orbital station Ollanius XIV.

The young woman officer's face was streaked with blood and oil. She was a junior officer, probably from the communications support crew whose duties involved making sure the officers were tended to during the months they were wired into the *Sanctis Chirosian*. 'Admiral, what is happening? Who is attacking us?'

'I don't know,' said Thalak, breaking his own rule of never revealing any ignorance or weakness to his crew. 'Someone who was waiting for us. It's not just us, they're going for the whole system.'

'You've heard from Vanqualis?'

'I don't need to,' replied Thalak bleakly. 'It's the Trooping of the Warding Standard. The whole damn army's in Palatium. That's what the attackers were waiting for.'

The officer pushed a strand of bloody hair back from her face and looked up at one of the monitors. It was showing a great chunk of burning wreckage drifting above the pitted metal surface of Ollanius XIV, venting streams of burning fuel and air. 'The *Skystrider* is down,' she said.

'I know,' replied Thalak. The *Skystrider* was a grand cruiser, the largest and most powerful ship in Battle-fleet Scaephan. Without it, the battlefleet's power to oppose an invasion was cut in half. 'The *Defence of Phantis*, too. They've hurt us. But we're not down yet.'

As if in reply, the *Sanctis Chirosian* was wrenched over savagely. The ship's gravity suddenly shifted and snapped into reverse, the floor becoming the ceiling. Thalak grabbed onto the doorframe as he fell, stomach lurching as the din grew. Massive map

tables heavy as boulders crashed into the chandeliers of the Cartographers' Hall, and bodies broke
against the decorative bosses of the ceiling.

The communications officer fell past him and
smashed into the monitors on the ceiling of the
communications helm, her body spasming as electric current ran through her and spat sparks from
her fingers. The smell of cooking blood turned Thalak's stomach one final time and he vomited,
heaving up his guts as he clung grimly to the doorway. He heard a grisly snap above him and a pair of
booted feet hung beside him. The comms officers,
hard-wired into the ship's systems, had fallen down
but they were still attached by the interface units
clamped around their heads and their necks had
snapped. Like a scene from a mass execution, they
all hung silent and dead in a ring above Thalak.

A new sound, louder and even more appalling,
battered against Thalak's ears. It was a rhythmic
scream of metal through metal. Something was biting through the ship, crunching through decks and
bulkheads.

Thalak looked through at the Cartographers' Hall
and somewhere in his battered mind it all made
perfect sense. He was in hell. The Imperial creed had
many hells, although some priests argued they were
all one and the same, but one of them definitely
looked like this. Bodies impaled on shards of metal.
Corpses guttering in the flames, some of them still
alive and writhing. Great wet streaks of blood
sprayed up the walls. Lights flickering, screams cut
off, the boom of escaping air shuddering through

the ship. Thalak had served his Emperor, but it had not been enough, and now he was in hell.

As if to prove him right, the ruined side of the Cartographers' Hall was forced open like a great metal mouth with teeth of jagged steel. Bodies slid into it as it howled, metal against metal screeching. Guttural voices yelled from inside and dark shapes clambered out, misshapen, hulking forms.

Thalak snarled and clambered back into the burning ruin of the Cartographers' Hall. He took his laspistol from its holster – it was a good gun, and it had been his uncle's before Thalak had followed him into the Imperial Navy.

There were more of them. Dozens. A hundred. Dark and monstrous, swarming into his ship.

'For the Emperor!' yelled Thalak, and fired. The crimson las-blasts streaked past gnarled dark green skin and flickered in tiny, furious red eyes. Gunfire opened up in response, heavy-calibre fire sprayed at random, splintering the panelling behind Thalak. Thalak dived to the floor, rolled and came up firing, forcing himself to ignore the pain.

He was terrified. The fear inside him was like a chunk of ice where his heart should be, freezing his mind. But the rest of him kept fighting, because some part of him told him that was what an officer did.

A fist slammed into him and he was driven into the floor. The shattered remains of a chandelier cut into him. A brutal face with tiny violent eyes above a huge mouth filled with filthy tusks roared down at him and a kick crunched into his ribs. One of the creatures stamped down on his hand and the laspistol was gone.

Greenskins. Orks. Animals, killers, the oldest enemy that mankind had among the stars. They were on Thalak's ship, and they were killing him.

An ork bellowed and the creatures bearing down on Thalak parted for one of their number, easily twice the height of a man and hugely muscled. Its face was so deeply scarred it was barely a face at all but in the midst of the ugliness, there was a glimmer of intelligence and malice in its eyes far more terrifying than a hundred ignorant killers.

There was no part of Thalak now that felt anything other than terror. The greenskin leader reached down and gripped Thalak by his shoulder. Its other arm was artificial, a bionic so crude it looked like it could have been powered by steam. Metal claws fixed around Thalak's elbow and tore his arm off at the shoulder; white horror flooded through him and his body reeled with the shock.

The greenskin held Thalak up into the air. For a moment he could see the ocean of orks flooding into the *Sanctis Chirosian*, butchering injured crewmen where they lay, blazing away with crude deafening guns at those few still on their feet. The orks seemed completely at home amid the destruction and death. They were a natural part of this hell.

Thalak was held high and shaken like a standard to rally the orks. The leader roared and the orks roared with him, cheering the death of the ship and the mutilation of the fleet's commander. Then Thalak was thrown back down and a dozen feet stamped down on him, shattering his bones and battering against his head. Finally the *Sanctis Chirosian* was gone, and there was only blackness.

It was just after the Warding Standard was unfurled that the attack came.

The first blast hit the Processional Quarter square on, throwing broken bodies and severed limbs into the air, a hundred men blown to bits in a split second and dozens more sliced apart by shards of shrapnel. The Warding Standard itself, stitched together from a dozen regimental banners and festooned with battle honours and campaign ribbons, fell tattered and bloody to the ground, draping itself over the chunks of uniformed meat that remained of the honour guard regiment escorting it.

The second blast hit the Aristarchical Pavilion. Lord Globus was vaporised. Lady Akania was beheaded by a shard of missile casing and tumbled down onto the square. Counts and barons were shredded. Lords and ladies were thrown broken against the front of the Herald's Chapel and the Lord Magister's Basilica.

It was an orbital artillery strike. Guns high up in orbit above Vanqualis threw explosive shells down at Palatium. It came utterly without warning, because with Battlefleet Scaephan stationed in the system nothing could possibly have got through to threaten Vanqualis. And yet it had, because now enemy spaceships were spitting fire and death down at the jewel of Nevermourn.

In the moments that followed, the Warders of the Vanqualian Republic reacted to the shock. Guns were hurriedly loaded, officers yelled for battle order, and cavalry tried to control their starting horses. The gates leading from the vast parade grounds of the Processional Quarter were jammed as thousands of troops tried to get out and take cover among the lofty civic buildings of Palatium. In the panic, few of them took heed of the shadow now cast over the parade ground, or of the dark spot that appeared in the air and got larger and larger.

The third blast was not a missile or bomb. It was the impact of a huge dark slab of rock, pitted like an asteroid, that slammed into the centre of the parade ground so hard it drove a deep crater into the ground. The front of the Herald's Chapel collapsed and the roof of the Lawkeeper's Chamber fell in. Spires fell with the impact, buildings spilling their floors out into the parade ground.

Through the choking dust, the survivors could see hundreds of bodies and scores of groaning wounded. They helped their brother soldiers, dragging them towards the scrum at the processional gates. Cries went up for regimental medics, only a few of whom had been permitted to carry their bulky, inelegant medi-packs on procession. Men screamed, shorn of limbs or with their abdomens split open by shrapnel. Some tried to claw their way out from beneath the dead. Others bit back the pain and waited to die, knowing no one would come to save them. Many looked to the scions of House Falken to deliver them, but House Falken's proud sons and daughters were mostly dead in the burning wreckage of the pavilion.

The dust began to settle. The outline of the rock itself could be seen. It wasn't just a rock – its underside had been heavily plated with slabs of metal to help it survive the impact and it was studded with crude engines that had directed its fall. A gunshot rang out, and a screaming man fell silent.

Shapes emerged from the deep pits in the rock. At first they were just more bodies, the inhabitants who had died in the impact being kicked out to make way. Then a terrible cry went up from inside, a deep animalistic war-bellow echoed by hundreds of bestial voices.

As one, the attackers charged out of the rock. They surged forward with their guns blazing, raking through the bodies, great rusted blades dispatching the wounded as their hulking shapes lurched through the near-darkness.

Some of the soldiers turned and readied their autoguns, bayonets fixed. The attackers crashed into them and the Wardens of the Vanqualian Republic saw their enemy for the first time – huge, brutal, green-skinned with murderous red eyes, maddened with battle. Orks, someone yelled – aliens, foul xenos come to defile Nevermourn and the world of Vanqualis.

The battle at the gates was short and bloody. Blades fell on uniformed flesh. Autoguns chattered in response but the orks had the numbers and the momentum, and hundreds of troopers fell. More were crushed as the retreat forced its way through the gates and out into the civic districts of

Vanqualis, the orks hacking into the backs of the troopers as they turned to run.

The resistance in the Processional Quarter collapsed, but the orks did not stop. As more rocks slammed into Palatium and disgorged their alien passengers, the orks surged forwards into the streets of the city.

SOVELIN COULD HEAR Palatium dying. From his position by the Malcadorean Gate he could see huge columns of dust and flame spewing from all across the city as more asteroids smashed into it, and more bombs streaked down from above. The sky was almost dark, only a blood-red tinge across the horizon remaining of the daylight, and Sovelin could see silver specks hanging high above in orbit. Spaceships, he realised – and it wasn't Battlefleet Scaephan. The battlefleet was gone. Vanqualis was alone.

'You!' he yelled at an artillery crew trying to manhandle their bulky mortar carriage towards the gate. 'Unlimber the damn thing and carry it!'

Hundreds of troopers swarmed around Sovelin, all from his regiment, the Vanqualian Rearguard Artillery. He had got them off the parade ground as soon as their part in the Trooping of the Warding Standard had been done with. He had known that something was wrong, and he had known that no one would listen to him. They would not put the army on alert; certainly not break up the Trooping, on the word of someone like Sovelin who was barely senior enough to be spared the marching. So he had got his artillery out of the Processional

Quarter and had been taking them to man the walls, just in case, when the first bombs had hit.

The sound was horrible. From far across the city he could hear more explosions mixed with screams. People were in the streets now – the Terran Avenue was lined with the homes of functionaries and house servants, and they knew that something terrible was happening to their city. Another rock streaked down from above and slammed home, the closest yet to the Malcadorean Gate, kicking up a plume of wreckage. Chunks of stone and red roof tiles scattered across the street. More and more civilians filled the streets, emerging from their homes or running from the areas of the city already under attack.

'Get up on the wall!' shouted Sovelin to his men. 'Protect these people!' The soldiers began to turn their artillery pieces to face the street and ready their guns, sheltering behind the monuments that flanked the Malcadorean Gate – a great stone serpent, the heraldic symbol of the Falken family, and an eagle representing the Imperium to which Vanqualis paid fealty.

Sovelin heard the orks and knew then what the forces of Vanqualis were facing. There was nothing else that could explain the war cries and the shrieks of raw terror that moved in front of them like a bow wave. Panic filled every face Sovelin could see as gunfire stuttered from the alleyways and windows smashed.

Closer. Sovelin could hear their grunting alien tongue and the screams of people who fell beneath their blades. Closer still and a building along the avenue collapsed, its front spewing rubble and shattered furniture into the street. Dark green forms scrabbled over it, blazing gunfire. More of them, thick like a green tide, flooded down the street.

People were pouring from their homes, running and screaming. They were heading for the Malcadorean Gate, beyond which was the jungle and the hope of safety. Perhaps they could make it to the coast, and from there reach the cities of Herograve.

But they would not make it. Not unless the guns of Sovelin's artillery made a stand, and bought them time with their lives.

'What do we do, sir?' said Captain Laesc, who had his laspistol and sword drawn as he crouched down by the closest autocannon mount.

Sovelin couldn't answer for a moment. Thousands of people were now crowding the street and the orks were surging forwards. Sovelin could see the crude totems, festooned with severed hands and heads that the orks carried ahead of them, the gleaming bone of their tusks, the savage glee in their eyes as they cut down the civilians who straggled behind.

'We run,' said Sovelin. 'Run! All of you! Now! Go!'

The Vanqualian Rearguard Artillery broke cover and ran, Sovelin at the heart of them, hauling their autocannon and mortars with them as they headed between the monuments of the Malcadorean Gate and out into the deep green mass of Nevermourn's jungles.

As Sovelin's troops broke and ran a great cry went up from the fleeing civilians of Palatium. They were the men and women who served the Falken family, for Palatium was not a city like the towering hives elsewhere on the planet but a place that had been built as the seat of the Falken family's reign. Its civilians had given their lives to House Falken and now the army, led by scions of that same family, was fleeing before them.

Many gave up and died beneath orkish blades, trampled by the booted feet of the xenos. Others scrambled over one another and trampled fellow citizens, even friends and loved ones, in the scrum to escape. Those who made it to the Malcadorean Gate were crushed against the huge stone pillars of the gate itself or the podiums on which the statues were mounted. The serpent and the eagle looked down sternly on the carnage and panic.

Then the orks overran the gate and the butchery began in earnest. Thousands died in a few moments and the orks plunged into the crowds and emerged again covered in gore, exhausting the magazines of their crude guns and laying into their prey with swords and cleavers.

Survivors streamed from the Malcadorean Gate, a fraction of those who had fled the orks. The screams followed them and many of them, like Admiral Thalak, were sure that they had indeed already died to an orkish bullet and were now simply fleeing further into hell.

THE HUGEST AND greatest ork to ever emerge from the war-worlds of the Garon Nebula strode towards the pulpit of the Temple of Imperator Ascendant. The temple was a riot of howling orks, ripping down the tapestries that depicted the founders of House Falken taking their first steps on the shores of Herograve or forging through the jungles of Nevermourn. The greenskins blew the faces off statues with their guns and smashed the bronze plaques that showed scenes from the lives of Imperial saints. They smeared blood on the pale stone walls, blood from the temple's clergy now being dismembered by the small slave-creatures who followed the orks everywhere. Dung and gore were heaped on the temple's altar and the image of the Emperor now lacked a face, the intricate altarpiece scarred with gunfire.

One cleric was still alive and the slave-creatures were toying with him, kicking a gun away from his outstretched hand as he reached for it to take his own life. Again and again he reached haplessly for the skittering gun, and each time the lean, scurrying creatures howled with laughter. They looked up as the great ork's shadow fell over them and their faces fell, cruel red eyes widening in fear above their sharp wicked little faces, and they scrambled out of his way to hide between the dark wood of the temple's pews.

The other orks bellowed their triumph as their warlord walked among them. The warlord was bigger than any of them, twice as tall as most, its great gnarled head thrust brutally from between his shoulders and its huge jaw scowling around the forest of broken tusks. Its skin was as dark and gnarled as the bark on an ancient tree, and its eyes, even sunk deep into its bestial skull, burned with an intelligence and drive the other orks lacked.

The warlord only had one normal arm, with which he batted the closest slave-creature out of the way. His other arm was a contraption of metal and steam that spurted hot gouts of vapour as he moved, and ended in a great three-fingered claw large enough to rip the turret off a tank. The machinery encasing his ribcage and his spine was a rusted ladder of metal chunks that hissed black lubricant as he moved. Thick green cords of muscle had grown around his mechanical parts, loosening and contracting as he moved. To have survived the replacement of half his torso with such crude replacements suggested a level of toughness abnormal even for an ork.

The warlord roared, but not with the triumph and gloating bravado of the other orks. The orks fell silent, even the burliest of them shuddering at the warlord's displeasure. The warlord glowered at the greenskins and his eyes fell on one of them, who was slashing up one of the temple's tapestries with the rusted, bloody blade of his cleaver.

The warlord darted forward with speed far too great for something of his size, and seized the vandalising ork with his natural hand. His fingers closed around the ork's muscular throat and lifted the creature off the ground. The warlord shifted the ork to his mechanical hand and threw it across the temple. Its body slammed into the far wall leaving a crumbling dent in the stone, and slumped to the floor unconscious.

The warlord turned back to the slashed tapestry, pulling it off the wall closer to his face as he examined it. It showed the earliest Warders, the troops of Vanqualis who first protected the shores of Herograve as the planet's cities were settled under the banners of House Falken. The soldiers were capturing a ridge, their stylised uniforms bright and their autoguns held high. The bodies of orks, cut up into pieces, were piled beneath their feet. The artist had shown them as weak and skinny, pathetic creatures barely worthy of Vanqualian bayonets.

The warlord yanked the tapestry off the wall and held it high, so the assembled orks could see the slain orks trampled by human feet. He yelled at them, spitting the hateful syllables of the orkish tongue.

The Vanqualians had won this planet from the orks. This planet belonged to the orks. This world, like so many of the worlds across which the warlord had strode, was green – and it would be green again. But these humans, the same humans now being slaughtered in the streets of Palatium, had once crushed the orks just as surely as the orks were crushing them. They were resilient and resourceful. They were driven. They believed in things that made them perform extraordinary tasks. To underestimate them, to treat them as blade-fodder and playthings, was a way to ensure the same defeat that had befallen the first orks to claim Vanqualis as their own.

If the orks in the temple understood this, any sign of it was hidden under the fear the warlord's smouldering anger instilled in them. The warlord threw down the tapestry and spat on it. He noticed the only surviving cleric hiding behind the pew beside him.

The man was elderly, his creased, terrified face smeared with blood and dirt, his fingers bloody and his dove-grey priestly robes tattered. Near him lay the gun he had been trying to grab off the slave-creatures.

The warlord bent down and picked up the gun. He crushed it in the fingers of his mechanical arm, and threw it back down at the cleric's feet. The cleric looked down at it, then stared up at the warlord, terrified tears filling his eyes.

As the warlord stomped towards the pulpit the slave-creatures fell upon the cleric and the temple filled with noise again, the cleric screaming, his robes and his flesh tearing, the slave-creatures cackling as they slicked themselves with his blood. The orks took the racket as a signal to continue destroying the icons of the human enemy and gunfire roared again, blasting censer globes from the ceiling and blowing holes in the pews.

The warlord ignored them. Perhaps once, he had been the same, a simple and brutal creature with nothing but the love of war burning inside him. But the warlord was not like that now, Even the cleric, in the last horror-filled moments of his life, had realised that. He was not an ork, for an ork was a simple thing. An ork was not driven by convictions that equalled those of his most zealous human opponent. An ork did not live by cunning as well as strength, the lust for supremacy as well as the desire for violence and carnage. The warlord did.

He stomped to the top of the pulpit, which overlooked the main nave of the temple. Instead of facing the rows of pews as the temple's preachers

had done, the warlord looked the other way, past
the ruined altarpiece and through the smashed window that still had fragments of stained glass
clinging to its frame.

Palatium stretched out before him. It was a small
city, built as a place for the planet's human leaders
to rule from instead of a centre of population and
industry. Even so, the speed with which the orks
had overrun it was impressive. Tiny green figures
cavorted on distant rooftops, tearing down the banners of House Falken, hurling masonry and roof
tiles into the streets below. Buildings burned, and
through the palls of black smoke descended huge
ponderous craft, daubed with the crude glyphs of
the many ork clans united under the warlord.

Many such craft were already disgorging thousands more orks to fuel the invasion of Vanqualis.
Some of the orks were specialists in the warlord's
army, sought out and won from their own warlords
in fighting pit duels or all-out battles. There were
orkish veterans in massive suits of powered armour,
heavy and brutal as walking tanks. A squad of expert
infiltrators, faces smeared black with camouflage,
moved with silence and economy unbecoming of
the more raucous ork warriors – these were the
scouts and assassins whose natural habitat was a
jungle war zone. Masked slavers with barbed whips
lashed forwards squabbling crowds of slave creatures, who would be herded in front of the warlord's
main force to absorb bullets and set off mines.
Other ships were lowering down rickety, tempera-
mental war machines and tanks, with slaves

scrabbling all over them to tighten screws and oil joints.

The humans who had slain the first orks to inhabit Vanqualis doubtless had no idea that orks could muster such soldiers. They assumed that the greenskins were nothing more than a horde of animals, all alike in their crudeness and brutality. For the most part they were right, but then for the most part the orks did not have leaders like the warlord to marshal them into a fighting force as deadly as anything the humans could field.

The warlord looked beyond the city, to the jungles. Beyond those jungles was the sea, and beyond that the coast of Herograve, the polluted rocky wasteland with its teeming cities and billions of humans. Weak, cowardly, doomed humans, for whom the cleaver or the bullet was too honest an end. Nevertheless, that was how they would die, because Vanqualis belonged to the orks and no greater desire burned behind the warlord's eyes than to see it in the hands of the greenskins again.

FOR A LONG time, the countess was silent. The only sound was the hiss of the air recyclers pumping stale, cold, dry air into the pinnacle chamber. Her small, frail frame swamped by the sweeping pearl-studded gown, her hollow-cheeked face framed by the tiara of diamond spines, the countess seemed to sink deeper into the juvenat throne.

The chamberlain waited politely. He was a small and officious man who had lived a lifetime of service and delivered his share of bad news to the sons and daughters of the Falken family, but never had the news been this bad. He kept his composure and cast his eyes to the floor, awaiting the countess's reply.

Countess Ismenissa Falken took a deep breath that rattled through her aged body. 'When did this happen?'

'But less than an hour, my lady.'

'And of my husband?'

The chamberlain had evidently expected this question. 'Nothing is known of him. With the grace of the Emperor it may be that he still lives...'

'Spare me not, chamberlain,' said the countess, cutting him off. 'Is my husband dead?'

The chamberlain swallowed. 'Lord Globus was on the Aristarchical Pavilion, my lady, and it was thought destroyed in the first attack.'

'Then he is dead.'

'Very probably, my lady.'

'I see. Are there any of the family left?'

'We do not know. Many citizens have escaped Palatium but with little order. Perhaps there are some scions among them. I fear I have little to tell you that is certain.'

'It is certain that the greenskins have returned,' said Countess Ismenissa. 'And it is certain that our world is invaded. It is also certain that we cannot stand alone.'

The countess stood up. From the black slabs of metal that made up the juvenat throne snaked several thick cables that fitted into the rear of the jewel-studded bodice of her dress. Several children, dressed in the same crimson coattails as the chamberlain, stepped out from the shadows behind the juvenat throne, some holding the hem of her long skirts off the floor, others gathering the cables as they slid from the throne so they did not become tangled as the countess walked regally towards one of the tall arched windows that ringed the chamber.

The shadows behind the throne could not hide their blue-grey skin and hollow black eyes, nor the way they walked hunched or on all fours like animals. The wives of House Falken dutifully produced many children, not all of whom survived their childhood, and it was from those lost sons and daughters that the countess's hem-bearers were created. The servitor technology leased to House Falken by the Adeptus Mechanicus was complex and flawed, so the half-living children fell well short of the cherubic ideal.

The chamber was at the pinnacle of one of Herograve's hives and from it could be seen the vast slope of the city, studded with lights against the night's darkness, sweeping down towards the polluted plains that surrounded the city. In the far distance could be seen another mountain of scattered lights, smudged through the polluted air – a neighbouring city, one of the several that studded the continent of Herograve. Billions of Vanqualians lived within those cities, and in a few hours they would start to learn that their ruling class was all but destroyed and aliens had invaded Nevermourn.

In the sky above, just visible through the layers of smoke from the hive factories, were the tiny specks of light reflected from the undersides of the orbital defence network. Thousands of turbolasers and missiles speckled the sky above Herograve's cities, protecting them from bombardment. Vanqualis did not have the resources to protect its entire orbit in such a way, and so had chosen to spare its cities from enemy bombardment. That was the reason that orks were not raining down on the hive cities, but that would be little comfort to the survivors of Palatium who had seen their loved ones butchered in the streets on distant Nevermourn.

'We must ask for help,' said Countess Ismenissa. 'With the Warders broken and House Falken decimated, we are alone. We are isolated here, far from the worlds of Imperial dominion, but it is only the Imperium that can help us. Now is not the time to be proud. We will beg if we must.' The countess looked away from the window at the chamberlain. 'Summon the astropath and bring him here. He must be ready to transmit immediately.'

'Of course, my lady,' said the chamberlain. 'Should I take steps to inform the populace?'

'Of the invasion?' The countess waved a hand. 'Yes. Give it to the Lay Parliament. Have them debate it. It will give them something to do.'

The chamberlain did not scurry off to his duties, as the countess expected.

'Yes?' she said.

'There remains one further matter. With Lord Globus... gone, you are the only representative of House Falken in a position to assume leadership. You are the ruler of Vanqualis, my lady.'

The countess sighed. She had never looked older than she did in that moment, framed against the blackness of her city, swamped by her finery. 'Very well. I am sure there is a ceremony for it somewhere. Have the archivists dig it out.'

'It shall be done.' The chamberlain bowed briskly and hurried out to his duties.

The countess was well over two hundred years old, thanks to the efforts of the house physicians and the constant attentions of the juvenat throne. In all that time it had never been this bad. She had lived through the Hive Scorcid revolt, the scandals of her uncle Baron Malifiss Falken, and the schism forced by the emergence of the now-defunct Cult of the Terran Resurgence. She had seen upheavals and unexpected deaths, conflicts with the governors of the Scaephan sector and crises where the hive cities were starved of food or water. But never anything as bad as this. She was an old woman, and she felt every year.

And now, for the first time in its history, Vanqualis would have to beg for help from the Imperium, that distant power to whom House Falken had paid the tithes of its cities' riches in return for sovereignty over their world. The orks had their foothold on Nevermourn now, and there was no doubt where they would head next. With Nevermourn infested Herograve would follow, with its cities and its teeming billions.

The countess walked to an ornate bookshelf, which held several large volumes. Her dear Globus had always been more concerned with military than planetary matters and the countess had felt it prudent to

become familiar with the history and geography of
her world, in case she had to take a more active part
in the governing of Vanqualis. Now, the entire
responsibility for that government fell on her.

Countess Ismenissa took a heavy book from an
upper shelf, the children crawling like obedient pets
to carry her skirts around her. The book was an atlas,
presented to her by one of the hive universities in
return for some state function she had performed half
a century ago. One of the children turned a handle
that reeled her cables back in as she returned to the
throne. She sat down, feeling the juvenat liquids flowing through her veins again, holding back the effects
of ageing on her bones and organs. She laid the book
open on her lap as the children took their positions
behind the throne again, and began to read.

Maps of Nevermourn flickered past her eyes. At
that very moment, refugees and greenskin filth alike
were streaming through those valleys and hills,
fighting, killing, making for the shore and then
Herograve beyond them. There would be a war, long
or short depending on how the countess led her
people in the following days, and perhaps at the
end of it all Vanqualis would still stand and House
Falken would still rule. But the centuries had taught
Countess Ismenissa to be pragmatic, and she knew
in her heart that Vanqualis and all those billions of
citizens would probably not survive.

# CHAPTER TWO

'Against whom will the battle at the
end of time be fought?'

'Know only that it will not be against
enemies from without.'

– Daenyathos, *Catechisms Martial*

DEEP IN THE heart of the hulk, so far from the massive churning warp engines and the tramping of power-armoured feet it might have been deep underground on some forbidden planet, lay the sanctum. Its original purpose was uncertain – presumably it had been a part of a spaceship at one time, because the hulk was an amalgamation of spacecraft welded together into strange and ugly shapes by the forces of the warp. But it was stone, not metal, and its elegant, simple temple was not built in a cargo hangar or a ship's bridge, but in a dark half-flooded cave dripping with stalactites. The temple was partially submerged, the roof of a long covered processional leading up to it now forming a tiled walkway just breaking the surface. Dim lights glowed under the water, glow-globes that had been lit when the cave had been discovered and had probably been lit for hundreds or thousands of years, patiently waiting for its worshippers to return.

Chaplain Iktinos walked along the path, the lower edges of his purple and black Space Marine power armour lit strangely by the light from below. He wore a grim skull-faced helmet, its eyepieces black and expressionless, and an eagle-topped mace, his crozius arcanum, hung at his waist. Iktinos, like any Space Marine, was huge, not much shy of three metres tall in his armour, but even so it was with humility and reverence that he passed over the threshold into the temple itself.

The sanctum within the temple was also half underwater, the lights below the surface casting strange shifting lights along the ceiling. The altar, along with slabs of carved stone that had fallen from the above, broke the surface and Iktinos used them to reach the large slab of fallen ceiling in the centre of the temple. Beside it a statue reared up from the water – it had the upper body of human woman and the head and lower body of a snake, and had its arms raised crookedly towards the ceiling. It was from a cult or religion that had probably been forgotten for centuries. Iktinos ignored its broken, accusing gaze as he kneeled down by the collection of monitoring equipment piled incongruously on the platform.

This place was Iktinos's sanctum, as sacred to him as it had been to whichever worshippers gathered there before their ship had been lost in the warp and become a part of the space hulk *Brokenback*. Iktinos removed his helmet to reveal a smooth, unmarked face with larger, more expressive eyes than deserved to belong beneath the sinister grimace of the skull. Shaven-headed and with light brown skin, Iktinos's real face had just as much presence as the Chaplain's skull. It was rare for Iktinos to take off his helmet, as it was a badge of office, an indicator that he was a man apart from the rest of the Soul Drinkers Chapter. Here, in his sanctum, it was safe for him to do so.

Iktinos checked one of the monitor screens. A single green blip jumped across it. He pulled a long spool of parchment with various readouts scrawled on it from the base of the monitor and cast his eyes over its information, evidently satisfied. Then he walked to the edge of the platform and reached down into the water.

A Space Marine's strength was awesome. Iktinos planted one foot on the stone and hauled a large rectangular slab of stone from the water. With a bang that echoed off the rocks of the cave beyond the slab slammed onto the platform, splintering the marble beneath. On the upper surface of the slab was carved the image of a stern-faced, bearded man dressed in ornate, archaic armour, such as might be found on the noble warriors of feral worlds. He had a crown on his brow and his hands were clasped over his chest holding the pommel of a double-headed axe. All around him were carved letters from a language that Iktinos did not recognise, one that had probably been forgotten as long as the temple's snake-headed god. The slab was a stone coffin for a long-dead king, and the image was carved on its lid.

Iktinos opened some metal clasps, evidently late additions, holding the lid closed, and hauled the lid off the coffin. The muffled screaming began instantly.

Inside the coffin was a wretched, skinny, filthy figure. Its robes were black with dirt and it had a bag over its head with tubes and wires snaking from it, wires that were ultimately connected to the monitors beside Iktinos. The figure reached up and groped blindly at the air in front of it, the skin on its hands pallid and sagging from the damp, wrinkled and rotting. The stench was awful.

Iktinos pulled the bag off the figure's head. The face of the man underneath was swollen and white, splitting along the seams of his features. A wide tube ran down his throat and another up his nose. His eyes were wide and blind, pure white without iris or pupil.

Iktinos pulled the tube from the man's throat and the man could scream properly now, howling sobs of desperation and fear. For several long minutes, the man could only scream. Then there was not enough left in him to scream any more.

'Please…' gasped Astropath Minoris Croivas Vel Scannien, voice hoarse and feeble. 'Please… oh, my Emperor, stop… just… just let it end…'

Iktinos looked down at him, his face as expressionless as the skull-masked helmet at his feet. 'Stop?'

'The nightmares. Let me out. Or… let me die. Please.'

'You begged us for this.'

'I didn't know!' The words came out as a sob, like that of a child. 'How would I know?'

'You begged us to take you,' continued Iktinos. 'You said you would do anything to get away from Dushan, from the Multiplaeion.' He held out his hands to indicate the coffin. 'This is what you are doing.'

Croivas Vel Scannien put his hands over his face and sobbed. There was barely anything else left in him, no words, not even terror or hatred now. There had been a man inside Croivas Vel Scannien once, but he was almost completely gone.

'Why?' he said, voice just a whisper. 'What do you want?'

'You know what I want.'

'Throne of Earth, what… what do you want me to tell you?'

'All of it.'

Croivas took his hands down from his eyes. 'You know I can't do that. I've told you, why won't you listen? It's… every one of us does it differently. It has to be directed at you, you have to know the codes… With me it's dreams, and at the best of times…'

'You said you were the best,' replied Iktinos, interrupting him. 'You said you could do it when I took you away from Dushan. It was why I took you at all.'

'You really... you really think I wanted this?'

'I don't care what you want. You mean nothing. Which is why you will do as I tell you.'

Dushan had been a world of mutilations. Deep scars across its continents, great ravines splitting its cities apart. Volcanic and tortured. Herds of slaves mined the perfect, flawless gems, forged in the fury of the planet's mantle, for use in precision equipment like cogitators and spaceship sensors. Those slaves had revolted and murdered the Imperial classes – classes that included Croivas Vel Scannien, an astropath, the planet's link to the Imperium at large. The Soul Drinkers had arrived there to draw recruits from the rioting slaves and in doing so they had been approached by Croivas, who wanted to go with them too. It was to the Chaplain, the spiritual leader of the Chapter, that Croivas had gone with his offer. The Chaplain had accepted. The rest of the Chapter had never known.

Since then Croivas had been Iktinos's prisoner. He had been in the coffin for longer than he could remember and his mind was broken. Croivas began to beg, offering Iktinos things he could not possibly deliver or claiming he had a loved one, a woman, back on Dushan who might still be alive. Iktinos calmly explained that there was nothing Croivas possessed that Iktinos could want, and that even if there was a woman she would be buried in the mass graves of the mine pits where the Imperials had been thrown by Dushan's slaves.

Then Croivas began threatening Iktinos, and so desperate was he that some of his threats even sounded realistic. He would strip Iktinos's soul away from his body, drive him mad, wipe his memory so he turned into a drooling infant. Tell the rest of the Chapter what Iktinos was doing. But Iktinos knew that, as powerful a psyker as the astropath was, he would have long ago enacted his threats had he really been able to pull them off.

Eventually, after almost an hour of ranting which left Croivas raw-throated and exhausted, the astropath gave in to Iktinos and sank back down into the nightmares. Astropaths sent and received psychic messages, the only means of sending information across the Imperium's immense interstellar distances, and every one had a different method of doing so. Croivas did so through dreams, receiving the complex symbolic messages while asleep and rebuilding them according to astropathic codes when awake. It was while he had slept in the coffin, sealed underwater, that fragments of communications from across the Imperium had flickered through his mind.

Cadia was at war. It was the lynchpin of Imperial defences around the Eye of Terror but now its commander Ursurkar Creed had demanded assistance from all who could render it to fight off the hordes of traitors and abominations spewing from the Eye. Dramatic news, to be sure, but Iktinos demanded that Croivas move on.

Aliens, of a type never encountered before by the Imperium, had carved out an empire for themselves on the southern fringe, among worlds evacuated or wracked by the century's wars against the tyranids. To Iktinos, such things were irrelevant. The millions of citizens begging for deliverance meant nothing. Less than nothing – they were a distraction. Or would have been, to someone without Iktinos's superhuman dedication.

Skeletal mechanical creatures were slowly infesting a cluster of stars close to the galactic core in the Ultima Segmentum. An entire empire had seceded from the heartland of the Imperium, along the western spiral arm of the galaxy, and the call had gone out for the upstarts to be crushed. Religious schisms had plunged the planets near holy Gathalamor into war, and the diocese of Gathalamor itself was begging for assistance in keeping the conflict from its sacred shores.

No use. None of it. Iktinos pressed Croivas harder, but Croivas was falling apart. His lips were bloody from the effort of speaking and the cacophony of symbols forcing their way through his mind was driving him insane. Iktinos did not care, and demanded that Croivas continue.

Daemons summoned to the streets of a world isolated by warp storms. Greenskins flooding through the jungles of a planet deep in the Segmentum Tempestus. Mutants rioting, burning the crops of agri-worlds and threatening hive planets with starvation. Fleets of xenos pirates preying on pilgrim ships, devouring the very souls of their captives.

Alien gods demanding worshippers, plagues of insanity and heresy, a hundred thousand wars burning across a million worlds...

'Stop,' said Iktinos.

Croivas gasped and coughed up a clot of blood. His lips still worked, mind festering with the symbols that had bombarded him as he lay in the cold stone coffin.

'Go back. The greenskins.'

'The... the great beast,' gasped Croivas. 'Came without warning. Shattered them. Without help they'll die.'

'Where? What about the black stone?'

'The... symbol. The code. Black stone. Onyx. And... glass.'

'Volcanic glass,' said Iktinos. 'Obsidian.'

'Yes.'

'What else?'

'Now this land is ours, we shall never mourn again,' said Croivas. It sounded like a quotation from somewhere, not Croivas's own words.

'What else?'

'The world. A grave for heroes. Van... Vanqualis. A stone serpent rules. Pride.'

'And the beast?'

'Thousands of greenskins raining down from the sky. Too many to count. Destroyed their armies in a heartbeat. And their fleet is... gone.'

'Is it an exaggeration?' Iktinos's voice was not lacking in emotion now. There was steel in it, an implicit threat so powerful he could have been holding a knife to Croivas's throat.

'No. No, they will die without help.'

'Will they get it?'

'They are far away from anyone. Perhaps there was an answer.'

Iktinos stood back from the coffin. He glanced down at the monitors – Croivas's heart would not take much more.

'I expect more,' he said. 'You told us you were the best.'

'Then let me go,' gasped Croivas.

In reply, Iktinos picked up the tube he had taken from Croivas's throat and forced it back into the man's mouth. Croivas reached up to fend off Iktinos but Iktinos simply grabbed his flabby claw of a hand and crushed its softened bones in his fist. Croivas's scream was strangled and weak. His remaining hand flapped against the lid of the coffin as Iktinos forced it over him again and the shadow fell back over Croivas Vel Scannien's blinded eyes.

Croivas's whimpering was barely audible as Iktinos put his shoulder to the side of the coffin and pushed it back into the water.

Iktinos glanced back down at the readouts, made a few adjustments to the air mix and sustenance regimens, and then walked back out of the sanctum and towards the cave entrance. As he did so he pulled his helmet back on and his face was replaced with the grimacing Chaplain's skull.

Iktinos had served well and never given up where even stout-hearted Space Marines, even fellow Chaplains, had chosen to discard the sacred word and turn their back on the traditions of their order's foundation. Now Iktinos would be rewarded – not with riches or peace, but with the chance to play a part in the greatest work all mankind had ever known. Space Marines, and the Soul Drinkers in particular, were immensely proud, but Iktinos had gone beyond that and it was not pride that swelled his heart as he went to do his duty among his fellow Soul Drinkers.

It was the knowledge that when he was done, nothing in this galaxy – in this universe – would remain unchanged.

CHAPTER MASTER SARPEDON of the Soul Drinkers took to the centre of the auditorium, watched by the hundreds of fellow Soul Drinkers. He was a horrendous sight. From the waist up he was a Space Marine, a psychic Librarian, with his purple power armour worked into a high collar containing the protective aegis circuit and the golden chalice symbol of the Chapter worked into every surface. He was an old man by most human standards and his shaven head was scarred by war and sunken-eyed with the things he had seen. From the waist down, however, he was a monster – eight arachnid legs, tipped in long talons, jutted from his waist where human legs should be. One of his front legs was bionic, the original having been ripped off what felt like a lifetime ago.

'Brothers of the Chapter,' he began, his voice carrying throughout the auditorium. 'We have come so far it is difficult to imagine what we once were. And I am glad, because it shows how far we have left that time behind. Some of you, of course, have never known the Chapter other than as it is now. And I am glad of that, too, because it shows that in spite of everything the galaxy has thrown at us we can still recruit others to our cause. We have never given up, and we never will. The new initiates, and those who have now earned their armour, are proof of that.'

Sarpedon looked around at the assembled Soul Drinkers. There were faces he had known for a long time, back into the earliest days of his service in the Chapter before he had led it away from the tyranny of the Imperium. Others were new, recruited by the Chapter in the days since the schism.

The auditorium had once been a xenobiology lecture theatre on an explorator ship that had become lost in the warp. Large dusty jars containing the preserved bodies of strange alien creatures were mounted on the walls, and Sarpedon himself spoke from on top of a large dissection slab with restraints still hanging from it.

'We have been apart for some time,' continued Sarpedon. 'Captains, make your reports. Karraidin?'

Captain Karraidin was one of the most grizzled, relentless warriors Sarpedon had ever met. A relic of the old Chapter, he wore one of the Soul Drinkers' few suits of Terminator armour and had a face that looked like it had been chewed up and spat out again. He stood with the whirr of both his massive armour's servos, and the bionic, which had replaced his leg after he lost it in the battle on Stratix Luminae. 'Lord Sarpedon,' said Karraidin in his deep gravel voice. 'Many of the novices have earned their full armour in the Suleithan Campaign. They intervened in the eldar insurgency and killed many of the xenos pirates. They have done us all proud.'

'What are your recommendations?'

'That Sergeant Eumenes be given a full command,' replied Karraidin.

Sarpedon spotted Eumenes himself among the Soul Drinkers – he knew Eumenes as a scout, one of the new recruits of the Chapter, but now he wore a full set of power armour and he seemed perfectly at home among its massive ceramite plates.

'Sniper Raek has distinguished himself in scouting and infiltration duties,' continued Karraidin. 'I recommend that he remain a scout and take command of other novice forces. Given our current situation I believe the Chapter would benefit from veteran scouts like Raek.' The slim-faced, quietly spoken Raek was the best shot in the Chapter – as good, some said, as the late Captain Dreo.

'Then it shall be so,' said Sarpedon. 'And of the latest recruits?'

'The harvest has been bountiful again,' said Karraidin with relish. 'They are born soldiers, every one of them.'

The Soul Drinkers recruited new members from among the oppressed and rebellious people of the Imperium and turned them into Space Marines as the old Chapter had done, but without such extensive hypno-doctrination – Sarpedon wanted to ensure their minds were as free as the Chapter itself. For the last several months Karraidin's novices had been earning their place in the Chapter, intervening to fight the

Emperor's enemies around the scattered worlds of the largely desolate Segmentum Tempestus.

'Then we are winning our greatest victory,' said Sarpedon. 'The forces that deceived once wanted us broken and desperate, whittled down one by one, reliant on those forces to keep us from sliding into the abyss. We have clawed our way out and built ourselves a future. Some of our best have been lost to win this victory, and I have no doubt there are those who will still try to stop us. As long as we take new novices who believe in our cause, and those novices earn their armour fighting the Emperor's foes, our enemies will never win.

'But those enemies never tire. Ever since Gravenhold we have had to rebuild ourselves and now I believe we are ready to fight as a Chapter again. The Eye of Terror has opened and Abaddon has returned, it is said. More and more of the Imperium's military are diverted to countering the tyranid fleets. The underbelly is exposed and the Imperium is too corrupt to defend itself. We are sworn to do the Emperor's work, and that work is being neglected in the galaxy's hidden and isolated places.'

'Such as the Obsidian system,' said a voice from among the assembled Soul Drinkers. It was that of Iktinos, the Chaplain, distinguished by his black-painted armour and the pale grimacing skull that fronted his helmet. He was surrounded by his 'flock', the Soul Drinkers who had lost their sergeants and gone to Iktinos for leadership.

They accompanied him in battle and often led the other battle-brothers in prayers and war-rites.

'Chaplain?' said Sarpedon. 'Explain.'

'The *Brokenback* picks up many signals from across the galaxy,' said Iktinos. 'We are far from the Imperial heartland but nevertheless there is chatter, transmitted from ship to ship. I have been sifting through it to find some indication of the Emperor's work remaining undone.'

'And I take it you have found somewhere?'

'I have, Lord Sarpedon. The Obsidian system, in the Scaephan Sector, to the galactic south of the Veiled Region. The planet Vanqualis has been invaded by the greenskin scourge. The people there have begged for assistance from the Imperium but as you well know, the Imperial wheel is slow to turn and the orks will surely devastate their world.'

'So there is the Emperor's work to be done?' asked Sarpedon.

'They are people of an independent spirit,' said Iktinos. 'They have resisted the Imperial yoke and remained true to their own traditions. They have survived for a long time alone, and we may find adherents to our cause there. Certainly there are many billions of Emperor-fearing citizens who will perish without help.'

'We are not a charity,' said Librarian Tyrendian sharply. Tyrendian was a lean and handsome man, seemingly too unscarred and assured to have seen as many battles as he had. Like Sarpedon he was a powerful psyker – unlike Sarpedon his power manifested as devastating bolts of lightning, like psychic artillery, hurled at the enemy. When Tyrendian spoke his mind it was with a self-important confidence that won him few friends in the Chapter. 'There are countless worlds suffering.'

'This one,' said Iktinos, 'we can help.'

'We should be at the Eye,' continued Tyrendian. 'Chaos has played its hand.'

'The whole Inquisition is at the Eye,' retorted another voice, that of Captain Luko, the Chapter's most experienced assault captain. 'We might as well hand ourselves over to our enemies.'

'It is also the case,' said Iktinos, 'that our Chapter is not rich in resources. We are lacking in fuel and ordnance. The *Brokenback* cannot go on forever, and neither can we. The Obsidian system has a refinery world, Tyrancos, from which we can take what we please. Tyrendian is correct, we are not a charity, but we can both help secure our future and help an Emperor-fearing world survive without being ground down by the Imperial yoke.'

'And it's better,' said Luko, 'than sitting on our haunches here waiting for battle to come to us.' Luko was known throughout the Chapter for the relish with which he approached battle, as if he had been born into it, and Sarpedon could see many of the Soul Drinkers agreed with him.

'Lygris?' said Sarpedon, looking at the Chapter's lead Techmarine.

'The Chaplain is correct,' said Techmarine Lygris. Lygris's armour was the traditional rust-red and a servo-arm mounted on his armour's backpack reached over his shoulder. 'Without significant re-supply soon we will have to reconsider using the *Brokenback* as a base of operations. We would have to find ourselves another fleet.'

'Then I believe the Obsidian system may be our next destination,' said Sarpedon. 'Iktinos, assist me in finding out whatever we can about Vanqualis and its predicament. Lygris, prepare the warp route. We must be ready for…'

'Let them rot,' said yet another voice from among the Soul Drinkers.

It was Eumenes who had spoken, the sergeant who had recently earned his full armour. He pushed his way to the front, close to the anatomy stage at the centre of the auditorium. He was a brilliant soldier and looked it, sharp intelligent eyes constantly darting, face as resolute as it was youthful.

'Scout Eumenes,' said Sarpedon. 'I take it you disagree?'

Eumenes grimaced as if the idea being discussed left a bad taste in his mouth. 'The people of Vanqualis are no better than any of the rest of the Imperium. They will be as corrupt as the rest of them. You say you have turned your back on the Imperium, Sarpedon, but you keep dragging us back into its wars.'

'On the Imperium,' said Sarpedon darkly. 'Not the Emperor.'

'The people *are* the Imperium! These vermin, these murderers, they are steeped in the corruption we are fighting against! If we have to bring the whole damned thing down, if we have to set worlds like Vanqualis aflame, then that is what we do! The

Imperium is the breeding ground for Chaos! The Emperor looks upon this galaxy and weeps because none of us have the courage to change it.'

'Then what,' said Iktinos darkly, 'would you have us do?'

Eumenes looked around the assembled Soul Drinkers. 'The underbelly is exposed. You said so yourselves. We strike while we can. Break it down. The Adepta, the bastions of tyranny. Ophelia VII or Gathalamor. Imagine if we struck at Holy Terra itself, blotted out the Astronomican! This tyranny would collapse around us! We could help rebuild the human race from the ashes! That would be the Emperor's work.'

'Eumenes, this is madness!' shouted Sarpedon. 'If the Imperium fell the human race would follow. Destroying it is not the way to deliver its people.'

'If what I say is madness, Sarpedon, then a great many of us are infected with that same madness. Do not think I am alone. And we could do it, Sarpedon! Think about it. The Imperium has been on the brink for thousands of years. We are the best soldiers in the galaxy, and we know what the Imperial vermin fear. We could bring it all down, if we only made the choice!'

'Enough!' Sarpedon rose to his full height, which on his arachnoid legs put him a clear head above the tallest Space Marine. 'This is insubordination, and it will cease. I am your Chapter Master!'

'I have no master!' Eumenes's eyes were alight with anger. 'Not you. Not the Imperium. No one.

You cling to the ways of the old Chapter so dearly you are no more than a tyrant yourself.'

No one spoke. Sarpedon had fought the Chapter before – he had led the Chapter war when he had overthrown Gorgoleon and taken control of the Soul Drinkers, he had battled adherents to the old Chapter's ways and even faced one of his own, Sergeant Tellos, who had become corrupted by the dark forces against which the Chapter fought. But a conflict like this had never come into the open so brazenly.

'I see,' said Sarpedon carefully, 'that the Chapter does not unite behind me and cast down the rebel.' He cast his eyes over the assembled Soul Drinkers, reading their expressions – anger and offence, yes, but also apprehension and perhaps some admiration for Eumenes's boldness.

'Then you cannot ignore me,' said Eumenes. 'As I said, I am not alone.' The young Soul Drinker smiled and stepped forward into the centre of the auditorium, face to face with Sarpedon himself. 'They used to say that the Emperor would give strength to the arm of His champion. That Rogal Dorn would counsel victory to the just. Do you believe He will lend you strength, Sarpedon, if we settle this in the old way?'

The old way. An honour-duel. One of the Soul Drinkers' oldest traditions, as old as the Imperial Fists Legion, the Legion of the legendary primarch Rogal Dorn, from the ranks of which the Soul Drinkers had been founded almost ten thousand years before.

'First blood,' said Sarpedon, with a steely snarl on his face. 'I would not grant you anything so noble as death.'

IN THE HEART of the *Brokenback* lay the dark cathedrals, the baffling catacombs and ornate sacrificial altars that once adorned the *Herald of Desolation*. Nothing was known of the *Herald* except that it had at some time in the distant past been lost in the warp and become a part of the ancient space hulk, and that its captain or creator must have been insane. Hidden cells and torture chambers, steel tanks scarred with acid stains, tombs among the catacombs with restraints built into the stone coffins – the purpose of the *Herald of Desolation* was lost amid the hidden signs of madness and suffering, smothered by the dark, ornate magnificence that blossomed in the heart of the *Brokenback*.

The dome that soared over Sarpedon's head was crowded with statues, locked in a painful, writhing tableau of contortion and violence. Below the sky of stone agony was a thigh-deep pool of water broken by oversized figures that had been sculpted to look as if they had fallen down from above, and reached up towards the figures of the dome as if desperate to return. The dome was vast; easily the size of the Chapel of Dorn in which the last honour-duel among the Soul Drinkers had taken place.

The Soul Drinkers, stood observing around the edge of the circular pool, seemed distant and dwarfed by the strange majesty of the place. In the centre, Sarpedon and Eumenes stood, armoured but unarmed.

This was their fight, and theirs alone – when it was done the results would affect the whole Chapter, but for now it was a matter between them.

'Why have you brought us here, Eumenes?' said Sarpedon. 'You could have come to me earlier. There was no need to bring the whole Chapter into this.'

'It's not just me, Sarpedon.' When Eumenes spoke there always seemed to be a mocking note in his voice, as if he couldn't help but scorn those around him. 'There are dozens of us. And you can't hold out forever.'

'Are you just here to threaten me, Eumenes, or to decide this?'

Eumenes smiled. 'No witchcraft, Sarpedon.'

'No witchcraft.'

Eumenes darted forwards. Sarpedon ducked back and raised his front legs to fend off Eumenes but Eumenes was quick, far quicker than Sarpedon anticipated. Eumenes drove a palm into Sarpedon's stomach and though the impact was absorbed by his armour Sarpedon tumbled backwards, talons skittering through the water to keep him upright. Eumenes jumped, span, and drove a foot down onto Sarpedon's bionic front leg. Sparks flew as the leg bent awkwardly and Sarpedon, off-balance again, dropped into the water and rolled away as Eumenes slammed a fist into the floor where his face had been. Stone splintered under his gauntlet.

Eumenes had learned to fight twice. Once, among the brutalised outcasts amongst whom he had grown up – and again with the Soul Drinkers, under the tutelage of Karraidin. He was dirty as well as quick, brutal as well as efficient. And he really wanted to kill Sarpedon. Sarpedon could see that in his every movement.

Eumenes followed up but Sarpedon was on his feet, backed up against a huge broken stone arm that had fallen from above. Eumenes struck and parried but Sarpedon met him, giving ground as Eumenes tried to find a way through his defence. Sarpedon's front bionic leg dragged sparking in the water as he skirted around the fallen arm, watching Eumenes's every flinch and feint.

'What do you want, Eumenes?' he said. 'Why are we here? Really?'

Eumenes ducked under Sarpedon's remaining front leg and darted in close, spinning and aiming an elbow at Sarpedon's head. Sarpedon grabbed him and turned him around, using the strength of Eumenes's blow to fling the young Soul Drinker over his shoulder. Eumenes smacked into an oversized sculpture of a contorted figure, his armoured body smashing its stone head into hundreds of splinters. Eumenes slid down into the water on his knees but he leapt up immediately. His face had been cut up by the impact and blood ran down it as he snarled and charged again.

This time Sarpedon reared up, bringing his talons down on Eumenes and driving him down so he sprawled in the water. Eumenes struggled under Sarpedon's weight as Sarpedon reached down to grab him.

A stone shard, sharp as a knife, stabbed up from the water. Sarpedon barely ducked to the side in time as Eumenes tried to stab him in the throat. Eumenes swept his legs around and knocked Sarpedon's talons out from under him, and now Sarpedon toppled into the water.

Suddenly he was face to face with Eumenes. Eumenes had the knife at his throat, Sarpedon gripping his wrist to keep the weapon from breaking his skin. He was looking right into the youth's eyes and what he saw there was not the emotion of a Space Marine. Eumenes might have been implanted with the organs that turned a man into a Space Marine, and he might be wearing the power armour so emblematic of the Astartes warriors – but Eumenes was not a Space Marine. Not in the way that the old Chapter understood it. Sarpedon had not understood what he was doing when he began the harvest anew and made Eumenes into the man fighting him now.

Eumenes tried to force the point home but Sarpedon was stronger and the stone blade was slowly pushed away. Sarpedon held up his free hand, which had a dark smear of blood on one finger. Blood from the cuts down Eumenes's face.

'First blood,' said Sarpedon. He held up his hand so the watching Soul Drinkers could see. 'First blood!' he yelled, signifying the end of the fight.

For a few moments Sarpedon saw nothing in Eumenes's eyes but the desire to kill. The honour-duel was forgotten and Sarpedon was not a fellow Soul Drinker to Eumenes – he was an enemy, something to be destroyed. Eumenes really believed in his own cause, Sarpedon realised. To him, Sarpedon was as foul an enemy as the daemons that preyed on mankind.

Eumenes's grip relaxed and the stone shard fell into the water. Gauntleted hands took Eumenes's shoulders and pulled him back away from Sarpedon. The hate in Eumenes's face was gone, replaced with something like triumph, as if Eumenes believed he had somehow proven himself right.

'Take him to the brig,' said Sarpedon, pushing himself up out of the water with his seven remaining legs. 'Post a guard.'

Apothecary Pallas hurried up and shook his head at the ragged state of Sarpedon's bionic. 'This will take some fixing,' he said.

'Be grateful it's the same one,' replied Sarpedon. Had Eumenes shattered one of his mutated legs and not the bionic, Eumenes would have won the duel to first blood. It had been that close. Sarpedon might be stronger, but Eumenes's ruthlessness had almost brought him out of the duel as the victor.

'Your orders, Lord Sarpedon?' said Techmarine Lygris.

Sarpedon looked up at Lygris. Like Pallas, Luko and others, he was one of Sarpedon's oldest and most trusted of friends, veterans of the Chapter War who had been with him through everything the Chapter had suffered. He realised then that such old friends were becoming rarer, and the Chapter would have to rely on its new recruits.

'Take us to the Obsidian system,' said Sarpedon. 'Find out everything we have on it. And make the Chapter ready for war.'

# CHAPTER THREE

'But what of the masses of humanity,
the Emperor's flock?'

'Pay them no heed, for their greater
number is already damned.'

– Daenyathos, *Catechisms Martial*

'DOWN! EVERYONE DOWN!'

General Varr had barely yelled the words before
the first shots slammed home, bursting among the
soaring trunks and branches of the Wraithspire
Palace, filling the air with shards of burning wood.

The men of the 901st scrambled for cover. The
grounds of the palace were magnificent, the riotous
jungles of Nevermourn manicured into stands of

flowers and ornamental lakes, but in that moment they became just another battlefield. Varr dived into the cover of the massive tree trunk beside him as debris rained down, dark sheets of shrapnel shredding the palace lawns and more ordnance exploding among the branches.

Varr saw one man cut in two, the halves of his body flopping into an ornamental pond in a burst of pink foam. Another stumbled by with one arm missing, clutching at the bleeding stump as another trooper dragged him into cover behind a cluster of statues. Varr tried to see where the fire was coming from. The enemy must have artillery beyond the tree line that formed the border of the palace gardens – dull orange flashes between the trees were followed by great dark explosions in the gardens. Varr couldn't see the enemy, only hear the reports of their guns and feel the thunder of the shells ripping into the gardens.

'Report!' yelled Varr into the vox-unit's handset, struggling to hear his own words over the bombardment.

'Hundreds of 'em!' came the yelled reply, broken up by static. 'Kullek's seen 'em on the ridge! All of them, full frontal assault!' Kullek's positions were further forward, closer to the tree line, and he formed the first line of defence.

Varr handed the vox-unit back to the trooper beside him. He turned to Lieutenant Fulgorin who stood with his back to the tree trunk. 'Fulgorin, they're charging. Get the men ready to receive the enemy.'

'They'll be caught in the bombardment...' began Fulgorin.

'Of course they will!' snapped Varr. 'Why do you think they sent us here?'

Fulgorin hesitated for a moment. He was an aristocrat, someone used to being respected, and he made a natural officer. But he still believed that the men of the 901st were human beings in the eyes of the Imperium.

'The greenskins'll kill us quicker than the damn bombs. Get to it!'

'Yes, sir!' Fulgorin ran across the palace grounds, yelling at the men to ready for the charge. If Fulgorin had ever been an Imperial Guard officer then he was an old-fashioned one who led from the front, taking his place among his men with his lasgun and bayonet. Troopers of the 901st braved the falling artillery to set up firepoints among the raised plant beds and splashed through ornamental ponds to take up firing positions on the banks. Thousands of men, thousands of guns, the drab green of their fatigues almost lost among the greenery. On the far side of the battlefield were the Warders, a small contingent of artillery that had escaped the first ork attack on Palatium. They were commanded by a noble-born officer that Varr had only spoken to over the vox – Lord Sovelin Falken, his name was, and Varr had little doubt that he would prove to be every bit as outclassed in battle as the officers who had been slaughtered in Palatium's streets. Varr could see the Warders' deep blue uniforms and colourful sashes from where he stood, and pick out the brass and silver of their gun mountings. They would not last long, he thought, but the 901st needed all the manpower they could get.

In front of the 901st and the Warders, the tree line of Nevermourn's jungle rose like a dark green curtain thirty metres high, its deep shadows giving way to the soaring fronds of the canopy like a roof spread over the world. It seethed with life, and as General Varr watched a torrent of creatures streamed from between its roots and branches, a dark cloud of birds, lizards and insects driven from the jungle.

The jungle knew what was storming through it to take the Wraithspire Palace.

The Wraithspire Palace, which the troops were defending, speared up from those jungles like a hand reaching for Vanqualis's turquoise sky. Wrought from the mightiest of the jungle's greatwood trees, enormously enlarged and moulded by some forgotten bioscientific technique, the Wraithspire Palace was the most spectacular man-made sight on Nevermourn. Its state rooms and audience chambers, nested like the chambers of a seashell, were hollowed from the living wood, and from the enormous spread of branches that ringed the palace like a collar hung chapels and private landing pads like ornate baubles. The Wraithspire Palace was a symbol of human mastery over the jungles and, had the greenskins not struck during the Trooping of the Warding Standard, many of House Falken's senior aristocrats would have been sheltering amid the palace's finery at that moment.

Shells burst against the side of the Wraithspire Palace, sending slabs of burning bark and shorn branches tumbling lethally into the palace grounds. Varr drew his own laspistol and took up position alongside his command squad as another man died within earshot, his screams mingling with the explosions overhead and the orders barking back and forth. The fallen trooper had been impaled by a falling branch and squirmed like a pinned insect, gore spurting.

Varr looked away. Once, a very long time ago, it had been hard to watch the deaths of his men. It still was, in a way, but he had come to understand that dying in the Emperor's service was a victory of sorts for the men of the 901st, and given the scale of the ork forces it might well be the only victory they could win.

Varr turned to his vox-operator, Mekrin. Mekrin's face was covered in knife-shaped black tattoos that doubled as urban camouflage and ganger markings. The first rule of the 901st was that you never asked what the other guy did to get sent here, but in Mekrin's case it was obvious.

'Where's Lieutenant Kullek?' Varr asked Mekrin.

'By the lake, sir,' replied Mekrin, the vox-set handset held tight to his ear. 'The one with the bridge. Says he's gonna race the men to a hundred greenskin ears.'

'Here,' said Varr, taking the handset. 'Kullek!' he yelled into it as more ordnance burst in the grounds, throwing clouds of dirt and tumbling bodies into the air.

'I can smell 'em, sir!' came the roar from Kullek.
Varr peered through the falling earth and saw
Kullek's mob, the Butchers, crowded around the
shores of an ornamental lake with a bridge leading
across it. He could even pick out Kullek himself, a
bear-like man with a shaven head who seemed
completely at home surrounded by a mob of murderers who aspired to match the depths of his
brutality. Kullek's crime was no secret – he was a
multiple murderer, a taker of skulls, a predator. He
loved war.

'Pull your men back into the line, Kullek! We
draw them in and catch them in a crossfire! Get
firepoints to your flanks and bring your centre level
with Trox's position!'

'Smell 'em, sir!' continued Kullek, as if he hadn't
heard the general at all. 'Like… like livin' gone bad,
like all them murders stood up and come to life!
Gonna be a good one, lads! Gonna taste like all our
old days at once!'

Varr could hear the Butchers roaring in agreement. There had been a time when Varr would have
made a point of rooting out men like Kullek and
having them executed before their savagery infected
the rest of the regiment. But that was a different
time, a different regiment, and now Kullek was one
of the forces that held the 901st together.

Gunfire spattered from the tree line. 'Hold!'
yelled Varr, hoping Kullek would pass the order on
to his men and keep them from running off into
the jungle. 'Kullek, get your men back, form a line
and…'

A tremendous sound boomed from the jungle, a monstrous trumpeting accompanied by the crash of splintering trees. Varr saw the shadow of it first, a great blackness seething from the heart of the jungle. Then it burst out into the open air, mighty greatwood trees crushed before it, a horde of howling greenskins charging around its feet.

It was immense, maybe fifteen metres high, covered in shaggy matted hair. It was a four-legged creature with enormous tusks and a vast maw so crammed with teeth it couldn't close it. Violent red eyes flared with pain and anger, for on a platform precariously lashed to its back were scores of smaller greenskins goading it forward with spears. Its front legs ended in huge shovelling claws that lashed around it as it reared up, carving gouges from the ground and throwing orks aside.

Varr saw Kullek's Butchers break from cover and open fire, crimson las-blasts criss-crossing the zone of the destruction in front of the beast. Orks were pouring out of the jungle now, guns blazing, visibility cut by the volume of gunfire and shrapnel.

'Heavy weapons!' ordered Varr. 'Every big gun on the beast! Get Lord Falken's men to hit it with the artillery!'

Mekrin began to relay the order to the 901st's officers, and to Lord Falken on the far flank. The other troopers of Varr's command squad hunkered down with their guns up, ready to defend the general from the advancing orks – Shenshao with his plasma gun ready, even the medic Morn with his laspistol drawn. Varr himself drew his sword – not the power sword he had once wielded as a Guard commander, or even a chainsword, but a simple infantryman's blade he carried to distinguish himself in battle.

Gunfire sprayed up at the monster as the green-skins goaded it into the palace gardens, flowerbeds and stands of manicured trees disappearing beneath its claws. A missile streaked into it and blew a boul-der-sized chunk of flesh from its shoulder, igniting the matted hair, but the damage was superficial and it would only make the beast angrier. It lowered its head and drove its lower jaw along the ground, churning up turf and soil, and wrenched its head back up flipping two or three troopers into its maw.

Varr's heart was pounding. He had no idea that anything like the orkish behemoth existed on Never-mourn. He hadn't been expecting it, and any plan he had for the defence of the Wraithspire Palace was falling apart in his mind. But he had reached his pre-vious rank by being able to read a battle and react to its ebb and flow. He tried to do that now, even as Shenshao fired a plasma blast towards the indistinct forms of the greenskins rampaging through the 901st's forward line.

'Mekrin, get to Trox,' ordered Varr.

Mekrin fiddled with the various dials and switches on the vox-readout and passed the handset to Varr.

Trox, inevitably, was praying. '...from the Throne on high, for He who watches us in our wretchedness, for Him do we seek redemption in the blood of His foes...'

'Trox!' shouted Varr into the handset. 'Fall back to the palace gates!'

'The xenos are amongst us, general!' came the reply, Trox's throaty preacher's voice quavering with fervour. 'The Great Beast looks upon us and hungers!'

'Fall back and give them the centre, that's an order!'

Varr's guts were knotted. He had known that this would be a hard fight, one they might not win. The beast was one thing, but the sheer number of the orks was the real deciding factor – hundreds were already among the 901st, duelling in point-blank firefights or leaping among the troops, cleavers rising and falling. He could see men dying amid the carnage and clouds of fire and debris, here one with his torso blown apart by ork gunfire, there a man dismembered and held high by his orkish killer like a gory standard for the other aliens to rally around. Falken's flank was embattled, too, the artillery firing sporadic bursts of mortar shots over the battlefield as the loaders fended orks off the gun with bayonets and autogun fire.

Then, Varr saw the ork warlord amid the chaos. The warlord was substantially larger than any other greenskin – Varr understood that orks tended to grow larger and stronger as they achieved battlefield successes and that the biggest of them were invariably the leaders, creating a cycle that resulted in truly immense killing machines leading the orkish hordes. But the warlord wasn't a hollering, battle-lusting killer like the other orks now rampaging through the palace grounds – he moved with grim determination, stalking through his own lines, observing the flow of the battle in much the same way as Varr himself was doing. The warlord had a crude mechanical arm and had the tiny, sharp-faced creatures – gretchin, some of the Guard called them, or grots – scampering around his feet, but it was the warlord's glowering presence that struck Varr. This was not just a horde that wanted to kill and destroy. The warlord wanted something more than simple destruction.

The 901st were falling back. Varr could actually hear Trox preaching, bellowing the praises of the Emperor even as his grenade launcher punched glittering bursts of shrapnel through the charging orks. The men were scrambling back over the cratered, scarred mess the palace grounds had become, keeping up lasgun fire with the battleground discipline that Varr had tried so hard to instil in them.

The waves of greenskins were blunted by the storms of fire but they kept pressing, the gargantuan creature ripping its way through the ornamental lake and crunching through its bridge as the orks forced the 901st back towards the doors of the Wraithspire Palace.

It wouldn't work. Varr could see it, even as he gave the order for the flanks to push up and surround the orks, catch them in a crossfire at the palace threshold. There were too many orks, and they were filling the palace grounds like water filling a chalice, fighting through one another to get to grips with the 901st. The huge shaggy beast was out of control now, rampaging through the 901st towards Lord Falken's artillery. Varr had little regard for Falken, who after all was a part of the planetary defence force that had so spectacularly failed to blunt the invasion of Palatium – but even so the idea of the behemoth trampling its way through the Warders turned Varr's blood cold.

Varr's thoughts were broken in a rush of movement and noise. His flank surged forwards and the orks turned to face them, roaring with appreciation that the 901st was giving them a proper battle. Lasgun stocks shattered under ork cleavers. Las-blasts bored through gnarled green flesh. Heads were struck from bodies, torsos were blown open by bursts of gunfire, corpses were trampled underfoot. The 901st roared as they charged but the orks drowned them out with discordant battle-cries.

Through the devastation a massive dark shape loomed towards Varr. Varr shot it through the eye with his laspistol but another one followed it, bringing an ugly serrated blade down at him. Varr caught it on his own sword but his blade shattered under the ork's assault and Varr was on his back, rolling under what seemed to be a tonne of writhing orkish muscle. He jammed the broken blade into the back of the ork's head and felt it spasm as it died. Varr rolled the stinking body off him in time to be almost blinded by a plasma blast fired by Shenshao into the face of an ork following up to kill Varr on the ground.

The ork's charred body toppled into the mud and Morn grabbed Varr's collar, dragging him free as lasfire sprayed over their position, fending off the charging greenskins.

'Anythin' need fixin'?' asked Morn.

Morn's grin showed a mouth full of missing or blackened teeth, and the man's skin was so lined it looked like it was covered in knife scars. His thinning hair was straggly and grey, and Varr once again marvelled that Morn was alive at all, let alone a medic.

'Not yet,' gasped Varr and got to his feet, snapping shots off at the hulking orks looming through the thickening smoke and showers of falling debris. The troopers of the 901st were crowded more densely around Varr's position beside the main trunk of the palace, and Varr knew that many of them were meeting their redemption there in bursts of gunfire or welters of blood, or suffocated down in the mud under bodies and trampling feet.

An ork flamethrower incinerated a trooper standing just a few metres away, sending him tumbling to the floor, spreading guttering flame along the churned turf. Blood sprayed over Varr as another man was carved open by an ork cleaver, and across the battlefield the behemoth trumpeted as it threw a dozen Vanqualian Warders into the air with a toss of its immense head.

They were all going to die there. A new clarity came over Varr's mind and the carnage seemed to slow down around him. This was his punishment. He had been sent to Nevermourn to die. It really was that simple.

A roar of engines streaked overhead. Varr just saw twisting contrails rippling through the air above him, coiled through with leaves torn from the branches of the Wraithspire Palace. A split second later the explosions kicked in, chains of deafening impacts that sent enormous columns of pulverised earth and broken greenskin bodies high into the air.

Lieutenant Fulgorin tumbled into cover beside Varr. His face was streaked with blood

'What in the hells was that?' he asked breathlessly.

'Thunderhawks,' said Varr, unable to keep the note of wonderment out of his voice.

THE CANYON-LIKE STREET of the hive was crowded with people, silent in their mourning, thousands of pale faces turned up in pleading towards the countess as she passed. Palace guards carried her aloft on a palanquin, her attendant children skulking along beneath the platform carrying the various elements of the juvenat equipment, which invigorated her ancient body when she was forced to travel outside the security of her pinnacle chambers. The children had the customary strange, feral look in their eyes and they hissed at the crowds, snapping at the ankles of the palace guards carrying their mistress as if jealous of them.

Countess Ismenissa could see the tears in the eyes of the citizens watching her pass by, and with a faint nod of her head gave silent approval for their vigil. All over the city they were out in the streets, clogging all the hive's thoroughfares in their billions, silently praying for deliverance. This was the way of Vanqualis's commoners – stoicism and acceptance, their sorrow always silent, their fate always accepted. Tragedy was kept within.

'They're killing us!' cried a solitary man's voice from the crowds. 'What are you going to do? What will save us?' The voice was silenced as the crowd rippled around the protestor and he was cut short in a mercifully brief flurry of punches and kicks.

The palace guards shoved the crowds aside and carried the countess through the sea of longing faces into the entrance hall of the Basilica Praector. The basilica, like much of the hive, was built in the style favoured by Vanqualis's founders – pious and industrious, solid dark steel girders and mesh floors embellished with columns and devotional plaques. The whole city spoke of labour and prayer, the two activities that should make up the whole of a commoner's existence.

The senior archivist hurried from among the towering data-stacks that filled the Basilica's main dome. His long, aged face bobbed above the data-slate that had replaced his hands, constantly spooling out a stream of printed parchment. He bowed as best he could, his nib-tipped fingers scribbling information down as he spoke.

'Countess,' he said hurriedly. 'I had not thought, with the current situation... I had not believed that you would be here... that is, to attend person-ally...'

'This is a matter I must see to myself,' replied the countess. The children scuttled to their places behind her as she stepped down off the palanquin, the palace guards in their brocade and finery shouldering their riot shields. 'When our very world is at stake, one can trust only oneself.'

'Of course,' replied the archivist. Behind him a gaggle of other archivists, some of them even more aged and bent with their hands and faces replaced with writing or sorting devices, hurried around the datastacks. Above them, the black-clad soldiers of the Archive Regiment walked the tops of the stacks, their carbines ready to defend the precious historical information. With war and chaos looming, every institution on Herograve was on high alert.

'You will wish to see the document,' continued the archivist.

'I will,' said the countess.

The archivist led the countess between the stacks, the children scurrying behind carrying the long trailing hem of her dress and the juvenat units connected to her by cables through the back of her bodice. The archivist did his best to hide his revulsion at the dead children shambling and crawling along, but the countess was the only person who had ever really got used to their presence.

The data-stacks were crammed with thin black sheets of crystal, the medium on which the commoner authorities of Herograve's cities recorded their histories and decisions. House Falken, however, used the more reliable and traditional method of illuminated tomes, created by house retainers whose lives were spent recording the words and needs of Vanqualis's nobles. These tomes were contained deep within the refrigerated heart of the basilica, where the cold created a layer of freezing vapour underfoot and the shelves glowered with endless lines of heavy books, some of them many hundreds of years old.

The book that Countess Ismenissa sought was in a void-safe in a small clearing among the stacks, held aloft by a pair of winged steel cherubs.

'The safe is gene-locked, countess,' explained the archivist. 'I cannot open it. Such a thing would be above my station.'

A look of mild distaste came over the countess's face. She disliked any activity that might damage or violate the physical form she had kept in good repair for so many centuries. Nevertheless, these were extreme times. She ran a finger over the reader on the top of the safe, wincing as the tiny laser pulse drew a drop of blood from her finger. The micro-cogitator inside whirred for a moment, trying to unravel the countess's genetic code from the jumble of age-reversing drugs in her system.

The void-safe slid open and the countess took out the slim, steel-bound book inside. The cover was engraved with the twin symbols of the serpent and the griffon, emblems of House Falken and of those who owed House Falken a debt.

'This document is one of our most precious house relics,' said the archivist. 'Though some are older, none of them are of such importance to...'

The countess silenced him with a look, before opening the cover. Pages of flexible crystal covered in shining, flowing script slid past her as she turned them. They spoke of honour, of oaths so crucial they were sacred, binding the authors to the soil of Vanqualis and the soul of House Falken. They were powerful words, and in the darkness on the edge of the Imperium it was rare indeed to find honour held so deeply.

The final page bore two signatures. One was that of Heradane Falken, a mighty noble lord from decades past who reigned when Nevermourn was still largely untamed and Herograve's cities were just scrapes in the dirt, struggling to find a foothold on Vanqualis. The other was that of a man named Orlando Furioso, his mark embellished with the symbols of the eagle and the griffon.

'I had never looked upon it till now,' said the countess quietly. 'I wonder now if I really believed it was true.'

'It is in order?' asked the archivist.

'Of course it is,' snapped the countess. 'The house's retainers spent years crafting every word. And honour of this strength allows no failure. I had to see it for myself before I could really understand the debt I was to call in.'

'Then, countess, what is your decision?'

The countess paused for a moment, running her age-dried fingers over the signatures. 'Bring forth the astropath,' she said.

The palace guards muscled forwards a lean man in shackles, his face dominated by the yawning hollow sockets where his eyes had once been. Symbols were incised into the pale skin of his cheeks and shaven scalp and they glowed faintly, as if power smouldered within the man. His hands and feet were shackled and he wore black robes marked in crimson.

The countess despised witches, as did all Vanqualis's Emperor-fearing folk. But an astropath, though psychic, was the only communication with the Imperium at large. The dead eyes of the countess's children followed the astropath as he approached. The countess stroked the head of the nearest child as if comforting it in the presence of the hated witch.

'I must have a second message sent,' said the countess. 'It must be received, and quickly, but the symbols given are very precise and the receiving astropath must be powerful indeed. I expect it to be received and acted on with all haste, so inaccuracies will not be accepted. Understood?'

'Understood,' said the astropath, shivering in the cold. 'But you are as aware as I am that our art cannot be precise. The call for help I sent out two months ago was only received by a few, and only the 901st Legion was close enough to act. To reach a specific recipient, in addition, requires a great deal of power and skill, and the most precise symbolic discipline on both ends. Our isolation here means that...'

'It means you must do better,' snapped the countess. 'You have one purpose here, and that is to connect us to the Imperium outside. I had expected our call for help to bring forth the Imperial Guard and Navy, not the smattering of criminals that were sent in their stead. Now you have a chance to redeem yourself for that failure. This message will get through. Vanqualis will accept nothing less.'

'Of course, my lady,' said the astropath grimly.

'The message,' said the countess, 'is that Vanqualis is doomed by the orkish scourge and the Imperium has sent us nothing but a gaggle of criminals to defend us. House Falken of Vanqualis is therefore compelled to call in an ancient and grave honour debt. I do not take this step lightly, but I take it in the name of House Falken and all the peoples of Vanqualis. Without help, we shall all surely perish and the unholy xenos will have dragged another world from the Emperor's light.'

'It shall be done, countess,' said the astropath. 'To whom is this message to be sent?'

The countess held the document in front of the astropath and he ran his fingers over it, his psychic near-sense reading the script on its crystal pages. They told him of the exact details of the debt, and the people who owed it.

His mouth hung open. Had he still possessed eyes, they would have been wide in wonderment, and not a little fear.

'Can it be done?'

'It can, countess,' gulped the astropath. 'It is a strenuous task to communicate so urgently across the gulf of the immaterium, but as you say, their own astropaths will surely be of the highest quality.'

'Then again, I will accept no failure,' said the countess. She snapped the document shut and put it back in the void-safe. 'Now that the decision has been made, I must return to the people. They must see their countess unafraid.' The palace guard brought forth her palanquin and she was conveyed back through the basilica to where the huge crowds held their endless vigil, expressing their fears and hopes with the silence appropriate to the commoner.

The astropath knelt on the floor of the basilica, visualising the images that formed the coded message to be received and decoded by another of his kind far across the interstellar gulf.

The debt had been called in. There would be no going back now. If Vanqualis survived, it would be because honour had overcome the brutality of the xenos. It was a slim thread on which to hang the hopes of a world, but when the Imperium was so distant and the enemy was so close, it was all Vanqualis had.

# CHAPTER FOUR

'What of the times when the enemy is stronger, in body or in numbers?'

'No xenos is more cunning than humanity. No traitor has the courage of the pious.'

– Daenyathos, *Catechisms Martial*

THE THUNDERHAWKS ROARED over in another pass. Heavy bolter fire was stuttering down, kicking up crescent sprays of dark ork blood. Varr could see the Thunderhawk gunships banking, their nose-mounted heavy bolters boring streaks of fire down into the orks as their engines kept them hovering above the battlefield. They were painted dark purple and he caught a symbol on the tailplane of one – a golden chalice. Varr wasn't familiar with the Chapter, but he had served in Imperial armies long enough to know what the gunships' appearance meant.

Space Marines. The Adeptus Astartes.

Following the long space voyage after receiving Vanqualis's distress call, the 901st had been on Nevermourn for two weeks, and Varr had always known that if the full force of the ork horde ever hit them the 901st would fall and Vanqualis would be lost. Now, for the first time, it looked like Vanqualis might be worth fighting for after all.

One gunship swooped low, behind the mass of orks crowded in front of the palace gates. The Thunderhawk's side doors slid open and bolter fire chattered out. One Space Marine leaned out, bareheaded, and pointed down at a space in the throng with his lightning claw. The Thunderhawk tipped almost onto its side and maybe twenty Space Marines dropped out, bolt pistols blazing and chainswords raised up ready to strike.

'Astartes!' shouted one of the 901st's soldiers. 'Tears of the Throne! They've sent in the Astartes!'

The effect on the soldiers was instant. Even these impious criminals had heard of the Space Marines, either as figures of the Emperor's wrath in preachers' sermons or as whispered soldierly legends. They said a Space Marine could do anything – rip a man apart with his bare hands, live forever, take on the most horrible aliens and win. Some didn't believe they really existed, but treated them as a symbol of the power the Emperor instilled in His citizens. Others spoke of them as the soldiers who fought the battles that really mattered, far away from the pits of war where the Penal Legions were sent to die.

Now they were here, fighting alongside the 901st.

For a moment Varr could only watch them, the gunships firing streams of explosive death into the orks as their payloads of huge, armoured Space Marines made ready to drop into the fray. Then the officer in him took over again.

'All fronts advance!' he yelled. He held his broken sword high, standing clear of cover so as many men could see him as possible. 'Charge!'

'WHO ARE THEY?' asked Sarpedon over the vox, trying to block out the roar of the Thunderhawk's engine. Through the open door beside him swung the view of the battlefield – the handsome grounds in the shadow of the Wraithspire Palace, now seething with a mass of orks and the thin cordon of soldiers trying to contain them.

'Not the Guard exactly,' replied Lygris, his voice transmitted from the *Brokenback* in orbit over Nevermourn. 'There are a couple of troop transports in deep system space, staying out of the way. Looks like the Penal Legions. The Chapter archive won't have any records.'

'I'm not surprised,' said Sarpedon. Penal Legions rarely lasted long enough to amass a regimental history – they were sent into the teeth of vicious conflicts and were considered fortunate if they existed in any form afterwards. 'This is the Imperial response?'

'Looks like all of it,' said Lygris. 'There isn't much in the way of military build-up here. Vanqualis is lucky to have what has turned up.'

Sarpedon looked down at the motley collection of killers and criminals, united only by their mud-spattered dark green uniforms and their collective failure to serve the Imperium.

'They're here to die,' said Sarpedon, more to himself than to Lygris. 'This is their punishment.'

'Engaging!' came Luko's voice over the vox, against a backdrop of clashing blades and gunfire.

Soul Drinkers units were making landfall among the orks, taking the greenskins by surprise. Sarpedon could see the shockwaves rippling through the mass of orks as they turned to face the threat suddenly boring through them.

'Take us down!' Sarpedon shouted and the gunship banked low, fire stuttering down from its nose and door mountings. Sarpedon glanced back into the passenger compartment – Squads Salk and Graevus were unhooking themselves from their grav-restraints, bolters ready. Sergeant Salk was rapidly earning the status of a veteran among Sarpedon's most trusted officers, and Graevus led his assault squad with a quiet authority that contrasted with the brutality and skill with which he wielded his power axe. Graevus was also one of the more obviously mutated members of the Chapter – one of his hands was grotesquely huge and taloned, a fleshy vice that let him wield the bulky power axe one-handed as lightly as a fencer's sword.

Sarpedon could see the off-white glint of orkish tusks amid the gnarled green flesh, even the hateful red eyes and spatters of human blood on their blades. He could smell the stink of ork sweat and blood.

'Go!' he shouted. He had his force staff gripped in both hands as he pushed himself out of the Thunderhawk on his mutated legs, the mass of orks sweeping up towards him. Salk and Graevus followed, bolters chattering even as they fell.

Sarpedon took the fury inside him built up over a lifetime of battles, first the wrath at the Imperium's foes, then his rage at the Imperium itself that had betrayed and tried to destroy his Chapter. He took it all, concentrated it until it was white-hot, and let it flood out of his mind, around the spiralling aegis circuit of his armour, and out into the reality around him.

Sarpedon was the most powerful psyker the Soul Drinkers Chapter had ever fielded. He had no finesse, no fine control, but he made up for that in raw power.

His hate flooded out of him, and a great many orks learned for the first time what fear really was.

GENERAL GLAIVAN VARR had never fought in a battle like the one the 901st fought for the Wraithspire Palace, and he was grateful for it. He had seen many terrible, soul-scarring things, especially at the Eye of Terror where he had held his last command as a free Guard officer. But none of them could quite compare to the vast, dark figures that strode over the battlefield, more imposing than even the Wraithspire Palace itself. Their bodies were made of shadow and their eyes burned with purple flames. Fire leapt between them, as if a hellish reality were layered over the battlefield, somewhere populated with figures crafted from pure fear. Their hunched shapes and violent eyes, and the splintered maws which opened up in their faces, gave them the looks of malevolent orkish gods, come down to punish the greenskins.

Varr had witnessed enough psykers using their powers on the battlefield, and yet the spectacle had still struck fear into him on a primal level. The effect on the orks was astonishing. A terrible wailing went up from the orks, something Varr had never heard before. He saw greenskins running, and volleys of gunfire cutting them down.

'They've got the greenskins scared!' shouted Varr as loud as he could. All around him the men of the 901st were pressing forward, and Varr was well aware that he was one of the few factors keeping them going. 'Put them to the blade! Put them to the gun! Show them why the Emperor sent you here!'

The battle was a blur. Varr was aware of the fighting around him, of hot ork blood spraying up his arm, of a rusted combat knife in his hand in place of his discarded sword hilt. Part of him registered the flamethrower-wielding ork who fell, its face blasted open by Varr's pistol, and Varr's command squad falling on it to finish it off. Another part saw the arcs of fire streaking from the centre of the battle where the Space Marines were laying waste to the ork centre, and how the orks weren't charging towards the 901st's troops now – they were fleeing into them, throwing themselves into firefields and bayonet lines to get away from the Astartes assault.

But most of Varr simply marvelled. He couldn't direct the battle any more – he had set it in motion and done everything he could to direct the men well, but now it would unfold on its own. There had been a time when Varr could manage every unit and every manoeuvre of his regiments, when he was leading seasoned and disciplined men who treated his words as that of the Emperor. But the 901st were not those men, and Varr's role now was to fight with them and lend what he could to the battle with pistol and knife.

The huge shaggy monster that had so nearly broken Lord Falken's artillery was rampaging through its own lines now, driven mad with the psychic fear looming over the battlefield. Even the monster was overshadowed by the huge dark shapes, and in terror it had thrown off the gretchin goading it and was trampling orks beneath its huge front claws. The Thunderhawks were hovering over the battlefield and firing streams of fire into it, blasting one side raw and bloody, and Varr could glimpse broken bones jutting up through the mass of gory muscle.

The beast fell, and what resolve was left in the ork push fell apart. The 901st surged forwards over the ground that the centre had given up and Varr saw Kullek, somehow still alive, he and his butchers taking on the orks at their own game of close-quarters murder.

'Trox, Kullek, take the centre forward! The whole line will advance to the tree line! Fulgorin, hold the rear!' Varr wasn't sure who had shouted the order until he realised that it was him.

'A THOUSAND, GIVE or take,' said Mekrin matter-of-factly. 'Another five hundred will be dead before we move out.'

Varr looked out across the lines of Imperial dead. Fifteen hundred sinners had done the Emperor's work for the first time in their lives, by dying. That left about five thousand in the 901st and Van-qualian Warder artillery. If the line had not held, there would have been far fewer left to carry on the fight.

Varr turned to Lord Sovelin Falken, who shared the makeshift command post in a reception chamber just off the entrance hall of the Wraithspire Palace. The place was spectacular, the living wood trained into decorative swirls and staircases spiralling up through the trunk, but its majesty was dulled by the drab-uniformed penal troopers using it to regroup and treat their wounded.

'Your men took a mauling,' said Varr.

'I cannot deny that,' said Sovelin. He was a young man, slightly too pasty to look like a real soldier. He was always moving, too, his eyes darting and his hands wringing.

'Half your planet's inhabitable land is covered in jungle and your men weren't trained to fight in it.'

Falken looked as if he might bristle at that, but his pride had taken enough of a battering at Palatium to let him swallow it for the moment. 'The Warders were founded to defend the cities of Herograve and put down uprisings by its commoners. Nevermourn was our haven. There was no need to defend it.'

'A haven? It's the underbelly, Falken! Herograve's covered by orbital defences, enough to put off any invader. But the jungles have nothing, and once the greenskins reach the coast it is just a short hop across the sea and they'll be in your cities. Nevermourn was begging to be invaded–'

'Do you think I don't know that, Varr?' snapped Falken. 'This planet has been alone for centuries. The only outsiders we ever saw were Administratum collectors come to take away our tithes. Is it any surprise we ended up blind to the outside?' Some of Falken's surviving artillerymen were tending their own wounded in the palace entrance hall, their blue uniforms spattered with mud and blood, their brocade and uniform brasses dull. 'I saw Palatium die. I know what our failures were.'

Varr didn't need to ask Falken to elaborate. He had seen more planets fall to ignorance and complacency than to the brilliance of an enemy commander. 'How many Warder regiments got out of Palatium?' he asked.

Falken shrugged. 'Mine. Apart from that, some civilians who might make it to the coast.'

'That's it?'

'The greenskins knew just when to hit us.'

'And the Space Marines knew just when to hit them,' said Varr. 'The Space Marines are the best soldiers in this galaxy. This world isn't lost yet.'

'My world is,' said Falken, and Varr could see in the nobleman's face that he considered the responsibility for the fall of Palatium to fall on his own shoulders. 'I have men wounded, I should see to them.'

Falken headed off to where his Warder artillery-men were patching up their wounds. The 901st and the Warders were not mixing, which was under-standable since in every sense they came from very different worlds. Elsewhere Varr could see Brother Trox preaching to a group of men whom he had adopted as disciples. Trox was deeply religious and had been some kind of a preacher before he had been condemned. As ever the exact nature of his crime was a secret but the rumours tended towards something to do with women. Trox had a haunted look in his hollow eyes as if he was certain the Emperor's wrath would fall upon him at any moment, and his followers gradually ended up the same, fatalistic and grim, not caring much if they lived through the next battle.

For a moment Varr wondered if these men were really alive at all in the eyes of the Emperor, or if they were just marching through drawn-out deaths to make their existence worthwhile. They included Varr himself, of course – maybe he was already dead, and he had simply not found an appropri-ately reverent way to die yet.

'General!' called someone behind him. Varr turned to see the Space Marine walking in through the palace's grand doors and into the command post. None of Varr's command squad or officers dared to challenge the new arrival – the Space Marine's incongruous size and the heraldry of his power armour gave him an air of power that simply brushed men away from him. It was the Astartes that Varr had seen leaping from the Thunderhawk, still wearing his lightning claws blackened with scorched orkish blood. His helmet was still off – his hair was shaven into a single dark strip down the middle of his scalp and instead of the stern granite face Varr expected of the Emperor's finest, he had a wide face that broke easily into a triumphant grin. 'Captain Luko of the Soul Drinkers. We sent those greenskin vermin packing, did we not?'

Varr returned Luko's greeting with a slightly bitter smile of his own. 'I don't know how much we had to do with it. I am not afraid to admit that we were lost until your battle-brothers waded in.'

'Commander Sarpedon sent me,' continued Luko. 'The gunships have taken a pass over the tree line. It looks like the orks have retreated into the jungle and are regrouping.'

'So they'll be back.'

'That they will.'

'We've blunted them, though, and that's more than they expected. I suggest we take the chance to fall back in good order. Give them the palace and find another point to defend. The orks will be heading for the coast so we make them pay for every step they take.'

'Sarpedon agrees.' Luko indicated the battlefield outside the palace doors. The grounds of the Wraithspire Palace were heaped with greenskin dead. 'There can only be so many of them, eh?'

Varr had imagined that Space Marines would all be grim, devout warrior-monks but Luko had something like savage joy in him. Maybe Luko actually enjoyed what happened on the battlefield – Varr couldn't imagine anyone actually looking forward to battle, but then Space Marines were said to be the perfect soldiers.

'There are always more,' said Varr. 'That's how the greenskins fight. Always more of them. The Guardsmen used to say they grew out of the ground, just to spite us.'

'Then we'll kill them faster than they can grow them,' replied Luko. 'How long before you can move out?'

Varr glanced back at his men. 'If we take all the wounded, an hour. I can't speak for Lord Falken's men, but they'll just have to keep up.'

'What are your numbers like?'

'In total, just under five thousand men plus some armour. The jungle won't make supply any easier but I can keep them going for long enough.'

'That's five thousand more soldiers than the orks were expecting,' said Luko. 'The 901st fought well today, general. These are some tough men you have here.'

'We are scum, captain.'

'That's what I said. And the ork might never retreat for long, but he can be killed. As you said, we draw them in, kill them off, and by the time we reach the coast there won't be enough left to hit Herograve.'

'I wish I shared your confidence, captain. The truth is that my men have been condemned to death and the 901st was sent here to die. We weren't selected to defend Vanqualis because of our skills in battle, that's for sure – we were the only unit close enough to the Obsidian system when Vanqualis sent out the distress call. I knew two weeks ago that this was not a particularly winnable campaign. With your Chapter here that has changed, but my men are still here on Vanqualis as a punishment.'

Luko stepped closer and Varr felt dwarfed by the size and presence of the Space Marine. 'No. You were sent here to save this planet. If you think these men can serve their Emperor by dying, think how much better they can serve Him by surviving.'

'All respect,' said Varr, 'you do not know what it means to be declared beyond the Emperor's light. Many of these men are looking for death.'

'Then you will command them to survive,' replied Luko. 'And do not presume to know what the Soul Drinkers have gone through.'

Varr was not in the habit of backing down, but somewhere inside him he knew that Luko could be right. There was more than just punishment facing him and his men. Perhaps there was some redemption on Vanqualis for the men of the 901st Penal Legion. Not the nebulous, abstract thing the preachers spoke about – actual, honest-to-Throne redemption that washed away your past. 'Then we'll be with you,' said Varr.

'If,' said Luko slyly, 'you can keep up.'

'Is that a challenge, captain?'

'Only if you accept it.'

'Then we have a deal. The 901st will put the Space Marines to shame.'

'And the Space Marines will show the 901st how to fight.' Luko held out his gauntleted hand. Varr shook it, acutely aware that Luko had to take care not to crush the man's hand.

'We move out in an hour,' confirmed Luko. 'I hope the greenskins enjoy their new palace. Your men made sure they paid enough for it.'

Luko walked off back towards where the Soul Drinkers were mustered, among the smouldering craters and heaped dead of the palace grounds where they were watching for the orks to return.

'One thing,' said Varr.

'General?'

'The witchcraft.'

Luko grunted a laugh. 'Commander Sarpedon is a powerful psyker, General Varr. He takes what he thinks the enemy will fear and throws it out there, a hundred metres high. Usually works, too.'

'My men are a superstitious lot. They'll say psykers are bad luck.'

'Bad luck it is,' replied Luko, turning again to leave. 'For the orks.'

THE HUMANS HAD thrown the orks back into the jungle and slain the huge monster that the horde had driven before it. Death and destruction had come with the humans, and worse things besides – gods. The gods of the greenskins, suddenly angry at the orks. They had loomed over the battlefield, dark and terrible, but instead of roaring their approval at the bloodshed they had spat down wordless curses and refused to crush the weakling humans.

The orks skulked through the jungle, thousands of creatures lurking in the dense undergrowth among the mud and vermin. Word passed rapidly about what they had seen, their gods turned against them, the humans breaking the charge of the unbeatable horde. Anger and fear were like a disease, spreading from ork to ork in an instant. Guns flared in the darkness. Blades flicked into the shadows and came out wet with blood. That fear and anger turned an ork against its fellow greenskin, started brawls, started wars, and enough orkish worlds had burned because the orks turned on themselves.

Crude, brutal voices were raised, barking the base insults that made up the bulk of the ork language. One mighty ork, a scarred warrior with one eye missing and dozens of kill-trophies hanging from rings stuck through its skin, bellowed its rage through the jungle. Other voices were raised, now emboldened. Bones were broken and scores settled. Dissatisfaction rippled out and for a moment it felt like the horde would surely fracture.

A mechanical hand closed around the mighty ork's head. He had not seen the massive shadow looming behind him, silent and glowering. The rusted, bloodstained steel claw closed around its skull, the thick bone fracturing. Its remaining eye popped out and its teeth shattered, spilling from its mouth before its head crunched flat and the claw let go. The ringleader slid down into the mud. Insects, smelling blood and brains, scrabbled over its ruined skull.

The warlord stepped out into the open. Las-burns, like charred craters in his skin, still smouldered. Silver glinted where a bayonet had broken off unnoticed in his shoulder. His mechanical parts were slathered in greasy mud and gore, steaming with the heat of the engines built into his chest.

He reached down into the mud and picked up the veteran's body, its head a twisted mess. The warlord shook the body like a rag doll and threw it down again, stamping on it and shattering its ribs in an insult so crude even the most blunt-minded ork could not fail to get the message.

The warlord was in charge. His goal was the goal of the horde, and of every ork there. He was a creature of vision, a creature of drive and willpower that none of them possessed. Without him, the orks would never have left the Garon Nebula, and would still be squabbling over meaningless feuds waiting for a warrior to rise and lead them onto something greater. Without him, they would be nothing. Only the warlord understood how to make the orks more than mere animals, only he knew how to take away what the humans loved and inflict that which they feared.

He barked his anger at the orks, who fell prostrate before him or scrabbled out of sight. The slaves who followed him melted away into the undergrowth, tiny beady eyes watching him with fear, for they knew he was willing to kill again and again if that was what he had to do to make his will known. The warlord might be more than an animal, more than an ork, but that did not mean he had ever shown anything like mercy or leniency. He was more ruthless than the most bloodthirsty of his orks, for his killing was driven by more than just the joy of battle and the desire to be strong.

The gods had not come to the battlefield to taunt the orks. It was a trick! It was a lie spun by the humans! For that was what humans did, they won by lies and trickery, baser than the cruellest slave-creature. The ork gods were watching them, and they had not come down to lend them strength because the orks did not deserve it. They had fallen upon Palatium when its defenders were unawares, and then been thrown back by the unexpected arrival of the humans' armoured elites. They had done nothing to deserve the presence of the gods, for good or ill. They were nothing yet, and only when they had proven their worth in the burning cities of Vanqualis would the gods even deign to spit upon them.

The warlord ceased his ranting. How many of the orks understood what drove him? Very few. Perhaps none of them. But as long as they fought for him, it did not matter.

He strode through the undergrowth, kicking slaves out from underneath his feet. He could see, through the trees, the battlefield in front of the enormous palace the orks had tried to capture. The orks rarely bothered with burying their dead so the warlord paid no mind to the heaps of ork bodies piled up around the ruined palace gardens. What made him growl and glower were the armoured forms among the carnage, the human elites, who had snatched a victory away from him. They had struck from above like lightning, and destroyed the victory that the warlord had all but grasped. The false gods aside, they had used strength and skill to defeat the orks, and that was what offended the warlord the most. These armoured warriors had not tricked him or led his army astray – they had simply been too strong for his orks. It was that simple. None of the horde would ever admit it, but it was true. These purple-armoured humans, much taller and far braver than any other human he had fought, had beaten the warlord in a straight fight.

From the depths of the jungle, the low booms of distant explosions shook the canopy overhead. More roks and crude ork spacecraft were making landfall, depositing thousands more orks into the jungles. The warlord had brought many tribes with him, far more than had participated in the strike on Palatium. The destruction of the city had been about timing, throwing the forward elements of his horde at the humans when their guard was down. The conquest of the jungle, and the destruction of this planet's cities, would be about numbers, willpower and strength. That was the battle he had forged his horde to win. He had been on the planet for more than sixty days and nights, and it was only the force of his will that had kept the horde together while the main bulk of it was deposited in the jungle.

When the whole horde came to grips with the humans, even the armoured warriors and their witchcraft would not save them. Then, the whole of Vanqualis would burn.

# CHAPTER FIVE

'How must we honour our fallen?'

'With every bullet and every blade,
with every moment of victory and
pain.'

— Daenyathos, *Catechisms Martial*

THE ORK SHIP tumbled in a bright fiery arc towards
Vanqualis, far more graceful in destruction than it
had ever been in life. The guns that bristled from the
twisted prow of the *Brokenback* threw a further volley of lance fire and ordnance shells into the ork
wreck and it came apart, spilling ribbons of burning
fuel and vented gases as it dissolved into thousands
of chunks of flaming wreckage.

'Not enough,' said Lygris to himself. The sight through the great bridge viewscreen was astonishing but there were plenty more ork craft in the invasion fleet and the *Brokenback*, formidable as it was, simply couldn't destroy them all. In any case their real damage had been done – they had disgorged smaller landers, and even hollowed-out asteroids, to bring hordes of greenskins down to the planet's surface.

The bridge of the *Brokenback* was dark, so Lygris could concentrate on the image from the viewscreen. Lygris knew the ship so well he could control most of its systems from the command pulpit that faced the screen. Everything was lined in the screen's harsh light, dense shadows were cast every time another explosion burst amid the wreckage of the ork ship. Lights winked on the data-lecterns dotted around the bridge and in the cogitators and data-engines under the grille of the deck.

'How goes the battle, Techmarine?' came the voice of Chaplain Iktinos.

Lygris was surprised that the skull-faced Chaplain had remained on the *Brokenback* – Iktinos had elected to lead the reserve force of a hundred or so Soul Drinkers, who would be sent down to Vanqualis in case the main force could not react to a threat in time. 'Good. But not well enough.' Lygris waved a hand dismissively at the image of the ork ship breaking up. 'There are many more like this and most of them have already served their purpose. The jungle is too dense for us support the battle on the ground. We're just cleaning up here, the real war is on Vanqualis.'

'And the rest of the Obsidian system?'

'The orks only seem to care about Vanqualis itself.' Lygris pressed a few keys on the command pulpit's instrument array, and called up a diagram of the Obsidian system on the main screen.

The closest planet to its sun was Proxiphan, a dead, scorched ball of rock, then the boiling firestorm of the gas giant Infernis Magna. A great gulf of space separated Infernis Magna from Vanqualis itself, the only planet in the system with a significant population. Beyond Vanqualis was Voiderhome, a small rocky world that saw exploration from the early colonists of Vanqualis before they discovered there was nothing on Voiderhome but suffocation and cold. The final planet in the Obsidian system was Tyrancos, another gas giant, orbited by a few refineries and processing plants built in an attempt to draw some wealth from the titanic blue-green mass of the planet. Beyond Tyrancos there was just Ollanius XIV, the monitoring station that had seen the Battlefleet Scaephan annihilated at dock by the first ork attacks.

'What is here that the greenskins want?' wondered Iktinos aloud.

'What do they ever want? Conquest and battle.'

'And there isn't anything to conquer in the system other than Vanqualis?'

'It appears so.'

'Then this system would seem a strange choice of destination. There is only one planet's worth of slaughter here for the orks.'

'Perhaps,' said Lygris. 'But then greenskins aren't known for strategy. Maybe the Obsidian system was the first place they came to.'

Lygris's vox chimed. 'Bridge here,' he said.

'Techmarine Lygris, we're picking up a communication,' came the reply. It was one of the Chapter's scouts, manning the comms helm towards the hulk's prow.

'From Vanqualis?'

'No, sir. Tyrancos.'

Lygris glanced back up at the diagram of the Obsidian system. Tyrancos was just a footnote to the Obsidian system – its refineries were abandoned and it had a population of zero. 'Who is it from?'

'I can't tell. But it's powerful. Looks Astartes.'

'Send it through to the bridge.'

Screens lit up on the pulpit's array in front of Lygris.

'Anything?' asked Iktinos.

'It's us. It's the Soul Drinkers.' Lygris fiddled with a few controls and a blip appeared on the screen, showing a point in orbit around Tyrancos. 'There. It's a Chapter code.'

'We have no men on Tyrancos.'

'I know. And it's an old signal, too. From the days of the old Chapter, before Sarpedon took over. A lot of our sensors were salvaged when we scuttled the old fleet, which is why the *Brokenback* can decode them.'

'The old Chapter? That makes little sense, Lygris.'

'But it's there.'

'Perhaps Commander Sarpedon is not telling us the whole truth about why we have come to the Obsidian system.'

Lygris turned to Iktinos, his face stern. 'No, Chaplain. We know everything he knows. This is something else.' He looked back at the monitor. 'It's a distress signal, standard. Probably automated. I'd suggest investigating it, but…'

'I shall go.'

'You, Chaplain? You might be needed here.'

'It may be that contact with the old Chapter, in whatever form it takes, could be hazardous to the Soul Drinkers, particularly to the newer recruits who never knew the days before Sarpedon led us away from the Imperium. As Chaplain, it is my duty to become aware of such moral threats and eliminate them where I can. I should go.'

'I see. Take one of the Thunderhawks, then. And I suggest you not go alone.'

'Of course. I shall speak to the men, and lead the rites. Then I shall be gone.'

As Iktinos left the dark sphere of the bridge, Lygris brought up the image of Tyrancos on the viewscreen. It was a gas giant, no more or less remarkable than millions of such worlds in the galaxy. A few decrepit refineries, on platforms or refitted asteroids orbiting the unforgiving gas giant, were all that suggested that anyone had been anywhere near it. And yet, the old Chapter had been to Tyrancos in some capacity. Lygris had fought alongside the old Chapter for many decades before Sarpedon took over the Soul Drinkers and he had

certainly not heard of any involvement in the
Obsidian system.

As Iktinos had said, it made little sense. But it was
also less pressing than the battle for Vanqualis. The
targeting array had locked onto another ork ship,
larger this time, a bloated construction of flaring
engines and melded asteroids typical of orkish technology so crude it was a wonder the greenskins
managed space travel at all. Lygris put thoughts of
the old Chapter out of his mind and sent the *Brokenback* towards the target, ordnance chambers
reloading and lance batteries recharging, ready to
bring a taste of the Emperor's wrath to the greenskins.

'THE JUNGLE LOVES war,' General Varr said.

'You believe so?' said Luko.

'I know it. The men who fight in wars want them
to end, but war itself wants to continue. The jungle
helps keep wars alive. It doesn't give you battlefields
where you can settle things with a single conflict. It
keeps us killing each other one at a time, never winning or losing decisively, always being dragged
deeper in.'

Squad Luko stood watch around the edges of a
clearing formed by a fallen greatwood tree, which
Varr had chosen as a temporary command post
while the whole of the 901st and the remaining
Warders caught up with him. The dark purple of the
Soul Drinkers' armour melded with the shadows
that flooded the bases of the vast gnarled trees. Captain Luko himself stood by a portable

communications unit, its viewscreen folded out. General Varr sat beside him on a fallen tree trunk. Darkness was all around as were the sounds of the jungle, the whistling of birds high up in the canopy and the creaking of the trees. Kullek, the bear-like man who had somehow contrived to survive the battle for the Wraithspire Palace, stood toying with a serrated combat knife beside a pale and weak-looking Lieutenant Fulgorin. Fulgorin's left arm and shoulder were heavily bandaged, and the fear in his eyes probably came from the fact that the jungle was a very bad place to pick up any kind of wound. Nevermourn's legions of insects loved the smell of blood.

'Sometimes you don't have a choice,' said Luko.

'Well, someone did,' replied Varr. 'The greenskins chose the jungle. They love war, and the jungle helps them wage it. Any officer worth his stripes will avoid the jungle at all costs if he can, especially if he's up against greenskins.'

'Maybe so, general,' said Luko. 'A Space Marine would take this jungle and make it into his weapon.'

'Can the Soul Drinkers do that with Nevermourn?'

'Watch us.' Luko smiled as only he could, as if battle and bloodshed were a hearty joke to him. 'Commander,' he said into his vox.

The communications unit flickered into life, its screen now showing Sarpedon's gnarled face. The high collar of his aegis suit was obvious – what was not clear were his horrible mutations. Luko knew that Sarpedon had to be wary of the reaction his mutations would gain from other Imperial soldiers. If nothing else, they would suggest that the Soul Drinkers were renegades, a fact that could turn Emperor-fearing troops (and even the assorted scum of the 901st) against them.

'General Varr,' began Sarpedon. 'It was good to know you survived the Wraithspire Palace.'

'I appreciate that, commander,' replied Varr, 'but that survival will not mean a great deal if we let the orks surround us. They're bringing more into the jungles and we won't be able to stop them so bluntly a second time.'

'Very true,' said Sarpedon. 'So we take the fight to them.'

'Are you… are you sure that can be done?' It was Lieutenant Fulgorin who had spoken. Fulgorin had probably never seen a Space Marine in the flesh before, and Luko was no doubt as intimidating to him as the greenskins.

'Anything,' said Sarpedon with a look like steel, 'can be done.'

'What do you suggest?' said Varr, ignoring Fulgorin.

'My scouts have gone ahead of us and identified high ground, the only such ground for many miles around. The ork army is large and unruly and they need a relatively defensible place to regroup. The heights is it. They'll head there and capture it, and use it as the base for their push on the coast.'

'Bit brainy for orks,' said Kullek, who seemed to show no qualms about speaking out of turn in front of the Space Marines. But then, Kullek was crazy.

'These are different,' said Varr. 'They had the intelligence to fall on Palatium when it was at its most vulnerable. And they have a leader who seems to know what he is doing.'

'We know where they are going,' continued Sarpedon. 'So we trap them. To get such a large body of men to the heights, they will need to negotiate a long valley, half filled with swamp.'

'Kullek,' said Varr. Kullek took a battered, blood-stained tactical map out of his filthy fatigues. Varr took it and spread it out as best he could on the fallen trunk beside him. 'Here,' he said, indicating the long, narrow depression which swept up towards a cluster of hills. 'The Serpentspine Valley. If we position our troops along the head of the valley below the heights we can trap the green-skins.' The valley was just one feature in a vast swathe of jungle, broken here and there by ruins or outcrops, but mostly unbroken canopy and marsh. At the top edge of the map the jungle met the seas in a rugged coastline broken by sandy beaches that would have been a vision of paradise in peacetime, but which were now set to be the scene of a bloody endgame in the defence of Herograve. 'We can keep them pinned, but not for long.'

'You won't have to,' said Sarpedon. 'We'll bombard them into the dirt.'

'With what? My ships are just troop transports and they're orbiting Voiderhome to keep out of the sights of the ork ships. Falken's artillery could do some damage but it won't nearly be enough.'

'With our fleet,' said Sarpedon. 'With the orks hidden by the jungle there isn't much the big guns can do. But when they're pinned down in the valley, we can carpet them with ordnance.'

'You mean…'

'Wipe them out,' said Luko with relish. 'Kill them all. That's how we'll beat the jungle.'

Varr was silent for a moment. The boldness of the plan was the opposite of the way war was normally conducted in such an environment. 'We'll lose a lot of men,' said Varr. He glanced up at the huge armoured forms guarding the clearing. 'Well, I will.'

'You'll lose them anyway,' said Sarpedon. 'This jungle will take them.'

'I know. But it means that we won't get many shots at this.'

'In the Adeptus Astartes, we are accustomed to only needing one.'

'Then it will be done,' said Varr. 'I'll have the men make for the valley as soon as the stragglers are in. I'll have to get them moving at the double if we're to keep ahead of the greenskins.'

'Good. We will regroup below the hills and form the line,' said Sarpedon. 'I'll have men towards the rear of our lines in case the greenskins try to slow us down. I shall have my men move out immediately.'

Varr folded the map back up and Mekrin picked his way through the mud and undergrowth to pack away the comm-unit. Varr motioned for him to stop.

'Commander Sarpedon,' said Varr. 'I fought through the Eye of Terror with the Kar Duniash

Heavy Lancers and never saw a single Space Marine. For every one of you there might be a million of us. Why are the Soul Drinkers here?' Varr looked into the comm-unit's screen – even on screen, few normal men were able to look Sarpedon in the eye.

'Because no one else can do it,' said Sarpedon. 'I'll see you at the Serpentspine Valley, general.'

THE SHIP WAS a great temple to honour and to fallen comrades, the pale marble of the walls and floor inscribed with thousands of names, and times and places of death. Braziers lit every corridor and shrine, so no fallen battle-brother's name ever fell into shadow. The high ceilings and wide spaces made the spacecraft more like a place of reflection, quiet and sombre, and in every great gallery and mustering chamber a huge ever-burning fire hung in the air like a caged sun. It was said that every single fallen brother had his name inscribed somewhere on the *Cerulean Claw*, thousands of battles remembered in the endless march of names. Many names had been added in the recent past, for the Chapter and the *Claw* had settled a grudge that had stood for many hundreds of years, and paid in the blood of their brethren to do so.

Chief Librarian Mercaeno of the Howling Griffons knelt to examine one such name, newly cut into the floor of the Manse of Furioso. It was a captain of the Fourth Company, who had fallen to the daemon Periclitor in the final bloody struggles. So many had fallen to the daemon's blade, so many had their minds shattered by its evil.

But not Mercaeno. Mercaeno had survived, because it had been Mercaeno who killed Periclitor.

'How many were lost?' came a voice that was not that of a Space Marine.

A man stood on the smooth tiles that wound their way between the inscribed marble slabs of the floor, forming a path so that no Howling Griffon would have to tread on the names of his fallen brothers. He had the face of a scholar or an academic, his thinning brown hair swept back and speckled with grey, his eyes hollow enough to suggest his recent past had seen trauma, too. He wore a long dark flak-weave coat over black clothing. He did not wear the stylised 'I' to show his affiliation, but the fact that he spoke to Mercaeno as an equal was enough to demonstrate his rank.

'It is of no concern.'

'I think it is.'

'To you,' said Mercaeno. 'The destruction of Periclitor was one of the most sacred tasks of this Chapter's recent history. Many old vengeances were made good. Many new ones were born. These matters do not go beyond the Chapter. Our oaths are our own to uphold.'

'I understand you killed Periclitor, Mercaeno.'

Mercaeno fixed the man with a withering stare. Mercaeno had immense presence, his long, leathery face dark with the years, his eyes black like flint, all surrounded by his massive power armour in the gold and deep red of the Chapter. Oaths, some of them unfulfilled since the day he first took up a bolter for his Chapter, were inscribed into the armour, endless lines of obligations and honour-debts that tied Mercaeno into the Howling Griffons. But in spite all this, the inquisitor did not flinch. 'Why are you here, Thaddeus?'

'I like to know a little about my hosts.'

'You are not a guest. Were you not an inquisitor you would never have been permitted to set foot on the *Claw*.'

'But I am,' replied Thaddeus. 'And as an inquisitor, I'm inquisitive. For instance, I'm glad you're heading with all speed towards the Obsidian system, but I'm still curious as to why. Inquisitive, you see.'

Mercaeno couldn't tell if Thaddeus was trying to be amusing. Very little amused Mercaeno, who after all had seen more death, destruction and dishonour than most men could comprehend. 'We permitted you to journey with us, inquisitor. That is more than the Howling Griffons would grant anyone else.'

'We're close,' said Thaddeus. 'It won't be long before we're in the Scaephan sector.'

'We will not drop out of warp until we are in-system,' said Mercaeno.

'Within the Obsidian system?' Thaddeus cocked an eyebrow. 'It'll be infested with ork ships.'

'The greenskin has nothing that can compare to a Space Marine strike cruiser,' replied Mercaeno bluntly. 'We shall appear among them and scatter them. We do not give our enemies the luxury of seeing us coming. You have much to learn about the Astartes way of war.'

'You'd be surprised what I know,' said Thaddeus.

Mercaeno was about to round on Thaddeus, but

seemed to think better of it. Instead, he walked a little way across the manse to where one wall was
dominated by a carved mural of a Howling Griffons
commander, magnificent with the spiked arc of an
iron halo around his head and an axe with blades
like the wings of a hawk.

'Inquisitor, do you know who this man was?'

'He was more than a man,' said Thaddeus. 'That's
Orlando Furioso.'

'Chapter Master Furioso, indeed. What do you
know of his death?'

'I do not...'

'No, you do not. Inquisitor or not, we keep our histories to ourselves. Chapter Master Furioso died by
the hand of Periclitor, whose name you will no
longer speak in the presence of my brethren. We were
gathering to celebrate the fifth millennium since our
Chapter was founded from Guilliman's sons. Traitors
ambushed us. Renegade Astartes. Their leader was
named Periclitor. Chapter Master Furioso threw them
back from his flagship but it was crippled and
crashed onto Arios Quintus. There Periclitor's traitors
fell upon the Howling Griffons and butchered them.
Periclitor mounted Chapter Master Furioso's body on
the prow of a Thunderhawk and set it adrift, so that
we would happen upon it when we came to search
for our brethren. An oath of vengeance was sworn by
the Chapter, to be borne by every battle-brother that
followed until it was made right. That was more than
three thousand years ago, inquisitor, but to a Howling Griffon Furioso's murder was as raw a wound as
if it had been committed yesterday.'

'So you killed Per… the traitor,' said Thaddeus.

'No,' said Mercaeno. 'We fought as the sons of Guilliman and of the Emperor. We quelled rebellion and battled aliens. We threw daemons back into the warp. We took on a hundred oaths, a thousand, and every one of them burned as bright as the oath of vengeance against Periclitor. Some of them still stand, and every one of them is a shame that I cannot articulate. Came the time that Periclitor rose again, this time at the Eye of Terror, and in the millennia that had intervened he had committed countless atrocities and become elevated to a daemon. The Howling Griffons hunted him across the Eye, from daemon world to dead space, and when we finally came to battle his army it was only the raw wound of Furioso's death that kept us fighting until we were victorious. Periclitor, a prince of daemons, a champion of the foul gods, did not comprehend the determination of a Howling Griffon to fulfil the oaths he has sworn. Chapter Master Furioso did not die three thousand years ago. He died the moment Periclitor fell and he was avenged. Only then could we grieve for our lost brother. Do you understand now, inquisitor, what manner of men you are dealing with?'

'I do, Lord Librarian. And I have my oaths, too. I have sworn them only to myself and to the Emperor, but I must still pursue them.'

'This is the way of the Inquisition, then?'

Thaddeus gave a bleak smile. 'No, it certainly is not. But it is my way.'

'Very well,' said Mercaeno. 'I have settled some of your curiosity. I have questions of my own. What interest does the Inquisition have in the Obsidian system?'

'None,' replied Thaddeus. 'The Inquisition does not exist. Only inquisitors do, each one doing the Emperor's work in his own way.'

'Then what interest does Inquisitor Thaddeus have there?'

Thaddeus paused, looking up at the face of Chapter Master Orlando Furioso. 'I failed to do my duty a long time ago,' he said.

'You seek redemption, then?' said Mercaeno.

'You could say that. Unfinished business, if you like. Any more than that, Lord Librarian, is for Inquisitorial ears only.'

'So be it, inquisitor.'

'I take it that your mission to Vanqualis is a matter of honour, too?'

Mercaeno gestured towards the image of the Chapter Master. 'Lord Furioso himself gave his word. Were it not kept, all we have done to avenge him would be for naught. Deliverance must come to Vanqualis and it must be the Howling Griffons who bring it. You understand now why I must take so many of my Chapter to fulfil this obligation.'

Inquisitor Thaddeus looked around the Manse of Furioso, the place dedicated to the fallen Chapter Master. Several squads of Howling Griffons were in the huge room, paying their respects at shrines to fallen heroes or gathered overlooking the inscribed names of their brethren, performing rites to cleanse the soul and prepare them for the battles to come. Mercaeno's force consisted of more than three hundred Howling Griffons, a major force by Astartes standards, and the fact that the rest of the Chapter was still fighting in the battles around the Eye of Terror suggested the importance of Furioso's oath to Vanqualis.

'We are all here because we believe,' said Thaddeus. 'And because we cannot back down. It's what the Imperium is built on.'

'Quite so, inquisitor. Now, if you are satisfied, we shall shortly arrive in the Obsidian system and I must attend to the Rites of Detestation. There will be a great deal there that we must be prepared to hate.'

Mercaeno left Inquisitor Thaddeus in the Manse of Furioso. If the inquisitor still did not understand the depths of the Howling Griffons' determination, then he would once they fell upon the greenskins and showed them how the Griffons kept their promises.

## CHAPTER SIX

'How must the alien be met on the battlefield?'

'The alien fears our purity and nobility. He must therefore be met with the most pure and noble hatred.'

– Daenyathos, *Catechisms Martial*

'WHAT IS THIS place?' said Raek, advancing warily through the harsh stripes of shadow that lay across the asteroid's surface. His sniper rifle was shouldered and he held his bolt pistol in front of his face, ready to snap shots at anything that moved.

'Nowhere,' replied Chaplain Iktinos.

Behind Iktinos was the colossal boiling disc of Tyrancos, a swirling blue-green mass so immense it almost overwhelmed the void around it. The shadows were cast by the Obsidian system's sun, a hard painful diamond hanging in space, undimmed by an atmosphere. Raek and Iktinos were on one of the many asteroids orbiting Tyrancos, on which refineries had been built to create useful fuels out of the gases piped up from Tyrancos itself. The asteroid rolled out before them, small enough for the horizon to curve round as if distorted, its surface broken by thousands of intake spines and bulky cylindrical refining units. Nearby was an enormous ragged hole as if something immense had taken a bite out of the asteroid, exposing torn layers of stone and metal underneath.

'Why would the old Chapter have come here?'

'Perhaps they did not. It is our task to find out.'

Raek lowered his pistol and knelt down, one hand on the red-black rock of the asteroid. Raek was a natural scout, attuned to his surroundings. Even through the faceplate of the voidsuit worn over his scout armour, he could taste the environment. If there were enemies waiting, hiding, Raek would know where. He would know which paths the bullets from their guns would take. He knew how to move unseen, even when the star Obsidian was bathing the asteroid in diamond-hard light.

'The place has gravity,' said Raek. 'At least two-thirds Terran standard. So something here still works. But no one's been here for a long time.'

Iktinos looked closer at the nearest intake spine. The asteroid had been fitted with the spines to draw in gases from Tyrancos's upper atmosphere, which could then be refined into fuel or materials. The spine was corroded – not rusted, but crumbling and pitted from the stark solar radiation and the biting of particle winds whipping up from Tyrancos.

'There may still be fuel,' said Iktinos. 'The *Broken-back* can re-supply here.'

'Maybe,' said Raek, 'but I don't like the look of that.' He nodded towards the hole that bit down deep into the horizon. 'It's not a meteor or a weapon impact. Looks like it was dug.'

'Then let us be certain,' said Iktinos, and walked away from the Thunderhawk docked behind him.

The hole was bitten deep down into the asteroid's crust, thrown into pitch-black shadow by the harsh light. The guts of the refinery had been sliced through, melted machinery sagging from between layers of scorched rock.

A suspended walkway of stone slabs led down into the interior of the asteroid, not suspended by wires or supports, but hanging there in space.

'Anti-grav,' said Raek. 'Someone built this. They hollowed it out and built something inside.'

Raek kept his pistol ready to come up and fire as he took the first step onto the walkway. It stayed firm beneath his feet. Chaplain Iktinos followed just behind, his augmented sight picking out the ragged mess of the crater giving way to polished, smooth stone beyond the threshold of the interior.

'Throne above,' said Raek quietly. He had seen what was mounted above the threshold, like a signpost warning against delving into the heart of the asteroid.

It was pitted with corrosion, but still unmistake-able. It was a golden chalice, marking the entrance to the asteroid. The symbol of the Soul Drinkers.

'Chaplain?'

'We move on, sergeant.'

Raek continued into the shadows. Around him opened a spectacular sight. The whole asteroid had been hollowed out and filled with an astonish-ingly complex mass of floating columns and arches, as if a hundred temples had been broken up and haphazardly reconstructed inside the aster-oid. The blocks constantly tumbled and moved around the asteroid's centre point, at which, half-glimpsed, floated a building of gold and obsidian like a tomb. The asteroid's gravity suddenly reversed as Raek crossed the threshold and the inside of the hollowed-out asteroid became the floor, Raek now looking up at the tomb floating high above him through concentric floors of shift-ing architecture.

The chalice was everywhere. The Imperial aquila, too, the two side by side emblematic of the old Soul Drinkers, before Sarpedon renounced the Imperium and made his Chapter renegades. Carved faces tumbled by, perhaps the images of past Soul Drinkers, while friezes of battle scenes could have been lost campaigns from the Chapter's past.

'What do you know of this?' asked Raek.

'I checked the Chapter archive before we left the *Brokenback*,' replied the Chaplain. 'There was no mention of Tyrancos, or of anything like this.'

'That's not what I asked,' said Raek.

Iktinos turned to Raek, the rictus of his helmet's faceplate falling on the sergeant.

Raek was shaken. He was good at hiding it, but he was surrounded by the unknown. 'Chaplain,' he continued. 'Why did Sarpedon bring us here? We are your battle-brothers, even if we did not all fight through the Chapter War as you did. We deserve to know.'

Before Iktinos could answer, movement flickered in the floating temple. Amid the ponderous shifting of the temple's architecture, it was as bright as day to a Space Marine's enhanced vision. Raek's pistol was holstered instantly and the sniper rifle was in his hands, his raw instincts turning to the weapon with which he was most comfortable.

Lights danced. Silver gleamed. Dead greyish flesh corded between slabs of armour decorated in gilt and flaking purple. Glowing red eye lenses flickered into life as blades and gun barrels unfolded from bodies. They were everywhere.

'Gun-servitors,' said Raek as more shapes unfastened themselves from layers of architecture, like blocky metal locusts on thrumming anti-grav motors. Beams of reddish light swept through the temple, seeking out movement and body heat. 'Someone wanted to keep us out.'

'No,' said Iktinos. 'Someone wanted us to be worthy.'

The first shots spattered down, rapid storms of laser spattering between the slabs orbiting above the two Soul Drinkers. Raek threw himself to one side. Iktinos drew his crozius and plasma pistol.

'So the old Chapter has not done with us yet,' he said calmly, as Raek opened fire.

THE WARLORD BELLOWED and the horde surged on. The beasts of the jungle swarmed before them, even mighty predators panicked by the war-cries of the orks and the tramping of feet. The horde had swollen with the arrivals from orbit and they boasted crude war machines, tracks churning through the undergrowth. Walking machines, with massive guns for arms and armoured bodies like great metal barrels, stomped through the mud with insane gun-happy orks at the controls. Snarling attack beasts, their bodies no more than fang-filled maws and a stomach, strained at the leash as their handlers whipped them forwards. And thousands upon thousands of orks tramped forwards, firing into the air or waving their cleavers with joy at the impending bloodshed.

Some of them had replaced their teeth with chunks of gold, or covered their bodies in war paint. Others wore skull masks, or carried the biggest, flashiest custom guns they could afford, or wore the body parts of their enemies as trophies. They were showing their affiliation to their clans, but in truth, there were no clans in the jungle. The warlord had welded them into one army – while back on their homeworlds in the Garon Nebula they would have been murdering each other over a look, under the warlord they were one horde, united in war. Only in battle did the orks put aside their weaknesses, and become what they were born to be.

The warlord, for the first time on Nevermourn, allowed their spirit of battle-lust to infect him. He hollered as he marched alongside them, snapping his enormous mechanical claw and letting the billows of steam hiss violently from the vents in his torso. He was a greenskin like them, a born killer, sent by the orkish gods to conquer the galaxy and exterminate everything that stood in their way.

The horde poured into the valley like a flood. The valley was choked with trees and the rotten remains of dead plants and animals that had tumbled down from above, waist-deep in the swamp in places, tree roots reaching overhead like arched doorways and venomous serpents writhing through the blackness. But the orks surged forwards, too powerful a force to be slowed down by the jungle. Fighting machines dragged down trees that had stood for centuries and tank tracks ground through the mire. Orks fell, sucked down by the mud or devoured by lurking predators. But they were a drop in the green ocean.

The warlord was at their head, storming towards the heights. Once they had the hills, the horde could group up and be strengthened, ready for the final bloody push on the coast. The orks were too set on murder and destruction to realise the relative subtlety of such strategies, but the warlord did. That was why the greenskins would raze the cities of Herograve, and why Vanqualis would be theirs.

An ork fell, a hole bored through his torso by a long-las shot. Snipers' targeting beams flickered through the dense foliage. Another shot coughed through the leaves and blew the side off an ork's head.

They were here. The humans. This time, not even the armoured warriors and their false gods would save them from the orks. The warlord bellowed like the hate-fuelled beast he was, and the orks charged into battle.

'COLD AND FAST, Soul Drinkers!' yelled Luko as the horde roared up from the green-black depths of the jungle. He could smell them, rotting meat and gunsmoke, old blood and choking exhaust.

Graevus was beside Luko, the power field around his axe crackling as he weighted it in his grotesquely deformed hand. Luko's own power claws leapt into life, spilling arcs of blue-white power off the ends of the blades. 'Don't get lost down there, Luko,' said Graevus. 'Just draw them up here, in and out. You don't have to kill them all yourself.'

Luko grinned savagely. 'Don't tempt me, Graevus. I might have to wipe these xenos out just to teach you a lesson.'

Then the time for talk was over. With a scream of escaping steam and the crunch of gears, a lurching machine of metal three times the height of a man tore out through the trees. One arm spat gunfire through the jungle, sending the Astartes of Squad Graevus and Squad Luko throwing themselves to the sloping ground of the valley. On its other hand was mounted a screeching circular saw, slicing through a tree trunk as it slashed towards the nearest Soul Drinker and sending the trunk crashing down through the canopy.

'Cover!' yelled Graevus as torn wood and gunfire rained down. 'Leave it for the guns! Take the green-skins!' Graevus's assault squad re-gathered their wits in a moment and suddenly they were a tide of armoured bodies and roaring chainswords, diving down the valley slope towards the dark tide of orks scrambling towards them. With a crunch of blade on flesh Graevus's men slammed into the orks and dark greenskin blood sprayed up from the carnage.

'Open fire!' cried Luko, but he didn't need to. Already the bolters of his tactical squad were blowing charred holes in the side of the war machine. The machine's metallic foot stamped down and crushed the leg of Brother Zalras – Luko dragged his battle-brother away but the act only grabbed the machine's attention. As it turned towards him Luko saw the glyphs stencilled onto the machine's cylindrical hull, stylised ork skulls and fist symbols, kill-markings and clan glyphs. Teeth and rotting, severed hands hung from leather thongs looped across its chassis. The blade carved down at Luko and he barely threw Zalras aside before it bit deep into the ground.

The difference between a Space Marine and a normal man was far more profound than just a suit of armour and physical size. The true difference, the one that made a man a Space Marine, was that a Space Marine was never ruled by fear. Fear clouded the judgement of normal men and made them do insane things – showing their back to the enemy, trying to hide, lashing around at enemies who weren't there. A Space Marine's mind was not so clouded. He knew what fear was, but when it sparked in him it never caught light. He mastered his fear and pushed it down, banishing it from his mind and never letting it take control. He knew that he was safest not running away from the enemy but toe to toe with it, face to face, where his strength and wargear counted for the most. So Luko ducked under the war machine's gun barrel and raked down at its leg mounting with his power claw. His arm jarred as the blades met metal but he forced them further down, the power field rupturing metal like a normal weapon tore flesh.

The machine lurched, gears inside it grinding angrily. Luko was barely able to throw himself aside as the saw blade scythed up at him again, carving a slice out of his shoulder pad. He rolled through the mud, exposed roots crunching beneath him, instinctively skidding into the cover of a massive thick tree trunk. Gunfire from the machine tore into the trunk, shredding wood and pulp, chewing through the tree's girth.

Squad Graevus tore through the branches and foliage above, their chainswords spraying ork blood as they churned, the flaring exhausts of their jump packs carrying them away from the orks surging forward to avenge their dead. Graevus himself twisted in mid-air and dropped down behind the war machine, carving a deep gouge out of the back of its armour with his power axe.

Luko rolled out of cover and lunged at the machine, punching his claws so deep into the machine's chassis that he felt muscle and bone giving way inside. The machine screamed, steam gouting from its churning engines.

Luko reached up and dug one claw into the machine, pulling himself up to the top of its body. He slammed his other claw into the metal and pulled, the power field flaring as it shattered the machine's hull. Every scrap of strength went into wrenching the top of the hull off and in a shower of sparks it came free.

The machine toppled over, fire and sparks spraying from its ruptured engines. Luko tumbled to the ground, as did the machine's pilot, a soot-blackened ork, torso torn open, violent red eyes gleaming above an insane grin. In its hand was a bundle of explosive sticks tied together with a detonator at the top. The ork ripped the pin out of the detonator and began to cackle at Luko.

Graevus hit the ground behind the ork and grabbed it with his free hand. His jump pack gunned into life and he soared up towards the canopy above, crazed ork in his hand. With tremendous strength he hurled the insane greenskin towards the ragged line of orks charging up the slope, following Graevus's assault squad. The ork slammed into his fellow greenskins and exploded, blowing apart a dozen aliens, throwing sundered limbs and spinning shards of wood through the jungle.

The war machine was down. Luko picked himself up as the gunfire stuttered from Luko's squad, even Brother Zalras propping himself up against a torn tree stump to snap bolter fire into the green mass seething into the bloody gap left by the explosion. Orks were falling but more were clambering over the top of them, eyes bright with hatred and the lust for revenge.

Luko glanced at Graevus. His battle-brother was sprayed from head to toe in ork blood. While Luko was fighting the war machine, Graevus's squad had been butchering orks down the valley slope, knowing their skill and the range of their jump packs would let them hit the ork line hard and pull back before they were surrounded.

'Didn't have to kill them all,' said Luko with a grin. It was his way of thanking Graevus for saving his life.

'Think we got their attention,' said Graevus.

'Pull them back,' said Luko. 'Squad! Suppression fire and fall back!'

The Soul Drinkers moved back through the forest, keeping volleys of fire thudding down through the trees. For every ork that fell two or three more scrambled over its body and stormed forwards. Luko led the squad back up the valley slope to the top of the ridge, thinning out the orks' front ranks, breaking up their charge, and even as the greenskins bellowed their hate the momentum was flooding out of them. They were slogging through their own dead, the front runners isolated enough for Luko's men to pick them off with bolter shots.

'Now!' yelled Luko. 'Volley fire!'

Squad Luko dropped to the ground. Graevus's men leapt up into the air on their jump pack exhausts, arcing back towards the ridge.

'Redemption!' yelled a voice belonging to a man Luko had heard named as Trox, the Penal Legion officer in charge of the flank force. 'Seek it now in the eyes of the xenos! Tear it from his bloodied hand!'

Lasgun fire opened up in a crimson storm. Three hundred troopers of the 901st, stationed at the top of the valley slope, fired as one. Lasers scoured bark from trees and leaves from branches. The orks in the front rank were shredded, bodies riddled with scorching holes, limbs sheared from bodies. Fire stuttered back up from them but the determination to charge up the slope had left their fire scattered and ineffective. A couple of Penal Legion troopers fell, but they meant nothing.

Luko's men continued to fire from prone, bolters punching great gory holes in the orks as laser fire streaked over their heads and they writhed back towards the ridge, still firing. A few of the 901st's shots fell short but Space Marine power armour was among the best in the galaxy and lasguns, appallingly deadly against exposed flesh, could do little more than scorch the paint from the Soul Drinkers.

'Scourge this stain from the Emperor's sight!' yelled Trox, his fanatical ranting a constant background to the gunfire. Silvery bursts of shrapnel exploded among the orks from his grenade launcher. A heavy bolter thudded shots into the orks and gradually the horde was masked by smoke and shrapnel, a veil of superheated earth and vaporised blood. Shapes loomed through the smog, a particularly large and violent ork leading a party of tough veteran greenskins towards the 901st's line. As Luko's Soul Drinkers took their place alongside the Penal Legion troopers, Graevus's squad charged forward to blunt the ork attack. Their leader's axe flashed down and the ork leader fell, carved nearly in two.

'Luko here!' shouted Luko into the vox. 'The flank's holding! We're drawing them off and keeping them pinned!'

'Well done, captain,' replied Sarpedon over the vox. 'Hold the line and let it bend if you have to. The main force will hit us soon.'

BLACK WATER, LIKE sweat, beaded on the walls of the brig. The *Brokenback* had plenty of places to hold prisoners – almost every one of its component ships had a brig, and some of the craft were entirely given over to cells and torture chambers. Some of them were bafflingly alien, while others were grimly prosaic in the manacles hanging from their walls and the channels cut into their decks to drain away the blood. The brig currently used by the Soul Drinkers on the *Brokenback* was more down-to-earth, part of a gigantic prison hulk sectioned off and reinforced, its bleak corroded steel corridors protected by sentry guns. Bones, decayed almost to grey sludge, still lay in the furthest corners, for the prison ship had evidently been full of inmates when the warp claimed it. Now, however, only one living thing was locked up there.

Brother Theylanos's last thoughts were of those final moments, when the otherworldly madness of the warp had rolled down these corridors like poisonous mist. The *Brokenback* brimmed with such stories, horrors implied by the strange dark corners of the hulk, and the screams of those chained prisoners still seemed to echo through the mass of blackened steel.

It was a dangerous thing to imagine. Too much thinking about such matters could be dangerous. It corroded the mind. In a sense, the whole of the *Brokenback* was a moral threat – without the Soul Drinkers' strength of will, it could have rotted their sense of duty and destroyed them. But they were strong enough. The screams of men long dead did not eat away at them as it would normal soldiers. The Soul Drinkers were better than that.

As the point of the knife slid in between the corded muscles of his throat, Theylanos thought for a terrible weak moment that the warp had come to the prison ship again, that silvery fingers of insanity were reaching from beyond realspace to drag him down.

Then the blade passed through his spine and wrenched up into the base of his brain, and the last image in his mind was the screaming faces of the prisoners welcoming him as one of their own.

Scout Nisryus pulled the blade free of Theylanos's neck and let the body slide to the ground. Nisryus was pallid and seemingly far too thin-faced to be a Space Marine, and his eyes wouldn't stay still, constantly focusing on things no one else could see.

Scout Tydeus crouched down and checked the wide wound on the Soul Drinker's throat. Blood was already crusting around the wound. 'He's gone,' said Tydeus with customary shortness. 'Is there anyone else?'

'Not that I can feel,' said Nisryus. The Space Marine had precognitive powers and one day, perhaps, he would be able to tell the future, an exceptionally rare talent – and very dangerous in every respect. Nisryus's studies with the Chapter's other Librarians had been slow as his power was unusual and risky to use, but he could still see eddies of time and space that let him react quicker than the laws of physics allowed. 'If there is, they won't find us for a while.'

'Move up and let's do this,' said Tydeus. 'Scamander?'

Lexicanist Scamander was watching the corridor behind them, in case more Soul Drinkers detailed to guard the brig were about to happen upon the scouts. Though he wore the power armour of a full Space Marine, Scamander was very much one of Tydeus's men. Scamander was psychic, too, but while Nisryus's power was subtle and complex, Scamander's was very simple. He was a pyrokinetic, the results of his power showing in the scorched skin around his eyes and the sides of his face. His eyes had turned dark red and smoke constantly coiled from the joints of his armour. 'We're clear,' he said. 'Stand aside.'

Scamander moved up to a cell door set into the wall of the corridor. The door was a massive slab of age-blackened steel solid enough to have held firm for thousands of years. Scamander put one hand against it, the gauntlet blistered and blackened. The metal under Scamander's hand hissed and began to glow cherry-red. His face hardened and faint flames licked from his eyes – the armour down his other side was becoming frosted, crystals of ice forming where water dripped on it from the ceiling. The heat created by Scamander had to be drawn from some-where and he took it from his own body, so that his flesh and armour became deathly cold as the metal softened and parted beneath his touch.

Within the cell, a single prisoner sat on the bench that protruded from one wall. He stood up as the metal came apart under Scamander's hand. The dim light from the corridor fell on his face – it was Eumenes, stripped of his armour and locked up on Sarpedon's orders.

'Is it done?' said Eumenes from within the cell as the door came apart.

Scamander stood back, breathing heavily, the flames around his eyes replaced with a coat of hoary frost. Tydeus stepped forwards. 'Not yet, sergeant.'

Eumenes's face darkened. 'Where is Raek?'

'Called away to investigate a distress signal from Tyrancos. He went with the Chaplain.'

Eumenes suddenly smiled darkly. 'That will save us a task, then. With Iktinos on board we would have trouble. Have you had to kill anyone?'

'One,' replied Tydeus.

'Then they'll miss him soon,' said Eumenes. 'We have to move fast. And get in contact with the surface, too. What news from there?'

'The greenskins are pressing home. Won't be long before Sarpedon gives the order.'

'Then we'll have to be finished here before it does.' Eumenes nodded at Scamander. 'Good to see you, scout. How are things in the librarium?'

'Lexicanist now,' said Scamander, still catching his breath. 'Tyrendian has big plans for me.'

'So do I,' said Eumenes. 'Nisryus, are we still clear?'

'We get out of the prison ship just fine,' said Nisryus, the flickering, restless look in his eyes showing he was reading invisible psychic currents around them. 'I can't see further than that.'

'I can,' said Eumenes, clambering through the ragged, smouldering hole torn through the door by Scamander's power. 'I know exactly how this is going to end. Send the word to the others, it begins now. Nisryus, take point, and Scamander stay with me. We hit the bridge first.'

THE WARLORD'S HORDE poured through the Serpentspine Valley, crashing into the foothills of the heights beyond like a wave. The 901st were positioned along the side of the valley, herding the greenskins towards the cliffs at the head of the valley where the first foothills of the heights rose over the dense green canopy.

The Soul Drinkers and the tougher elements of the 901st drew off parts of the horde in diversionary attacks. Luko and Graevus drew hundreds of orks up into a savage crossfire, while on the other side of the valley Salk held an outcrop of lichen-covered rock that anchored the 901st's line. Countless greenskins died, but there were many, many thousands more rampaging towards the cliffs. The 901st's line bent but did not break and the Soul Drinkers held firm, but they were fighting secondary battles that only stacked the odds. When the orks hit the cliffs, the real battle began.

'OPEN FIRE, LYGRIS!' yelled Sarpedon, throwing another ork off the cliff.

'Yes, commander,' replied Lygris from orbit. 'The guns are hot. Fire's coming in a few minutes.'

Sarpedon stabbed with his force staff, discharging its build-up of psychic power into the chest of an ork rearing up at him.

Sarpedon's Soul Drinkers were holding the first foothills of the heights, the long dense green mass of the Serpentspine Valley rolling out before them. The whole valley seethed with greenskins and it was funnelling their advance towards the cliffs held by Sarpedon's line. Orks were clambering up the vine-covered cliffs and Sarpedon was throwing them back down. Soul Drinkers around him were empty-ing bolter magazines down over the lichen-covered rocks, blasting wet ragged holes in the orks who tried to scramble up them.

It was a short climb and the orks were tenacious, and every time one tumbled down into the canopy the greenskin behind it got a little further towards the cliff top. Fire was hammering back up at the

Soul Drinkers, too, thousands of guns pointed upwards firing wildly, turning their air hot and metallic with flame and shrapnel.

'They've broken through!' cried Karraidin, the Master of Novices, who commanded a crowd of scouts and newly inducted Soul Drinkers guarding against the orks forcing through the 901st's line and around the cliffs. 'Hold them off! Hold them! For Dorn and the Emperor, earn that damned chalice on your shoulder!'

'They'll get to the artillery,' voxed Sarpedon as he knocked another ork down off the cliff-top. They were in chainsword range now and the Soul Drinkers were fighting the greenskins hand-to-hand at the top of the cliff. 'Keep them off the Vanqualians, we need every gun we can get.'

Sarpedon stabbed down with one leg, pinning an ork's hand to the rock with his front talon before spearing its head with his staff. Another clambered over the dead ork's body and three rapid shots from another Soul Drinker, one of Karraidin's novices, blasted it off the cliff to send it tumbling back down through the canopy.

Sarpedon was about to thank the young Space Marine when a terrific roar rose up from below the cliff, huge and monstrous. A sudden surge pushed the Soul Drinkers back from the cliff, orks throwing themselves on the Space Marines' guns and chainswords to force them back. Sarpedon lashed around him but was forced onto his back legs and had to scuttle back from the edge to keep himself from being isolated. Orks were all around him, hulking veterans with twisted faces almost hidden amongst scar tissue, all power and violence.

Behind them rose a true monster. It was huge, huger by far than any other ork on Nevermourn – bigger than any ork Sarpedon had ever seen. Its body was half mechanical and its eyes were so full of hate that Sarpedon knew instinctively it was not just a near-animal like all the other greenskins. It was old, the years etched onto it in scar tissue, and its sheer power was made obvious as it threw orks aside and stormed towards Sarpedon.

But Sarpedon was a monster too. He braced his many legs against the rock beneath him and squared himself, holding the head of his staff towards the warlord like the point of a spear. The warlord bellowed like a bull, lowered a shoulder and charged, and Sarpedon stood firm.

The warlord's mechanical fist slammed down with a sound like a meteor strike. Sarpedon barely stepped aside but his force staff hit home, the eagle-winged tip forced deep into the warlord's chest with the weight of its own charge.

Sarpedon's staff was carved from very rare psychoactive wood, and it served to conduct the massive reserved of psychic power he could call upon. When he focused his mind and drove the staff home, the discharge of power would rip the target apart and blast its soul from its body. Sarpedon focused like that now, driving every drop of power from the depths of his mind into a white-hot spike driven towards the warlord's burning bestial soul.

But the warlord's willpower was stronger than anything Sarpedon had ever felt and his power splintered against its soul. The ork wrenched the staff from its chest and closed its mechanical claw around Sarpedon's upper body. The Space Marine forced an arm inside and held the claw open as steam sprayed from the pistons trying to close the claw around him. Sarpedon was exceptionally strong, but the warlord was nothing but muscle and rage, and for an awful moment he knew the claw would shatter his bones and crush him to death.

A piston blew and a great gout of smoke and flame sprayed from the elbow joint of the ork's arm. The pressure was suddenly off and Sarpedon fought back, trying to force the claw open to escape. The warlord roared and hurled Sarpedon with all its awesome strength. The Soul Drinker crashed through branches and tree trunks, tumbling as he fell, fighting to keep a grip on his force staff.

Sarpedon rolled as he landed, flipping rapidly upright on his agile legs. He could hear the warlord charging towards him. He was deep into the jungle that covered the foothills of the heights now, and close behind him was the Vanqualian artillery. He couldn't take another step back; he had to stand and fight. The ork was one of the few things Sarpedon had fought that was physically stronger than him, and toe to toe he might fail. He turned on the Hell.

The warlord was almost upon him, crunching through the trees. Sarpedon had tasted its willpower, and knew it would not be frightened by the parlour tricks that had shaken the greenskins at the Wraithspire Palace. It had to fear something. Everything did. Somewhere in this galaxy was something that the warlord feared, something that would distract it long enough for Sarpedon to get onto the front feet and beat it.

It wanted Vanqualis. It wanted this world. But if this world was gone, it would have failed. That was what it feared – failure. It was probably the only thing that Sarpedon himself feared, too.

The Hell tore out from Sarpedon, rippling through the trees, and to his psychic eye the jungle was blasted away, stripped down to the bare blackened earth. He tore the sun from the sky and the life from the earth. For him and the warlord, Vanqualis was a barren, worthless place, only unforgiving stars in the sky and torn, dead land stretching in all directions. The Hell showed Vanqualis as a meaningless prize, a place where thousands of greenskins had died for nothing, a pathetic memorial of failure to the warlord's horde.

The warlord was upon him. For a moment the giant ork faltered, the Hell showing him a terrible truth about the futility of his greenskins' crusade. That was all Sarpedon needed. He squared his back legs and dived forward, and he and the warlord crashed together with a sound like thunder.

# CHAPTER SEVEN

'What is the greatest sin?'

'The greatest of them is treachery, for it
is a sin against the very soul.'

– Daenyathos, *Catechisms Martial*

LORD SOVELIN FALKEN ground his face into the mud,
ears ringing from the explosions. He writhed
through the muck under the closest mortar carriage
as the ground shuddered under the explosions, and
for a moment everything was blackness and deafening white noise.

He pushed himself onto one knee to see what was
happening. Most of the Vanqualian Warders had
also taken cover from the fire that had burst down
through the ragged canopy and exploded among

the artillery pieces. Men lay dead, one beheaded by shrapnel, another with both arms torn off lying face-down in the undergrowth. Another was still alive, just, the lower half of his body a foul gory mush. His face was bone-white and his eyes were open in fear as the life leached out of him into the mud.

Dark shapes were lurching through the trees along one side of the clearing. Several of them were lugging huge guns, barrels still glowing hot in the darkness. The orks had got their artillery out of the valley and had shelled Sovelin's own artillery positions, which meant that they were about to charge and butcher the Vanqualian Warders so they could no longer fire on the main ork horde below.

'Form up!' yelled Sovelin. 'On me! Form the line!' He could barely hear his own voice through the ringing but soon men were scrabbling towards him, their uniforms covered in mud and their faces pallid with fear.

He was in charge. That fact hit him. If he didn't lead these men, they would die.

Somewhere amid the chaos Sovelin gave the order to fire. The firefight was brutal, ork gunfire rattling off the gun carriages, autoguns replying. The orks were trying to set their heavy weapons up for another barrage but most of them were shot down as they did so. Others drew cleavers and charged, running across the clearing to be cut down. One made it to the line and suddenly Sovelin was fighting the alien itself – a foul thing with half a face, the rest of it blackened grinning skull. Sovelin's autogun stock shattered as he brought it up to block the ork's cleaver and the alien barged him to the ground. It hacked down at him with its cleaver and Sovelin couldn't roll out of the way fast enough – the cleaver missed his head but the ork's huge weight was on him, crushing him. Panicking, Sovelin wrenched his laspistol from its holster and unloaded it at point-blank range into the greenskin's abdomen. The creature spasmed on top of him, grunting its foul breath into his face, and for a moment Sovelin was sure it would chew his face off with that huge scarred maw.

Then the ork slumped down and breathed out a long death rattle. Hands reached down to haul it off Sovelin – two of the Vanqualians dragged it away and Sovelin saw the huge wounds he had blown in its stomach. He had probably severed its spine. Sovelin had never killed anything, certainly not up close, before.

'We need…' said Sovelin, catching his breath, 'we need to group up. Like a firing squad. We can out-shoot them but we have to keep them away.'

But they were all around. Hundreds of them. Thousands. The orks had broken through some-where and they were attacking the artillery. Sovelin was going to die, and all his men with him.

A deep bass note in the back of Sovelin's mind suddenly rose to a roar and the world changed. Another image was laid over the jungle – a bleak, endless wasteland, a tortured and lifeless world with black void for a sky. Sovelin couldn't focus, and both the Vanqualians and the orks reacted the same.

The firing stopped and men took cover, holding their heads as the strange images pounded at them.

It was witchcraft. The Space Marine psyker who had terrorised the orks at the Wraithspire Palace was here. That meant the Space Marines were here, too, and that the Vanqualian artillery might be saved.

Sovelin stood up and tried to find another gun so he could carry on leading the Vanqualians. His mind wouldn't focus – he could barely grasp the gun that lay at his feet and the world was swinging around him as if he was dizzy or drunk.

A monster crashed through the trees, wrestling with a Space Marine. It was an ork, bigger than Sovelin had believed possible, half its body a smoking mechanical horror. But no matter how huge and foul the alien, Sovelin realised with a lurch in his stomach that the Space Marine was worse.

The Space Marine was a mutant. The lower half of his body was a horrendous parody of nature, with eight articulated legs like those of a spider or a scorpion. He moved with speed and viciousness alien to a human. Strike by strike, step by step, the mutant battered the ork back into the forest. The other orks advancing on the artillery let out a terrible howl as they witnessed their leader being matched, and even bested, by the mutant.

But the orks were the last thing on Sovelin's mind now. Horrifyingly, he saw the truth. The mutant. The witchcraft. The sudden appearance on Vanqualis. And for the first time, he saw clearly the chalice symbol these 'Soul Drinkers' wore on their shoulder pads. It all made perfect sense. An awful cold horror filled Sovelin more profound even than the fear of death the orks had brought with them.

And Sovelin was the only one who knew.

'You!' shouted Sovelin, pointing to the nearest Vanqualian. 'Get me the field vox! Now!'

'Sir?'

'We have to warn Herograve,' said Sovelin. 'The Black Chalice have returned.'


TECHMARINE LYGRIS REALISED there was something wrong when he saw the guns.

The scouts had surrounded him on the bridge. There must have been thirty of them and Lygris instinctively knew that Eumenes, who stood in the centre of them with his arms folded in an attitude of complete confidence, was in charge. They had their bolters aimed at Lygris and he was covered from every angle.

Lygris turned from the viewscreen, which was showing the target area in the Snakespine Valley for the *Brokenback's* guns. 'Eumenes. What is the meaning of this?'

'We're taking the ship, Lygris,' replied Eumenes smoothly.

Lygris was tough, and he had fought in plenty of actions under Sarpedon and with the old Chapter before that. But there were too many Soul Drinkers with Eumenes, scouts and full Space Marines, among them some veterans whose experience rivalled Lygris's. Eumenes himself was an exceptional soldier. 'Why?'

'You know why, Lygris,' sneered Eumenes. 'It's over. We're taking this Chapter from Sarpedon. We should be bringing down the Imperium instead of losing our brothers down on Vanqualis for a world the Emperor doesn't care about.'

'This is treachery,' said Lygris, his voice hard.

'I know,' replied Eumenes steadily. 'That's why we're not doing you the insult of asking you to join us. Just step down from the pulpit and let us take the ship, and you will live.'

Lygris walked down the short flight of steps onto the bridge deck. As he moved, he thumbed a control stud on the instrument array, praying silently that none of Eumenes's men saw him. 'You know I can't give you the bridge, Eumenes.'

'And you know I have to give you the choice.' Eumenes cocked the action of his bolter. 'Shall we do this?'

Lygris rapidly scanned the faces of Eumenes's Soul Drinkers. He recognised Scamander and Nisryus, two new psychic recruits who were supposed to be the future of the Chapter Librarium. He saw a few more experienced battle-brothers, but most of Eumenes's men were from the recent intake of recruits. Then Lygris's hearts skipped a beat when he saw the white armour trim of an Apothecary,

'Pallas,' he said, unable to keep the shock out of his voice. 'What are you doing?'

Apothecary Pallas had been there from the start. He had fought on the Star Fort, when the Adeptus Mechanicus had stolen the Soulspear from the Soul Drinkers and started the terrible cycle of events that led to the Chapter War and the break with the Imperium. It had been Pallas who had diagnosed the rampant mutations threatening to destroy the Chapter, and who had helped save the Chapter and make the recruiting of new Astartes possible. Pallas was as fundamental to the Soul Drinkers as any of them, and yet here he was standing alongside a traitor.

Lygris tore his mind away from Pallas. Beneath the deck, amid the cogitators and electronics, a red warning light blinked and he could just hear the thrumming of heated metal buckling.

'You won't understand, Lygris...' said Pallas.

'This is betrayal, Pallas! Of all of us!'

'I don't believe, Lygris! I don't believe in Sarpedon, not after what happened to Tellos. We're falling apart and Sarpedon can't see it. It's either this or watch the Soul Drinkers die out. Eumenes has a lot of us on his side, Lygris, a lot, and if it comes down to it he's going to win. This is the only way.'

'No,' said Lygris dangerously. 'There is always another way.'

'Enough,' said Eumenes. 'Kill him.'

Lygris had no more warning than those two words before bolter fire stuttered towards him. He threw himself behind the command pulpit, the bolter rounds slamming into the delicate machinery, showering him with sparks.

Heated metal below the grille of the deck flared cherry-red, and the only warning was a screech as the outer casing of one of the cogitators fractured and superheated air sheared out.

The last control Lygris had activated on the command pulpit had dumped enormous amount of information, all the input from all the *Brokenback's* sensors, into one cogitator beneath the deck. The volume of information had overloaded the equipment to the extent that its physical shell shattered, and a moment later an explosion of flame and razor-sharp data-crystal shards burst up from below the deck.

Eumenes's men took cover. Lygris jumped out from behind the pulpit and sprinted for the glowing hole now torn in the deck. Gunfire ripped around him, shots smacking into the pulpit and thudding into the viewscreen. Lygris tumbled through the tangle of smouldering equipment, turned end over end, until he felt the solid floor of the bridge sphere beneath him. He felt in the near-darkness and found an opening where one of the floor's panels had been removed to allow thick cables to snake through into the cogitators. Lygris grabbed a handful and pulled them free, opening up enough room for him to clamber into the network of conduits and tunnels beneath the bridge.

'Hold fire!' Lygris heard Eumenes yelling. 'You'll hit the equipment! You'll blind us!' The voice got quieter as Lygris pulled himself further down, and finally fell down into a wider tunnel.

Beneath the bridge was a long, winding tunnel of steel, bored through the mass of the *Brokenback* like the lair of a vast worm. Lygris had used it to lay cables from sensors and engine clusters all over the hulk, and he was the only person in the

Soul Drinkers who had any idea where its various branches led. Lygris ran, head down, into the darkness, as the last few bolter shots rang dully through the metal.

Eumenes had betrayed the Soul Drinkers. Pallas too, and Throne knew how many others, were with him. And now they had the *Brokenback*. Lygris was the only one who could take it back off them, but he couldn't do it alone, and for the time being alone was exactly what he was. So he kept running, seeking the darkness in the heart of the hulk.

EUMENES KNELT DOWN to peer into the smouldering hole in the deck, through the equipment below the bridge, where Lygris had escaped.

'Don't bother,' said Pallas behind him. 'Lygris knows this hulk like the inside of his helmet. He can run forever.'

'But he won't,' said Eumenes. 'We've betrayed him. And you're with us – he's known you since long before Sarpedon ever led us astray. That's the worst kind of treachery there is. He won't just hide out as long as he thinks there's something he can do to hurt us.'

Pallas's expression was impossible to read behind the faceplate of his white helmet. 'Maybe,' he said. 'But he won't be easy to find. Certainly not by blundering after him.'

'I know you'd like your old friend to escape this,' said Eumenes. 'But he had his chance and didn't take it. He dies, Apothecary.'

Pallas didn't speak for a moment. 'Very well,' he said.

'And you know him best. Take a squad and find him. And Nisryus, go with him. Lygris can't hide from you.'

'Not from a precog,' said Nisryus, as if to himself. 'Not when I can see him first.'

Pallas left the bridge, the young psyker Nisryus behind him. Eumenes turned back to the rest of the bridge. The command pulpit was bleeding sparks and smoke was still coiling from the hole torn in the deck. 'Tydeus, do we have any ordnance control?'

Tydeus was crouched by one of the bridge helms. 'Just,' he said. 'We can aim the guns from here. It's not perfect, but...'

'It doesn't have to be,' replied Eumenes sharply. 'Target the heights. Then open fire.'

SOVELIN CROUCHED AGAINST the bole of a huge great-wood tree as he tried to pick out a voice from the static spooling from the vox-unit's handset. His artillery still held the clearing behind him. Sporadic gunfire was still spattering from the jungle and Sovelin's Vanqualians had formed a firing line among the artillery pieces, and when Sovelin had finished raising the warning he would join them to hold the hill. Sovelin should have felt proud that they were showing such discipline in the face of the enemy, taking the fight to the orks instead of abandoning the guns and running. But there was no room left amid the horror for anything like pride.

The Black Chalice. The very thought of it turned his gut. He had heard the stories as a child, everyone on Vanqualis had, and he had thought they were some kind of allegory – a personification of evil and corruption. But the Black Chalice was real, and its bearers were here, on Vanqualis, just a gunshot away.

'...palace of the countess,' said an officious voice, transmitted from the distant cities of Herograve. 'Unless you have an appointment, I am afraid...'

'No!' shouted Sovelin. 'No! I am Lord Sovelin Falken! I am commanding the Vanqualian Artillery in Nevermourn! Listen, the countess is my... she's my great aunt. Yes, great aunt. I spent summers at her retreat on the shores of Lake Felandin. She never thought I'd make it in the Warders. Ask her.'

'Sir, I...'

'Listen, damn you! There are orks everywhere and I might never be able to repeat this!'

'Very well,' said the voice, evidently trying to regain its composure. 'I shall be sure the correct members of the countess's household are informed.'

Sovelin gulped, and told the countess's chamberlain of the Black Chalice.

He was almost finished when a column of red-white fire lanced down from the sky and incinerated his artillery.

The handset still in his hand, scalding air battering against him, Sovelin Falken watched open-mouthed in horror as a pillar of coruscating laser blasted his Vanqualian Warders into dust and melted the mortar and autocannon pieces into sprays of white-hot liquid metal. Pulses of laser blew a deep crater in the ground and ignited the leaves of the trees ringing the clearing. The skin on Sovelin's face blistered in the heat and he was barely able to drag himself behind the tree, tongues of flame licking past him.

'It's started!' Sovelin couldn't hear his own voice and he was sure the link had gone down, but he had to try, he had to tell them. 'They have a fleet up there! They're killing us!'

The betrayal had begun. The Bearers of the Black Chalice had manipulated Vanqualis's defenders into position, and now they would wipe them out. Sovelin curled into a ball amid the storm of fire, and prayed to the Emperor that he would survive long enough to seek revenge.

SARPEDON SHOULDER-CHARGED THE warlord with every last drop of his strength, slamming into the beast's chest. Step by step he had forced it back, ground his way through the fight keeping the green-skin on its back foot, striking hard and fast without giving it a moment's respite. They had fought through the dense trees that swathed the hill, past the clearing where the Vanqualians were holding out, and back into the open ground that ran along the top of the cliff.

The warlord met Sarpedon's charge like an immovable wall of flesh and steel. It was wreathed in smoke, flame bursting from the joints of its metal-caged arm and chest as the mechanics of its repaired body burned hotter to keep it matching Sarpedon.

Sarpedon and the warlord were face-to-face now, their conflict boiled down to a test of strength. The warlord's muscles writhed beneath its green-black skin and its eyes were narrowed to hateful red slits, its claw pressing against Sarpedon's chest while the creature's natural hand tried to dig its claws into Sarpedon's throat.

Sarpedon's ears were ringing with white noise as he poured everything into forcing the warlord back. He could smell the blood hissing against the red-hot mechanical plates of the warlord's body, and hear the huge bestial heart thudding in the ork's chest.

Sarpedon looked into the warlord's eyes. There was something horribly human there, something that echoed Sarpedon's own hatred of this alien who had come to Vanqualis to burn and destroy. The thought that there was something human about the creature's hatred filled Sarpedon with a sudden flood of rage and disgust.

With that final burst of raw anger, Sarpedon barged the ork off the cliff's edge. The warlord bellowed as it fell, reaching up with its mechanical claw. But it was too late – the claw closed on thin air and the warlord fell back down towards the canopy below. Its flailing knocked other orks off the cliff and everywhere there rose a terrible orkish cry of rage and sorrow as they saw their leader bested.

Pride swelled in Sarpedon's hearts. He had beaten the best the orks could throw at him. The defence of Vanqualis looked a little closer now, and the greenskins looked weak for the first time.

As if in reply to that thought, a lance of fire bored down through the sky behind him. Sarpedon turned in time to see the flash as the Vanqualian artillery was vaporised and flame rippled through the treetops. The shockwave almost knocked Sarpedon off the edge of the cliff and the nearby Soul Drinkers, who had been holding the cliff edge as Sarpedon battled the warlord, dived to the ground to take cover. The laser pulsed and rings of flame washed off the impact site, shredding the surrounded trees into flurries of burning leaves. Sarpedon held his ground, keeping an arm in front of his face to keep his skin from being scorched by the flame-hot wind tearing through the jungle.

'Lygris!' voxed Sarpedon as soon as he could hear himself think. 'What in the hells was that?'

There was no reply from orbit. 'Lygris? Was that from our guns? Lygris, come in!'

'Sarpedon!' yelled a familiar voice. It was Karraidin, his huge Terminator-armoured form crashing through the trees towards Sarpedon. 'Lord Sarpedon, it's...'

His voice was cut short by a volley of gunfire that slammed into the back of his enormous Terminator armour. Karraidin turned and fired back into the trees behind him with his storm bolter, rattling off a fearsome spray of fire. The replying fire didn't let up, and more and more shots smacked into Karraidin's armour, slamming deep scars into the ceramite plates, thudding into the thick armour encasing his torso.

'Captain!' yelled Sarpedon, sliding behind a boulder for cover.

'It's treachery, Sarpedon,' grimaced Karraidin. Sarpedon saw there was blood on his lips. 'They've got the ship. We're next.'

'Who?'

A bright flash of plasma burst from the trees and hit Karraidin square in the abdomen. The super-heated liquid plasma ate through his abdominal plate and pushed Karraidin backwards, his armoured boots digging into the rock beneath him. But Karraidin did not fall – with awesome strength he held his ground, and when the flare of the plasma blast died down there was a great crater melted in the armour covering his stomach. Amid the metallic stink of vaporised metal, Sarpedon could smell cooked flesh.

'Us,' said Karraidin, reloading his storm bolter.

Treachery, realised Sarpedon, betrayal from among the Soul Drinkers. With a sickening lurch in his stomach, he realised that could be the one enemy that he couldn't defeat.

Fire battered into Karraidin, so heavy it tore chunks out of his shoulder pad and greave. Karraidin took a step forward, defying the enemies firing at him, the captain's form almost lost amid the explosive impacts that tore into him. Sarpedon could not help him now – if he left cover he would be shredded too. He could only watch as Karraidin carried on firing even as burning loops of entrails began to hang from the massive plasma wound in his stomach.

Slowly, agonisingly, Karraidin's steps faltered and he sank to one knee. He yelled wordlessly as he fired, and he was still firing as his white-hot storm bolter misfired and exploded in his hand.

'Fall back!' ordered Sarpedon to the rest of the Soul Drinkers holding the cliff-top. 'On me! Fall back!' He backed away from Karraidin, trying to keep cover between himself and the enemies firing on Karraidin. A few stray shots hit the rocks around Sarpedon, but it was Karraidin they were after.

Sarpedon had to watch as Karraidin literally fell apart before his eyes. Fire tore through one shoulder pad and Karraidin's arm came apart. Sparks flew as his bionic leg was shattered and buckled beneath him. The ammunition left in his storm bolter burst and took his other arm with it. He was still bellowing his defiance as he toppled backwards, the massive blocky form of his Terminator armour falling as slowly as one of the greatwood trees that rose around him.

As he fell back, Sarpedon could see shapes moving in the tree line. Space Marines, scouts and full battle-brothers in power armour, the barrels of their bolters glowing with the heat of sustained fire as they skulked forwards to finish off Karraidin. He was still breathing, gasping curses and threats, as the purple-armoured forms closed in on him. Sarpedon was too far away by now to see the old captain's final moments, but he could hear the point-blank bolter shots into ceramite and he knew that Karraidin was finally dead.

Sarpedon reached the tree line, and saw the Soul Drinkers he was leading closing around him. They were following him back, away from the cliffs. The traitors were following them and fire was falling on them now, zipping between the trees.

'Luko,' voxed Sarpedon. 'How's your position?'

'Quiet here,' replied Luko. 'The greenskins got tired of dying and joined to push on the heights.'

'Then be prepared to defend it. We're falling back to your position.'

'Falling back, commander? What happened?'

'We have been betrayed. Make ready, Luko, there is more at stake than greenskin blood now.' Sarpedon switched channels as he moved with his fellow Soul Drinkers towards the side of the valley held by Luko. One Soul Drinker, Brother Farlumir, fell, his leg blasted open by a bolter shot. A volley of shots chewed through him as he struggled on the ground. A neat kill, fast and sure. A Space Marine's kill.

'All Soul Drinkers!' ordered Sarpedon over the vox. 'All loyal sons of Rogal Dorn! Fall back to Captain Luko's position! General retreat, and watch your backs!'

Acknowledgement runes flickered. Questions, too, flashing over the vox – why were they falling back? What had fired on the heights? Several officers did not reply at all – perhaps they, like Karraidin, had already been executed, or perhaps they were in league with the betrayers.

Sarpedon led his men into the trees and the dark green shadows closed around them. Everywhere there was chaos – gunfire from the orks and the troopers of the 901st as the greenskins scaled the cliffs again unopposed, the chanting of the aliens as their warlord readied them for another attack, bolter fire spattering through the trees as brother turned on brother in the darkness.

Betrayal. Sarpedon could barely believe it. Yet he had heard Karraidin die and known his fellow Soul Drinkers had fired the shots that killed him. And the *Brokenback* had fired on the Soul Drinkers' own lines. It had to be true. And that meant that Sarpedon had failed, because the traitors had laid the groundwork for this rebellion behind his back.

'I just had to kill Brother Gerontos,' voxed Luko. 'He was one of our new recruits. He tried to shoot Graevus in the back.'

'Then I failed,' said Sarpedon. 'I was supposed to teach them. I didn't teach them well enough. This is my doing.'

EUMENES WAS A natural fit for the *Brokenback*'s bridge. He looked like he had been born to direct the unfolding battle on Vanqualis. The stern industrial feel of the armoured sphere, and the finery of the battle honours hung from the curved ceiling, gave him trappings of power that suited his air of absolute confidence.

'Is it done?' said Eumenes into the vox-unit mounted on the command pulpit.

'Yes,' came the reply, transmitted from the surface of Vanqualis.

'Scout-Sergeant, seeing him fall is not enough. Karraidin is the toughest son of a grox I have ever met.'

'He's dead,' replied Scout-Sergeant Hecular. Hecular had been brought into the Soul Drinkers at the same time as Eumenes, but unlike Eumenes he had remained with the scouts. 'I turned his body over myself. There isn't much left.'

'Good.' There was satisfaction in Eumenes's voice. 'Karraidin was the bane of our lives. We couldn't cock a bolter without him telling how Sarpedon was leading us towards the promised land. Killing Karraidin was the first step in taking back the Chapter.'

'Then what's the next?' said Hecular. There was gunfire in the background of the transmission, and howls of static from the interference caused by the lance strike on the heights.

'Killing Sarpedon,' said Eumenes.

'Hah! I'll leave that one to you, Eumenes.'

'That's the plan. For now, get your men back, Hecular. The next strike is incoming and you're not important enough to hold fire for.'

Hecular signed off and Eumenes glanced up again at the screen showing the head of the Snake-spine Valley. A huge crater smouldered on the crown of the lowest foothill – many men had died there, destroyed in the blink of an eye, and all Eumenes had done was give an order.

Eumenes had never claimed to be driven by a need for power, but it could not be denied that he had ended so many lives with nothing more than a word. Many, many more would die, of course. And it would take more than a simple order to kill Sarpedon.

'What news is there from the rest of our units?' said Eumenes.

'It's good,' replied Tydeus, who was manning another of the lecterns at the back of the bridge. Lygris had done his job well, and almost all the important systems on the hulk could be accessed from the bridge of the *Brokenback*. 'The Soul Drinkers are falling back towards the eastern ridge. Hecular drove them off the cliffs.'

'And the eastern ridge?'

'Salk's holding out there,' said Tydeus, with a smile. 'But our big gun's got the rest of it locked down. The penal troopers didn't stand a chance.'

'Then that's our strongpoint. Our brothers can gather there then strike out for the forest. We'll send down the Thunderhawks to pick them up once they're in a defensible position.'

'The 901st haven't broken down yet,' said Tydeus. 'There's a chance they could regroup and make things hard for us.'

'I don't think that will be a problem,' said Eumenes coldly. He flicked an activation stud and the whole of the *Brokenback* shook as the power coils of its laser batteries brimmed with power again.

The pict-screen in front of him flared again as a massive pulse of laser smashed down into the ground. This time the strike hit the cliffs themselves, boring through the rock and blasting shards of stone like meteors in every direction. A huge pall of smoke billowed up from the strike, and there could be no doubt that hundreds of greenskins as well as any Soul Drinkers and soldiers nearby had been killed instantly.

The cliffs collapsed, a massive drift of shattered stone flooding like water down over the canopy and into the valley. For several long moments there was stillness save the billows of smoke dissipating over the valley.

Then there was movement, tiny at first, from the high viewpoint looking like ants crawling over the long tongue of spoil that now reached into the valley. Orks, first hundreds then thousands of them. The collapse of the cliffs had created a slope leading up to the foothills, the perfect route for the greenskin horde to take the heights for which so many orks had already died. The army seethed forwards, covering the slope in dark green bodies, the thousands of orks bottled up in the valley suddenly free to charge forwards and raise hell among the soldiers who had kept them penned in.

'The 901st are dead,' said Eumenes as the orks poured up the slope into the heights. 'So is this planet.'

Most men would have thought twice about approaching a cordon of Space Marines, standing guard around an Astartes command post. But General Varr, spattered in mud and blood, walked straight towards the ring of Soul Drinkers standing guard in the dense jungle beyond the western ridge of the valley.

A gauntleted hand gripped his shoulder. The Soul Drinker looked down at Varr, the general's muddied face reflected in the eyepieces of the Space Marine's helmet.

'Halt,' said the Soul Drinker.

Varr was about to remonstrate with the man when a familiar, weary voice came from the clearing beyond. 'Let him go, Brother Kallidas.' It was Sarpedon's voice, but it didn't sound as confident or fearless as when Varr had spoken with him while planning the Serpentspine Valley operation.

The hand left Varr's shoulder and the general proceeded more carefully through the dense bank of trees ahead and emerged into a dank clearing, drenched in the permanent rain of water running off the almost solid canopy overhead. Several Soul Drinkers were on guard, ready to shoot – bolters swept over Varr before it was confirmed he wasn't an enemy. In the centre of the clearing stood Sarpedon.

Varr stopped dead. He had witnessed mutations on corrupted traitor soldiers before, and even sometimes hidden among his own men – tentacles for hands, extra eyes, vestigial tails, scaled skin and much stranger things besides. But he had never seen a mutation as spectacular as Sarpedon's arachnoid lower half, his eight legs of jointed exoskeleton packed with dark muscle.

'Throne above,' said Varr. It was all he could think to say, as if his ability to speak had been all but struck from him. It wasn't disgust that he felt, or even fear. It was a cold, disbelieving shock, for the combination of Space Marine and mutant monster was so utterly incongruous that for a moment Varr didn't properly register what his eyes were telling him. But the moment passed and Sarpedon the mutant was still stood in front of Varr

'General Varr,' said Sarpedon. 'You see now why I spoke to you through Captain Luko. I can never predict what a man's reaction will be when he sees me.'

'You know why I came here,' said Varr, swallowing back his shock. 'Your Space Marines deserted my lines and your fleet destroyed the Vanqualian artillery. Now the greenskins have run rampant. I have a thousand men dead at the very least, and half the survivors scattered around the valley. If I can regroup them I'll be fortunate to have half an army left. I want answers, commander.'

'Our Chapter has been betrayed,' said Sarpedon. 'Someone is usurping my command. One of our own. The Soul Drinkers are in revolt. The traitors have seized our ship and are trying to destroy us on the ground. Does that answer your questions, general?'

Varr looked at a loss. 'Betrayed? You are Space Marines! Do you mean to say the Emperor's finest have mutinied? You were… you were an inspiration! I saw the looks in my men's eyes when they realised the Angels of Death were on their side. They thought we could really save this planet. But no, Vanqualis will fall and my men will all be lost because you're no better than the scum I command. Hells, you're worse – my men are killers and thieves but at least they're all on the same damned side!'

Sarpedon reared up, and at his full height he was almost twice as tall as Varr. 'Do not presume, general, to know what manner of men we are.'

'There are those who worship you,' said Varr. He had gathered his wits now after witnessing

Sarpedon's appearance, and the pride still left in him refused to be cowed by Sarpedon's presence. 'Do you know that? You are the Emperor's will! You are supposed to be the defenders of this Imperium!'

'No,' said Sarpedon gravely. 'Not us.'

Varr paused. 'You're not Imperial.'

'Not for a long time,' said Sarpedon. He indicated his mutated legs. 'The Imperium would hardly tolerate the likes of us defending it, do you not agree?'

'Then... what are you?'

Sarpedon settled down again, his legs folding down beneath him so he was just the height of a normal Astartes. 'That, general, is a more complex question than you realise.'

'You're renegades.'

'That's the short version, yes. We rejected the Imperium. Now we do the Emperor's own work, not the will of the Lords of Terra. Dark powers tried to corrupt us to their own will, but we broke away from them for they are the Emperor's enemies. That struggle resulted in the mutations you see.' Sarpedon looked Varr in the eye. 'The Inquisition has killed men for knowing less than I have told you. The concept of the Emperor's finest going rogue is a dangerous piece of knowledge.'

'I have seen many things,' said Varr. 'This is not the strangest of them.'

Sarpedon allowed himself a smile. 'And you are a renegade yourself,' he said. 'Of sorts.'

'The Inquisition took exception to the bravery of my men,' said Varr bitterly. 'The Kar Duniash Heavy Lancers. Elites, armoured cavalry. An honour to command. We were stationed near the Agrippina system and we fought... I don't know what we fought. I can't describe them. Daemons, I suppose.'

'In the days before we split from the Imperium,' said Sarpedon, 'we saw it often. When the Imperial Guard fought against the servants of the Dark Powers, the Imperium would decide that they might have seen too much.'

'They wanted them dead,' continued Varr. 'Executed. The Inquisition ordered me to lead them into the middle of the desert where they would be bombed from orbit. They would be wiped out because they had not broken and fled like everyone else, they had fought and gone face to face with the Great Enemy. So I led my men into the mountains instead, into the caves, where the bombs wouldn't find them.'

'And for that, you were condemned. That sounds like the Inquisition I know.'

'Hah! More than just that, commander. The Inquisition had to send a regiment of stormtroopers down to that world to kill us. We gave them a hell of a fight. Months, it took them, up there in the mountains, to kill us all. It cost them a good few lives to take me alive. That's what sent me to the Penal Legions. That's why they didn't just shoot me on the spot. I humiliated them, so they wanted to humiliate me in return.'

'And did they succeed, general?'

Varr waved a dismissive hand. 'That,' he said bleakly, 'is for the Emperor to decide. In any case, even if you do the Emperor's work as you say you do, that does not change the fact that half your Astartes seem to have different ideas. And my men are still trapped on this world surrounded by orks.'

'I am afraid I cannot give you the answers you want to hear,' said Sarpedon. 'My Chapter is at war. I cannot fight my own brothers and save Vanqualis at the same time, nor can I help the 901st. I have no wish to see you and your men die here. But you have to fight this battle yourselves. Soon my men will move out to hunt down the traitors and fight them before they can get off-world, and it may be that very little of this Chapter survives. If there was another way to do this, Varr, I would take it, but you and your men are on your own.'

Varr shook his head as he turned to leave the clearing, to rejoin the men of the 901st and try to fight their way out of Nevermourn. 'We always were,' he said.

# CHAPTER EIGHT

'How can we know when the battle is won?'

'Know only this. There is but a single battle, and it will never be won.'

– Daenyathos, *Catechisms Martial*

LASER FIRE RANG around Raek's head as he ducked down behind a stone pew. The pew jutted absurdly from a chunk of chapel wall that orbited the gilded obsidian sarcophagus in the centre of the asteroid's bizarre temple. He was about halfway up, clinging on as the architecture shifted and laser fire lanced through the air towards him. The gun-servitors were old, and that meant they were good – they were fast and accurate, their targeting cogitators far more agile than those of the lumbering tech-constructs Raek had fought on the *Brokenback*'s training decks.

Raek leaned out a fraction and brought his rifle's barrel up swiftly, instantly drawing a bead on the servitor firing at him. The red of its metallic eye blinked as it registered Raek as a target, an instant before the sniper rifle's bullet sliced neatly through one of the servitor's anti-grav units. The servitors' shells were armoured but the anti-grav units were not and the machine tumbled down towards the curving polished floor below.

'Iktinos!' shouted Raek.

'Almost there,' came Iktinos's calm reply. He was somewhere above Raek, climbing through the precarious shifting layers of the temple as the gun-servitors flitted around him.

An icon flickered against Raek's retina. It was an incoming vox – and not one that Raek could ignore.

'Sergeant,' said Eumenes, the superiority and determination in his voice obvious even through the background noise.

'Eumenes,' said Raek. 'We're under fire here.'

'It's started,' said Eumenes. 'The rebellion is in the open now.'

'Then you need me to…'

'Yes. And bring me back something the Chaplain can't live without. Iktinos will be difficult to kill. Don't leave it to chance.'

'Chance, Eumenes? I don't believe I'm familiar with that concept.'

'And make it quick. I need to get the *Brokenback* out of this system as soon as I can.'

'It will be done. Raek out.'

Raek flicked the vox-link shut. Eumenes had been correct, of course – the first Space Marines had been created by the Emperor to be difficult to kill, and Iktinos was tougher than most. But no matter how superhuman, Iktinos would go down just like everyone else with one of Raek's bullets through his eye.

Raek's thoughts were broken as every muscle in his body tensed on instinct. He had been born with his senses hard-wired to throw him into maximum alertness at the slightest stimulus, like a hair trigger in his mind.

It was the silence. The gunfire had stopped.

The gun-servitors hung in the air, the red target-lights extinguished. The spindly barrels of their lasguns hung limp below them like the folded legs of hovering insects. Slowly, they floated back towards the metallic pods set into the chunks of floating architecture.

Raek scanned carefully, rifle high. The servitor pods hissed closed and there was silence again, roaring in his ears.

'Chaplain?' he called out. 'What happened to the defences?'

'I shut them down,' said Iktinos from above. 'We are safe, novice.'

Raek stood up, keeping the rifle high. Iktinos, he thought, was anything but safe.

The Chaplain was somewhere above him. Raek climbed, keeping his footing on the marble and granite, his gun held in the crook of one arm so he could bring it up and fire in an instant. He reached up and pulled himself onto the next chunk of architecture as it drifted past above him – it was a section of an arch, almost upside-down so it was like Raek was now sitting on a crooked crescent moon of stone.

He could see Iktinos, on a lip of obsidian jutting from the entrance to the tomb around which the rest of the shattered temple orbited. Raek brought up the rifle and against any other target he would have sent a shot right through the spine or the back of the head. But Iktinos wore artificer power armour, and only a shot through one of the critical weak spots – the eyepiece, the tiny spot over the throat, the joint under the arm where a shot from the right angle would pierce both hearts – would produce the guaranteed kill Raek needed. Iktinos walked into the tomb, and Raek's chance was gone.

Raek was a patient man. He could wait for days, for weeks, before taking a shot. The only thing he really remembered from his childhood was the baking heat of the desert sun as he lay on the hot sands for days, the scope of his hunting rifle scanning the horizon for that one shot. He had been the best hunter on that planet even before the Imperial Guard had arrived to take away the many mutants of his tribe, and his family and friends, and he had learned the kill-spots that would take down a guardsman. He had learned quickly how even a disciplined soldier will take risks to save his fellow trooper when that trooper has a bullet in the gut or a shot through the knee. And he learned to recognise when only a headshot would do.

They had never found Raek. Even when his people were gone, the adolescent Raek had survived to kill again. They had sent whole squads, whole platoons after him, and they had never got him. It had been Iktinos who had heard the tales of the invisible killer, and gone out into the desert to find him. The fact that Iktinos was now his target meant nothing at all to Raek, no more than the Guardsmen whom Raek had murdered from kilometres away over the sand dunes.

Raek jumped lightly up onto the next level of the floating, shattered temple, close enough to see a little way into the tomb. A faint pale bluish glow came from inside. The cut obsidian of the walls was gilded with symbols of the old Chapter – the chalice of the Soul Drinkers, stylised images of Space Marines more like hieroglyphics telling a story than portraits of Astartes. Gilded letters ringed the images, but Raek didn't recognise the language.

Raek made it to the threshold of the tomb. He pulled himself onto the ledge outside the doorway and gravity suddenly shifted. While the gravity in the rest of the temple had pulled towards the inside surface of the great spherical chamber, it now pulled Raek to the floor of the tomb, as if the tomb were a normal building on solid ground on any other world.

The tomb was big, bigger than it had looked from the temple entrance. Space seemed to flow strangely in the asteroid. Raek's enhanced vision struggled to pierce the veil of darkness inside. Raek pulled the hood of the voidsuit back from his face – there was a breathable atmosphere in the tomb, and he didn't want anything between his target and the naked eye.

'Chaplain?' he said, hoping to gauge Iktinos's location from the reply. But there was none.

Beyond the tomb's threshold, the darkness lifted. Inside the tomb was even larger, the ceiling high above Raek, the cavernous space criss-crossed with walkways and ladders. It was a library, and thousands upon thousands of books must have been stacked on the miles of shelves and cases, made of gold and black glass, that covered every surface. Soaring pillars were encrusted with shelves groaning with scrolls, and overhead hung huge smouldering censers that bathed everything in a deep amber glow.

At the far end was a golden chalice, five metres high and flanked by the images of two Space Marines, rendered in gilt against the obsidian wall. There were gun-servitors, too, standing mute guard over the library, hovering over bookcases or high up near the gilded ribs of the vaulted ceiling.

Iktinos had known how to shut them down. The library was defended by extensive security systems, but Iktinos had simply walked in. He had known all along what was in the asteroid.

Raek had thought that he was the traitor here. But perhaps Iktinos had betrayed them all.

Raek's rifle played between the bookcases and pillars, seeking out Iktinos on the high walkways and among the shadows that pooled around the ground level. The air here was dry and cold, no doubt to preserve the books, some of which looked very old indeed. But there was no movement save the slow, pendulous swaying of the censers overhead, and the corresponding shadows that flowed across the floor like the waves of a black sea.

'Novice,' came Iktinos's voice behind Raek. 'Do you now understand what it means to be a Soul Drinker?'

Raek froze, every nerve wound up tight. Iktinos had got behind him. That was impossible. No one had ever managed such a thing before, not against Raek. The place must have addled his senses somehow, dulled his mind or deceived him.

'We are the inheritors of a tradition as old as the Imperium, novice,' continued Iktinos, his voice so calm and level it was almost hypnotic. 'This Chapter is more than an army. It is the instrument of the Emperor, His hand lain upon the Imperium. In blindness we have gone for so long, but now we are free, the final stages can begin.'

Raek could feel Iktinos behind him, standing close among the shadows by the threshold. He could leap back and drive the stock of his rifle into Iktinos's throat, or whirl around and hope he was quick enough to fire before Iktinos got out of the way. Against a normal human opponent there would have been no question, but Iktinos had a Space Marine's reflexes and a lifetime of battle experience.

For the first time Raek cursed himself silently. He should have seen this coming, he should have accounted for Iktinos being one step ahead. He should have just been better.

'But the details elude you, novice. You do not know what all this means. You do not know the future. This revelation is all you will ever know. The Chapter's destiny will be written without you.'

Raek dropped to the floor, bringing his rifle round to blast Iktinos in the midriff. His senses slowed time down and the library swung around him ponderously. Iktinos's black-armoured form came into view, his bone-white grinning mask, the venom-green glint of his eyepieces.

Iktinos was faster. He caught Raek around the throat and tore away his rifle barrel. Raek tried to pry his captor's gauntleted hand away as his air was cut off.

'If you understood,' intoned Iktinos as Raek struggled, 'you would beg me to be a part of it. But you never will.'

Iktinos dropped Raek and the rifle. Raek hit the ground hard and lunged for his gun. Quicker than thought, Iktinos had his crozius in his hand. The power field flared, edging the obsidian and gold of the tomb in harsh blue-white. The crozius fell in an arc – again, time slowed down, so Raek had to watch it as it followed its, deep, pure crescent through the air towards his head.

The crozius cracked into the side of Raek's skull and took his head clean off. The head thudded wetly into the side of one of the bookcases and the body slumped to the black stone floor, pumping blood out into the darkness, one hand a few centimetres from his rifle.

IKTINOS LOOKED DOWN at the novice's body. There had been a rebellion, of course – it had been prophesied that another Chapter War could occur, and pose a threat to the grand plan. In some ways it was a shame that a novice had to die – the novices were a foundation of the next phase in the Chapter's history. But Iktinos had to survive. He was the last of the Chaplains, and everything depended on him.

Iktinos looked up at the library, the weight of the knowledge held inside like a stone slab on Iktinos's soul. Some men, had they known what knowledge was contained there, would have broken down and wept when they imagined what appalling devastation would be wreaked if it ever became known by the Imperium at large. But nothing caused Iktinos fear. He had faith. That rarest of commodities – true, pure, absolute faith.

Iktinos walked to the closest bookcase and took a book down from its upper shelf. The chalice embossed on its cover told him everything he needed to know. He opened it and began to read, and the blessed truth flowed through him like blood.

THE HALL OF Commanders was dominated by monumental sculptures of the Howling Griffons' great past – commanders and Chapter Masters who had orchestrated the Chapter's most glorious campaigns. They loomed over the circular hall, jewelled eyes focused on the huge tactical holomat like a round table in the centre of the room. The images of these legendary commanders were there to remind the assembled officers of the Howling Griffons to show humility, that there was always something the Chapter's fallen heroes had to teach them.

'A trap,' said Mercaeno, 'is the only way.'

Mercaeno stood over the holomat, which was showing a three-dimensional map of Nevermourn, along with the short stretch of sea and the coast of Herograve. The hives were glittering jewels of projected light, and it was obvious from their size how many billions of people would die if the orkish tide reached Herograve.

'The greenskins landings are confirmed here,' continued Mercaeno. Indicators appeared all over the map, angry red blips that signified where ork asteroids had come down in Nevermourn's jungles. 'The first landings were at Palatium. The planetary defence force was destroyed and the orks are opposed only by a Penal Legion. It is unlikely the troops will do anything more than slow the orks.'

'Jungle is their ground,' said Captain Darion, of the Ninth Company. His red and gold armour was studded with gemstones, each one signifying a notable kill. 'War has to be up close. Greenskins love it.'

'That is why,' said Mercaeno, 'we give them Nevermourn.'

A murmur went around the Hall of Commanders. A dozen or so officers were gathered there, resplendent in the heraldry of the Howling Griffons, each one proudly displaying kill markings or inscribed oaths on his armour. Mercaeno commanded the whole force, along with the veterans of the First Company. Darion had the Ninth, a company heavy in assault units – Darion himself was a formidable assault captain with hundreds of kills to his name. Captain Borganor led the Tenth Company, which had until recently consisted of newer recruits and scouts. The bloody battlefields that had led the Chapter to Periclitor had seen most of those young Astartes attain the rank of full Space Marine, and the Tenth was now as battle-hardened as any other company in the Chapter.

'Give it to the alien?' said Borganor, a leathery and allegedly unkillable veteran whose body was loaded with bionics to replace the many body parts he had lost.

'Orks are simple creatures, captain,' said Mercaeno. 'Their strategies can easily be predicted. They will surge towards the coast and assemble there to strike against the shore of Herograve.' The holomat showed a stretch of coastline. 'This is where they will land. The crossing is easiest here. With the Warders gone the orks will have no reason to think it will be defended by anything more than a handful of civilian militiamen.'

'But it will be defended by us,' said Captain Darion.

'Exactly. The greenskins will be at their most vulnerable when landing. We will meet them there and gun them down. The surf will be choked with their dead and the scourge will be thrown back into the sea. A drawn-out, purposeless conflict in the jungles will be dispensed with and the enemy will be destroyed with one stroke. This is the way of Roboute Guilliman, and the word of the Codex Astartes.'

'There is risk,' said Captain Borganor. 'We will only have one chance. The greenskins do not have enough tactical acumen for anything other than a single massed invasion of Herograve. If we do not stop them there...'

'We *will* stop them,' said Mercaeno. 'This Chapter swore an oath. It will be kept.'

'The orks will take a far greater risk with the invasion,' said Darion. 'It is they who will be punished for it.'

'Then I agree,' said Borganor. 'This is the way of Guilliman.'

'No,' said a voice from the back of the Hall of Commanders. 'It is not. Guilliman never gave ground to the enemy. He never threw away the lives of Imperial citizens.'

The eyes of the officers turned to Inquisitor Thaddeus. In spite of his rank, Thaddeus was still just a man, and as such he was dwarfed by the Astartes around him.

'You talk out of turn,' said Mercaeno sharply. 'Guilliman would sacrifice a billion lives if it would save a billion and one. You know that as well as I do.'

'Exactly, Lord Librarian,' said Thaddeus, approaching the holomat. 'Sacrifice. Tens of thousands of refugees from Palatium and elsewhere on Nevermourn are making their way to the coast. If we hold back, they will never make it. These are Imperial citizens, those same citizens of Vanqualis you swore your oath to defend. This Chapter should be down there in the jungles now, ensuring their safety.'

'Your tone,' said Darion dangerously, 'suggests we are lacking in courage. Inquisitor, you should know by now that such a thing is ill-advised in the company of Astartes.' Darion's hand strayed towards the sword at his hip.

Mercaeno raised a calming hand. 'Darion, there is no need for offence. The inquisitor here does not understand honour as we do. To him, honour consists of succeeding in his mission no matter who must break their oaths or fail in their duty, so long as this exalted agent of the Inquisition succeeds.'

Thaddeus didn't return Darion's offended glare. 'Lord Librarian, the fact remains that if the orks gather strength in Nevermourn they might never be defeated. Every hour more land in the jungles of–'

'I command three companies of the finest army this Imperium has ever fielded!' barked Mercaeno. 'No greenskin vermin can threaten our victory! You know as well as I do that fighting on Nevermourn is a waste of battle-brothers' lives. No man worthy of the Inquisition would be so foolish. Why are you here, Thaddeus? You care nothing for Vanqualis or its people. What do you seek on Nevermourn?'

Thaddeus was silent for a long moment, the officers of the Howling Griffons staring at him accusingly.

'That,' said Thaddeus at length, 'is for the Inquisition to know.'

Borganor banged a fist on the edge of the holo-mat table. 'Enough of this!' he sneered. 'The inquisitor is privileged even to be here. The trap will be laid.'

'Yes,' said Mercaeno. 'The trap will be laid and the greenskin will die. Inquisitor Thaddeus, it is clear to me that your mission here does not coincide with ours. Your authority has little foundation here. You are very far away from your colleagues and among us you are just a man. I had hoped that we had come to understand one another, but it seems that you cannot change. Be grateful that I have not yet ejected you from the fleet.'

'Take your leave, inquisitor,' said Captain Darion darkly. 'My tolerance has its limits.'

Thaddeus looked around the room, at the dark eyes looking back. 'Very well,' he said. 'This battle is yours to command, Lord Librarian.' Thaddeus turned and walked out of the Hall of Commanders.

Mercaeno and his captains looked back to the holomat, and plotted out the details of the trap that would end tens of thousands of greenskin lives in the name of the Emperor.

VANQUALIS'S MOON WAS a sinister green eye with a great dark crater as a pupil, glaring down at Nevermourn. Its thin greenish light barely penetrated the jungle canopy and dappled the mud-spattered dark purple armour of the Soul Drinkers squad as it advanced through the murk.

'Damn this filth,' said Sergeant Salk bleakly. 'This place will never clean off.'

Among the roots and mud around him, the rest of his squad slowly, quietly advanced to the top of the small ridge, their armoured feet sinking knee-deep into the near-liquid mud. 'We'll have to leave some scars of our own, then,' said Brother Karrick, Squad Salk's heavy bolter gunner. Karrick sported a bionic arm, strong enough to let him carry the bulky heavy bolter with ease. 'To make it even.'

'Visual,' said Brother Treskaen, lying on the slope of the ridge so he could see beyond. Salk scrabbled up beside him and followed his gaze.

In the centre of a large clearing in the jungle ahead of Squad Salk stood a fortress. The fortress was very old, probably dating to the time of the earliest colonies on Nevermourn when House Falken was only just beginning to carve out its safe havens in what had been then an unexplored jungle paradise. It was a crumbling edifice of reinforced rockcrete, rusted bands poking through the pitted surface like ribs, its blocky cylindrical base surmounted by ugly, brutish battlements. Varr and Sarpedon had not expected the fortress to mean much to the orks, who weren't in the habit of capturing strongpoints or holding ground. But it wasn't orks that Squad Salk were stalking.

'Is there movement?' asked Salk.

'None yet,' said Treskaen, sighting along his bolter.

'Wait,' said Karrick, sliding into the mud beside them. 'There. South-west. Light.'

Salk could see it. It was the laser sight in a sniper rifle, typically used by the best shots among the Chapter's scouts. It was playing along the foliage that crowded up against the side of the fortress, and as Salk followed the thin crimson line he could see the scout crouched down, almost in pitch darkness, among the brutal battlements.

'It's them,' said Treskaen. He spat into the mud to the side of him. 'Traitors.'

'They're dug in,' said Karrick. 'Look at that place.'

'There will be a way in,' replied Salk. 'There always is, unless Dorn himself designed it.'

'If we had the *Brokenback* we could burn them out,' said Treskaen, with hate running deep in his voice. 'Burn them all. Let them rot in the mud.'

'These are our brothers,' said Karrick.'

'*Were* our brothers,' hissed Treskaen. 'Now they're no better than the xenos filth we came here to kill.'

'I know,' said Karrick defensively. 'But it wasn't long ago we fought alongside them.'

'It wasn't long ago, brother, that we fought for the Imperium.'

'They are both traitors and brothers,' said Salk as he watched the scout move along the battlements, keeping a careful watch on the jungle around the fortress. 'Somewhere along the line we made this happen. One of us made a decision that led to this, and the rest of us accepted it.'

'You mean Sarpedon?' said Karrick.

'This is no one man's responsibility,' replied Salk.

'Tell that to the betrayers,' said Treskaen, little of the venom gone from his voice. 'Sarpedon's the one they want. Karraidin was a warning. The first chance they get they'll kill him.'

'No,' said Karrick. 'First chance they get they'll make it off this planet and strand us here. Maybe take a few pot shots with the *Brokenback* before they disappear.'

'Then we shall not give them the chance.' Salk flicked onto the command vox-channel. 'Salk here. I've got a squad to the fortress perimeter.'

'Any sign of them?' came Sarpedon's voice.

'The traitors are holding it. It's in bad repair but it's still solid enough.'

'Make a circuit if you can,' said Sarpedon. 'We need to know entrances and exits. But don't be seen.'

Salk looked back towards the squad fortress, its dark grey mass picked out in sallow green by the glaring eye of Vanqualis's moon. 'They'll know we are coming, commander.'

'I know,' said Sarpedon, something like resignation in his voice. 'But this is how it has to be done. I'll have the rest of the men move up towards your position and make ready for an assault. They could be gone by morning.'

'Understood. And commander?'

'Sergeant?'

'Do we know who is leading them? Who instigated all this?'

'I have some guesses, sergeant, as do you. When I see the answer with my own eyes, then I will be sure enough to tell it as the truth.'

'Should we have seen it coming?'

Sarpedon paused before replying, a moment too long. 'We gain nothing from looking for failures in our past. Our duty now is to put it right.'

'Understood,' said Salk. 'I'll take my squad around to get the layout of the place.'

'Good work, brother,' said Sarpedon. 'We will be with you soon. Be ready to fight at dawn.'

# CHAPTER NINE

'What is it that makes us Astartes?'

'Our augmentations and battlegear are as nothing compared to the mastering of our own fears. It is this that places us above the human race.'

– Daenyathos, *Catechisms Martial*

THAT NIGHT, THE stars that shone down on Herograve shone down on blood. The city reeked of fear, and in countless places that fear blossomed into death. One of the great squares, where the hive city's grand avenues intersected, saw such a blossoming, and Vanqualis's ice-green moon stared impassively as men and women died in fear.

185

The people were piled up in the square, clambering over one another. At the walls and in the corners they formed huge quivering mounds of human forms, writhing through limbs and bodies to reach higher up the smooth unforgiving walls. They thronged the avenue behind, shoving forward, and even from the balcony high above their screams could be heard. But they kept coming, streaming from their homes, climbing over the bodies of their fellow citizens to scale the walls of the square into which the packed avenue emptied. At the top of the walls were spiked battlements with firing slits manned by House Falken's family retainers, who watched bemusedly as thousands upon thousands of citizens died in the crush below.

'Why do they do this?' asked Countess Ismenissa.

'It is said that a cardinal has arrived from off-world,' said the countess's chamberlain, stood beside her on the balcony. 'And that he will bless all who file past his throne with the Emperor's beneficence. He is supposed to be beyond that wall, in the vault of the Temple of the Imperial Soul.'

'And is this true?'

'No, my lady, it is not,' replied the chamberlain. 'It is not known whence this rumour came.'

The countess sighed, and shook her head. 'Send a detachment of house troops,' she said, 'with gas grenades and water cannon. Disperse the crowds in the street and start clearing the square.'

'Yes, my lady.'

'And keep telling them to stay in their homes. Some of them may listen.' Countess Ismenissa waved a hand at the square below the balcony, where many men and women were dying beneath heaps of their fellow commoners. 'I must take my court from this tower. I do not dare imagine the stench come morning.'

'It shall all be done. With your leave, my lady.'

'To your duties, chamberlain.'

The chamberlain left the balcony, walking through the grand windows, which stood open onto the astonishing view of the hive, marred by the tragedy unfolding below. It was not the first such occurrence among the cities of Herograve. Word had got out about a shipment of food and weapons for the house enclave in Hive Scendalean, and the riotous looting of the convoy had turned into an all-out battle in the streets. It was still smouldering among the soaring, age-blackened hab-towers that rose from Hive Scendalean like nails driven into the city.

An apocalyptic cult had proclaimed the orks to be a scourge sent by the Emperor to punish the sinners of Vanqualis, and had set off bombs and committed massacres in Hive Lastrantus and the Ashcoast Colonies to kill as many citizens as possible and spare them the terrors of the greenskins' wrath. In every hive commoners were being seized by an insane desperation, and were killing themselves and their families to end the horror. Random killings and lootings were spreading faster than any disease. The orks had ended countless lives among the people of Herograve, and not one greenskin had even set foot on the continent yet.

Countess Ismenissa turned away from the grim sight below and walked from the balcony into her state rooms. They were lavish, with deep carpets and expensive drapings everywhere, gilded and hard-wood furniture, and many of the tapestries in the style for which House Falken was famed. Though the rooms were fully furnished and had an impos-ing four-poster bed, they were purely for receiving diplomats and other family members – Countess Ismenissa lived day to day in the far humbler rooms on the level below. A couple of the countess's chil-dren stared down at the carnage below, though their dead minds could not understand the suffering unfolding down in the square.

A House Falken retainer, in the emerald green and deep orange silk uniform of a herald, was waiting for her inside the room. The countess had planned to spend some time reviewing the situations in each of Herograve's major cities, and she had not expected to be interrupted.

'What do you want?' she asked sharply. The count-ess realised with a start that she had not slept for some time, and her temper was frayed.

'My countess, Lord Sovelin has contacted your court. He said his was a matter of the gravest urgency.'

'Sovelin? I do not recall the name.'

'He left instructions that you be told about the summers on Lake Felandin, should you not remem-ber him.'

'Sovelin. Yes... yes, one of Althelassa's brood. Slated for the Warders, though that skinny sickly boy could never have held a gun, I thought. He's alive, you say?'

'As of an hour and a half ago, my lady,' said the herald. He was young, and obviously did not relish his task of passing on what was sounding more and more like bad news. The countess's children hissed at him quietly from behind their mistress's skirts.

The countess held out her hand expectantly. 'Then let us see what he has to say.'

The herald handed her a folded parchment on which Lord Sovelin Falken's message had been transcribed. The countess's eyes flickered over the fragmented message transcribed from Sovelin's own words, which in many places had been unintelligible thanks to the gunfire and explosions in the background.

The mention of the Black Chalice made her hands tighten around the parchment, and her face become even paler and more skeletal as if her skin was translucent and her face was the skull beneath.

'The Black Chalice,' she said to herself. She heard the children flinch behind her.

'They are here?' said the herald, shocked into speaking out of turn.

Under other circumstances the countess would have had the herald chastised, but this time she could not blame him. Every child of Herograve was taught of the Black Chalice – fairytale monsters from the planet's blackest past, monsters from beyond reality of whom the vilest of heretics and cultists were but mere shadows. Preachers used the Bearers of the Black Chalice as allegories for evil and corruption, and mothers told their children fanciful stories of how all evil on Vanqualis flowed from it. The countess knew, and most commoners suspected, that the Chalice had its foundation in reality, some horrendous trauma that had wounded Vanqualis so deeply that the stories of the Black Chalice and its bearers had never ceased to be told.

'Open up a link with the *Cerulean Claw*,' said the countess. 'It should be close enough to forgo the need for an astropath. This is no longer just about the greenskins, the Dark Powers have their eyes on our world and our allies must be warned. Go!'

The herald hurried out of the state rooms. The countess was left alone with Sovelin's message in her hands. Who would have thought that Sovelin, that pasty wretch banished to the artillery, would have a part to play in the return of the Black Chalice? The Emperor's will could be obscure sometimes.

The screams from the square below were getting louder, mixed in with gunfire and the engines of riot control vehicles. The countess closed the grand windows to shut out the sound, as she contemplated how to tell Chief Librarian Mercaeno of the Howling Griffons that his Astartes would be going to battle with something far worse than the greenskins.

DAWN BROKE THROUGH the jungle, tinting everything a dark green as Vanqualis's sun forced its rays through the canopy. The greenish light turned the purple armour of the Soul Drinkers black as they gathered in a broad crescent echoing the curve of the fortress's southern wall.

'In position,' came Salk's vox. Salk held the western end of the Soul Drinkers' line.

'Ready here,' voxed Captain Graevus, whose assault unit anchored the eastern point of the line.

'Good. You two are the ends of the line. If the traitors counterattack and get round you, they will surround and crush us.'

'If they get past me then I'm dead,' said Graevus. He didn't speak with bravado – it was a simple statement of fact.

'Soul Drinkers,' said Sarpedon over the all-squads vox channel. He could see his Astartes all around him, beetle-black in the breaking dawn light, crouched down deep among the undergrowth and looping roots, huddled in the cover of the massive gnarled tree trunks. 'Every battle we have fought has brought us a new test. Nevermourn has led us to the sternest test yet. The enemy are our brothers, yet they are also traitors who must be defeated. Let there be no doubt – our objective is to kill them, those Space Marines alongside whom we have all fought many times. Some of you were there for the first Chapter War. All of you have heard tell of the depths we had to reach to come through it. This battle will be no less terrible. Nevertheless, a Space Marine must know neither fear nor doubt in the midst of battle. Know the traitors are telling themselves exactly the same thing. The next time we are together in peace, we shall be celebrating our victory and mourning those who had to die. This is the way of Rogal Dorn and of the Emperor. Cold and fast, Soul Drinkers, and move out.'

As one, the line moved forwards towards the great dark shape of the fortress. Over the years the fort had sunk into the waterlogged soil and it was surrounded by a mass of sucking mud, thick and deep enough that anyone weaker than a Space Marine would have been dragged down and trapped there. Sarpedon's talons cut through the morass as he moved forwards shoulder to shoulder with the men he could still call battle-brothers. It was dark in the shadow of the fortress, its glowering battlements only edged by the sun's first rays, but the sharp, enhanced eyes of the traitors' scouts would surely spot Sarpedon's Soul Drinkers advancing and start the battle well before they got to the walls.

The southern side of the fortress had a wide, pitted rockcrete causeway leading to an enormous gate of age-stained plasteel. This was the Soul Drinkers' objective, and it would surely be the place most heavily defended by the traitors. If Sarpedon wanted to get inside and deal with the traitors face to face, he would have to fight a battle they had prepared, throwing his men at the gates to force the traitors to face him.

It was ugly. No sane general would have accepted it. But Sarpedon was not a general of the Imperial Guard, who had to cope with the weaknesses and indiscipline of their men. He was a Space Marine, and so were those under his command. Tactical insanity, the willingness to fight battles that no commander of lesser men would contemplate, was the weapon of choice for the Space Marines.

With bleak inevitability, the first streaks of gunfire thudded down through the overhanging foliage into the mass of mud and rotting vegetation through which the Soul Drinkers were advancing. Sniper fire whistled down into the mud. A Soul Drinker stumbled and fell, and was dragged forwards – alive or dead – by one of his squadmates so he was not left behind by the advance. Movement up on the battlements showed the traitors were preparing, gathering for the sacred moment when the enemy came within bolter range.

Sarpedon had been there many times. That range was etched into the consciousness of every Space Marine – the place where war turned from big guns and artillery to cut and thrust, single shots, volleys of fire and diving for cover.

More fire. Another battle-brother fell. A missile streaked down from the battlements and threw a black claw of mud into the air. Bolter range hovered closer, and the Soul Drinkers were sighting down their bolters ready to open up. Sarpedon's psychic powers did not allow him to receive telepathic messages or read minds, but even his latent power picked up the tension, the wound-up intensity that replaced human fear in a Space Marine's mind. He could feel it from the traitors, too, vibrating through the jungle, and he knew then that these were his brothers, fighting because they believed as completely as he did.

The advancing Soul Drinkers crossed bolter range. 'Charge!' ordered Sarpedon, and his voice was drowned out by a curtain of burning shrapnel as hundreds of bolters opened up as one.

Brothers fell. A body tumbled from the battlements. The noise was appalling. More and more traitors were joining their brothers on the walls.

'Demolition teams forward!' ordered Sarpedon over the vox. Several squads ran onwards through the mud as the rest of the Soul Drinkers covered them, hunkering down behind shattered tree stumps or knots of rock-hard roots.

But the fire was too heavy. The traitors had won too many of the Soul Drinkers over to their side. The demolition teams were pinned down, and more of Sarpedon's battle-brothers were dying with every moment. Brother Phokris died, his helmet blown wide open even as he pressed the firing stud on his missile launcher. Brother Wrackath fell to the ground by Sarpedon's side, his leg sheared off by heavy bolter fire. Sarpedon himself folded his legs beneath him to crouch down behind the trunk of a massive fallen tree, mud spraying all over him as bolter rounds smacked into the ground.

The closest demolition team, led by Sergeant Salk, was prone in the mud, surviving only thanks to the slope of the low rise ahead of them. They couldn't advance. None of them could. The ruined jungle around the fortress was becoming a no-man's land, and the traitors' fire was too heavy for the Soul Drinkers to make it across.

Against any other foe, the Soul Drinkers would have stormed the place, cold and fast, just as their philosopher-soldier Daenyathos had described in his *Catechisms Martial*. Against human rebels or alien scum, they would have braved the fire and relied on the shock of their assault to carry the day. But not against fellow Space Marines. No more dangerous opponents existed in the galaxy.

Through the gunfire, Sarpedon could hear a scream of engines from overhead. He glanced up and saw a flare of engines through the canopy, bright against the darkened dawn sky.

With no further warning, the Thunderhawk gunship plunged down through the canopy, its nose-mounted guns instantly opening up and raking the battlements of the fortress with fire. A side door opened and a figure leaned out – black-armoured with a faceplate of pale bone. Iktinos.

Iktinos leapt out of the gunship, trusting in his battlegear to protect him from the long fall. As he hurled himself out of the door the gunship's engines flared and the Thunderhawk hurtled towards the battlements.

Traitors dived for cover among the huge rockrete slabs of the battlements. Some of them were too late. The Thunderhawk slammed into the battlements, the back of its armoured body breaking against the fortress, and skidded along the top of the wall. Ammunition cooked off inside the shattered craft and its fuel load followed, erupting in a great orange-black bloom.

'Forward!' yelled Sarpedon, as the fire from the battlements faltered.

The Soul Drinkers line advanced, the demolition teams breaking cover and running. Sarpedon could hear war cries going up from his battle-brothers. He followed them, feeling the aegis circuit of his armour pulsing as he drew on the great well of psychic power inside him.

Fear. That was Sarpedon's weapon. He delved into the lower reaches of his mind to dredge up that which caused him an emotion most resembling the fear that normal men were cursed with.

The primarch Rogal Dorn strode over the battlements, the golden yellow of his armour burning with hatred at the traitors. Great gilded eagles, vast and terrifying, loomed down from the canopy. From the burning wreckage of the Thunderhawk strode the heroes of the Soul Drinkers, those who had died to make the Chapter free – and among them was Daenyathos, the philosopher-soldier who had written out the Soul Drinkers' way of war thousands of years before.

The traitors, like all the Soul Drinkers, had trained with the Hell to help steel their souls against the hallucinations Sarpedon could conjure – and even without that experience, as Space Marines they were difficult men to shake. Sarpedon forced the Hell higher, casting wrathful flames into the eyes of the Chapter's dead and making Dorn tower over the fortress, his rage like lightning tearing down through the jungle.

Salk's demolition team threw themselves against the base of the wall beside the gate, where the overhang of the battlements shielded them from the guns of the traitors. Sarpedon spotted Salk attaching a large metallic device to the side of the gate. Other teams were making it to the wall, too, while some were still pinned down by fire from the traitors who had stayed at their posts.

Iktinos strode through the mud and carnage, bolter shots flying around him. He was battered and covered in mud, but the presence the Chaplain brought with him was undiminished.

'Chaplain!' said Sarpedon, as he ducked behind a bullet-scarred rock to concentrate on the Hell. 'It is good to see you alive. I feared the traitors would do for you.'

'Not for want of trying, commander,' replied Iktinos. 'They sent one of their scouts to kill me. They were not successful.'

'Do you know who is in charge?'

'I have my suspicions.'

'And they are?'

'Eumenes.'

Eumenes. Of course. Eumenes was brilliant – brave, decisive, intelligent and ruthless. The scouts would be on his side, which was why so many of the Chapter's new recruits had joined the rebellion. And Eumenes was persuasive. He had been an officer of the future. Sarpedon had even imagined Eumenes leading the Chapter when Sarpedon himself was gone.

If Sarpedon failed here, that was exactly what would happen. Eumenes would command the Soul Drinkers into a future of treachery.

'Ready,' voxed Salk.

'Ready here!' echoed Sergeant Dargalis, who had taken his assault squad through the storm of fire to the other side of the gate.

Sarpedon checked the status of the other forward squads. Some were not in position, still pinned down. Others didn't respond at all. It would have to be enough.

'Do it!' ordered Sarpedon.

Twin explosions ripped through the wall either side of the fortress gate. The ground shook, felling trees weakened by shredding gunfire. Thunderheads of dust and vaporised mud roared forwards. Chunks of rockcrete fell as thick as rain, and even a Space Marine's eyesight could not penetrate the solid mass of dust and smoke that rippled from the gate.

'Forward!' ordered Sarpedon. With Iktinos beside him, and the rest of his Soul Drinkers half glimpsed through the sudden hot gloom, Sarpedon scuttled over the fallen tree and towards the shattered gates. The gunfire was quiet – the bolter exchanges from the flanks of the Soul Drinkers' lines might as well have been on a different world. The din of battle was gone for a brief moment as the smoke and dust clung to no-man's land.

On the battlements, the traitors would be recovering rapidly from the detonation of the demolition charges. They would be getting back to their posts, checking their bolter loads, ready to massacre the loyal Soul Drinkers emerging from the gloom. The Hell would be dying down, Rogal Dorn's titanic figure turning distant and the glowering heroes of the Chapter's past just dim ghosts against reality.

Sarpedon had trained them too well. Any other enemy would crumble. Not the traitor Soul Drinkers.

Sarpedon could see the wall now, dark against the filmy grey of the clearing dust. The gate had fallen completely, massive slabs of corroded metal lying twisted on the shattered rockrete causeway. The battlements over the gates had crumbled, forming a great drift of rubble choking the gates. Armoured forms were moving over the top of the rubble, taking cover ready for battle.

Sarpedon recognised the high collar of an aegis circuit and the double-handed force sword in the hands of one traitor on top of the rubble slope. It was a Librarian, one of Sarpedon's fellow psykers among the Soul Drinkers, and a man who had seen everything that Sarpedon had, from his earliest battles at Quixian Obscura to the Chapter War and everything beyond.

Sarpedon strode into the open. 'Gresk!' he yelled.

Librarian Gresk looked down at Sarpedon, and held up a hand to halt the fire of his fellow traitors ready to attack from the ruined battlements. 'Commander!' called back Gresk. 'Though you cannot call me a brother, we are still Soul Drinkers. We still have a duty to one another. I have no wish to see you die here. You can still turn back and there will be no battle here.'

'You know I cannot do that, Gresk,' said Sarpedon. Around him, the Soul Drinkers were taking up positions at the end of the rubble slope, sighting down their bolters over slabs of rockrete and the lips of impact craters on the causeway. 'This ends here, either way. But you are correct, you have a duty. A duty to tell me why.'

'This had been happening for a long time, Sarpedon,' said Gresk. In the eerie pause in the battle, his voice carried as clear as thunder. 'Even since we discovered what we were, since the death of Abraxes. Look at where you have led us. We are on this Emperor-forsaken place, fighting for an Imperium you claim to despise. Our own brothers were nearly our downfall on Gravenhold. We barely survived Abraxes's curse, and the Inquisition nearly did for us on Stratix Luminae. Your rule is leading us towards destruction. We cannot survive with you in charge any more. Just as you usurped Gorgoleon, we are usurping you in charge.'

'"We?" You mean Eumenes,' said Sarpedon.

'Eumenes organised the scouts right under your nose. After Gravenhold he had the loyalty of all the new recruits. He is brilliant, Sarpedon, and he leads as if he was born to it. He has beaten you for the soul of your own Chapter. Those of us who have sided with him are simply joining the winning side.'

All around the two Librarians, the tension was being ramped up again. One gesture, one word, and both sides would be consumed by the kind of murderous short-range slaughter at which Space Marines excelled. Sarpedon could see fingers tightening around triggers and thumbs ready to activate the exhausts of jump packs. That was all it would take – one word. Gresk was a master of the

Quickening, a psychic power that enhanced the metabolism of his allies so they moved with incredible speed and grace. In such a battle, the power could turn the tide.

'I thought you must be dead,' said Sarpedon. 'Because I could not imagine you joining this rabble. You still have a chance to abandon this madness before the killing begins.'

'You do not understand, Sarpedon,' replied Gresk, and there was genuine sadness in his voice. 'I have no wish to see you die, but Eumenes wants your blood. My task here was to hold you in place. To keep you at the walls, to give you ground as long as I slowed you down long enough. There will be no more battle. Turn back. Do you understand?'

Sarpedon realised why they were there. The canopy of the jungle petered out just before the fortress walls – the Soul Drinkers were open to the grey-green dawn sky.

'The *Brokenback*,' said Iktinos beside him.

'Fall back! All units!' ordered Sarpedon. 'Retreat!'

The Soul Drinkers were not used to the order to retreat. No Space Marine ever took it lightly. But Sarpedon was still their Chapter Master, and they broke cover to fall back into the chewed-up battle-field of mud and fallen trees. Sarpedon himself scuttled backwards, watching Gresk turn back from the battle and walk back into the body of the fortress.

The first lance strike hammered down, shearing deep into the ground where Sarpedon had stood. Superheated air slammed into Sarpedon like a wall and he barely kept his footing as the ground shuddered and split. Another strike, bright as a second sun, hit home and Sarpedon saw a body flying, half-chewed away by the immense power of the laser bolt.

The bombardment was ripping down all around them, awesome in its power. Had the Soul Drinkers been advancing on the gates, they would have been annihilated completely. Many of them still died, torn apart by the columns of laser that burst into being in front of the fortress gates.

'Chaplain!' shouted Sarpedon over the din. 'This battle is over! Regroup with the men in the jungle!'

'Yes, commander,' replied Iktinos. He was an icon of the Chapter, more so perhaps than even Sarpedon himself, and if the Soul Drinkers would follow anyone now, it was him.

As Sarpedon ran through the destruction, lit by the strobing pulse of the lasers firing down from the *Brokenback* in orbit, he realised that the thought of another man, such as Iktinos, leading the Chapter was more and more acceptable to him. Gresk was correct – Sarpedon had led the Soul Drinkers almost to destruction. He had seen them all but torn apart, and all because he believed he knew what path the Chapter should take. If he was wrong, if the traitors were justified, then Sarpedon did not deserve to rule the Soul Drinkers.

'FOR GUILLIMAN, SON of the Emperor! For the Founding Father!'

Mercaeno's voice was echoed by the hundreds of Howling Griffons gathered in the vast Battlecry

Cloister, the spectacular vaulted temple of war that served the *Cerulean Claw* as a mustering deck. The floor was tiled with trophies – scraps of xenos armour, fragments of shattered traitorous skulls, alien bodies crushed like specimens on a slide, stamped flat beneath millennia of Howling Griffons' boots.

'For the oath and the word! For the honour that men fear! Howling Griffons, what say you to the oath sworn by your brothers long dead?'

'Honour them!' cried the men, ranked up by company and squad, their officer out in front of them leading them. And in front of them all was Mercaeno, voice as proud and rousing as a preacher's.

'Even though it may cost your life?' bellowed Mercaeno, challenging as much as encouraging. The wordless roar of approval that came back at him was answer enough.

'Though your soul be rent and your bodies broken? Shall you honour this oath, Howling Griffons, inheritors of Guilliman?'

The roar again, louder, more insistent. The fervour of the Howling Griffons to honour the Chapter's ancient oaths bordered on mania. The fire inside them flashed in their eyes. It was only the merciless discipline of the Adeptus Astartes that kept them from rioting, from expressing that power within them in random violence.

'Then make your oaths, Howling Griffons.'

Captain Darion stood out in front of the assembled Howling Griffons, his power sword held high so all could see him. At his side trundled a scribe-servitor, its hunched form carrying a long spool of parchment and twin electroquills quivering on armatures extending from its eyes sockets. It would take down the oaths made by the battle-brothers of the Howling Griffons as they made them to Captain Darion, as was the tradition among the Howling Griffons. Their oaths were sacred, and to return to the Chapter without having fulfilled them brought great shame. Howling Griffons had stayed away from their Chapter for years, even decades, seeking ways to fulfil oaths they had made before battle. Some of them were still out there in the galaxy, questing until they settled their matter of honour, or until they died.

'What is the meaning of this?' came the harried-sounding voice of Inquisitor Thaddeus as he ran across the trophy-laden floor of the Battlecry Cloister. He was still pulling on his long flakweave coat.

Mercaeno turned to the inquisitor and stepped in front of him, so he was kept away from the oath rites that were specific to the Chapter.

'No doubt you will rejoice,' said Mercaeno, although there was no congratulations in his voice. 'We are landing on Nevermourn.'

'What changed?' said Thaddeus.

'The oath we swore to Vanqualis was to do more than simply defend it. An ancient enemy has returned, perhaps in league with the greenskins, perhaps manipulating them. The force must be destroyed.'

'Who?'

Mercaeno shook his head. 'That, inquisitor, is not even for your ears.'

'Wait, Lord Librarian,' said Thaddeus. 'There may be forces at work here that you do not understand.'

'Your words grow tiresome, inquisitor. Whatever your mission here it cannot compare to the fulfilment of our oath to Vanqualis. It is one of the most ancient of…'

'You seek the Grail of Damnation,' said Thaddeus.

Mercaeno was silent for a moment. Behind him the Howling Griffons crowded around Captain Darion, swearing they would take an enemy's head or avenge a lost battle-brother, or be the first man to set foot on the ground of Vanqualis.

'Or whatever you call it,' said Thaddeus. 'There are many names, but they all mean the same thing. Please, Lord Librarian, you cannot just-'

'You know nothing of the Black Chalice!' roared Mercaeno. 'Whatever devilry you intend on Vanqualis, you shall not interfere in our mission!'

'I know a great deal about the Black Chalice, Lord Librarian, more than any man alive. And I cannot allow you to take your men into a battle you do not understand.'

'Allow? You do not allow us anything, inquisitor! You have no authority here, Inquisitorial seal or not! The Black Chalice is an evil that has blighted Vanqualis in ages past and vowed to return. Now that time has come, and it must be destroyed. Not studied, not contained, not negotiated with – destroyed, utterly and forever, with honest gunfire and chainblade.'

Thaddeus's eyes were wide with horror. 'You do not understand what you are fighting, Lord Librarian.'

'Then that is where you and I differ, inquisitor. I do not have to understand my enemy. I must merely destroy. Stay out of our way, Thaddeus, lest you become that enemy.'

Mercaeno turned back to his men, hearing the oaths that they would defeat a bearer of the Black Chalice in single combat, or that they would walk upon the shores of Herograve and proclaim to its people that they were at last free.

'This is your last chance, Lord Librarian,' said Thaddeus.

Mercaeno glanced back at him, a hand on the force axe at his belt. 'You wish us to let the Black Chalice live, Thaddeus. I have battle-brothers here who would kill you on the spot for voicing such a thought. Should I call them forth, or would you rather face me here?'

For a moment Thaddeus looked like he would draw a weapon from beneath the flakweave panels of his coat, and accept Mercaeno's challenge. The oaths of the Howling Griffons faded out and the only two men in the cloister were the inquisitor and the Librarian, ready to settle their differences in the oldest way.

'Then may your oaths be fulfilled,' said Thaddeus, backing down before Mercaeno as all men did. 'And may the Howling Griffons find victory.'

Mercaeno did not reply, instead joining the rest of his Astartes and making his own oaths to be recorded and fulfilled as was the Chapter's way.

Mercaeno swore that Vanqualis would be saved.

And that the Black Chalice would be finally shattered forever.

# CHAPTER TEN

'How can we tell our friends from our enemies?'

'It is said that all but our battle-brothers will become our enemies in the end.'

– Daenyathos, *Catechisms Martial*

'I THOUGHT YOU were dead, brother!' said Sarpedon, with a joy in his voice that had not been there since the catastrophe at the Serpentspine Valley. His voice echoed strangely in the cave, where he had made the Soul Drinkers' temporary command post. He spoke into his vox-unit and the signal was poor, for it had to be transmitted from the *Brokenback* in orbit to the surface.

'It was a close thing, commander,' replied Lygris. 'But by the Emperor's grace I live still.'

'Where are you?'

'In the ruin of the *Abandoned Hope*,' replied Lygris. His voice was severely distorted by the ancient vox equipment he was using and the interference from Vanqualis's atmosphere. 'It's a part of the *Brokenback* that only I have explored. Eumenes and his men are hunting me down but I know this place too well.'

Sarpedon looked around the cave, at the primitive scrawlings on its walls and the skull symbols carved over the entrance. It was hidden in the depths of the jungle, dark, damp and choked with moss and weeds, and had probably not seen sentient life for hundreds of years. 'We're not much better off, Lygris,' said Sarpedon. 'The traitors are led by Gresk down here. They're holding a fortress and the orks are everywhere. It's bedlam on the surface.'

Around the cave, and the natural defences of rocks and trees outside it, the Soul Drinkers were standing guard and tending their wounds, cleaning the jungle filth from their battlegear and performing the personal rites of battle and devotion. They had been beaten, and defeat had its own traditions just like victory – silent, personal rites of shame and atonement, appeals to the Emperor for the chance of redemption, and promises of vengeance. Deeper into the cave were the ruins of a small shrine or perhaps the simple tomb of an ancient ancestor, where Apothecary Karendin was setting broken limbs and transfusing blood.

'Librarian Gresk? Throne preserve us, I never thought Gresk would side against you. Pallas, too.'

For a moment Sarpedon was shocked that Pallas had joined Eumenes's rebellion, but in a way, it made sense. 'Tellos,' said Sarpedon. 'Pallas was the closest thing to a friend Tellos had. And I failed Tellos as much as I failed any of us.'

'I've been keeping a watch on the *Brokenback*'s communications,' continued Lygris. 'Eumenes is making ready to bring the traitors off the surface and onto the ship. Without me it'll be at least two days before he can get the warp engines on-line. Then Eumenes will send the Thunderhawks down to the surface and pick up Gresk and the rest of them.'

'Then we need to be victorious by then,' said Chaplain Iktinos. Iktinos was standing nearby, studying the carvings on the cave wall. They were primitive depictions of warfare, humanoid shapes butchering one another and standing atop piles of skulls. 'For Eumenes would maroon us here, to die amongst the criminals and the xenos.'

'All this means we have the advantage, then,' said Sarpedon.

Iktinos turned from the cave wall. 'How so, commander?'

'We know what Eumenes wants. He wants to get his fellow traitors off Nevermourn. He has to do it before he can escape here. That's how we'll get them out into the open and onto our battlefield.'

'Then you have not yet given in, Sarpedon,' said Iktinos.

'No Soul Drinker has ever given up at anything, Chaplain,' said Sarpedon sharply. 'I have led this Chapter into Nevermourn and I will not rest until I have led it out again. You know me better than to doubt that.'

'Then you do consider yourself responsible for this rebellion,' said Iktinos. It wasn't phrased as a question, more a statement of fact, not quite challenging Sarpedon but coming close.

'Command means responsibility,' replied Sarpedon. 'Wherever this Chapter goes, I have led it there. Whatever obstacles it faces, I have chosen to face them.' Sarpedon's voice was sharp, and for a moment it seemed he would take Iktinos to task for questioning him – but Sarpedon's face softened as he backed down from a confrontation. 'Tellos taught me that,' he said. 'I hope he knew that at the end. I should have watched Tellos more closely, and I should have watched Eumenes, too. And Pallas and Gresk, and everyone else who had joined forces against me. I could have stopped this from happening, so it is my duty to stop it now.'

'Eumenes doubts that you are fit to rule this Chapter,' continued Iktinos, relentlessly. 'With the doubts that so clearly lie within you, can you be sure he is not correct?'

'This is my Chapter,' said Sarpedon. 'I won it from Gorgoleon and led it from corruption. I saved us from Abraxes's curse and the Inquisition, I brought us out of Gravenhold. No one has earned the right to command this Chapter as I have. I have no doubts, Iktinos. There is nothing I will not do to save this Chapter and do the Emperor's work. And to do that, I must see out what I started. I must stay in command.'

For a long moment, the two Space Marines faced one another as if about to strike. Sarpedon was not backing down now, and nothing in Iktinos's grim, skull-faced gaze suggested he would accept he was wrong.

'This is my Chapter, too,' said Iktinos. 'And you are my Chapter Master. I shall fight by your side until the end. And I, too, have no doubts.'

'Commander, Chaplain,' said Lygris over the vox, evidently relieved to have heard any conflict averted. 'The plan.'

'Yes, the plan,' said Sarpedon. 'Lygris, I have two tasks for you. Firstly, I need some images of the fortress and the area around it. Topographical data. Can you do that?'

'Certainly,' said Lygris. 'I can still get into the bridge cogitators remotely, for a short while at least.'

'Secondly, do you have access to the flight decks?'

'The primary decks, yes,' replied Lygris. 'It may not be easy. I'm being hunted down here and the flight decks will be guarded, but there are a few back doors I can use.'

'Good,' said Sarpedon. 'I need you to destroy the Thunderhawks.'

THE LOWER DECKS of the *Cerulean Claw* were a celebration of the fallen Howling Griffons. The greatest heroes were remembered in places like the Manse of

Furioso, but the lower-ranked battle-brothers who had died performing some heroic deed were commemorated in the Remembrance Decks. Memorials to dozens of Howling Griffons stood, crowned with statues of them in the full heraldry of their armour, standing guard over one another in marble or polished granite. They stood in halls remembering the dead of a particular campaign, or of an era in the Howling Griffons' history, and each one was like a weight pinning the past down upon the Chapter.

Inquisitor Thaddeus moved through one of those places now, and it was like a quiet, imposing forest of stone with statues of Space Marines watching him on every side.

Thaddeus had scouted out the layout of the *Cerulean Claw* early on in the voyage, because he knew that he might one day have to steal through it, unseen and probably hunted, looking for a way to escape. He knew that the ship had a secondary shuttle bay and that the complex circuitry in his Inquisitorial seal would probably open it and let him take a shuttle down to Vanqualis. He was an inquisitor, and the best of his kind planned for when everything went wrong.

Thaddeus crept past a statue of a Howling Griffon carrying twin chainblades, the statue's face turned mournfully towards the floor. At the far side of the hall he saw an archway with a blast door leading to the shuttle deck. A few more moments and Thaddeus would be off the *Cerulean Claw*.

'Inquisitor,' said a deep, commanding voice from behind Thaddeus. Thaddeus span around and saw a

Space Marine across the tomb chamber. The gold and crimson of his armour marked him out from the forest of stone Space Marines around him. Thaddeus scanned the Space Marine rapidly – he recognised the heraldry and ostentatious oath-texts of Mercaeno's command squad, veterans who acted as his hands and eyes among the Chapter.

'Eyes everywhere,' said Thaddeus. 'Damn Astartes, I swear sometimes you can see through walls.'

'Inquisitor Thaddeus,' said the Howling Griffon, 'Chief Librarian Mercaeno has ordered you confined to your quarters.'

'Does he now? And what's his excuse?'

'He does not trust you.'

Thaddeus smiled bitterly. 'The Lord Librarian is honest, at least. Which one are you?'

'Brother Rhelnon,' replied the Howling Griffon. 'Lord Mercaeno sent my battle-brothers and I to find you, inquisitor. You are being deliberately elusive. I think Mercaeno was right to suspect you.'

Thaddeus moved carefully, keeping the plinth of the closest memorial between him and Rhelnon. 'I bear the authority of the Immortal Emperor of Mankind,' he said, 'and the Adeptus Astartes are subject to that authority whether they like it or not. Worlds could die at my command, Brother Rhelnon. The mighty could be dragged away in chains.'

'None of us dispute the Inquisitorial mandate. But here, you are just a man, and you are alone. Power does not stem from the Inquisitorial seal you carry with you. It comes from this.' Rhelnon patted the barrel of the bolter he held across his chest. 'You are trying to escape, which means you oppose the will of the Howling Griffons. Therefore, you are our enemy. As you are a guest here, Lord Mercaeno has permitted for you to be captured rather than killed. This is not an offer the Howling Griffons regularly make to their enemies.'

'All this because you made a promise you cannot keep,' said Thaddeus. 'Brother, do you even know what the Black Chalice is?'

Rhelnon seemed slightly taken aback by the question – no doubt he had been expecting Thaddeus to either give up or attack, not question Rhelnon back. 'The Black Chalice is a daemon,' he said. 'A thing of the warp, a puppet of the Dark Powers. The Bearers of the Black Chalice are the human vermin who worship it.'

'And they were on Vanqualis a long time ago, and they will one day return,' said Thaddeus. 'No one knows where they went or what happened to them but the Black Chalice is so deeply ingrained on the minds of the people of Vanqualis that it must have been something terrible indeed. Am I right?'

'Inquisitor, your words will do nothing to sway us from our–'

'Brother Rhelnon!' snapped Thaddeus. 'Am I right?'

Rhelnon did not answer. His grip tightened on his bolter and his finger slipped inside the trigger guard.

'They call it the Grail of the Damned,' said Thaddeus, 'halfway across the galaxy in the Scorpanae

Cluster. It's the Obsidian Skull on Phylax Minor, where they say it's a drinking cup made from the skull of a daemon and that anyone who drinks from it lives forever. Mercaeno doesn't know what he's dealing with – no one in this galaxy does. The only one who comes close is me.'

'I have my orders, inquisitor,' said Rhelnon.

'I know,' said Thaddeus, a trace of sadness in his voice. 'But what kind of a man would I be if I didn't try to make you understand before?'

'Before what?'

'You know what.'

Rhelnon sighed. 'It can be done without this, inquisitor.'

'Maybe in a perfect galaxy,' said Thaddeus.

Rhelnon moved first. His reflexes were sharper than any man's, even an inquisitor's. Thaddeus dropped to his knees and a short, tight burst of bolter shots zipped over his head and cracked into the stone plinth beside him. Shots burst against the statue above him and a broken chainblade fell, sheared from the hand of the stone Space Marine by the impacts.

'Thaddeus, I will take you in if I can but your death will give me few regrets!' shouted Rhelnon. He snapped off another shot, which nearly took off Thaddeus's foot before he pulled it back behind the statue.

Thaddeus reached into his voluminous flak-weave coat and pulled out his gun, a modified autopistol chased in brass and silver. Heavy shots thunked into the chamber as he cocked it.

Thaddeus dived out from behind the plinth, firing as he went. The shots were snapped blind and flew wide. Rhelnon rapidly judged that a mere autopistol would do little against power armour and stepped into the open again, trying to draw a bead on his prey.

Thaddeus flicked a selector stud on the weapon and a single round clicked into the chamber. It was the last of his archeotech rounds, very old, very valuable bullets crammed with circuitry too old to be replicated. Once he had loaded his whole gun with them, back when he had the backing of his fellow inquisitors. But that felt like a long time ago. He had been saving that last bullet for a special occasion, and now that Rhelnon was bearing down on him, Thaddeus decided that the occasion had arrived.

He rolled between two of the memorials and fired. The bullet zipped wide again but then its ancient technology kicked in and it flitted around in a wide arc, arrowing back towards Rhelnon.

Rhelnon threw himself to one side but too late, the bullet smacked into his armour, boring deep inside. He yelled in anger and pain as his right arm was shredded, the bullet ricocheting around inside his armour like an angry trapped insect. His blood spattered up against the stern obsidian Chaplain statue standing over him.

'Traitor!' yelled Rhelnon, opening fire even as he stumbling with the impacts. Bolter shots sprayed in a burning fan. Statues fell, their legs shot out from beneath them, stone heads smashed on the floor.

Thaddeus ducked down, the tough flakweave of his coat deflecting shrapnel and knife-sharp shards of obsidian.

Thaddeus had been out in the galaxy for a long time. He had learned never to rely on any weapon he could not carry on him at all times, and never to spare any expense in securing the best. He had known that sooner or later, doing his duty to the Emperor would rely on his ability to survive a close encounter with a hostile Space Marine.

Thaddeus fired more shots, emptying the mundane rounds from his autopistol. Rhelnon was in the open now and shots thudded into his greaves and abdomen, but they did little more than kick sparks from the Howling Griffon's armour.

The pistol's action snapped closed on an empty chamber. Thaddeus dropped the gun and pulled out an ornate hilt from inside his coat. From the hilt extended a shimmering blade, warping the air around it with it strange energy field. He couldn't see Rhelnon now – both men were keeping the memorials between them.

'We should have killed you!' shouted Rhelnon, his voice straining with anger rather than pain. 'Mercaeno should have never let you on board! We should have thrown you out of the damned airlock!'

'If I had told you the truth, you would have done just that,' said Thaddeus as he skulked between the statues, sword in his hand. He could hear Brother Rhelnon moving a few statues away. 'I do what I must. I lie because I serve a greater truth.'

'My Emperor rules from a throne of gold,' replied Rhelnon. 'Your kind sit upon a throne of deceit.'

Both men were trying to distract the other to win the advantage. Thaddeus listened to Rhelnon's armoured feet on the floor. There were only two statues between him and Rhelnon now.

Thaddeus ran first, headlong between the tombs. Rhelnon's huge armoured form reared up over him, the knife flashing down. Thaddeus had learned his swordcraft from the death cultists who served Lord Inquisitor Goldo, during Thaddeus's apprenticeship as a lowly interrogator. The swift, sharp parry he learned there kept Rhelnon's blade away from his heart and now the Space Marine was in his face – Thaddeus could see the anger in his eyes, smell the hot iron of the blood congealing around his many wounds.

The blade in Thaddeus's hand split into dozens of fluttering shards, like a swarm of lethal butterflies. Rhelnon reared up as monomolecular shards sheared through the ceramite plates of his armour, scored deep red lines across his face and punched right through his back.

Rhelnon roared like a wounded animal, slashing wildly at his foe. Thaddeus rolled away as the sword shards flittered around Rhelnon, opening up dozens of wounds. One by one the force in the shards died and they fell to the floor, the last of them spiralling around Rhelnon until he batted them away. Thaddeus used the time they bought him to roll out from beneath Rhelnon's assault and take cover three tombs away.

He couldn't help but glance up into the face of the statue above him. It was sculpted with the high collar and ornate force sword of a Librarian. For a moment Thaddeus was aware of ancient traditions of the Howling Griffons, and of how he had violated them to the core by lying to Mercaeno about why he had sought passage aboard the *Cerulean Claw*. For an insane moment he wondered if the Howling Griffons buried their dead here, if beneath these memorials were coffins containing the skeletons of those Space Marines, watching him with empty sockets, cursing him for turning on the Howling Griffons in their very own burial place.

Thaddeus chased the thought from his mind. There was no more room for doubt. Rhelnon must have summoned help by now. Thaddeus had to be quick.

'Inquisitor!' yelled Rhelnon. 'You cannot kill me! You are just a man. We are the Emperor's hand. There are three hundred of us on this one ship. You are trapped like a rat. We will try you and kill you, but it will be quick and there will be honour. Down here there is none. You will not be given a second chance.'

'The Emperor's inquisitors do not need second chances,' replied Thaddeus. The words meant nothing – they were just there to fill the hateful void, as if both men were fending off the fact that death would come to one of them in moments.

'I do not know what you want of us,' said Rhelnon, 'or what you seek by coming to this planet. But it is not the Emperor's work that you do.' He was moving again, stalking Thaddeus.

This time Thaddeus could hear him flicking the selector of his bolt gun – he wouldn't try to take on Thaddeus up close again.

The hilt of Thaddeus's sword was reforming, the shards liquefying and flowing across the floor like quicksilver, but Thaddeus knew the same trick wouldn't work twice. He had found the sword in the hands of a xeno-cult on the galaxy's eastern fringe and carried it ever since, knowing that one day it would make the difference between life and death. He deactivated the blade and holstered the hilt.

'Die!'

Rhelnon charged, right through the statues. With a terrific sound the obsidian Howling Griffons shattered beneath him as he leapt between the tombs, bolter blazing.

Thaddeus did not move. He did not try to roll out of the way or flee – that would not work.

Light flared around him, almost blinding. The conversion field he wore could absorb a couple of bolter shots, maybe three or four if its power coils, hidden in an archeotech amulet beneath Thaddeus's clothes, held out. The armour field was another relic of the days when he could still count on the support of his fellow inquisitors, and again, he had known that one day he would rely on it to keep him alive for a few seconds longer.

Thaddeus reached inside for the small coin-shaped device clipped innocuously to his belt. He flicked it out, depressing the charging stud with his thumb. The grenade hit the statue above Thaddeus, and just as the conversion field generator shattered with the strain of absorbing Thaddeus's gunfire, it exploded.

The grenade's detonation tore the statue of the Librarian apart, throwing stone shrapnel into the face of Brother Rhelnon as he bore down on Thaddeus. Rhelnon's charge never hit home and he fell to the floor beside Thaddeus, his bolter clattering across the stone tiles.

The light from the conversion field died down, Thaddeus's eyes adjusting from the glare. He looked down at Rhelnon, who was convulsing and gargling as one hand reached helplessly for the bolter.

The stone force sword from the Librarian statue had impaled Rhelnon through the chest. Thaddeus knew with one glance that the stone blade had cut through his lungs and the ruination of his internal organs was enough to fell even a Space Marine.

Rhelnon was dying. He was covered in blood, dozens of small wounds all over him. Blood ran from his mouth as his shredded lungs struggled to breathe.

'For the Emperor, Brother Rhelnon,' said Thaddeus. Then he turned from the dying Space Marine and headed for the shuttle bay.

There had been a time, as a young interrogator filled with the Emperor's fervour, that Thaddeus would have never accepted the death of a good Imperial servant as a necessary evil. But he was much wiser now.

DEEP IN THE crumbling fortress, all was decay. The faded heraldry of Vanqualis's conquerors, the founders of House Falken, hung on the walls, stained by the rain that dribbled through cracks in their ceiling and pulled apart by the roots and creepers forcing their way up from below. The scouts and Space Marines who had sided with Eumenes stood guard around the chamber, which had been a command centre for the House Falken forces who had originally won the jungles of Nevermourn. Sergeant Hecular stood guarding the doorway – its thick metal blast doors had rusted open, revealing the rotting cavities of crumbling rockrete beyond.

'The scouts on the battlements have the antenna up,' said Hecular.

'I've got a signal,' said Librarian Gresk in the centre of the room. The field vox in front of him was powerful enough for a boosted signal to reach the *Brokenback* even from inside the fortress. 'Bridge? Bridge, come in. This is Librarian Gresk.'

'Eumenes here,' came the voice from the vox. 'I have been watching your progress from orbit, Librarian.'

'Then you'll know we fended off Sarpedon. We can hold the battlements for another day at least before he regroups and tries again, if he dares. We're waiting for pickup now.'

'That was exactly my concern, Librarian.'

'What do you mean, Eumenes? We were victorious.'

'The Soul Drinkers were thrown back into the jungle. That means they are alive. Your orders were clear, Gresk. Keep the Soul Drinkers in place and engage them at the gates so the orbital bombardment would destroy them.'

'I did what I could, Eumenes. Sarpedon retreated before the *Brokenback* could open fire. I gave the signal to fire as soon as I–'

'Sarpedon retreated, Gresk, when he should have pushed on. He could have forced the gates. I saw you two talking, Gresk, breaking cover when both sides should have been fighting for their lives. And I asked myself, why would Sarpedon fall back from his objective, and why should a Soul Drinker loyal to me be parleying with the man he is ordered to kill? I can come to only one conclusion, Gresk.'

Gresk sighed. He was one of the Chapter's real veterans – his psychic prowess might not have been the equal of Sarpedon's own but he made up for that with decades of experience. And yet, he was in a new world now. The old Chapter, and even the Soul Drinkers after Sarpedon's Chapter War, had at least been united in purpose. They had fought as one hand. Now, there was treachery all around him. Eumenes was the expert at treachery – Gresk was the novice now.

'It is enough,' said Gresk, 'that Sarpedon be stranded here. He might never get off this planet and if he ever does we will be long gone.'

'You let him live.'

'I let him live, Eumenes. You might not be familiar with the way this Chapter does things, but there is such a thing as loyalty and it does not die so easily. Those men were my battle-brothers. There is no need to kill them.'

'There is every need!' The anger in Eumenes's voice was clear even from orbit. 'Sarpedon is our enemy! Do you really believe this Chapter will adhere to our cause if we let our enemies live?'

'I am not here because of your cause, Eumenes,' said Gresk. 'I am here because I cannot watch the Soul Drinkers being led into destruction. That is why I took up arms against Sarpedon, for the good of this Chapter. You cannot force me to kill my own brothers, Eumenes. My loyalty to you does not stretch that far.'

'Then you have no loyalty to me at all,' said Eumenes darkly.

'Eumenes, that is not what I–'

'Sarpedon will die. If you cannot accept that, Librarian Gresk, then the future of the Soul Drinkers has no place for you.'

Gresk was about to reply when he heard movement behind him. He glanced round to see Sergeant Hecular standing over him, his scout squad forming a semicircle behind Gresk. They had their bolt pistols drawn.

'Shall we do this, Gresk?' said Hecular.

'I don't–'

'You understand just fine. If you have to take some of us with you, then let's do it. Otherwise, I can keep it simple.'

Gresk was silent for a long moment, looking between the faces of Hecular's scouts. They were new recruits from the worlds the Soul Drinkers had visited, taken from among the Imperium's oppressed and brutalised. And Gresk did not know them at all.

'Very well,' he said. 'If this is what the Emperor's work means to you. Let us waste no more time.'

Hecular brought his gun up to point at Gresk's head, and the scouts did the same. Gresk could probably kill some of them before he fell, but what would be the point? Gresk didn't know which side he was on any more, only that one death was better than many.

He opened his eyes just in time to see Hecular smirk as he pulled the trigger.

EUMENES LISTENED TO the volley of gunfire transmitted from the old fortress on Vanqualis. It was impossible to tell whether he gained any satisfaction from the sound of bolter shells smacking into armour and exploding through flesh, or at the clatter as an armoured body fell to the floor.

'It's done,' came Hecular's voice.

'Keep me updated,' said Eumenes, and broke the vox-link. More equipment had been brought onto the bridge and Eumenes was surrounded by thrumming cogitator units and blinking readouts – the only light in the dark sphere of the bridge was from the readouts and pict-screens, so Eumenes's face was edged in hard greens and reds. The viewscreen was dark now, as if Eumenes didn't want any extraneous information distracting him.

The bridge doors slid open and Tydeus walked in. Tydeus had been Eumenes's second in command when Eumenes had led a scout squad in Gravenhold, and he was functioning in the same way now. Eumenes had issued orders that communications

with him went through Tydeus. He was a Chapter
Master now – he could not be distracted by every little problem that cropped up.

'Tydeus, good,' said Eumenes. 'The situation at the
fortress has been dealt with. It is time we left this
accursed system. Have the engines readied for the
warp. And send the Thunderhawks down to pick up
our brethren on the surface.'

'That is why I came here, Eumenes,' said Tydeus, a
trace of uncertainty in his voice. 'There is an intruder
on the flight decks.'

CROUCHED DOWN BY the hull of the gunship, Techmarine Lygris attached the demolition charge to the
ceramite plating just below one of the engines.
Lygris knew the structure of a Thunderhawk gunship inside out and he had known exactly where to
place the small engineering charge to breach a main
fuel line and render the craft useless. More importantly, he had known where on the *Brokenback* an
intact engineering deck could be found, which he
could raid for the tools and demolition equipment
he needed.

With a dull sound of collapsing metal the charge
on the next Thunderhawk along the line detonated,
sparks and fragments of charred metal spilling onto
the floor of the flight deck. The flight deck itself had
been some kind of combat arena, with one side
inexplicably taken up with a gigantic docking airlock. Rows of seats overlooked the deck, complete
with separate boxes for dignitaries and an entrance
tunnel that linked to a network of cells and cages

beneath the deck that the Soul Drinkers used to contain spare parts and fuel. Just what had happened in that arena before its parent ship had become a part of the hulk was just one of the thousands of mysteries on board the *Brokenback*.

Lygris slid the detonator core into the centre of the circular charge and thumbed its activation switch. A blinking telltale on the detonator told him the charge was armed – another switch would start the timer.

'Lygris,' said a too-familiar voice behind the Techmarine. Lygris span around, bolt pistol in hand, but the person who had spoken was hidden from view behind the Thunderhawk he had just disabled. There were more than a dozen Thunderhawks on the flight deck, some of them survivors of the old Chapter and some of them captured from forge worlds or Imperial battlefields, and their large armoured forms cut off the lines of sight around the flight deck.

Lygris knew the voice straight away, and his hearts sank.

'Lygris, they've got you surrounded. Eumenes's men are on their way. They'll be here in seconds.'

'They're too late,' replied Lygris. 'I'm done here. The traitors are trapped on Vanqualis, just like you meant to trap Sarpedon. It's too late for Eumenes's cronies to kill me now, Pallas.'

Apothecary Pallas stepped out from behind the Thunderhawk. Pallas was a brilliant Apothecary, a skilled scientist and surgeon who had played a major part in saving the Soul Drinkers from the mutations afflicted on them by the daemon prince Abraxes. Without him a part of the Soul Drinkers would die.

'Nisryus is close behind, Lygris,' said Pallas, 'and you cannot hide from him for long. Others are close behind him. Eumenes can flood this place with Soul Drinkers loyal to him.'

'And you expect me to give up?' Lygris's grip on his bolt pistol was tight. Pallas was a man he had trusted absolutely, but now he was an enemy. He hovered, agonisingly, between trying to kill Pallas and treating him as if he were still Lygris's battle-brother.

'No,' said Pallas. He held up his right hand, which was encased in the narthecium gauntlet, containing dozens of tiny needles and other surgical implements for battlefield treatment. A single silver spike emerged from the knuckle of the gauntlet. 'The Emperor's Mercy, Lygris.'

Lygris's voice caught in his throat. The Emperor's Mercy was administered to Space Marines or allies too severely injured to be saved. Its sharp, spring-loaded spike was driven into the back of the skull for a quick and painless death.

'Pallas, you cannot…'

'I do not know what they will do to you, Lygris,' said Pallas, urgency in his voice. 'I know the Librarium were training Nisryus to open up the minds of captives to interrogate them. At the very least they will do everything they can to make you talk. They need to know everything they can about the *Brokenback* and you're the only one who knows. I cannot go back to Sarpedon, not now, but I will do what I must to spare my friend's suffering. I can end it now, Lygris.'

Lygris shook his head. 'No, Pallas. I'm not giving up on my Chapter.'

'Then fight me!' snapped Pallas, but there was more sorrow than anger in his voice. 'If you die, I have spared you. If I die, then...'

'Then you have been spared, too,' said Lygris. 'You no longer have to take responsibility for the choice you have made. You don't have to look your friends in the eye again and tell them you have betrayed them. I won't do that for you, Pallas.'

'Damn it, Lygris,' said Pallas. 'This is the only way! Eumenes won't let either of us go without suffering!'

'You put yourself here, Pallas. You have to find your own way out.'

Pallas roared in frustration and anger, and Lygris was sure he could glimpse tears in the corners of Pallas's eyes as he drew back his narthecium gauntlet and charged. Lygris only dropped to the deck a fraction before the metal spike of the Emperor's Mercy snapped just over his head and embedded itself in the hull of the Thunderhawk.

The servo-arm mounted on the backpack of Lygris's armour reached up and closed on Pallas's head, wrenching him around so his back was to Lygris. Pallas slammed home an elbow into Lygris throat and both men fell to the floor, wrestling on the deck in the shadow of the Thunderhawk.

'Do it!' shouted Pallas as they fought. 'End it now!'

Lygris forced Pallas onto his back and was on top of him. A soldier's instinct brought the barrel of his bolt pistol up to Pallas's face.

Lygris's finger tightened. Pallas was his enemy. But Pallas was his battle-brother too. Those basic distinctions between friend and enemy had broken down. With Pallas bested and ready for execution, Lygris didn't know what to do.

Pallas sensed the moment of indecision. He sneered and threw Lygris off, stabbing down with blades that sprung from his narthecium gauntlet. Lygris rolled out of the way and barely got to his feet, stumbling against the Thunderhawk as he avoided Pallas's blow. Lygris put a hand against the hull below the engine for balance, Pallas's gauntlet dragging sparks from the ceramite.

Pallas kicked out at Lygris's leg and the Techmarine was on the floor again, bolt pistol skidding away from his hand.

'None of us are getting out of this,' said Pallas. 'It's over. The Chapter's over. If you won't spare me that suffering then I'll spare you, brother.' The Emperor's Mercy was primed again ready to strike and, flat on his back and unarmed, Lygris would have few ways to defend himself against a fellow Space Marine.

The explosive charge mounted on the Thunderhawk's hull, which Lygris had armed a moment before, exploded a few centimetres from Pallas's head. The Apothecary was thrown to the ground, sparks and shrapnel flying, smoke billowing from

the ruined engine above. The whole Thunderhawk
lurched and Pallas sprawled on the deck.

Lygris pulled himself to his feet, grabbing his bolt
pistol. He could see that shards of metal had been
driven into the side of Pallas's face and neck, and
into the armour of his chest and shoulder pad. His
face was blackened with soot from the blast and red
welts, like fat rubies, were growing where blood was
seeping from the cuts and congealing. Pallas stirred
very slightly – he was unconscious but not dead. As
Lygris had gambled, the blast had knocked him
unconscious but was nowhere near powerful
enough to fell a Space Marine for good.

Lygris could hear armoured feet clattering against
the deck – Nisryus and the other traitor Soul
Drinkers had arrived to trap Lygris and kill him. But
Lygris knew the flight deck area of the *Brokenback*
well, and in a way that no one else did.

Leaving Pallas lying on the deck to be found,
Lygris knelt down so his servo-arm could wrench a
drainage grille from the floor. Lygris slipped into the
shaft below and clattered down into a dark storage
chamber, once part of the cells below the arena
where gladiators or slaves, or even wild xenos creatures, had been kept before they were herded out for
the entertainment of the crowd. Lygris recalled for a
moment how he had helped clear out the cells, and
remove the age-encrusted skulls where they had
built up into ceiling-high piles in the ship's previous
life before it became a part of the hulk. He paused
to pull the grille back over the opening above him
with his servo-arm.

Beside him was a wide, yawning opening that led to an empty fuel tank deeper into the body of the *Brokenback*. Lygris could picture the warren of tunnels and pipes in his head, and he knew that he could hide there for days, weeks, even years if needs be.

'It's never over,' he said to himself, and disappeared again into the darkness.

# CHAPTER ELEVEN

'Who can we call our allies in the endless battle against corruption?'

'None but ourselves, our own souls
and discipline, our own bodies and the
weapons in our hands.'

– Daenyathos, *Catechisms Martial*

THE HEIGHTS OVER the Serpentspine Valley seethed
with activity. The clans had gathered and orkish
chanting drowned out the sounds of the jungle –
each clan had its own proud traditions, its own war
cries and chants, and its own brutal battle-rites from
ritual scarring to sacrifices. Here, thousands of
greenskins chanted as one around an ancient, wiz-
ened shaman who read the future from the entrails

of a dead slave. There, a clearing had become a glad-
iatorial pit, and two orks were settling some
overblown feud by trying to tear each other's throats
out with bare claws and teeth.

The symbols of dozens of clans were raised over
the heights. A clenched fist, a sword through a skull,
a stylised gun, daubed in paint and blood on banners hung from the trees. In their natural state those
clans would have been at war, intent on slaughter-
ing each other, because that was what orks were
born to do. But on Nevermourn, they fought as one.
Their old hatred broke out into scuffles and isolated
murders, but the instincts for full-scale war were
crushed. The orks' hatred was directed outwards,
towards the humans who infested this world.

The warlord knew that without him, the orks who
made up the horde would break up into dozens of
feuding factions and the humans would win.
Humans were a bad enemy to fight – which also
made them a good enemy, for orks made little dis-
tinction between the two concepts. No matter how
many humans were killed, there were always more to
take their place, shiploads of them brimming with
vengeance. Humans were like a weed, like a disease,
almost impossible to cleanse from a world. For a
greenskin that made them something more than an
enemy, for a fight against a favoured enemy was a joyous thing. Orks loved going to war with humans,
because defeating the humans meant something.

The warlord would cleanse them from this planet.
He would do to Vanqualis what the humans had
done to countless ork worlds. It didn't matter what

happened after the planet belonged to the orks – what mattered was the victory. The warlord would hurt them. They would remember him. That was the immortality promised by the orkish gods to the greatest of their warriors – the warlord would live on in the fear he planted in human hearts.

The warlord strode through the makeshift camp that had sprung up on the heights. Almost his whole horde was there, thousands upon thousands of orks. By the morning they would be itching for battle. The strange, insanely inspired ork engineers were fixing war machines or making new ones by cutting down trees and cannibalising parts. Ork medics, similarly crazed, were administering crude repairs to wounded orks, replacing limbs and removing damaged organs – the bellowing of their patients was drowned out by the clanking of war machines and the chanting of the greenskins.

The warlord walked right through the camp, barely acknowledging the cheers and raucous salutes as he passed by. He spotted a human soldier nailed up to a tree, being tormented by a pack of orks and slaves. Several others, now dead, hung from branches or lay in sorry bloody heaps in the mud. The humans were still out there in the jungle, and though they had lost many in the previous battles they were still a force on Vanqualis.

As far as the horde was concerned the humans had been sent fleeing like whipped dogs into the jungle and had been utterly defeated, but the warlord knew that they had sent some scouting parties onto the heights to monitor his army, and that there had been plenty of minor gunfights where humans and orks alike had been lost. The human commander must have been an enemy to admire in some small way, for refusing to give up. But the horde was greater by far, and there was no doubt that every soldier who opposed the warlord's will would eventually end up dead in the mud or nailed to a tree trunk being tormented to death by the greenskins. The human soldier died, and the warlord passed by as the slaves dragged the human's body down and began to cut it to pieces in the mud.

At the far side of the heights the trees gave way to provide a view across the jungles, north-west towards the coast. To some more emotional creatures the view would be breathtaking, an awesome rolling vista of the jungle canopy broken by rocky cliffs and the dark snaking ribbons of Nevermourn's rivers. But the warlord cared nothing for such things. The only meaningful feature was his objective – the coast, a dim strip of grey in the far distance just below the horizon. Soon his orks' lust for battle would be too much to contain and they would have to advance, and the warlord would use that momentum to drive them all the way to the coast. He could rely on his engineers, and the abundance of trees, to fashion a way across the ocean.

After that, he would take Herograve. Until now the horde had been given only a taste of battle, frustrating actions against a force that retreated before them and tried to trick them. In the cities of Herograve were millions – billions – of humans, terrified and primed for butchery. The human forces could do nothing to stop them now. In a matter of days the overture would be over, and the real killing would begin.

The warlord turned back to the horde, chanting and scrapping among the trees. None of them really understood what motivated the warlord. They did not understand the almost holy rage inside him, like an addiction that could not be sated until Herograve was drowned in blood. Perhaps, in that final slaughter, they would come to realise that orks existed to kill.

THE IMPACT OF the drop pod hitting home was heavy enough to shatter a normal man's bones. Chief Librarian Mercaeno didn't skip a syllable as he spoke the last words of the Rites of Detestation.

'...for the Enemy is within, as well as without, and it is within that he shall truly be defeated,' intoned Mercaeno. His command squad bowed their helmeted heads in contemplation of his words. One set of grav-harnesses was empty, for Brother Rhelnon had been killed on the *Cerulean Claw* trying to apprehend the rogue Inquisitor Thaddeus. 'It is only with victory that the Emperor can be praised. It is only with hatred that the victory can be won.'

'Only with hatred,' echoed the command squad in unison, just as the explosive bolts in the hull of the drop pod detonated and burst the pod open.

In a handful of seconds Mercaeno was out of his restraints, force axe in his hand. His command squad, eight Howling Griffons veterans with their armour festooned with oaths and kill-markings, was beside him, bolters and chainswords ready.

The drop pod had come down on target, on the slope of a low rise a short distance from the Serpentspine Valley where the trees were not so dense as to hinder the opening of the drop pods. Many other pods were already down, the Howling Griffons within already deployed and rapidly forming a cordon between the trees that soared overhead.

In an instant, Mercaeno appraised their situation. The jungle provided lots of cover but it also blinded them, so they could be surrounded in short order without knowing it. Speed was of the essence on a battlefield such as this, because other, lesser forces would be bogged down by the terrain.

'Lord Librarian,' said Captain Darion, hurrying across towards Mercaeno's squad. 'The area is secure. No hostiles. The sensor-readings were correct.'

'Then we must move with all speed before the greenskins get wind of our arrival and decide to challenge us.'

Darion held up a data-slate on which glowed a topographical map of the jungle. 'The last readings placed the Space Marine force seven kilometres from here,' he said, indicating a bright blip on the map. 'If we approach from the east they'll have heavy terrain at their backs, swamp and river.'

'Are they defending any fortifications?'

'None. It's just jungle.'

'Then they will not remain there for long. It is good that our enemy calls themselves Space

Marines. They fight as we do, so we can read their every move.'

More drop pods slammed home, kicking up showers of mud. The sides of the ovoid pods split open and more Howling Griffons emerged – Captain Borganor pulled himself free of his grav-restraints and began marshalling the Space Marines of his Tenth Company. Landers, rectangular and much larger than the comet-like drop pods, were making landfall a short distance away, crushing through the canopy and bringing down the branches of the trees. Birds took flight at the noise and devastation.

The landers in the jungle did not carry Howling Griffons. They opened to reveal the armoured hulls of vehicles in the Chapter's livery, embossed with the heraldic symbol of the rampant griffon that adorned the shoulder pad of every Howling Griffon. Engines gunned and the Chapter's tanks were disgorged from the massive landers. Rhino APCs, Predator tanks, and Mercaeno's command Land Raider rolled out, with more coming down behind them. The vehicular cargo was fitted with dozer blades and reinforced front armour to barge through the densest of Nevermourn's jungle.

'I had thought,' said Captain Darion, 'that there were oaths the Howling Griffons would never fulfil. I thought the Black Chalice must be so ancient that we would never have the opportunity to face it.'

'Then now you understand a little more about what it means to be a Howling Griffon,' replied Mercaeno. 'The barriers of possibility that restrain other men do not apply to us. Every promise we make, we will keep, though we must fight time itself to do so. We never give up, Darion. Never, at anything.'

'Of course,' said Captain Darion. 'I assume that tracking down Thaddeus is an oath you have made, too?'

'No,' said Mercaeno. 'When I kill him, it will simply be for vengeance.'

The tanks rolled towards the Howling Griffons' position, and the squads of Space Marines were already clambering into the Rhinos and Land Raiders. Mercaeno's command vehicle, a formidable Land Raider Crusader that bristled with automated boltguns mounted on its side turrets, rolled towards Mercaeno's squad and Sergeant Ossex ordered the squad inside. Mercaeno was last inside, surrounded by the many tactical readouts showing data from the other squads. He read off the readiness runes projected onto one pict-screen – the whole force had deployed and mounted up in a few minutes, with a speed and efficiency that no normal commander could hope for.

The Howling Griffons were the best fighting force that Vanqualis had ever, or would ever, see. And they were there with a mission, inspired by dedication to their duty and by the holy hatred that burned in the heart of every true Space Marine. As the Land Raider roared off at the head of the Howling Griffons' armoured column, there was no doubt in Mercaeno's mind that before his Chapter left Vanqualis the Black Chalice would be shattered at last.

\* \* \*

THE SAME SCANS from the *Cerulean Claw*, that Mercaeno was using to co-ordinate the Howling Griffons' attack, sped past the pict-screens in front of Inquisitor Thaddeus as the shuttle raced low above the canopy. The shuttle's engines stripped leaves from their branches as Thaddeus sped past, trying to keep his heart and hands steady as he approached the battlefield. Somewhere below the solid ceiling of greenery lay thousands of corpses from the battles that had already been fought for Vanqualis, along with thousands more living humans, orks and superhuman Space Marines who would still die no matter what happened. Palls of smoke still rose from the cratered foothills devastated by an orbital strike, and as the shuttle passed over them Thaddeus glimpsed charred bodies and shattered artillery pieces littering the hillside.

Thaddeus had to stay low in case the Howling Griffons had gunships in the air that would shoot him down – even the orks might be a danger if they had aircraft, which was not unknown in spite of the crudeness of their species. But Mercaeno's Space Marines were by far the greatest threat. Thaddeus had made yet another enemy, and they were one of the deadliest yet. There were fellow inquisitors out there in the galaxy who would gladly kill Thaddeus if they got the chance, as well as numerous members of the Ecclesiarchy and half the Adeptus Mechanicus. Few of them, however, could compare to Lord Mercaeno.

The pilot-cogitator did most of the work flying the shuttle, leaving Thaddeus to watch the sensor data from the *Cerulean Claw*. The Howling Griffons had found their prey, a concentration of Space Marines breaking across a patch of open ground created by the impact of an orkish asteroid. The shuttle had access to the data gathered by the *Cerulean Claw* in orbit – the crew had shut off the shuttle's access as soon as they realised it was missing, of course, but Thaddeus still had some old inquisitor's tricks up his sleeve. The Inquisitorial seal, which had opened the door to the shuttle bay, also had a code-cracking circuit that, for a few minutes at least, opened a back door into the shuttle's cogitator and let him see what the Howling Griffons were seeing. It wouldn't last for long, but then probably neither would Thaddeus.

The Griffons must have thought they had found the most hateful of enemies, Chaos Space Marines, renegade Astartes who followed the Dark Gods of the warp. Mercaeno wouldn't waste much time getting to grips with them, which meant that Thaddeus had to get there first.

Unfortunately, that also meant he couldn't pick his landing spot. He would have to come down in the heart of the renegade Space Marine force, and hope the jungle would forgive him for such a rude entrance.

Thaddeus could see the faint spray of smoke from the still-smouldering impact site on the target hill. In the earliest stages of the orks' invasion of Nevermourn, one of the asteroids carrying the first wave of greenskins had landed off-target, falling at a shallow enough angle to clip the top of a low hill and blast the trees and foliage off it before impacting at the foot of the hill and exploding. Thaddeus banked the shuttle and took over from the pilot-cogitator, gunning the craft's retros so it slowed dramatically and swooped down into the canopy.

Branches snapped and the shuttle was battered as it crashed down through the foliage, but Thaddeus knew he wouldn't be taking this ship off the surface of Vanqualis again. He would be lucky if he ever left the planet. He had enemies everywhere, and it was quite possible he was walking right into the hands of one of his oldest.

Thaddeus was gambling his life that Sarpedon wouldn't just kill him on sight.

'THE ONAGER ORBITAL shuttle,' said Sarpedon, 'is junk. There was a whole fleet of them on the *Brokenback* that we never used. They've got no armour and they need a landing strip. We lost all the old Scalptakers and Hammerblade fighter-bombers a long time ago, and without Lygris Eumenes has no way to fly the alien craft we found on the *Brokenback*. With the Thunderhawks disabled, Eumenes has only one choice left.'

'The Onagers,' said Chaplain Iktinos. 'That's how you know the traitors will be here.'

The Soul Drinkers were in position just inside the tree line. Beyond the tree line, the hilltop was charred and blasted. The taste of charcoal and smoke was heavy in the air and coils of smoke still wreathed overhead. Sarpedon's Astartes were in cover among the burned trees, smeared with ash as they moved along the tree line to get the best angles of fire. Their bolters, and the few heavy weapons they still had, could crisscross the open hilltop into a textbook killing ground.

'This is the only place Eumenes can land,' said Sarpedon. 'The Thunderhawks could have plucked his traitors off the roof of the fortress but the Onagers have to land here. That means the traitors will be here, too, and they'll have to get across open ground under fire to board and get off this planet.'

'My flock will relish it,' said Iktinos. 'Rarely do they have the chance to bring such decisive vengeance to the enemy.'

Iktinos had spoken of 'his flock' before, and the Soul Drinkers who made up his flock were gathered just behind him now, preparing their battle-gear for the coming fight. Iktinos had become the leader of a group of Soul Drinkers whose officers had been killed in the Chapter's various battles, and they were intense in their devotion to Iktinos. Now Iktinos was on Vanqualis they had their leader back, and Iktinos had led them in the rites and prayers they observed so keenly. Slowly, Iktinos's flock had become a unit of shock troopers, almost thirty Soul Drinkers strong, who now cared for nothing but the destruction of their enemies. If Sarpedon had been a stronger Chapter Master and elicited similar devotion from all the Soul Drinkers, the rebellion would never have happened and Vanqualis would be free of the orks.

'Luko here,' came a vox in Sarpedon's ear. 'Company.'

'Where?' Luko was just behind the front line, leading the reserve that would plug any gaps in the line and counter-attack if the traitors got into close assault range.

'Right over you at any second.'

Sarpedon could hear something crashing through the trees. The Soul Drinkers in the line were turning to face the new arrival, bolters sighting through charred tree trunks into the greenery beyond. A great dark shape came down, splintering through the branches, and Sarpedon caught a glimpse of red and gold livery on its hull.

The craft hit the ground, a short distance from the front lines. Its nose carved a deep furrow as it ploughed through the ash, its engines kicking out a wash of exhaust fumes and heat. It was a shuttle, short and stubby, not much more than a one-man craft for transporting dignitaries or officers between craft. Apart from its quartered red and gold colours, any identifying marks had been burned or scratched off. It certainly wouldn't be taking off again.

The shuttle smashed through the burned trees with a terrible sound, disappearing into the ash-black depths of the jungle past the far end of the Soul Drinkers' line.

'Hold!' ordered Sarpedon over the vox. 'Hold fire!'

A few minutes passed. A soft thud from the direction of the shuttle crash was probably a fuel tank exploding. The squads holding the end of the line reported no contacts.

Finally, a figure emerged, limping through the scorched trees. Sarpedon could almost hear fingers tightening on boltgun triggers. The figure was human – not a Space Marine but a normal man, wearing a long battered coat. Memory sparked in Sarpedon's mind. The man's face was older than he remembered, but he definitely knew the man. And it was someone he had been certain he would never see again.

'Hold your fire, Soul Drinkers,' said Sarpedon. 'Guns down.' Sarpedon stood up out of cover and clambered over the fallen trees and burned undergrowth. It took a few minutes for the man to reach Sarpedon and by that time, Sarpedon was certain. The man emerging from the crash site was the same man he had last seen on Stratix Luminae. It had felt like a lifetime ago, a time before the Soul Drinkers began to fracture and turn on themselves.

'Inquisitor Thaddeus,' he said.

'I'm afraid I don't have much time for pleasantries, Commander Sarpedon,' said Thaddeus. 'Although I should say I am grateful to you for not killing me.'

'Don't thank me just yet, Thaddeus,' said Sarpedon. The last time they had met, the two men had united to defeat the mutant overlord Teturact on the frozen tundra of Stratix Luminae. But they had been forced to co-operate in the face of their enemy, and previously Thaddeus had been dedicated to tracking down and destroying the Soul Drinkers. 'I had thought we would never meet again, inquisitor.'

'Your Chapter is certainly elusive,' replied Thaddeus, walking closer. Sarpedon could now definitely see that Thaddeus had aged rapidly. His hair was greying and starting to thin, and he had the slightly haunted, hollow look that Sarpedon had seen in the faces of many veteran Imperial servants. 'It took a lot to track you down to here.'

'Then the Inquisition has not given up looking for us?'

'The Inquisition? I don't know. I have not had friendly contact with a fellow inquisitor for some time, Lord Sarpedon. I am something of an outcast.' Thaddeus smiled, but with little joy. 'Perhaps we have become very similar. I had to anger a lot of superiors to find you on Stratix Luminae and they haven't forgotten it. I'm on my own here. And since the Inquisition ordered all histories of the Soul Drinkers deleted it is very difficult for a man on his own to find you. In truth it was only chance that brought me here at all.'

'Then why did you come here, Thaddeus? On Stratix Luminae we came to a truce and I thought that was the end of it.'

'Lord Sarpedon, surely you have some idea of what the Soul Drinkers mean? A renegade Space Marine Chapter is dangerous enough. The deletion order was carried out because mere knowledge of you could be corruptive. But to have a Chapter who was led astray by its own will instead of something from the warp or some alien power – Lord Sarpedon, there are inquisitors who would refuse to believe such a thing! They would say the very fabric of the Imperium would unravel if a Chapter of Astartes suddenly developed free will! That was the reason I was on my own when I hunted you. My superiors said it was for the good of the Imperium, but I realise now they were just afraid of the very idea of you, in case I found you and the resulting knowledge could not be contained.'

'Then what? You pursued us out of curiosity, Thaddeus? So that you could tell yourself you had found us when other inquisitors would not?'

'Perhaps at first,' said Thaddeus.

'Commander,' said Chaplain Iktinos. 'The scouts on our western flank report movement.'

'The traitors?'

'Most probably. Certainly not greenskins.'

'Then make sure they're watching the skies, too. Have all the men in position. This is the only chance we'll get.'

'Traitors?' said Thaddeus.

'Though I am loath to admit to an outsider,' said Sarpedon, 'some among us believe they should command this Chapter, rather than me.' Sarpedon took Thaddeus's shoulder and led him back from the tree line, into the cover of the burned forest.

'Then I might be too late,' Thaddeus said, with as much sadness as frustration.

'Too late? Explain yourself, inquisitor. And those traitors will be upon us in minutes. Be quick.'

'I could not search for you by normal means, since the Chapter's existence has been purged from Imperial records,' said Thaddeus. His voice was low and urgent now. 'So I had to try something more esoteric. I looked for traces of you left in the mythologies of primitive peoples, who might recall the Soul Drinkers' recent activity away from Imperial censors. And I found something.'

'What?'

'Legends, Commander Sarpedon. Legends of the Soul Drinkers. Ancient, too, thousands of years old.'

'About the old Chapter, then?'

'Perhaps. On an arctic world on the eastern fringes I discovered the legends of the Grail of the

Damned, used as the symbol of dark armoured warriors who drank men's souls. I made the connection.'

'I do not know of any wars the old Chapter fought in such a place,' said Sarpedon.

'Neither did I,' said Thaddeus. 'But the Grail of the Damned was not the only reference. I found a Drinker of Souls worshipped by cannibal tribes near the Storm of the Emperor's Wrath. This was across several worlds, Sarpedon, and these people were centuries behind developing space travel. Someone had left those legends there, and left a scar on those worlds so deep they became a religion.'

'Then the old Chapter left an impression on savage worlds,' said Sarpedon. 'This would not be the first time a Chapter has been the foundation of myths among such peoples. I do not understand why that should bring you here.'

'You will, Sarpedon, with just a little thought.'

'Salk here,' voxed Sergeant Salk from the end of the Soul Drinkers' line. 'My men have spotted contrails above us. Looks like Eumenes is sending the landers down.'

'The traitors are almost upon us!' voxed Sarpedon to his whole force. 'Final prayers and be ready for the fight! This time they fight on ground of our choosing, and they will be vulnerable as they flee. They chose to show us no mercy at the fortress. Now we must show the same to them.' Sarpedon could hear the murmured prayers up and down the line, verses from the *Catechisms Martial* and battle-rites older than the Chapter itself.

'Think, Sarpedon,' continued Thaddeus. 'What could bring you and I to this same Emperor-forsaken world?'

The Soul Drinkers were tensed for battle, all of them save Sarpedon himself at their position in the line. But Sarpedon realised the importance in Thaddeus's words.

'Vanqualis has its legends, too,' said Sarpedon.

'The Black Chalice,' said Thaddeus darkly. 'The fountain from which all evil flows. It is said to float in the warp, disgorging the stuff of Chaos. The Bearers of the Black Chalice are giant armoured warriors who wear the chalice as their emblem, and they will one day come down from the sky to claim Vanqualis as their own. Someone connected to the old Chapter came to the Obsidian system a long time ago and did something that left that scar on the minds of the Vanqualian people. I had reached this system to study the legends of the Black Chalice when I realised the Soul Drinkers were here, too. So I came to the surface to warn you.'

'Someone brought us here,' said Sarpedon. 'We have been manipulated.'

'You have an enemy here. I have made many sacrifices to hunt you down, Sarpedon, so I am an enemy, too. But the only thing more dangerous than a renegade Chapter is an enemy who can manipulate them to his will.'

Sarpedon thought rapidly. It was difficult to absorb what Thaddeus was telling him. It could be a trap, a lie typical of the Inquisition – but Thaddeus had let Sarpedon go once before, and there was a sincerity in him that Sarpedon could not ignore. The Soul

Drinkers had been brought into a situation that Sarpedon didn't understand, to ground prepared for them by someone in the old Chapter. That idea ignited an old hatred inside Sarpedon, something that had been near the surface ever since the daemon prince Abraxes had offered Sarpedon awesome power in return for a lifetime of servitude.

'No one owns this Chapter,' said Sarpedon darkly. 'We are no one's weapon.'

'I know,' said Thaddeus. 'That is why your Chapter has to live.'

The anger flared inside Sarpedon again. The treachery of Eumenes had brought him low, but now he was inflamed again. After all this time, after all these sacrifices made to secure the freedom of the Soul Drinkers, still there was a foe out there who thought he could use the Soul Drinkers for his own ends. Nothing in this galaxy, not the depredations of Chaos or the corruption of the Imperium, not even Eumenes's betrayal, provoked Sarpedon's anger like the knowledge he was being used.

'Vanqualis is lost,' he said. 'When the traitors are dead we will leave this place and hunt down whoever thinks they can bend the Soul Drinkers to their will. We will not rest until it is done.'

'That may not be quite so simple,' said Thaddeus. 'I needed help to make it this far, and my hosts were just as interested in the Black Chalice as I was.'

Sarpedon rounded on Thaddeus. 'What do you mean?'

'Contact!' voxed Sergeant Salk from up ahead. 'Armour sighted, incoming!'

'Armour? The traitors have no tanks,' replied Sarpedon on the vox.

'It's not the traitors,' replied Salk.

Sarpedon ran through the charred forest up to the edge of the tree line. On the far side of the clearing he could see dark shapes crashing through the burned trees. The hull of a tank rose up as it ground over the fallen trunks, and Sarpedon caught a flash of red and gold livery. It was a Rhino APC and a Predator battle tank followed it, autocannon turret swivelling towards the Soul Drinkers' position. Sarpedon could see the rampant griffon symbol on the tanks' hulls as more vehicles tore through the ruined forest and roared towards the Soul Drinkers.

'Your hosts, Thaddeus?' said Sarpedon to the inquisitor behind him.

'The Howling Griffons,' replied Thaddeus. 'They believe they are fighting the Bearers of the Black Chalice.'

'Are you armed?'

Thaddeus took his autopistol from beneath his greatcoat. 'Always.'

'Then take your place in the line,' said Sarpedon.

Chaplain Iktinos began intoning the final rites of battle, the final words that shielded a Space Marine's soul against the sins of despair and defeat. As one, the Soul Drinkers readied themselves to face an enemy that Sarpedon knew would not stop until they were all dead.

IN SPITE OF the roar of the Land Raider's engine, around Mercaeno it was calm. It was spiritual quiet before the storm, a few short moments of reflection before the killing began.

The axe that had slain Periclitor was heavy in Lord Mercaeno's hand, as if the magnitude of that deed weighed it down. Its head was covered in the scroll-work of the psychic circuit that ran through the weapon, focusing Mercaeno's psychic ability so tightly that he could wrench the very soul from an enemy it struck. The axe had been carried by a long line of Howling Griffons Librarians and like any such Chapter artefact it carried oaths and obligations of its own – admonishment for corruption and laxity, an undertaking to be merciless and intolerant of any failing even among his own battle-brothers, and an overpowering dedication to the utter destruction of the Emperor's foes.

The axe was a symbol of what the Howling Griffons had vowed to do thousands of years ago. It was not enough to defeat the Black Chalice, to hurl them back into the shadows and deny them whatever prize they sought on Vanqualis. No, while any normal soldier would call that a victory, to the Howling Griffons it would be a defeat for which the Chapter would never atone. The Howling Griffons had to destroy the Black Chalice itself, shatter it and cast it to the winds of destruction, and slaughter its bearers to a man. Nothing short of utter destruction was acceptable. The Lord Librarians who had carried the axe before Mercaeno had exemplified that ruthlessness. Mercaeno himself would outdo them.

'Enemy sighted!' came the vox from Techmarine Thol in the lead Predator tank. 'They are Astartes!'

Mercaeno looked up at the pict-screen on which was the transmission from Thol's Predator. Among the grainy darkness of the charred forest he could see purple-black armour like the carapaces of a host of beetles – power armour, Space Marines skulking in the darkness. He could even see the bone and gold chalice on a shoulder pad, emblazoned as if the enemy were proud of their corruption. Mercaeno's disgust was overshadowed only by his anger.

'Then it ends here,' said Mercaeno. Around him his command squad bowed their heads in silent agreement, Brother Rodrigo clutching the First Company's battle standard ready to let it unfurl.

'Howling Griffons,' announced Mercaeno to all his squads. 'The time for prayer and preparation is over. Clear your minds and prepare your souls to receive the wrath of the Emperor. The Black Chalice is before us, overflowing with evil, and we are the Emperor's own fist poised to destroy it! In this hour a thousand years of oaths are fulfilled, a great weight of duty is placed upon us, and it is with fury and hate that we will cast it off! Death to the Black Chalice! Vengeance to the Emperor! Victory to the Howling Griffons!'

Even within the armoured hull of the Land Raider, Mercaeno could hear the rest of his army cheering at his words as three companies of the galaxy's greatest warriors roared out of the forest and towards the Bearers of the Black Chalice.

# CHAPTER TWELVE

'What right to we have to pass judgment on a fellow human being?'

'I ask of you, what right have we to presume him innocent?'

— Daenyathos, *Catechisms Martial*

THE ARMOURED SPEARHEAD of the Howling Griffons crashed into the Soul Drinkers so hard the jungle shook with it. The humid winds of the rainforest turned hot and dry with fire as dozens of vehicle-mounted guns opened up. Autocannon shots from Predator tanks exploded among the charred trees, sending shards of fire-hardened wood flying like steel shrapnel. Lascannon spat fat crimson bursts of shimmering las-fire into the darkness, shearing tree trunks in two and gouging deep glowing furrows in the ground. The spearhead's detachment of Whirl-wind support tanks carpeted sections of the Soul Drinkers' line with rockets from their turret-mounted launchers, hammering gaps in the line for the Rhino APCs to streak towards.

The spearhead advanced into the teeth of the Soul Drinkers' firing line. As soon as the spearhead crossed the sacred line of bolter range the air was filled with explosive bolts, rattling in heavy scorching chains that battered against the hulls of the Howling Griffons' tanks. Heavy bolter rounds blew the track off a Predator so it carved a crescent gouge in the earth as it slewed round, more shots hammering against it and blasting the paint off one side.

A missile launcher sent an armour-piercing krak missile streaking into the side of a massive Land Raider and the ammunition for its sponson-mounted heavy bolter detonated, blowing the side off the vehicle and sending the Space Marines inside diving out to escape the burning wreck. The gunfire was so heavy the charred, flat ground was chewed into a pockmarked battlefield in a few moments, and the burned forest the Soul Drinkers held was reduced to a sorry mass of stumps and fallen trees, showered with shrapnel and burning branches.

The sky turned dark with smoke, like a new night falling on Vanqualis lit only by the scarlet of las-fire and the lightning flashes of explosions. Darkness fell, the ruined forest lit from beneath by the blazing of hundreds of bolt guns. Men died in that darkness, their deaths picked out frame by frame by

the strobing gunfire like images from a pict-viewer.
A torso reared back as a heavy bolter shell smacked
into a Soul Drinker's chest. A Howling Griffon was
crushed as a Rhino was blown onto its side by a
missile, spilling passengers from its sundered hull.
Bodies slumped over fallen tree trunks or were
blasted back through the forest as gunfire blanketed
the battlefield.

The first Rhino APC reached the line, its engine
gunning violently as its armoured hull rode up over
fallen trees and the bodies of Soul Drinkers who
had died in the first moments of the battle. The
Rhino's top hatch opened and a squad of Howling
Griffons vaulted out, blazing with their bolters
before they even hit the ground. One or two never
left the vehicle, their heads battered into bloodied
flowers of torn ceramite by bolter shots, and
another clattered to the ground with one arm and
shoulder blown off by a plasma gun blast. But suddenly the Howling Griffons were among the line,
and the battle was now the close-quarters murder at
which Space Marines excelled.

The Soul Drinkers' line bowed and held as more
Howling Griffons squads dived into the battle. Captain Luko bellowed and led the Soul Drinkers'
reserve into the fray, leaping over their own dead to
reach the enemy. Chainblades screamed against
ceramite and bolter shells thudded into flesh.

More Howling Griffons were deploying to support the assault, pumping bolter fire into the rest of
the Soul Drinkers' line to keep them from helping
their battle-brothers. Jump-packed squads arced

over the carnage, chainswords falling as they let themselves tumble down into the conflict. Bodies flew as power weapons flared, officers on both sides wading in to lead their men in the slaughter.

Just behind the tip of the Howling Griffons' spearhead, the standard of the First Company was raised, its bullet-holed banner depicting a resplendent griffon rending foul monsters beneath its claws. Lord Mercaeno and his command squad emerged from their Land Raider, the Lord Librarian's mere presence pushing the Howling Griffons forward a step. Mercaeno drew his axe, let the light that poured from it illuminate him as if a shaft of sunlight fell upon him from on high, and then charged.

Further along the line, Sarpedon commanded the Soul Drinkers' defence, ordering his Astartes to hold the line and trust their battle-brothers in the centre to repel the attack. He did not conjure the terrifying hallucinations of the Hell, because he knew that there would be nothing the Howling Griffons were afraid of. Not even the Black Chalice itself, pouring waves of evil and Chaos onto the battlefield, would deter the Howling Griffons from pressing home their attack.

He resisted the urge to plunge into the fight himself because he was needed here, in the line, ensuring the Soul Drinkers were not surrounded by the disciplined, relentless Howling Griffons squads advancing across the charred ground towards them. Iktinos's crozius arcanum, glowing like a beacon, told Sarpedon that the Chaplain was leading the way where the fighting was hardest, and he could even hear snatches of Iktinos's preaching amid the din of battle.

Sarpedon glanced about him, trying to pick out the shape of the battle through the darkness and chaos. He had left Inquisitor Thaddeus behind the front line, and at the periphery of his attention he realised that the inquisitor was now close to the thickest of the fighting, where the shining axe blade of the Howling Griffons' commander now flashed.

'THADDEUS!'

INQUISITOR THADDEUS heard his name bellowed through the din. Thaddeus was crouched down beside the bullet-riddled tree stump, autopistol hot in his hand. His muscles froze at the voice, because he knew it was Mercaeno.

Thaddeus glanced past the stump. A dead Howling Griffon lay just beyond him – the backpack had been blasted off and the huge armoured body lay on its front, a gory wet chasm torn into its back. Other bodies lay draped over fallen trees or battered down into the mud. Space Marines battled one another in the thick of the fighting, an astonishing sight – huge figures clashing with appalling strength and speed. And in the midst of them all was the crescent of Mercaeno's axe, rising and falling in the chaos.

Thaddeus drew his alien sword, its blade thrumming with the urge to break up into its component shards and kill. He knew he could not fight in this battle, not when the combatants were Space Marines. A few of the more martially minded and

experienced inquisitors were the equal of a Space
Marine in combat, and a handful of them were substantially tougher even than an Astartes. But
Thaddeus was not one of them. As the Howling
Griffons had told him, he was just a man. He also
knew that he probably would not have a choice
over whether he fought or not.

'Thaddeus!' bellowed Mercaeno's voice. The
Howling Griffon burst from the throng, throwing
Soul Drinkers aside and battering another to the
ground with a sweep of his force axe. Thaddeus
froze – even across the ruination he could see the
anger creasing Mercaeno's face, the wrath burning
in his eyes. Mercaeno, with a Space Marine's
enhanced vision and a psyker's insight, had picked
out the skulking Thaddeus from the shadows.
Thaddeus cursed himself for thinking he could
hide.

Most men would have fled. Thaddeus knew that
somewhere in the back of his mind. But most men
would not have understood, in the blind flare of
panic, that Mercaeno would have killed him as he
ran as surely as if he just lay down to die. So Thaddeus stepped out of cover and stood his ground,
sword and pistol gripped tightly as the huge form
of Lord Mercaeno bore down on him.

The gunfire was dim and muffled, as if its sound
was breaking through from a different world. The
battlefield was blurred and vague, its fighting Space
Marines just shimmers of half-glimpsed movement. There was nothing on Vanqualis now save
Mercaeno and Thaddeus.

Without even willing it, Thaddeus was firing, the autopistol shots smacking into Mercaeno's breast-plate in miniature starbursts.

Mercaeno didn't even notice. It was all Thaddeus could do to throw himself aside as the axe came down, its glowing blade burning with psychic fire as it cleaved down through the tree stump behind him.

The force of the impact threw Thaddeus to the ground. He rolled onto his feet, firing almost blindly at the huge, dark armoured form of Mercaeno above him.

'You slew my battle-brothers!' yelled Mercaeno. 'You betrayed us! And you are in league with the Enemy!'

'There is no enemy!' shouted Thaddeus in reply. 'There is no Black Chalice! All of this is lies!'

'You speak to me of lies? You, whose very soul is deceit!' Mercaeno slashed at waist-height with his axe and Thaddeus had to drop to one knee to turn it over his head with his alien blade, the force so strong it nearly broke Thaddeus's wrist. Mercaeno's form swept over him and Thaddeus lunged upwards, driving his sword into Mercaeno's body.

The blade hit ceramite just below Mercaeno's arm, and its tip sheared through his power armour with unnatural ease. Thaddeus willed the blade into action and as it slid through muscle and bone the blade fragmented, dozens of steel shards flying loose to shred Mercaeno's flesh. Like great steel insects, they burst from the armour of Mercaeno's chest and right arm, flitting through the air hungry for blood.

Mercaeno roared. Thaddeus twisted the blade and felt ceramite fragmenting under it. The pain and destruction wrought by the blade would have felled anyone, even most Astartes. But Lord Mercaeno's hand had taken the head of Periclitor, and he had seen every kind of combat on every type of battlefield. He had suffered worse and been victorious. What little hope still flared in Thaddeus's mind was extinguished as Mercaeno's left hand grabbed the back of his coat and lifted him off the ground.

Mercaeno flung Thaddeus with all his strength. Thaddeus flew through the air, his sword and pistol left behind, and charred branches splintered beneath his weight. He hit the ground hard enough to knock the breath out of his lungs and skidded insensible across the ashes.

Thaddeus forced himself to his senses. He had landed beyond the tree line, on open ground. The roaring beside him was the engine of a Rhino APC, one of its tracks blown off and its hatches left open where the Howling Griffons inside had disembarked. He reached inside his coat for one of the many weapons he still carried.

His hand closed around a small metal sphere and he drew it from beneath the folds of his coat. It would have to do.

Mercaeno charged towards him and Thaddeus rolled forwards so he slammed painfully into the Howling Griffon's armoured body. His hand reached up to clamp the magnetic grenade to the back of Mercaeno's armour. If Thaddeus was to die, he could at least help the Soul Drinkers escape destruction and find their true enemy, by killing the Howling Griffons' commander.

Mercaeno's gauntlet closed around Thaddeus's own hand. The Space Marine had seen Thaddeus's ploy coming and reacted with impossible speed. Bones cracked and tendons snapped beneath his grip. Thaddeus was filled with a cold, horrifying pain, echoing through his whole body, and his nervous system lit up with agony.

Mercaeno let go and Thaddeus's ruined hand dropped the grenade. Mercaeno kicked it contemptuously aside and grabbed Thaddeus by the throat. The grenade burst somewhere on the edge of Thaddeus's vision, harmlessly.

'You do not know…' gasped Thaddeus. 'None of you… you have no idea who you are fighting…'

Mercaeno slammed Thaddeus down against the sloping front armour of the Rhino. Thaddeus barely registered the cracking of his ribs, such was the pain from his crushed hand and the desperation running through him.

'By the oaths of justice,' said Mercaeno, ignoring Thaddeus's words, 'you have been judged a traitor to the Howling Griffons and an enemy of the Emperor. There is no punishment fitting your crimes. We pray that the Emperor shall accept death as sufficient.'

'By the authority of the Holy Orders of the Emperor's Inquisition…' gasped Thaddeus, desperately.

Mercaeno sneered and brought his force axe up. The intricate patterns on its surface were lit up with the force of his hate and he brought it crashing down into Thaddeus's body.

The last thing Inquisitor Thaddeus saw was his own blood spraying over Mercaeno's rage-filled face.

SARPEDON ADDED UP the dead. It had become a reflex action, a necessity of command. Acknowledgement runes were dim against his retina and he guessed that thirty or so Soul Drinkers already lay dead amid the furious melee in the centre of the line. The Chapter could not afford to lose a single Soul Drinker, and Sarpedon's stomach tightened as he watched the future of his Chapter dying amid the ruin and mud.

Sarpedon was further along the line from the close-quarters fighting where the Howling Griffons were trying to force their way through. The Soul Drinkers alongside him were keeping up an unending stream of fire at Howling Griffons half-glimpsed through the smoke and swirling ash. Howling Griffon tanks were firing on them, and return bolter fire was getting stronger with every moment as the Howling Griffons advanced their own firebase towards the trees. Soon the whole line would be enveloped in face-to-face slaughter.

Sarpedon had never given into despair before. He had been brought low, he had stared death and the destruction of the Soul Drinkers in the face. But he had never felt the coldness of sheer despair that reached up at him from the scorched ground.

'Luko!' voxed Sarpedon, snapping himself out of feelings that were so unbecoming of a Space Marine. 'Report!'

'They've got numbers and armour!' replied Luko. Sarpedon could hear the sizzle of Luko's power claws and the screaming gunfire all around the Soul Drinkers' captain. Luko was in the heart of the action, trying to plug the gap the Howling Griffons armour had blasted in the line.

'I need your honesty, captain,' said Sarpedon. 'Can we hold this position?'

Luko paused, a little too long. 'No,' he replied. 'Not here. Not against this.'

'Then get them out of there, captain.'

'Yes, commander.'

Another volley of bolter shots whipped around Sarpedon's head, shredding the sorry remains of the burned forest behind him. Sarpedon crouched further, folding his mutant legs under him. If he charged now, he thought, if he led the Soul Drinkers against the advancing Howling Griffons, they would all be destroyed and no one would ever have to know how far Sarpedon had fallen. It would be over, and he would never have to answer to anyone about how his Chapter had been split by treachery, and trapped on an Emperor-forsaken jungle world by the Howling Griffons.

Sarpedon choked the thought down, banishing it from his mind. In spite of everything, he was a Space Marine, and he had a duty to his battle-brothers that a normal soldier could never understand.

'Soul Drinkers!' called Sarpedon over the all-squads vox. 'The line will retreat! Forward squads disengage, line squads cover!' Sarpedon hefted his own bolter, ready to add his own fire to the effort. With every moment more of his battle-brothers were dying, and if this hateful strip of forest could not be held then they were dying for nothing.

The Soul Drinkers turned their bolters on the centre of the line as the forward squads, following the twin icons of Captain Luko and Chaplain Iktinos, disentangled themselves from the furious battle. The Howling Griffons tried to fall on them as they left but Sarpedon led the remaining squads in close, battering back the assaulting Howling Griffons with volleys of bolter fire. The forest around the line's centre was not a forest at all, just a broken wasteland blanketed with a caul of darkness and gunsmoke.

As the Soul Drinkers fell back to the cover of the still-standing forest behind them, Sarpedon could see the Howling Griffons' commander in the centre of the melee. Several Soul Drinkers had been surrounded in the last few moments before the covering fire weighed in and they were being butchered, the commander leading his Space Marines in those final acts of vengeance. The commander's axe rose and fell, cleaving limbs from bodies, and Sarpedon recognised the high collar and force weapon of a Librarian. He could even hear his adversary, roaring in frustration as the Soul Drinkers fell back down the slope of the hill towards the darkness of the valley below, where the jungle was too dense for the Howling Griffons' tanks to follow.

That same determination that Sarpedon himself had fought with time and time again was etched in the blood-spattered face of the Howling Griffons' commander. For a moment Sarpedon wondered if the Howling Griffon would recognise his own qualities in Sarpedon too – but then Sarpedon remembered that to the eyes of any Emperor-fearing soldier he was a hideous mutant, an abomination cursed by the Chaos gods and an enemy of the Imperium.

In storms of gunfire and hatred, the Soul Drinkers fell back before the fury of the Howling Griffons to seek their sanctuary in the jungle's depths.

THE FALSE NIGHT of battle had dissipated and true night had fallen. Slowly the creatures of Nevermourn's jungles were returning to places where gunfire and chaos had driven them off a few hours before. Sinuous, six-legged lizards wound their way back up tree trunks and flying creatures like winged snakes flitted into their treetop roosts. Beetles with shining emerald-green carapaces dissected the bullet-shredded leaves to rebuild the hives that had been crushed beneath tank tracks or power armoured feet. The night was punctuated by the shrill calls of tiny, brightly coloured birds and the whoops of ape-like creatures as they clambered back towards their territory in the canopy. The larger predators and herbivores that occupied the upper tiers of Nevermourn's ecosystem returned more slowly, nervously avoiding the patch of jungle where the Howling Griffons were encamped.

The Howling Griffons were guarding a knot of deep jungle at the foot of the hill where they had fought the Soul Drinkers. The jungle was dense here, too thick for anyone other than a Space Marine to forge his way through. The ground was sodden and as night fell rain had come with it, sending chutes of water shimmering down through the canopy like miniature waterfalls. Amphibious snakes slid through the standing water underfoot, writhing around the ceramite greaves of the Howling Griffons who held guard.

'Damn this,' said Captain Borganor. His Tenth Company troopers had formed the Howling Griffons' firebase and it was clear that he resented not being in the centre of the line, getting to grips with the enemy. 'They can't even pretend they're Space Marines. True Astartes would stand and fight. Now we've got to follow them through this Emperor-forsaken jungle before we can kill them.'

'They know we would have destroyed them,' said Lord Mercaeno. 'The Bearers of the Black Chalice are no fools. They have evaded justice for thousands of years. They know when they are beaten. And remember how the corrupt will always cling to life, even when death is an inevitability. They stave off their damnation, as if a few more days of freedom will somehow cleanse their lives of sin.'

Borganor and Mercaeno were in a small clearing formed by the hollow, rotted stump of an enormous fallen tree. Water cascaded down one side of the hollow, forming an ankle-deep pool choked with weeds and strange-coloured flowers. Mercaeno was enacting the wargear rites that the Howling Griffons observed, cleansing the taint of the Black Chalice from the holy axe. It had become besmirched with the blood of traitors, which had to be ritually washed away before the weapon was fit to strike through the oaths of the Howling Griffons. On a water-smoothed rock in front of Mercaeno was the axe, and he was slowly, painstakingly lifting off the scorch-dried blood encrusting the delicate patterns of the blade.

Normally the wargear rites would require Mercaeno to remove and purify his armour as well, but Nevermourn was too perilous to allow himself to go so unguarded. Beneath his armour, inscribed into his skin, were endless lines of text, smaller and denser than those on the armour. They were the most powerful oaths, the oldest ones, the promises that had bound him since before he had been fit to pick up a boltgun. Oaths to serve the Emperor, to honour his Chapter, and to guard his soul against the corruption the psyker's gifts could bring. They had been cut deep, so that every time Mercaeno felt pain in battle, he would be reminded of those oaths, and of how they were a physical part of him.

One oath, inscribed in flowing High Gothic across Mercaeno's barrel chest, was newer than the rest. The name of the daemon Periclitor was carved there – and the most recent cut was the line that struck through the daemon prince's name. That oath had been fulfilled. Those oaths, the old ones, remained hidden on Nevermourn. There was no need to display them when they were written across Mercaeno's very soul.

'If we could get the tanks through this terrain we'd have their heads already,' said Borganor bitterly. 'We would be delivering them to House Falken now.'

'The jungle is ours to use as well, captain,' said Mercaeno. He didn't lift his eyes from his task of cleaning Inquisitor Thaddeus's blood from the blade of his axe. 'You are familiar with our surroundings?'

'Of course.'

'Then you will be aware that ahead of the enemy is a swamp.' Mercano gestured at the streams of water falling all around them. 'All the rainfall flows through the jungle to the low ground ahead of them, and they will have to pass through that swamp to get away from us.'

'So we will have to follow them into it,' said Borganor. 'Shamed though I am to say it, it is not a battlefield I relish fighting upon.'

'You forget, captain, that we are not alone here. The enemy may be using this jungle to their advantage, but we have advantages of our own. We have the Emperor, and the blessed variety of His servants.'

Sergeant Ossex of Mercaeno's command squad was at the entrance to the hollow. 'Lord Librarian,' he said. 'We have contacted the general. His command frequency is patched into our vox-net.'

'Good,' said Mercaeno. He saw that Ossex had a new oath recently painted onto one of his vambraces, an oath to avenge the death of Brother

Rhelnon. The oath had a name that had been crossed out – that of Inquisitor Thaddeus, who had slain Rhelnon and been slain in turn by Mercaeno. The Howling Griffons had made good on another promise.

'Have they contacted the enemy yet?' asked Borganor.

'Not yet,' said Ossex. 'They do not seem aware of the nature of the enemy they face.'

'Of course not,' said Mercaeno. 'The Bearers of the Black Chalice are too grave a threat to become known to mere soldiers.' Mercaeno flicked through the channels of the Howling Griffons vox-net until he found the channel that had been newly patched in.

'General,' he said. 'This is Lord Mercaeno, commanding officer of the Howling Griffons.'

'General Glaivan Varr of the 901st Penal Legion,' replied a weary voice, rendered grainy through the substandard Imperial Guard vox. 'The Howling Griffons, you say? I had not thought Vanqualis was worthy of one Space Marine army, let alone two.'

'There are no Space Marines on this world save us,' replied Mercaeno sharply.

'Commander Sarpedon would disagree,' said Varr. 'He and his Soul Drinkers.'

'So that is what they call themselves,' spat Mercaeno, the venom clear in his voice.

Varr paused. 'There is something I do not know,' he said carefully.

'More than you can imagine, general. The creatures you know as the Soul Drinkers are traitors to the Emperor.'

'Renegades,' said Varr. 'Hunted by the Imperium. So they told me.'

'Then you should have exterminated them!' snapped Mercaeno.

'We were having something of an ork problem, Lord Mercaeno,' said Varr, tiredness and cynicism weighing his voice down. 'Fighting Space Marines on principle isn't a priority for me and my men.'

'They are no mere renegades, general. These Soul Drinkers are given over to the Ruinous Powers. The Dark Gods of the warp, corruption made flesh. They have come to take this world and give it over in sacrifice to their gods, and they have used the ignorance of you and your men to turn you into tools of wickedness. This is the work of Chaos, general, and you are a part of it, unless you redeem yourself and join us in destroying it.'

For a long time General Varr did not reply, and the only sounds were the trickling of the water and the low, constant calls of the jungle.

'Chaos,' he said.

'Chaos,' replied Mercaeno. 'It is nothing but lies. And believing those lies is the path to corruption. The Enemy has come to Vanqualis, and it is far deadlier than any savage greenskin horde.'

'We fought alongside them,' said Varr. 'We killed thousands of orks…'

'Because they want this world for themselves. The Bearers of the Black Chalice no doubt used the ork invasion to infiltrate Nevermourn. The greenskins be damned, the true enemy has revealed its head and it will be destroyed.'

'Then I take it, Lord Mercaeno, that you are assuming command of the Imperial forces on Vanqualis?'

'That is correct,' said Mercaeno. 'And with our combined forces we will butcher the Bearers of the Black Chalice here and now. What is your position, General Varr?'

'We're encamped on high ground about two kilometres north-west of the head of the Serpentspine Valley,' said Varr. 'We're still receiving stragglers from the battle in the valley. We've got two thousand healthy soldiers here, another five hundred to a thousand holding out in pockets between here and the valley. My scouts tell me the greenskins are moving north from the heights over the valley, which means they're making their push on the coast.'

'We have greater concerns than the orks,' said Mercaeno. 'The betrayers are fleeing from my Howling Griffons through the marshes south of the ruined fortress.'

'I know where you mean,' said Varr. 'I've got it flagged on our maps as dead man's ground. Nothing's getting through there, even the orks would give it a wide berth.'

'And that is where we will destroy the Black Chalice. My men are approaching from the east. You will take the 901st and block the western edge of the marshes. The traitors will be trapped.'

'Abandoning our positions here will give the orks free rein,' said Varr. 'They could get to the coast in three days unopposed.'

'General Varr,' said Mercaeno gravely, 'my Chapter swore to defend Vanqualis a long time ago. When we learned of the greenskins that infested it, I took my Chapter to cleanse these jungles of the xenos. But the Howling Griffons also knew that one day the Black Chalice would return, and until they are destroyed there is room for no other concerns. I despise the xenos as much as you do, Varr – the more so, for I have fought their kind in every corner of the galaxy. But believe me when I say that I would rather every single Vanqualian dies to orkish hands than a lone bearer of the Black Chalice escapes these jungles alive. Do not think to question me, Varr, nor even to guess at what drives us. We will stop at nothing to fulfil the oaths our Chapter has sworn. Nothing.'

'Then my men can be in position in half a day,' said Varr. 'If that is an order.'

'That is an order, general.' Mercaeno closed the vox-link.

'Penal Legions,' said Borganor with some distaste. 'The worst of the worst. Scum not fit to seek the Emperor's redemption.'

'Scum indeed,' said Mercaeno. 'But the greenskins will have weeded out the weaker-willed. Among those men will be the hardest-bitten of killers. And it barely matters if the 901st stand and fight or run like dogs, Borganor. All they need to do is slow the Black Chalice down. As soon as we get to grips with the enemy, the Black Chalice will be destroyed. Whether the 901st survive to fight alongside us is irrelevant.'

'Then they shall serve some purpose in death,' said Borganor. 'Far more than they ever did in life.'

'Have Captain Darion draw in the patrols and make ready to move. As soon as the 901st are in position we will tighten the noose.'

Borganor saluted and left the hollow, leaving Mercaeno to finish his wargear rites.

Finally it would be done and one of the Chapter's oldest oaths would be fulfilled. By the next nightfall another name carved deep into Mercaeno's skin would be struck through, so that every time Mercaeno felt pain he would be reminded of the day the Black Chalice fell.

# CHAPTER THIRTEEN

'How far must we compromise when victory is at stake?'

'The concept of compromise is alien to an Astartes. To die unrelenting is to be victorious.'

– Daenyathos, *Catechisms Martial*

WITH THE TWIN dramas of the ork advance and the Howling Griffons' pursuit of the Soul Drinkers, a great deal went unnoticed in Nevermourn's jungles. Tiny pockets of Penal Legion troopers held out against scattered bands of orks, both sides cut off from their parent armies, fighting miniature wars for survival. Stragglers were picked off by predators native to the jungle, crushed in the maws of enormous insectoid monsters or dragged down beneath the ground by the articulated tentacles of subterranean beasts. A thousand stories were played out away from Vanqualis's eyes, men and greenskins dying heroic or shameful deaths, prevailing against the planet or falling to one another's blades.

One of those unnoticed dramas saw a number of small, obsolete cargo landers flying down through the last vestiges of the night. They landed clumsily on the cratered open ground on the blasted hill. From the forest around the hilltop emerged the Soul Drinkers loyal to Eumenes, led by Sergeant Hecular. They had watched the conflict between the Howling Griffons and Sarpedon's Soul Drinkers with some amusement, relishing the irony that it was Imperial Space Marines who had seen off their enemy Sarpedon.

Silently, rapidly, the rebel Soul Drinkers embarked on the Onager orbital landers, which trundled around the hilltop and took off again. They rose into the sky as the first tinge of grey-green morning light edged the far horizon, heading for the *Brokenback* so they could finally leave this forsaken planet forever.

EVEN SARPEDON'S MUTATED legs made hard work of forcing his way through the foul, sucking swamp around him. It stank, for everything that died in the jungle eventually found its way into the swamp where it lay and rotted, forming a rank sluggish lake of decay and stagnation. The trees that grew there were like skeletal hands reaching desperately up from the swamp, and slime-encrusted roots arced overhead forming archways and tunnels among the filth. The Soul Drinkers had been forging on for several hours, knowing that the Howling Griffons would be matching their every step.

'Commander,' voxed Sergeant Salk from up ahead. Salk's squad included a number of tough field veterans and Sarpedon had found himself using them as forward scouts more and more often. 'We've got contacts up ahead. Half a kilometre from us.'

'Howling Griffons?'

'No. It looks like the 901st.'

'All units, halt,' ordered Sarpedon. The remaining Soul Drinkers, around two hundred Astartes strong, stopped forging on through the filth and held their positions, holding their weapons up out of the stinking water. Sarpedon himself halted and the sounds of the swamp settled around him – chirping insects, the hooting of birds roosting among the blighted trees overhead, and the slow, sluggish grind of the water itself.

'I could make contact, commander,' voxed Salk.

'No, sergeant,' replied Sarpedon. 'We don't know whose side they're on. The Howling Griffons could easily have taken command.' Sarpedon crawled a short distance through the swamp to the thick bole of a tree, which rose on a crown of overhead roots that resembled Sarpedon's own arachnoid legs. Sarpedon clambered up the tree – he could climb as nimbly as an insect, his legs tipped with long talons that dug deep into the bark.

From the vantage point, his enhanced Astartes eyesight piercing the filmy gloom, he could just glimpse the far edge of the swamp where banks of mud rose from the water and the jungle began again. The Penal Legion troopers were well disguised, smeared with mud and wearing improvised camouflage, but they were definitely there standing guard. They crouched down among the undergrowth or kept watch from the forks of trees, scanning the swamps. They were expecting an enemy to come through the swamps towards them, and that enemy could only be the Soul Drinkers.

Between the Soul Drinkers and the 901st's line, several enormous hunks of machinery lay half-submerged in the swamp. A few more were embedded in the far bank, hulks of rusting metal or lumps of scorched rock. They were the remains of the ork asteroid ship that had landed off-target and hit the hill behind them – it must have broken up and scattered itself all over the swamp and the valley beyond. The sight was a sudden reminder that the greenskins had brought the Soul Drinkers to Vanqualis in the first place, but that now the xenos were far from Sarpedon's mind, well down the list of priorities that now began with survival.

'They've been sent to trap us here,' said Sarpedon. 'Poor damned sinners.'

Sarpedon saw movement on the far shore. Chimera troop carriers, rugged APCs used throughout the Imperial Guard, rode up over the tangles of roots on the bank and tipped down into the swamp. Ripples rode through the filthy swamp water ahead of them as they forged forwards.

'They're moving to engage,' said Sarpedon. 'Soul drinkers! Advance as line!'

Behind Sarpedon, the Soul Drinkers moved forward in a long, forbidding line, each Space Marine an anchor keeping the line taut and relentless. Sarpedon joined them, scuttling down from the tree back into the water. The Chimeras of the 901st were slowing down in the sucking mud and one foundered in the shadow of the orkish wreck. Its top hatch swung open and the men inside vaulted out. The water was chest-high to an unaugmented human and they struggled to keep their footing in the swamp.

One of them shouted. The Soul Drinkers had been spotted. Hundreds of men were in the water now, lasguns ready, a few heavy weapons and plasma guns shouldered ready to fight.

It could be because they are brave, though Sarpedon, that they come forward to fight us. Or it could be that they do not believe they will get off this planet, and they are just looking for a good fight before it is over.

Sarpedon could see the lead Chimera, a command vehicle trailing a cluster of antennae and mounted with vox-casters. The command unit inside were clambering out, and they were just hitting the water when the firing began.

'Advance!' Sarpedon heard – it was Captain Luko, jogging through the swamp, leading a chevron of

Soul Drinkers through the spattering of las-fire. The 901st were sending out ranging shots, or perhaps hoping to break up the advance. Space Marine armour was all but proof against isolated las-fire, and it took far more to rattle the Soul Drinkers. As the first bolters rang out, Sarpedon put his head down and ran for the command Chimera.

Almost immediately, the 901st were dying. Dozens of them in those few moments, thrown back against the hulls of their Chimeras or thrown down into the bloodstained filth of the swamp. Sarpedon saw it all as if detached, as if he was watching on a pict-screen far away, the sound of the gunfire around him faint and tinny. These were his allies, the men who had come to Vanqualis to be redeemed, and to fight them was a betrayal. But there was no choice, on either side. The destruction of the 901st was a cruel inevitability, a grim, heartless business to be done quickly and without emotion, like the execution of a battle-brother.

Ahead of Sarpedon, the 901st's command Chimera rocked as a plasma blast bored through its side and flames billowed from the top hatch. The men sheltering around it threw themselves away from the vehicle, stumbling through the murk, their silhouettes hard-edged among the flames.

Sarpedon and General Varr saw one another at the same time. Scorched by the guttering flame enveloping his Chimera, Varr drew his sword – an ornate sabre he had probably taken from a dead Vanqualian artilleryman to replace the blade he had broken at the Wraithspire Palace.

'Fall back!' shouted Varr to the men behind him, without taking his eyes off Sarpedon. 'Give the order! Fall back and hold the shore!'

The command squad's vox-operator hauled his vox-unit through the murk and darkness, relaying the order to the rest of the 901st. Varr didn't follow the rest of his squad as they retreated from the giant armoured forms of the Soul Drinkers.

'Varr!' called Sarpedon.

'Sarpedon,' replied Varr. 'Change in the chain of command. You are the enemy now.'

'I know.'

'If it could end any other way I would take it. I hope you believe that. But my duty is to the Imperium, and on Vanqualis that means Lord Mercaeno.'

'I believe it, Varr. And if it means anything, I would change it, too, if I could.'

Varr dropped back into a guard position, blade held high. 'Make it quick,' he said.

Sarpedon's force staff was in his hand. In a few moments he had crossed the distance between them, and Varr's blade came forward to meet him.

'The Howling Griffons?' said Eumenes.

'The Chapter symbol is the same,' replied Sergeant Hecular. In the dim light of the Soul Drinkers' Chapter archive, Hecular's face looked even more hollow and cruel than usual.

Eumenes swung the pict-screen around on its armature. The Chapter archive still mostly consisted of datastacks that had been salvaged from the old

Soul Drinkers fleet before Sarpedon had scuttled it after the first Chapter War, and was housed in a ship's chapel with mosaics on the floors and faded frescoes on the walls and vaulted ceiling.

The history of the Howling Griffons scrolled by. 'Ultramarines successors,' said Eumenes to himself. 'Guilliman's brood. Guilliman was the primarch who built the whole mess of the Imperium in the first place. I hope Sarpedon kills a few of his sons before they get him.'

'I never paid much attention to Imperial history,' said Hecular.

Eumenes turned to him. 'Then start now,' he said. 'Know the enemy.' He turned back to the Howling Griffons' history. 'The Griffons are just another Chapter of lapdogs. They'll toe whatever line Terra casts out, by the looks of it. We have to be gone by the time they're finished with Sarpedon.'

Eumenes noticed another Soul Drinker approaching – Apothecary Pallas, his face still scorched and raw from his encounter with Techmarine Lygris. Pallas had recovered consciousness a few minutes after Lygris had escaped and torn the flight decks apart looking for him, but the Techmarine had fled. 'The last Onager has landed,' he said. 'All those loyal to us are on board.'

'Good,' said Eumenes. 'And the wounded?'

'There are some,' replied Pallas. 'But the apothecarion can cope as long as I have some of the others to help me.'

'And what of Lygris?'

'Still missing.'

'His escape rankles with you, Pallas,' said Eumenes.

'Of course,' replied Pallas tightly. 'He bested me.'

'You failed me,' said Eumenes. 'I expect more from my officers.'

'I will find him, Eumenes.'

'Eventually, yes, it is inevitable. That is not enough. I want his head, and soon.' Eumenes switched off the pict-screen and spoke over the vox. 'Tydeus? The rest of the Chapter is on board. How long before we can hit the warp?'

'A day at least,' replied Tydeus. The sounds of the engine decks were clear across the vox. Many of the *Brokenback*'s component ships had functional warp engines, which had been connected together so they could move the whole hulk into the warp.

Eumenes's face darkened further. 'A day? Explain yourself.'

'Lygris has been sabotaging the connections between the plasma generators and the warp coils. They can be fixed but it all takes time. It won't stop us, but it will slow us down.'

Eumenes cast a filthy look at Pallas, whose failure had let Lygris stay at large on the *Brokenback*. 'Time is becoming a factor. We will jump into the warp as soon as the engines are ready.'

'Where to?' asked Sergeant Hecular.

'It doesn't matter,' said Eumenes as he closed the vox-link. 'As long as we get away from this damned system. Then we can start planning for the next stage.' Eumenes indicated for Hecular to follow him as he headed back towards the bridge to prepare for the *Brokenback*'s departure.

For a few minutes Apothecary Pallas stayed behind, surrounded by the datastacks, which contained the history of everything he had betrayed. He had turned his back on the old Chapter when he sided with Sarpedon, and now he had turned it on Sarpedon himself. There was no history anywhere now which he could call his own.

Then Pallas, too, left for the apothecarion where the Soul Drinkers injured defending the fortress lay. They had joined Pallas in his betrayal, and now the apothecary's obligations were to help them. They were Pallas's battle-brothers now – Sarpedon, and the Soul Drinkers with him on Vanqualis, were lost to him.

GLAIVAN VARR'S FATHER had taught him to fight. That was why the lesson had stayed. His father had fought in the Locrasian 31st Light Infantry, a very old and distinguished regiment who took their swords as seriously as their guns. The Locrasian fighting style was fluid and rapid, as dangerous as it was elegant. Varr's father was a fair man, but one who knew how harsh the galaxy could be, especially to a son who would follow him into the military. Varr had borne the bruises of a sloppy guard or reckless lunge, and by the time he came of age he could hold his own with the sword against a veteran of the Locrasian Light Infantry.

One day his father left with his regiment to help put down a bloody rebellion, and he had not returned. All that remained of him was a catalogue of parries and thrusts, cuts and finishing blows.

They were all useless. With Sarpedon so huge and lightning-quick, even Varr's father couldn't help him.

Varr fended off the force staff again, his blade now battered and chipped, blunt and barely any use as a weapon. He stumbled and caught the butt of the staff in his back, sprawling forwards, barely able to keep a grip on the sword. He plunged into the water, got his footing and pushed up again. His eyes were full of stinking mud and he didn't know where his enemy was.

His father would have whirled around, brought the blade up in a glittering arc with such poise and confidence that it would have sheared through the guard of his opponent and put the tip at the enemy's throat. Varr did that now, swinging his weight around, all his strength bringing the Vanqualian blade towards his best guess at Sarpedon's location.

The blade shattered. Varr's wrist shattered with it, white, numb pain flooding through his arm. He looked up, the filth running from his eyes, and he saw the sword had shattered on the armour of Sarpedon's forearm.

Varr took a little comfort in the fact that there was a hint of real regret in Sarpedon's face as he drove the force staff through his opponent's chest.

VARR'S BODY SLID off the end of Sarpedon's force staff and into the water, foul swamp filth filling the hole torn through the general's chest. Sarpedon watched the body sink down into the blood-slicked water.

'Commander,' said Captain Luko. 'The 901st are falling back.'

'General Varr is dead,' replied Sarpedon.

Luko nodded towards the 901st's positions. 'Then the Penal Legion troops will be leaderless,' he said. 'Give the order and we'll break through them.'

Sarpedon glanced in the same direction. 'There is nothing to gain by that,' he said. 'They weren't put here to stop us, they were put here to slow us down. Even if we got straight through them, they will have achieved that objective. By the time we have broken them the Howling Griffons will be among us.'

'Commander?' said Luko, his face tinged with doubt and concern that rarely troubled a Space Marine. 'Do you mean to fight the Howling Griffons in this swamp?'

'No,' said Sarpedon. 'I have no wish to give Lord Mercaeno what he wants. Tell me, captain, are we still in contact with the *Brokenback*?'

'I don't know,' replied Luko. We haven't had any word from Lygris since–'

'I don't mean Lygris,' snapped Sarpedon. 'I mean Eumenes.'

EUMENES DEMANDED THAT he be left alone on the bridge with all communications down, so that only he would be party to the negotiations. More and more equipment had been moved onto the bridge so that Eumenes could command the *Brokenback* and his Soul Drinkers alone.

Eumenes took to the command pulpit. It suited him completely.

'Good day, commander,' said Eumenes.

Sarpedon's face dominated the viewscreen. Around him could be seen the twisted trees reaching up from the fouled waters of the swamp. Sarpedon was filthy with the slime of the swamp and the blood of General Varr.

'I want to negotiate,' said Sarpedon.

Eumenes laughed. 'With what? I have the *Brokenback*. The warp engines are primed. In less than an hour we will be gone. What could you possibly offer us that we need?'

'Survival,' said Sarpedon. 'A future.'

'I don't think I am the one whose survival is at stake, Sarpedon.'

'Damn you, Eumenes, don't you even understand what is happening here? I'm not the only enemy you have. The Howling Griffons won't stop until the Soul Drinkers are destroyed. That means your men as well as mine. And even if you escape this system, the Howling Griffons will hunt you down. They outnumber you, Eumenes, and they will destroy you.'

'Let them try.'

'Eumenes, I cannot pretend I do not despise you.' Sarpedon's face was set – he was forcing down the anger inside him. 'You have betrayed me and everything I have fought for. But I cannot allow the Soul Drinkers Chapter to die. All the Soul Drinkers are my battle-brothers, and I will not hand the Howling Griffons a victory they won only because we were divided. Choke down your pride for a second, Eumenes. You know what I am saying is true. As long as we are divided the Howling Griffons will destroy us, one faction at a time.'

Eumenes leaned forwards. 'These are the words of a dying man, Sarpedon. Again, what can you offer me?'

'The Chapter.'

There was nothing to fill the silence that followed Sarpedon's words. Eumenes thought deeply for several long moments, the only movement the blinking of the lights that studded the cogitators and readouts around him.

'The Chapter,' Eumenes repeated. 'The Soul Drinkers.'

'Yours to command,' said Sarpedon. 'I will relinquish my rank as Chapter Master. You will be the new Chapter Master of the Soul Drinkers. You will have everything – the secrets of the *Brokenback*, the battle-brothers who sided with me, everything.'

'They will never fight for me, Sarpedon.'

'They will obey me,' said Sarpedon. 'And I will obey you. '

A long, slow smile spread across Eumenes's youthful face. 'And for this you receive survival. Nothing more. Only survival. Like an animal.'

'Like an animal,' replied Sarpedon. 'If that is what you wish. As long as we can unite to defeat the Howling Griffons, that is what you will have.'

Eumenes's brow knotted in thought. 'I need a way to get you off the planet.'

'Lygris can help you,' said Sarpedon. 'As long as you are quick.'

Eumenes looked the pict-image of Sarpedon in the eye. 'I will hold you to this, Sarpedon. I defeated you once. I will defeat you again.'

'I keep my word,' said Sarpedon gravely. 'There is no limit I will not reach to ensure the survival of the Soul Drinkers. Kill me if it amuses you. Just keep the Chapter alive. If it costs me everything to save the Soul Drinkers, then I accept that.'

'It will,' said Eumenes. 'I accept your offer. We unite to fend off the Howling Griffons. In return I am the Chapter Master of the Soul Drinkers, from this moment on. Defy the terms of this pact, and you and your battle-brothers' lives will be forfeit.'

Sarpedon's shoulders sagged, and for perhaps the first time in his life as a Space Marine he looked truly beaten. 'Broadcast across the ship's vox,' said Sarpedon. 'Lygris will hear. Then we can end this.'

Eumenes rapidly patched Sarpedon's transmission through to the vox-casters mounted throughout the *Brokenback*. 'Done.' Eumenes smirked, no doubt imagining his reign as Chapter Master. 'I will not kill you, Sarpedon. I will bring you low. Everything you believe in will fall apart and you will be alive to see it.'

'I have no doubt that is true, Eumenes. But my word is my word.'

Sarpedon began to speak through the *Brokenback*'s vox-caster, calling on Lygris to report to Eumenes and offer his expertise in calibrating and aiming the *Brokenback*'s precision armaments.

The note of defeat and sorrow in Sarpedon's voice was profound. For a long time Eumenes just stood there at the command pulpit and listened, admiring the ruination he would wreak on the man he had usurped as ruler of the Soul Drinkers.

# CHAPTER FOURTEEN

'What can we learn from the ways of
the xenos?'

'We can learn how to hate.'

— Daenyathos, *Catechisms Martial*

LORD MERCAENO WATCHED in quiet fury at the bright
orange blossoms billowing up over the jungle
canopy. He stood on an outcrop of moss-covered
rock that rose from the slope near the bottom of the
hill, overlooking the swamp-filled valley. The viewpoint overlooked the drab, decaying canopy that
stretched over the swamp, dark vegetation like a
ragged olive-green blanket draped over the stinking
waters. Somewhere in that darkness had been the
Howling Griffons' quarry, the Bearers of the Black

Chalice and their leader Sarpedon, and the Howling Griffons had come so close to getting to grips with them down in the filth and shadows.

Another explosion tore up from the jungle just in front of the Howling Griffons' positions. It burst up through the canopy on the near edge of the swamp, just where Mercaeno would have been marshalling his forces at that very moment had the bombardment not begun. Time and again the lance strikes and artillery shots hammered down from the sky, stitching a line of smoke and flame along the near edge of the swamp, like a wall of fire that barred the Howling Griffons from advancing any further.

'More deceit,' spat Mercaeno to himself. The ground shook as another explosion rocked the valley, throwing hissing curtains of vaporised swamp water into the air ahead of him. 'More cowardice. The traitors do not have enough honour even to stand and fight.'

'Lord Librarian,' said Captain Darion, who stepped up onto the outcrop behind Mercaeno. 'I've pulled the forward units back. They say we certainly cannot advance until this bombardment is over.'

'I thought as much.'

'And the accuracy is exceptional. An orbital bombardment would normally carpet this valley at random. The Black Chalice must have some very ancient technology at its disposal to fire so close to their own forces with such confidence.'

'Take care, Captain Darion, not to admire the ways of the enemy,' said Mercaeno bitterly. 'Nor to ascribe him a capacity for destruction beyond our own. We are the Emperor's soldiers. This is nothing compared to the strength granted us by our Emperor.' Mercaeno turned away from Captain Darion and switched to the vox-channel of the *Cerulean Claw*. 'This is Lord Mercaeno. Come in, *Cerulean Claw*.'

'*Claw* here,' replied the voice of Flag-Lieutenant Scarlphan.

Scarlphan was not a Space Marine, but part of the Howling Griffons' support structure of unaugmented humans who performed functions like crewing the Chapter's spacecraft, and working in its artificer workshops and apothecarion.

'We are under orbital bombardment. Where is this coming from?'

'The ship's sensors are tracking a very large spacecraft,' replied Scarlphan. 'It's in low orbit. It was hiding on the far side of the planet from us and we have only just found it. It shows considerable speed for its size. It opened fire a few minutes ago.'

'Can we engage?' said Mercaeno.

'It is unlikely the fleet could engage it successfully,' replied Scarlphan. 'Its armaments are considerable and its sheer size would make it impossible to target effectively. There is no saying where its vital points might be.'

'I need everything you have on it,' said Mercaeno. 'Full scans. Risk the *Claw* if you have to get close enough.'

'We have already begun,' said Scarlphan. 'I'm sending it to your slate now, Lord Librarian.'

Mercaeno took a data-slate out from the wargear hanging at the waist of his armour. Its screen lit up, showing a diagram of the enemy ship. It was huge, asymmetrical and ugly. Figures and diagrams flitted by.

'A space hulk,' said Mercaeno.

A space hulk was the result of a number of ships becoming lost in the warp, and clumping together to form an abomination of fused metal, like a bloated parody of a true ship. Every now and again the warp would spit a hulk back out into realspace, usually infested with aliens, renegades, or even the daemons of the warp. It was entirely appropriate that the Bearers of the Black Chalice should travel around in such a craft.

'Life scans?'

'Almost complete,' replied Scarlphan. 'Less than one per cent so far.'

'The damn thing's empty,' said Darion.

It was indeed strange. Space hulks were often infested, either by predators from the warp or mundane xenos, usually mindless vermin that hungrily colonised these floating pits of corruption. The hulk in orbit over Vanqualis was, for want of a better word, clean.

'The Black Chalice do not like sharing their living space,' said Mercaeno. 'And they're alone up there. Captain Darion, how well do you know your Codex Astartes?'

Darion looked faintly offended. 'Like my own thoughts,' he said.

'Then you are familiar with the approved tactics for boarding a space hulk?'

'Boarding? Yes, Lord Librarian.'

Mercaeno waved a hand at the swamp valley below, still shuddering with the bombardment. 'The hulk is risking coming into orbit only now. That means the Black Chalice intend to leave Vanqualis and board it so they can escape. That is when they will be vulnerable. And more importantly, we can hit them all at once. All of them, even their spacecraft. We can destroy them for good, so there will be no doubt.'

'There are few actions as dangerous as boarding a hostile craft, Lord Librarian,' said Darion carefully.

'I know of one, captain. Allowing the enemy to escape. Is that far more dangerous than any risk to which we could possibly expose the Howling Griffons? Would it not be corrosive to the very soul of this Chapter to see the enemy gathered before us, and not move to fulfil the oath that requires their destruction? Boarding the hulk is a last resort, but the path of the Space Marine is lined with such choices. Many commanders would let the Black Chalice go, it is true. None of those commanders are here.'

'Of course, Lord Librarian,' said Darion. 'And I agree. But we must go into this fully understanding the risks.'

'And it is my duty to minimise those risks as much as I can,' replied Mercaeno. 'To which end, we shall not be doing it alone.' Mercaeno switched vox-channels. 'General Varr? Come in Varr, this is Lord Mercaeno.'

'Varr's dead,' came the reply. It was a brutish, coarse voice, a world away from General Varr's relatively cultured tone.

'Who is this?' demanded Mercaeno.

'Acting General Kullek,' came the reply. The voice sounded faintly amused at this.

'*Acting* general?' Mercaeno did not bother to hide his incredulity. 'What are you talking about?'

'Varr's dead,' said Kullek. 'Dead man's boots.'

'And you are his second in command?'

'There's no second, not in the Penal Legions. But I'm the one who's giving the orders now, so that makes me in charge. Acting general, like I said.' The man's voice had an ugly, gloating quality to it, as if the death and destruction on Vanqualis was entertaining and participating in it a sport. However, given that the Penal Legions indeed had relatively little command structure, what Kullek said was probably correct. A man could walk far in dead men's boots if he was good at staying alive. It was still abhorrent, of course that Mercaeno should have to relay orders through a man who had doubtless been condemned to the Penal Legions for some horrible sin against the Emperor.

'Very well,' said Mercaeno sternly. 'What contact have you had with the enemy?'

'Still waiting,' replied Kullek. 'The general gave the order to fall back in the first scrap, and then didn't come out himself. The boys are getting restless. Not much fun waiting to get blown up down here. They want to get stuck in.'

'Then they shall have their wish. Your Emperor has need of the 901st. Tell me, acting general, have your men ever fought in a boarding action?'

THE AIR TASTED of salt and stone, lashed up by the storm. Even in the green depths of the jungle the warlord could taste that victory. The humans had tried to stop them – they had died beneath the greenskin onslaught, solely to keep them from this point. But they had failed. Armoured killing machines had descended from the skies and tried to fend them off, but these finest warriors of humanity had failed, too. Even the cheap trickery, which had conjured the images of orkish gods to scare the greenskins off Vanqualis, had failed. Only the orks had succeeded.

The warlord normally permitted only his hunters and scouts to venture ahead of the main body of the horde. But now, when victory was so close, he surged through the dense jungle like an ork possessed. His mechanical arm tore up trees at the roots and crushed the trunks of the soaring greatwoods. He kicked through undergrowth that tried to snare his feet as he trampled through it. Steam and smoke billowed from his artificial torso, the fires stoked hot inside him.

He could taste it, the tang of salt and the electric crackle of the storm. The jungle around him shuddered as if afraid, the canopy high above lashed by winds, shredded leaves and broken branches falling like rain. The foliage parted in front of the warlord and he was confronted with the gnarled, iron-hard trunks of a nest of trees. On either side they formed an impenetrable barrier in front of him, blocking his path.

The warlord roared in frustration. A gout of steam spurted from the elbow joint of his huge metal claw as he flexed his artificial muscles angrily. With rage flaring in his eyes he charged into the trees, his metallic fist slamming again and again into the wood. The bark splintered and wood pulped. The warlord jammed his body between two immense trunks and pushed, forcing the trees apart as if they were the ribcage of an enemy. Roots splintered in the ground below and with an awful tearing sound the trunks fell, crashing deafeningly through the canopy down to the ground.

Cold, wet air lashed at him through the gap the warlord had torn in the jungle. He could hear the cries of birds thrown into the air by the commotion of the falling trees. There was grey, swirling sky overhead.

The warlord forged ahead, stamping up the rocky slope in front of him. The temperature dropped and stinging salt-heavy winds battered against him. Finally, after an age confined to the green cage of the jungle, the warlord finally broke through into the open air.

The jungle ended against a high broken ridge of dark stone, like a scar. Beyond that was the sea. The storm brewing overhead had whipped the sea into an expanse of shifting mountains, the cloudy sky reflected in a grim dark grey that merged with the horizon. The waves crashed into the rocks and flung plumes of salt spray over the edge of the jungle, and over the warlord.

This was the objective the greenskins had fought and died for on Vanqualis. The sea. The warlord gazed across the waters towards the horizon where a strip of hazy darkness suggested land. The sea was all that separated Nevermourn and the orks from Herograve, the continent studded with cities full of hateful humans all but begging to be put to death by orkish blades. The warlord could see it – actually see it, for the first time. Herograve, where the greenskins would have their revenge, and where the ork gods would finally have a slaughter worthy of their worship.

The warlord looked down the coast from his vantage point up on the rocks. The jungle hung over the rocky cliffs in many places, turned feeble and brown by the salt spray. Elsewhere spectacular waterfalls plunged down into the sea, their waters swallowed up by the churning white mass that roared around the foot of the cliffs.

A kilometre or two down the coast was a bulge in the coastline where twin spurs of stone, like encircling arms, formed the boundaries of a bay. Within the confines of the bay the waters were less ferocious, and the jungle reached almost to the very edge of a beach of black sand.

For the first time in what might have been a lifetime, a broad, savage smile split the warlord's face. His ancient gnarled face showed joy perhaps unheard of in a creature so driven by hate and rage. The bay was his final objective on Nevermourn. It

was the place where, generations ago, the humans
had first gained a foothold on the jungle continent.
Now all that remained of the human presence here
were a few ruined stone buildings and a half-col-
lapsed lighthouse on one of the spurs of the bay,
abandoned after the city of Palatium and its space-
port provided a safer way for the humans to arrive
on Nevermourn. But now, of course, Palatium
burned.

The warlord could already see the orkish boats
being built on the shore, sheltered in the bay until
the time came for the final charge onto Herograve.
The ingenuity and industriousness of the orks knew
no limits when the prospect of slaughter and conquest was held in front of them – the horde would
work ceaselessly, hewing trees from the jungle and
cannibalising engines and weapons from the
horde's war machines, until a ramshackle fleet was
built to make the short voyage across the sea to
Herograve. Many in the horde would be killed during the voyage, blown up by malfunctioning
engines or drowned as their vessels sank, but it did
not matter. There were always enough orks. And
more than enough would arrive on Herograve to
make victory inevitable.

It was done. The ork victory would happen. Herograve and its cities would burn. All that remained
was for the blood itself to flow.

The other orks of the horde were reaching the
edge of the jungle and clambering up the sharp
rocks to see the waters spread out before them. They
were hooting and cheering, bellowing war-cries

towards distant Herograve, jeering at the humans who did not realise just how close their destruction had come. Already the greenskins were in the bay, swarming over the spurs of rock and through the beachfront jungles to secure their base for the voyage. Smoke-belching war machines were driven to the water's edge and slave-creatures whipped and corralled ready to begin the work of building the fleet. Orks worked quickly and paid no heed to safety or sanity – the boats would be built in two or three days, overseen by the insane masters of the horde's war machines.

For a moment the warlord was prepared to stride down to the bay and force the whole horde to congregate before him, so he could crack heads and bellow at them about why they were there. He could tell them of the treachery that had seen the humans take Vanqualis from the orks in the first place, about the orkish gods and how they demanded revenge. He could try to instil in them the same passion and dedication which had brought the horde to Vanqualis and hammered it forward through everything the humans could throw at it.

But they could not understand. Just as some orks possessed freakish abilities for engineering or crude medicine, so the warlord was a born leader, capable of perceiving strategies and truths that passed well over the head of any other ork. They did not know what it meant to pursue a distant dream with a passion, to defy all obstacles in its way, and finally reach the cusp of it. They did not need to know, either – no matter what happened now the orks would cross the sea and destroy Herograve, because they had been born to seek out such slaughter.

Nothing could stop the horde now, not when its momentum had brought it so far already. The warlord himself, even if he had wanted to, could not have saved Herograve from destruction.

THE ONLY SAFE place in the city now was high above it, in the sky yacht owned by a scion of House Falken who now doubtless lay dead in the ruins of Palatium. It was an elegant craft, its broad wings designed to catch currents and send it gliding majestically across the sky. Inside, though small, it was comfortable, and at least it was large enough for Countess Ismenissa to house her chamberlain, a full crew and her hem-bearers. The yacht was permanently airborne now save for occasional refuelling stops, and the luxurious passenger compartment was bathed in the hum of the trim-jets and whistle of the wind under the wings.

Lord Sovelin Falken knelt before the countess. His shoulders slumped as if a weight had finally been taken off him. Though he had at least made some effort to clean up since he had arrived on the shore of Herograve, he was still unshaven and his uniform was torn and scorched. In any other situation Lord Sovelin Falken would have been a disgrace, unfit to present before the countess.

'My lady,' he said, his voice shaking. 'I bring news from Nevermourn.'

Countess Ismenissa Falken stood over Sovelin. Even in her current surroundings, which were less regal than she was used to, the countess exuded an air of majesty and authority.

'Then you have travelled far,' said the countess. She had changed into her mourning clothes to show her distress at the state of Herograve's cities. Behind her the tormented city, wreathed in its customary smoke, could be seen rolling out through the arched windows surrounding the yacht's passenger compartment. Riots had broken out, and been gradually replaced by pitched battles between angry, frightened civilians and House Falken's household troops. The battles had been bloody, and House Falken had not won them all. The countess's berth on the yacht had been hurriedly arranged to keep her safe from the rampaging crowds. The Countess's magnificent dress was now black trimmed with crimson and her face had been made up with exaggerated darkness around her eyes, to symbolise the sadness of these events.

'From Palatium itself,' continued Sovelin, his eyes still fixed on the floor. 'Through the jungle, where I fought alongside the Imperial Guard until we were betrayed by the Bearers of the Black Chalice. And then to the coast itself, to watch for signs of the greenskins.'

'I did not think you of any note among the members of our House,' said the countess. 'I imagined you would do but little service to your world, and then away from the fires of battle. I certainly did not think you would escape Palatium when men like my husband did not.'

Lord Sovelin wavered, unsure of how to answer. 'No, my lady,' he said.

'But you have survived. Please, what news is it that you bring?'

'I stayed on the coast to watch for them, my lady. The orks. And they came. Through the jungle like a... like a monster, driving even the greatwoods before them. I found a vessel at the old bay, barely seaworthy, and as soon as I saw them I made for Herograve. The greenskins have made it to the coast, a great host of them barely dented by the efforts of the Imperial Guard. They will surely invade Herograve soon. It is but a matter of days, my lady.'

Countess Ismenissa was silent for a long while. She looked down at the city below her, at how some streets were wholly ablaze, forming intricate mazes of flame coiling through the darkness. Her children carried the long strings of mourning beads that trailed from the hem of her black dress, cradling them in tiny dead hands. The portable juvenat units, newer and less efficient than those in her pinnacle chambers, filled the back of the passenger deck and emitted occasional spurts of freezing white vapour.

'Look at me, Sovelin,' she said.

Lord Sovelin looked up at the countess, almost unable to meet her gaze.

'You have journeyed across Nevermourn, and across the sea, and then begged permission to fly a shuttle up to this yacht,' she said, 'just to tell me that we are doomed.'

'No, my lady. Merely to tell you when the green-skins will arrive. If we face them at the coast we could fend them off. It is as they land that they will be most vulnerable.'

'I know this, Sovelin. It has always been the only viable plan for the defence of Herograve. But look!' The countess indicated the city below. Sovelin followed her gaze and saw the flames guttering in the darkness. An explosion toppled a great dark spire and it fell, as slow and powerful as any toppling greatwood, into the mass of the city below.

'The people of Herograve are going mad with fear,' she said. 'Lunatics are walking the streets shouting prophecies and they are believed. The slightest rumour sparks riots. The troops have banished me to this cursed flying contraption because they cannot guarantee my throne chambers will be secure. And the dead are piling up, Sovelin, the dead! Great piles of them, in the streets. The household troops cannot keep order as it is. With the Warders lost at Palatium, we have nowhere near enough men under arms to both keep Herograve's cities from burning, and to fight a battle with the orks at the coast. It cannot be done.'

'Now, my lady, you are the one telling me we are doomed.'

Countess Ismenissa looked at Sovelin sternly. 'Something of the greenskin has rubbed off on you, Sovelin. You forget your tongue. I do not blame you for bringing me this news. You did your duty, after all. But I cannot pretend it spells anything other than disaster for us. And what of the Black Chalice?'

Sovelin sighed. 'I do not know,' he said. 'I fled them.'

'You ran for the coast as soon as you could. You did not stand and fight them.'

'I am just one man, my lady! I knew I could not stand against them. So I concerned myself with the foe we could defeat on our own, with the greenskins.'

The countess did not look impressed by Sovelin's words. 'The Black Chalice will be dealt with,' she said. 'The Howling Griffons answered our plea. They are honour-bound to destroy the chalice and its bearers. The greenskins are another matter.'

'My lady,' said Sovelin, 'if I may beg your leave. At the next refuelling stop, let me off this craft again. I wish to go to the coast and do what I can there to prepare the defences. It is our best chance to defeat the orks. Perhaps a militia can be raised from the cities on the coast. I bear the blood of House Falken and the uniform of the Warders. My presence might make a difference.'

'Make a difference to the battle, Lord Sovelin, or to yourself? To place yourself in the path of the greenskins would be a fine way to absolve yourself from fleeing the challenge of the Black Chalice.'

Sovelin stood, anger and exhaustion getting the better of him. 'I nearly died, my lady!' he snapped. 'Time and time again. I writhed through filth to evade the greenskins, I marched day and night, and I all but drowned to reach Herograve, all to fulfil my duty to my planet and my house! What do you want of me?'

The countess looked down her regal nose at Sovelin, utterly unflustered by his outburst. 'For you to be gone, Lord Sovelin, and for my husband, or one of the other commanders of the Vanqualian Warders, to have survived in your place. That is what I want. Go to the coast and do what you can, if that is where you see your fate. I must stay here and see that my people do not kill themselves before the greenskins ever arrive.'

Lord Sovelin did not answer. He just bowed to his countess, turned and walked out of her makeshift throne room, into the crew compartment from which he could disembark at the next fuel stop.

The countess turned back to the arched window looking down on the city. Far below, the streets of Herograve continued to burn.

THE ALIEN CRAFT descended through the canopy of the swamp, its black metal mouthparts slicing through the branches. The light from the bombardment at the swamp's edge cast strange reflections in the liquid darkness of its hull.

Inside the ship, in the cockpit towards its upper surface, was Lygris. He was flying the ship with Eumenes's permission, and with many misgivings. None of the Soul Drinkers could be sure that Eumenes's offer, to let Lygris take them back onto the *Brokenback*, was not some kind of cruel traitorous trick. Only Sarpedon himself had convinced Lygris to take the alien ship from the depths of the hulk and fly it through the range of the *Brokenback*'s guns, down into the swamp.

The Soul Drinkers crouched in the filthy swamp water hurried to take up positions beneath the craft as it descended to chest-height, the alien anti-grav generators around the edge of its dome keeping it eerily aloft without disturbing the water. The first Soul Drinkers clambered up into the ship's belly.

Sarpedon would be the last on. He watched his Soul Drinkers embarking – the alien ship was unarmed and poorly armoured, and the operation had to go quickly and without a hitch lest the 901st or the Howling Griffons had time to aim heavy weapons. Sarpedon hated feeling this vulnerable – it was not the way of the Astartes to place themselves at such risk, but he had no choice.

'I pray, Sarpedon, that this was worth it,' said Captain Luko. Luko's squad were acting as the rearguard, watching for Penal Legion troopers or Howling Griffons who might get close enough to prevent the Soul Drinkers from escaping.

Sarpedon looked at the Soul Drinkers captain next to him. Luko had put on the most warlike face of any of the Soul Drinkers, behaving as if war was something he relished. He had little of that bravado now. 'The Chapter must survive,' said Sarpedon. 'We have made sacrifices before.'

'There is no Chapter any more, Sarpedon. The Chapter died when you killed Gorgoleon. All we have left are the principles for which we fight and when those die, we might as well be another band of renegades killing for no reason. Eumenes does not believe in the same things as you, Sarpedon. If he is in command we will be the Soul Drinkers no longer.'

'If we do not co-operate with Eumenes we will be hunted down and killed on this planet,' said Sarpedon. 'Would you rather die?'

'Yes!' snapped Luko. 'When the alternative is to live a life of dishonour, killing for something I never believed in? Following the man who betrayed me? I would rather die than fight on like that.'

'Then walk away, captain,' said Sarpedon. He indicated the spacecraft into which the Soul Drinkers were climbing. 'These men will probably follow you. Lead them back into the swamp and die down here. If that is what you want, be the one to defy me and die the death you choose.'

Luko couldn't answer straight away. For a long, awful moment he just stared at Sarpedon, trying to gauge whether Sarpedon would really let that happen.

'I do this,' said Luko at last, 'because perhaps it will give me a chance to avenge Karraidin, and our other brothers who died by Eumenes's hand. And because you are still my Chapter Master.'

'Commander, captain,' said Sergeant Salk, trudging through the swamp towards them. 'The men are on board and Lygris is ready to leave. It's time to go.'

The three Soul Drinkers made their way through the swamp to the underbelly of the spacecraft that hovered above them. Sarpedon's Soul Drinkers, almost two hundred of them, were crammed inside the craft, their armoured bodies packed close. One missile fired by the 901st's troopers, one good volley of bolter fire from the Howling Griffons, one misplaced shot from the *Brokenback*, would do for them all. Sarpedon hated the whole situation, the rebellion, this damned planet, which had conspired to make him so vulnerable. It was not just the journey to the *Brokenback* that exposed the Soul Drinkers – it was the fact that for the first time since the death of Gorgoleon they were commanded by someone else, who could order them butchered wholesale if he wanted.

Sarpedon was last onto the ship. The dark liquid metal of the ship's mandibles folded up under him, forming a strangely knurled floor like the carapace of a black beetle. He could feel the eyes of the Soul Drinkers on him – by now they all knew of the deal Sarpedon had made, of how Sarpedon had handed control of the Chapter to Eumenes. He was their battle-brother and their commander and none of them spoke as Luko had done, none of them challenged him. But Sarpedon knew that the accusation in their eyes would be far more stinging than any words.

Iktinos had said nothing. Of all the Soul Drinkers, Sarpedon had expected Chaplain Iktinos to defy him over Eumenes. He had even been prepared to fight Iktinos, to whom the Chapter traditions and the principles they fought for were so important. But Iktinos had quietly accepted the situation and boarded the ship to return to the *Brokenback*, and Sarpedon knew that in no small measure the Chaplain's example was what had convinced many of the Soul Drinkers to accept the deal Sarpedon had made.

'Lygris?' voxed Sarpedon.

'Ready to take off,' replied the Techmarine from the alien ship's cockpit, a cocoon of liquid metal like a quicksilver cyst overhead.

'It's good to hear your voice, Techmarine.'

'It is good to still serve, Sarpedon,' replied Lygris. 'We're ready to take off.'

'Then launch.'

The ship shot up into the sky, the force of the acceleration pressing down on Sarpedon. In a little over an hour they would be back on the *Brokenback*, and Sarpedon had no doubt about the battle he would have to fight there.

First, he would have to face Lord Mercaeno and the Howling Griffons. And then, if any of them survived, he would have to face justice at Eumenes's hands.

# CHAPTER FIFTEEN

'How does a Soul Drinker fight?'
'As cold as the void and as fast as the
bullets from his bolter.'

– Daenyathos, *Catechisms Martial*

FOR A FEW hours, it was quiet. By the standards of
the last few days a tense, prophetic silence held sway
over Vanqualis.

The greenskins built their ramshackle fleet on the
shore of Nevermourn, and the first casualties of ork
fire were inflicted on Herograve as orkish catapults
flung explosive shells across the sea. They were
barely a footnote to the scale of carnage that would
erupt as the greenskins made it into the teeming
cities.

On Herograve, far more were dying at the hands of Herograve's own citizens and the thinly stretched household troops of the Falken family. A massive riot was sparked by a child's claim to have seen the ghosts of Imperial saints admonishing the people for their sins. The Census-Takers' Offices were stormed by civilians who mistakenly believed that guns and supplies were being stored there. A whole district was set aflame and the household troops, busy keeping looters and rioters off the streets elsewhere in the city, had no choice but to let it burn.

Isolated knots of Penal Legion troopers and Vanqualian Warders struggled through the jungle, some of them fighting bands of orks left behind by the horde's advance. Others drowned in quicksand or were picked off by predators as they trudged exhausted towards the coast.

Tens of thousands died but again, it did not matter. The situation on Vanqualis had long since gone past the point where individual lives mattered. All the sides were waiting, either on the surface or in orbit, for the next stage – the final stage – to begin.

That moment came when ports opened up and down the hull of the *Cerulean Claw* like dozens of hungry mouths. They spat out a stream of silvery darts – assault boats, drill-prowed boarding craft, arrowing straight towards the hideous, misshapen form of the space hulk *Brokenback*.

'GREETINGS, SARPEDON,' SAID Eumenes, his voice loaded with superiority. 'It has been too long.'

Eumenes and his men stood ranked up on the arena flight deck. Eumenes had more than two hundred Soul Drinkers pledged to him, including most of the newer recruits and many older veterans, Apothecary Pallas among them. The Thunderhawks on the flight deck were in the midst of repairs, with Lygris's destructive handiwork being undone so Eumenes's Soul Drinkers would be as mobile and swift as before.

Sarpedon and his men were disembarking from the spherical craft onto the flight deck. Lygris clambered down from the craft's cockpit to join the battle-brothers assembling behind Sarpedon, opposite Eumenes and his men.

Sarpedon didn't answer Eumenes. There was nothing he could say. It was obvious who had the upper hand here.

'Your men will garrison the eastern craft,' said Eumenes, 'the engines and the archives. I shall command the west and the prow. That includes the bridge. Neither you nor your men shall be permitted anywhere near the bridge, and my men will shoot on sight if you try to take it. Understood?'

'Understood,' said Sarpedon. He could almost taste the anger within the Soul Drinkers behind him. For a moment he wondered if it would all end there, the Soul Drinkers falling upon one another until none of them survived. Then Chaplain Iktinos walked to Sarpedon's side and saluted Eumenes. Eumenes saluted back, and Sarpedon could feel his Soul Drinkers taking that step back.

'What then?' said Sarpedon. 'If the Howling Griffons are beaten. What becomes of us then?'

'I will have plenty of time to decide that,' said Eumenes. 'Those who accept my authority can stay. The others, I will rule on when we are safely out of this system.'

Captain Luko stepped forward. 'What happened, Eumenes, to turn you into this?'

Sarpedon put a hand on Luko's shoulder, suggesting he should hold back.

Eumenes smiled. 'I remember when you spoke to me in Gravenhold, captain. About how war was something you despised, how all your bravado was just a show and war was a suffering you underwent because you believed in what you were fighting for. Well, I believe, too, and so I fight. Nothing more. After all, I am a Space Marine. If we do not fight for what we believe, then what are we?'

Sarpedon heard the activation stud of Luko's lightning claws being flicked on, and the faint hum as the power field's coils warmed up. Luko tensed up, and Sarpedon realised he was about to charge.

'Sharks in the void!' came a voice over the vox-casters, transmitted from the bridge of the *Brokenback*. Sarpedon recognised it as belonging to Tydeus, one of Eumenes's scout squad. 'Thirty plus, heading straight for us!'

'How long?' voxed Eumenes.

'Twenty minutes, maybe less.'

'Then the time for talking has passed. Sarpedon, get these men to their posts. The rest of you, battle

stations. Bridge, get all defensive weapons online.
Make ready to repel boarders!'

FROM OUTSIDE THE *Brokenback* was utterly hideous.
Its very name came from the painfully twisted
nature of its appearance. Dozens of ships were
welded together into a single immense craft, in
some places grotesquely biological like bulging
organs of metal, in others desolate and ruined like
stripped-down skeletons of corroded metal. The
fused hulls were covered with rust and barnacle-like
encrustations, with wings and sensor clusters jutting
out at strange angles. Deep scars, as raw as fresh
wounds, bled shreds of wreckage, and the hulk's
dozens of engines sprayed glowing exhausts in every
direction. Weapon turrets swivelled like eyes in
sockets all over the hulk's surface.

Towards this monstrosity sped the shoal of Imperial attack boats, huge drills grinding beneath the
eagles emblazoned across their prows. More than
thirty of them skipped off the uppermost reaches of
Vanqualis's atmosphere, undersides glowing, as
ranging shots from the *Brokenback*'s weapons spat
between them.

The *Brokenback*'s main armaments, the torpedo
tubes and orbital barrage guns of its component
warships, had too long a minimum range to deal
with the relatively tiny attack craft, so power was
switched to the defensive turrets. More and more
opened up as the assault boats approached and suddenly a hail of fire was streaming from the hulk,

thick as rain. Forward shields flared and fell as
sprays of laser bolts hit the lead craft. The first one
to be destroyed exploded in a blossom of white
nuclear flame, the fire snuffed out a moment later in
the vacuum leaving a sad tangle of charred wreckage
and bodies.

Another fell, and another. But the surviving
assault boats streaked on through the fire, passing
into the shadow cast over them by the hulk drifting
in front of Obsidian's harsh diamond sun.

The first assault boat to hit the *Brokenback* was
destroyed, its prow-mounted drills skipping off the
encrusted surface and its hull smashing sideways
into the hulk. But the next found purchase, its drills
boring through the outermost skin of the hull,
engines flaring to push it deeper into the ship. Like
burrowing ticks the rest of the assault boats forced
their way into the hull. For the first time since Sarpedon and his Soul Drinkers had arrived to clear out
the xenos that infested it, the *Brokenback* was
invaded.

EUMENES LED THE way through the dark, ancient corridors and gun decks of the *Macharia Victrix*. The old
warship was one of the more recognisable parts of
the *Brokenback*, the symbols of Imperial allegiance
everywhere. Imperial eagles looked through the
darkness and prayers written on the bulkhead walls
by the crew could still be seen beneath centuries of
grime.

'Hecular, take our flank!' ordered Eumenes as his
Soul Drinkers reached the primary gun deck of the

*Victrix*. Enormous orbital guns, huge and rusted immobile like ancient monuments to war, loomed several storeys high in the semi-darkness. Hecular took his squad and hurried down the gun deck, into the shadows.

'Bridge,' voxed Eumenes. 'Do we have more information on where they're coming through?'

'None,' replied Tydeus from the bridge. 'Only that they're in that sector. Sensor coverage is stretched thin around there.'

'Damnation, Tydeus. What do I...' Eumenes paused. 'Quiet!' he hissed to the Soul Drinkers around him. They stopped stalking along the gun deck, guns up as they scanned the darkness.

Eumenes listened carefully. The sounds of the *Brokenback* were all around – the settling of ancient metal against metal, the thrumming of distant engines, and strange, haunted sounds that echoed around the most ancient parts of the hulk. But beneath it all, there was a faint buzzing, like the sound of an insect.

'Drills,' said Eumenes, indicating the direction of the huge orbital lasers mounted at the far end of the deck. 'That way.'

The Soul Drinkers moved in a disciplined firing line down the gun deck, bolters ready like a firing squad.

Eumenes aimed down the twin barrels of his artificer-crafted storm bolter. He had found the weapon in the Chapter's armoury deep inside the *Brokenback* – presumably it was being kept to reward a Soul Drinker for a promotion to captain or for some great deed of heroism, but Eumenes had taken it for his own now he was in charge of the Chapter. It was a relic of the old Chapter, the barrels nestling between the wings of a gilded eagle. Eumenes enjoyed the irony that he should be wielding an icon of the Imperium.

Eumenes and his Space Marines were level with the first of the truly vast laser cannons, the huge generator chamber slanting upwards towards the high ceiling of the gun deck. It had needed a hundred crewmen to fire it when the *Macharia Victrix* had first gone to war, turning the huge wheels to aim the laser or hosing down the generator chamber to keep it from glowing red-hot and melting with the heat of the las-pulse building within. Now it was silent and corroded, its parts cannibalised and used elsewhere in the *Brokenback*. A sad and crippled relic of a bygone age, just like the Imperium the *Victrix* had once served.

Eumenes could hear something else now. Voices, raised in anger and savage joy. Whooping and cheering. Singing, even. From what Eumenes had learned from the Chapter archives, it didn't sound like the Howling Griffons.

'Get to cover!' ordered Eumenes.

The Soul Drinkers took cover among the enormous machinery of the laser cannon. The voices got louder and an explosion wracked the shadows that clad the very end of the gun deck, throwing plates of corroded metal and a cloud of centuries-old dust into the air. The choking cloud swept over the Soul Drinkers and cut down visibility like a dense fog.

From the darkness, shapes were swarming. It was Eumenes who fired first, storm bolter rounds chattering into the shadows.

From the swirling dust emerged a mass of bodies. With a barrage of foul-mouthed battle cries, two thousand troopers of the 901st Penal Legion charged into Eumenes's Soul Drinkers.

IT WAS A feint. Lord Mercaeno had loaded the entire 901st Penal Legion into the assault boats on the *Cerulean Claw* and sent them to assault the far side of the space hulk. Taking them off Vanqualis in the *Claw*'s Thunderhawks and shuttles was risky enough, given that the jungles were still infested with bands of orks, but any risk was worth it to Mercaeno. The 901st gave the Howling Griffons something that Space Marines could not boast when fighting on their own – an expendable force, a buffer zone of bodies to keep the enemy occupied while the real threat bore down on them.

'They have definitely boarded?' said Mercaeno. He stood on the bridge of the *Cerulean Claw*, which was arranged around an altar to the Howling Griffons' dead. The altar stood on the top of a low-stepped pyramid with the captain's post at the top and the senior crew arranged at their helms around the lower tiers. The pyramid stood in a large circular room, the lower-ranking bridge crew occupying niches set into the walls.

'That is correct,' said Flag-Lieutenant Scarlphan. Scarlphan, being an unaugmented human, was utterly dwarfed by Lord Mercaeno. He had a long and distinguished face and grey hair, and had served the Chapter for a very long time – but it was obvious that no matter how devoted his service, he was always an inferior compared to the Space Marines themselves. 'Some of the boats were shot down but most achieved a breach.'

'Are we tracking any activity on the hulk?'

'The hulk's structure is too complex for detailed scanning. There is small arms fire near the boarding locations.'

'Then the enemy are engaged. The 901st may not last for long and the Soul Drinkers will soon realise the ruse. Bring the *Claw* into her final approach.'

'Yes, Lord Mercaeno,' said Scarlphan. 'Navigation! Ordnance! Final approach vectors, all shields to starboard!'

'Brothers,' voxed Mercaeno to the Howling Griffons squads now quietly observing the pre-battle rites with their officers, gathering on the embarkation deck for the final battle. 'Make ready your souls. The Black Chalice evaded us on Vanqualis and sought to flee from our justice. Now we will corner them like rats on their own space hulk and butcher them. Now they will learn how the Howling Griffons keep their word.'

THE CERULEAN CLAW seemed to move with slow majesty as it rose from the opaque storm clouds of Vanqualis's atmosphere, trailing coils of vapour as it slid into the vacuum. In truth it was travelling with all the speed the ship's crew dared squeeze from the sub-warp engines, but the ship's size made it seem to approach the mass of the *Brokenback* with almost apprehensive slowness.

The *Claw* had allowed its orbit to decay rapidly after releasing the 901st on their assault boats, and slipped into Vanqualis's upper atmosphere like a shark below the waters. Its journey through the storm clouds had been short but dangerous. Mercaeno had judged those risks to be justified if it meant a chance to close distance with the *Brokenback*. The *Cerulean Claw* emerged from Vanqualis's atmosphere directly below the *Brokenback*, twisting gracefully to bring the upper surface of the Howling Griffons ship's hull towards the lower surfaces of the hulk.

The *Brokenback*'s guns had been given enough time to fire on the assault boats in which the 901st had been sent hurtling towards the hulk. But with the distance now so narrow, few of them could draw a bead on the assault torpedoes and gunships that launched from the *Cerulean Claw*, bright in the livery of the Howling Griffons.

The turrets on the *Claw* and the *Brokenback* swapped fire and guns were stripped from the lower hull of the hulk. Mercaeno's orders had been to get the assault ships onto the hulk at all costs, even if that meant risking the *Cerulean Claw* itself. With short-range fire blazing from the *Claw*, the turrets had to split their fire between the huge shape of the *Claw* and the host of glittering assault craft streaking towards it.

The assault craft slammed home into the underside of the *Brokenback*. Las-cutters glittered, spilling showers of crimson energy as they sliced through the outer hull, engines powering them deeper like predators chasing their quarry down a burrow. The *Cerulean Claw* fell away, impacts thudding into its hull as it rolled back down towards the veil of Vanqualis's upper atmosphere. The *Claw*'s job was done now, for the Howling Griffons' strike force had made the perilous journey onto the *Brokenback*, and the second, decisive front had opened up in the final battle against the Black Chalice.

LYGRIS WAS THE only one who had any real understanding of the *Brokenback*'s layout, and even his knowledge was incomplete. What he knew about the space hulk was summarised in the sketchy dataslate map he was holding. Sarpedon looked over his shoulder at the diagrams of the *Brokenback*'s many component ships, contorted into the strange shapes that filled the hulk. The lights in the gilded, ornate orbital yacht were dim thanks to the power drain feeding the defensive weapons, so the lavish, faded surroundings were edged in the green of the dataslate's screen.

'They're hitting the underside of the ship,' said Lygris. 'That's what the bridge says. They've probably scanned us and want to head for the warp engines.'

'They're going to blow the whole damned hulk up,' said Sarpedon.

'It's what I'd do,' said Lygris. 'If I was in their position. Standard space hulk engagement tactic, straight out of the Codex Astartes.'

Sarpedon looked around the yacht. The yacht had originally been the lavish private vehicle of some extremely rich or powerful citizen, and its garish, tasteless designs contrasted with the air of decay that surrounded the old place. Sarpedon remembered standing with Lygris and watching the scuttling of the old Chapter's fleet through the observation dome in the ceiling. The yacht was sandwiched between several component ships of the *Brokenback* and formed a crossroads between many of them, making it a logical place to be stationed ready to react to the boarders. Sarpedon's Soul Drinkers were making the final checks of their battle-gear, and several of them were listening quietly to Chaplain Iktinos performing battle-rites.

'What news from Eumenes?' said Sarpedon.

'His men are engaged on the *Macharia Victrix*,' replied Lygris. 'The whole 901st are on board.'

'Divide us and destroy us,' said Sarpedon quietly. 'Mercaeno's sacrificed the 901st to make sure he only has to fight half of us at once. Codex Astartes again, but with some imagination behind it. Show me the archive.'

The image on the data-slate shifted. The Chapter archive was in Sarpedon's area of responsibility, within easy distance of a determined boarding force heading for the warp engines.

'They'll have to get through us to get to the engines,' said Lygris. 'But I don't know if we can hold the archive. Not if all of them attack.'

'That's not what I was thinking.'

'Do you have a plan, Sarpedon?'

'Perhaps. Captain Luko!'

Luko looked up from the blades of his lightning claws, which he had been cleaning in a meticulous pre-battle rite. 'Yes, commander? Have you griffon feathers for us to pluck?'

'In time, captain. Your squad will lead the defence of the archive. I want the Howling Griffons held there. While you hold, I will lead the rest of the force and fall back through the old medicae ship to here.' Sarpedon indicated a series of cavernous spaces inside the *Brokenback*, one of the last major features of the ship's twisted landscape before the huge cylindrical forms of the main warp generators.

'The *Herald of Desolation*?' asked Lygris.

'That's right. The Howling Griffons will have to head through it if they are to skirt past Captain Luko at the archives. There we will make our stand.'

'If I may be so bold, commander,' said Luko, 'the *Herald* is far from the most defensible part of the *Brokenback*.'

'It has its advantages, captain. Trust me on this. For your part, the Howling Griffons will send a force to oppose you so you cannot hit the flank of their main force. Fall back and give them the archive, but pin them down in there if you can.'

Luko smiled. He understood this part of Sarpedon's plan at least. 'With pleasure, commander.'

'Then gather your men and to your posts. Chaplain!'

Chaplain Iktinos looked up from his ministrations. 'Yes, commander?'

'I would have you and your flock at my side in the *Herald of Desolation*. We will need you there.'

'Of course. Come, Soul Drinkers. The Chapter needs you.'

Luko saluted as he led his smaller force out of the yacht towards the Chapter archive. The rest followed Sarpedon and Iktinos, their wargear and their souls prepared for the battle. Iktinos's flock followed him like students following a master, taking every cue from the Chaplain. Sarpedon was glad of it, because he was not certain that his authority alone could carry his Soul Drinkers onwards after the pact he had made with Eumenes.

The tension was so obvious and intense it was almost painful. The Soul Drinkers had faced the Howling Griffons once before and they knew the enemy force had superior numbers and equipment. But Sarpedon also knew that he had an ally on the *Brokenback* that Lord Mercaeno could not expect.

He had the *Herald of Desolation*.

'DIE!' YELLED EUMENES. 'Die, you vermin!' The storm bolter chattered in his hands and bodies came apart in front of him, chanting, screaming voices all around.

The gunfire echoed deafeningly around the gun deck of the *Macharia Victrix*, bouncing between the corroded metal walls until it became a wall of agonising noise. Eumenes's Soul Drinkers were in the cover of one of the orbital guns, crouching behind machinery or perched up on the body of the gun to get a good firing position. The Penal Legion

troopers surged forward again and again, led by
frenzied, blood-soaked killers who weren't even
afraid of the volleys of bolter fire thundering down
at them.

Another surge charged forward. Eumenes fired
and another trooper fell to his knees, chest blown
wide open, to be trampled beneath the feet of the
men behind him. A thousand of them had fallen
already, and the way back to the orbital laser was littered with torn bodies – but there were thousands
more, the entire 901st, all pouring down the gun
deck as if they were fighting for the chance to die
beneath the Soul Drinkers' guns. Hundreds of men
reached the foot of the gun where Eumenes was
positioned, suddenly within arm's reach of him.
Eumenes shot the first, blasting his head clean from
his shoulders. The chainblade in his other hand
stabbed forwards almost of its own accord and
skewered another man through the stomach, chewing through his guts and out through his spine. The
man's momentum pushed him forward up the
blade so he slumped, convulsing on Eumenes,
coughing up a gout of hot blood over his armour.
Eumenes flicked his wrist and threw the body off,
cracking the skull of another trooper with the heavy
body of his storm bolter.

The sound of preaching could just be heard
between the volleys of gunfire, a voice raised
confidently in spite of the gunfire. The words of the
Imperial Creed urged the troopers of the 901st to
give in to the will of the Emperor, to let the
Emperor's fury fill them, to cast aside the false

pleasures of long life and happiness in favour of the blessed joy of sacrifice. And incredibly, the men seemed to believe it. They wanted to die so desperately the Soul Drinkers just couldn't kill them quickly enough.

Up on the gun, fire bloomed. Eumenes turned in time to see Brother Scamander, the young Librarian who had once been part of Eumenes's own squad, raise his arms and bring down a rippling torrent of flame that rushed down the side of the gun like a waterfall of fire. The Penal Legion troopers clambering up towards him were smothered in flame. They tried to beat out the flames that suddenly covered them, falling to the deck where they were submerged in the roaring pool of fire forming there. Men ran, on fire, insane with pain – others writhed and screamed where they had fallen, and the smell of cooking flesh mingled with the gunsmoke and ancient dust that filled the air.

Bolter fire swept the 901st's troopers off the gun, throwing broken bodies back down onto the blood-slicked deck. They regrouped behind the next gun, dragging their wounded with them when they could but leaving many of their own mewling and dying on the floor. The preacher's voice was still strident, even now urging them on to attack again. Lasgun fire spat from their positions, ringing off the body of the gun as Eumenes's men snapped opportunistic shots at any head that showed above cover.

Sergeant Hecular slid in beside Eumenes. Eumenes looked up at the Soul Drinkers' positions – a handful of battle-brothers lay on the deck

behind the gun, dead or wounded by lucky shots
from the 901st.

'Give me an enemy who runs,' said Hecular. 'We
could shoot them in the back. But these maniacs
just keep charging forwards.'

'They have nothing to lose,' said Eumenes. 'Every
one of ours who dies, we lose someone we are hard
pressed to replace. But these men are worth nothing
and they know it. There are billions more out there
to replace them. They came here to die.'

'I don't know if we even have enough ammo left
to oblige them,' said Hecular.

'Tydeus!' voxed Eumenes to the bridge of the *Brokenback*. 'What's happening?'

'The Griffons are on board,' came the reply. 'They
brought their cruiser in close and boarded on the
lower surface, towards Sarpedon's positions.'

'Then the Griffons are heading for the engines,'
spat Eumenes. 'And we're here killing off these vermin.'

'What do we do, commander?' asked Hecular.

Eumenes risked a glance over the cover of the gun.
Crimson las-bolts spat back at him. 'I'll be damned
if I'll let a cheap trick like this get us. Tydeus, how
much control do we have over the *Macharia Victrix*?'

'Without Lygris here, not much,' came the reply.

Eumenes looked again towards the 901st's positions. They were massing for another surge. Every
time they charged, even if a hundred of them died
they won, because Eumenes's men were tied up
fighting them instead of getting to grips with the
Howling Griffons. One of the 901st was a great bull

of a man, a shaven-headed gore-soaked monster who bellowed foul-mouthed orders. The other troopers of the 901st followed his words as if they came from the mouth of the Emperor himself. The 901st wouldn't give up, and they wouldn't take any excuse to slack off attacking.

'Not good enough,' said Eumenes. 'Get more of the *Victrix*'s systems online and tell me when you have them.' He switched to his all-squads channel. 'Soul Drinkers!' he yelled. 'The next time they charge, we'll meet them in the middle! Every man to the fore! Scamander, you're our biggest gun. Give it everything you've got. The rest of you, knives out, chainblades ready. Charge on my order!'

The cry went up, and the 901st made ready to charge again.

'Damn you,' hissed Eumenes as the bellowing giant ordered his men forwards again and the preacher's voice rose once more. 'You vermin. You dogs. Now we're going to have to kill you all.'

LORD MERCAENO WAS the first of the Howling Griffons to set foot on the hulk. He ducked through the rent torn in the hull by the boarding drills of his assault torpedo and looked around him.

Great dark spaces loomed around him. The high ceiling and vastness of the place suggested it was a cargo bay, perhaps from a civilian ship. The hulk appeared to be made up of many ships welded together by the vagaries of the warp, and the Howling Griffons had reached an unpopulated and ill-defended part of it. Mercaeno waved forward his command squad who advanced out around him, bolters sweeping the vast shadows.

'No sign of them,' voxed Captain Darion, who had emerged through another rent in the wall. More tears were being opened up in the wall as the *Cerulean Claw* drew the hulk in closer and opened up more boarding passages through its outer hull.

'They are near,' said Mercaeno. 'The enemy is no fool. He will be waiting for us.' Mercaeno consulted the portable auspex scanner he held. It had been set to locate an area with great power and heat signatures, which the scanners on the *Claw* had determined were the main generators for the hulk's warp engines. The Howling Griffons had gained a foothold on the hulk a short distance from the generators, but the ground between them and the generators was sure to be held by the most resolute and foul of the Bearers of the Black Chalice.

'Darion, take our left flank. Borganor, our right. The First Company and I shall hold the centre. Howling Griffons, be wary of the enemy's tricks, and advance!'

Three companies of Howling Griffons emerged from the *Cerulean Claw*'s boarding units. They moved with the efficiency and confidence born of a lifetime spent studying the ways of the Codex Astartes and of their confidence in Lord Mercaeno's leadership. They moved through the cargo areas into the shattered, twisted interior of a half-crushed factory ship, through the ruined cells of a space-bound monastery and the silent autosurgeon theatres of a dust-choked medicae ship. Everywhere there were signs of the hulk's previous lives. Here was a soldier's last words, scratched into the wall above his bunk as a troop ship was dragged into the warp. There were a handful of time-darkened skeletons, huddled together in the store room adjoining a medical unit, deep scratches on their bones suggesting a violent death there as the warp consumed the medical ship and madness reigned.

The hulk was cursed. They all were. Lord Mercaeno directed his squads through the twisted remains of the hulk's ships, certain in the knowledge that such a place could only harbour the servants of the Enemy.

'There's something ahead,' voxed Captain Darion. 'Signs of occupation. Lights. They've cleared an area out. There's a temple or a vault up ahead.'

'I believe we have found them,' said Mercaeno. Ahead of him a series of arches looked onto the dim interior with gilded, sculpted walls and a great observation dome dominating the ceiling. It looked like the inside of a wealthy citizen's private craft. It had turned dark and mouldering with the years, but it had been cleared of wreckage and Mercaeno noticed vox-casters and a communicator handset on the wall, all more recently installed. The observation dome's controls had been replaced and it probably still functioned.

'They were here,' said Mercaeno. 'I can taste them. The psyker's eye never lies, they were here. We are close. Advance, at the double! Guns up! Fire at anything that moves! All of you!' Mercaeno's force axe was in his hands but his greatest weapon lay within

his head, honed and tested by the arduous training
of the Chapter librarium. Mercaeno's mind was
primed to attack, and it was the most powerful
weapon the Howling Griffons had.

'It's a library,' came a vox from Darion. 'An archive.
There are datastacks everywhere... Movement!
We've got contact!'

Mercaeno heard the first flashes of gunfire from
Darion's flank. 'Move up, Howling Griffons! Flank
the enemy and surround them!' As the centre of the
Howling Griffons' line moved rapidly through the
decayed finery of the yacht Darion's voice sounded
over the vox, ordering his men to advance. More
gunfire rattled, fiercer and fiercer.

The yacht's interior gave way to a vast space, brutal and imposing, a mighty span of blackened iron
spreading in a ribbed carapace overhead. The far
wall gave way to a series of tunnels, grim yawning
mouths brimming with darkness. Blocks of age-
stained iron stood along the centre of the huge
space, from which hung countless shackles and
spiked collars. Prisoners had been kept here before
they were filed off into the tunnels beyond, and the
place stank of old, old fear.

Mercaeno set foot on the floor of the prison, and
knew immediately what this place was, and why it
felt so fundamentally different, so utterly wrong.

The enemy was indeed no fool. He had chosen his
battleground well. But in doing so, he had chosen
the one place that Mercaeno himself would have
selected to fight on. It was the last mistake the Bearers of the Black Chalice would ever make.

'They're here!' yelled Sergeant Ossex of Mer-caeno's command squad. Instantly the line was in battle readiness, scattering for cover among the manacled blocks or fallen slabs of corroded iron, training their guns on the shadows clinging to the openings opposite.

Mercaeno saw them. The gloom made the dark purple of their armour look beetle-black, but there was no mistaking the armoured shapes of Space Marines or the chalice symbol on their shoulder pads.

'Charge!' yelled Mercaeno, holding his force axe high and letting his psychic force crackle through it so the blade glowed blue-white like a beacon for the Howling Griffons to follow. Mercaeno led the charge himself, and as the first gunfire stuttered across the great space of the prison the Howling Griffons charged with him.

'For Guilliman! For the Emperor!' Mercaeno was shouting, as he leapt over a fallen column and drove his axe down at the first of the enemy he saw.

# CHAPTER SIXTEEN

'What will our fight mean to the galaxy when we are dead?'

'It will mean that the galaxy continues, for without every drop of Astartes blood it would crumble and fall.'

– Daenyathos, *Catechisms Martial*

THE BLACK SHIPS were legends in the Imperium, dark tales told in hushed voices. Hardened, voidborn, lifelong spaceship crews, told tales in dockyard taverns about how they saw a Black Ship once, sliding from the warp as silent and menacing as a ghost. Starship crews had been telling stories since mankind first invented the warp engine, tall stories of the strange things that might be seen in the loneliest regions of space, and the Black Ships differed from those stories in only one way. The Black Ships were real.

The Imperium asked three duties of its worlds. Firstly, they were to pay the tithes due to the Imperium. Secondly, they must never harbour the enemies of the Imperium. And thirdly, and perhaps most critically, they were to control their psychic population and hand over all their psykers to the agents of the Imperium. This last duty was enforced by the Inquisition, whose operatives monitored the efforts of individual worlds in rounding up their psykers, and to the Adeptus Astra Telepathica, who tested psykers to see which ones were strong enough to be trained up for the use of the Imperium. The rest, those who were too weak to ever resist the perils of the warp – and a few who were too strong to control – were sent to Terra and never seen again.

It was the Black Ships that took them there. Of the countless millions of psykers who had been taken away on a Black Ship, only the slightest fraction ever survived, trained to survive the threat of possession and madness that was the bane of every psyker. The others were held in cells wound about with anti-psychic wards, their spacebound dungeons places of fear and pain. Many of them knew that once they reached their destination, they would never return. Others remained ignorant, often from feral worlds that had barely any understanding of the great empire in the sky, and were driven mad by the terror of the Black Ships. Many tried to mutiny, but the mind-wiped troops of the Inquisition and the psychic interrogators of the Adeptus Astra Telepathica rarely failed to put down such uprisings with brutality extreme even by the standards of the Imperium.

Knowledge of the existence of the Black Ships was proscribed among Imperial citizens. Only senior adepts knew anything but whispered legends about them, and then they rarely had any idea of what went on inside their sleek black hulls, or which planet the Black Ships would visit next. No one, not even the inquisitors who served grim tours of duty on the Black Ships, knew what happened to the hordes of psykers herded off when the ships reached Terra. All they knew was that there were thousands of Black Ships out there, making long, terrible voyages to Terra and back, bringing the vast harvest of psychic humans to the very heart of the Imperium. Each Black Ship was deeply scarred with thousands of years of psychic pain, the agony of fear and the torments of the endless testing. Many inmates died on board the Black Ships and never left, their souls imprinted on the scarred walls. Others poured their hatred and fear into the substance of the Black Ships so that part of them would always survive, echoing through the Black Ships forever.

Every now and again a Black Ship would fail to reach Terra, sometimes attacked by pirates ignorant of the superstitions surrounding the Black Ships, or waylaid by heathen aliens. Sometimes they were simply lost in the warp, even their elaborate wards failing to keep the predators of the warp from homing in on the precious psychic cargo. The psykers on board these ships suffered appalling fates, their very souls torn apart in a feeding frenzy as warp-spawned monsters devoured them alive. Such ships were the scenes of horror that a normal human mind could simply not comprehend.

And one of them was the *Herald of Desolation*.

SARPEDON FELT THAT pain seething along the sweating black steel floor, up the blade-like metal columns and across the dark ribcage of the corroded ceiling high overhead. The *Herald of Desolation* had once been filled with terrified men, women and children, psykers being delivered to Terra, and when the *Herald* had become lost in the warp the insane old ship had brimmed over with fear and pain.

The Howling Griffons were charging across the cloister, guns blazing. Sarpedon's men met them with a barrage of volley fire and men died in those few seconds, Howling Griffons blasted off their feet, Soul Drinkers falling to the first bursts of fire from their enemies. Sarpedon ducked down behind the fallen slab of ribbed ceiling he was using for cover and looked behind him through the high archway leading to the complex of cell blocks, a baffling dark maze that seemed to defy the rules of geometry and logic.

'Salk! Keep the flank! The rest swing back!' ordered Sarpedon. The firebase on his flank, commanded by Sergeant Salk, was rooted in a spill of fallen iron from the distant ceiling, the metal scarred with the imprints of the psychic wards that had collapsed when the *Herald* plunged helplessly into the warp.

Dozens of Soul Drinkers blazed away there as the rest formed up around Sarpedon, sweeping sheets of bolter fire ripping across the cloisters.

Sarpedon could see Lord Mercaeno. He recognised the shard of blue-white light, the blade of his force axe. A corona of power flickered around Mercaeno's head. For a moment Sarpedon could only focus on the leader of the Howling Griffons – finally they were face to face, and Sarpedon knew he would never have another chance to beat them. If this even counted as a chance at all.

The Howling Griffons were upon them, vaulting over the manacle blocks into the midst of the Soul Drinkers. Soul Drinkers lunged forwards to meet them. Sarpedon joined them and suddenly a Howling Griffon was upon him, an officer with a power sword flicking out as quick as a fencer's foil. Sarpedon recognised the marks of a company captain's rank, the kill-markings painted onto the gold and red plates of his armour.

The power sword knifed towards the throat of a Soul Drinker. It clanged off Sarpedon's force staff as he forced himself between the captain and his quarry.

The captain's helmet was off. He was a veteran, with more age inscribed on his leathery face than almost any Space Marine Sarpedon had ever seen and grizzled grey hair clinging to a skull scarred and rebuilt dozens of times.

The captain turned his blade around deftly, forcing Sarpedon's staff away from him as he kneed

Sarpedon in the midriff. Sarpedon was forced back onto his hind legs and had to scuttle backwards to keep his front legs being sliced off by the captain's reverse stroke.

'Captain Borganor, Tenth Company,' spat the Howling Griffon. 'A pleasure to kill you.'

Time stopped. Sarpedon forced his consciousness down into the very depths of his mind, the primordial place that boiled over with psychic power. There he could hear the screams of those who had died on the *Herald of Desolation*, and feel the horror in which they had drowned. Using the raw psychic power that Sarpedon possessed, he dragged those echoes, those blighted souls, bleeding from the very fabric of the *Herald*.

This was why Sarpedon had chosen the *Herald of Desolation* to make his stand. The psychic imprint left on it by the Black Ship's inmates amplified Sarpedon's own capabilities. Here, the Hell could rise higher than anywhere else.

The pale, screeching spectres of the dead rose in boiling thunderheads of shadow and pain. White faces loomed, their eyes black wailing pits. Borganor struck around him at the ghosts, face twisted in hatred and disgust. Sarpedon took the chance to dive inside Borganor's guard and drive his force staff forwards like a spear. It slammed into Borganor's chest, Sarpedon's psychic power erupting in a plume of black flame that threw Borganor off his feet. The Howling Griffon slammed into the manacle block behind him.

Borganor tried to raise his sword but Sarpedon stamped down on his wrist with a bionic front leg.

Sarpedon swung his staff like a hammer and smacked Borganor's head to one side, opening up a deep gash down the Howling Griffon's face. Spectral hands reached out of the stone towards Borganor, moaning figures looming from the shadows coagulating around Sarpedon.

Borganor yelled in blind fury and tore his hand free, slashing wildly at Sarpedon and the ghosts rising up around him. Sarpedon span on his back legs, drawing in Borganor and pulling him forwards off-balance. Sarpedon caught Borganor's arm as the Howling Griffon fell forward, twisted it around, and snapped the elbow back the wrong way.

Borganor fell to the ground, one arm hanging grotesquely twisted and useless. His power sword clattered to the floor. Sarpedon crouched low on his arachnoid legs, snatching up the sword with his free hand. As Borganor tried to pull himself to his feet Sarpedon cut his left leg out from under him, Borganor's own sword shearing through ceramite and bone. The severed leg clattered to the marble floor in a spray of dark blood.

Gunfire flared all around. More Howling Griffons were pressing forwards, clambering over the cover to get at the Soul Drinkers. Sarpedon stepped back from a spray of gunfire as Howling Griffons saw his mutations and marked him out as a priority target.

'Through the arches!' cried Sarpedon. 'Now! Salk, keep the flank, the rest of you through the arches! Back into the cell blocks!'

Through the smoke and gunfire, Sarpedon could see that Salk's firebase was holding, dozens of Soul

Drinkers maintaining their position grimly as the
rest gave ground under fire. The Howling Griffons
were advancing heedless of the bolter fire sweeping
over them. And there were many more of them than
the Soul Drinkers could handle here.

Two Howling Griffons were dragging the crippled Borganor back from the front line. 'Witch!'
yelled Borganor as the shadows of the Hell died
down around Sarpedon. 'Mutant! Kill me, break
me, but you can never corrupt this son of the
Emperor!'

Sarpedon couldn't deny any of that. He followed
the Soul Drinkers back from the cloisters, through
the bullet-scarred archways into the closer network
of cell blocks. Around him rose a dark, rust-red
room, its floor covered with manacles where
dozens of people could have been shackled, kneel-
ing, in front of the stern altar to the Emperor that
took up one wall. Here psykers had been forced to
kneel before their master, the God-Emperor who
alone knew what fate lay for them on Terra.

Their cries came unbidden to Sarpedon now,
begging for mercy from the warp, or for interven-
tion from an Emperor whose will it was that put
them on the Black Ship in the first place. A corridor lined with dismal one-man cells led off in one
direction, tasting of pain and anguish. Another
gallery that led off had iron frames equipped with
restraints along one wall. Madness echoed from
that place, minds gradually worn away and broken.

'Fall back and cover!' ordered Sarpedon. 'Draw
them in!'

Already the Howling Griffons were following them. There was less space to fight here, the architecture designed to segregate prisoners and confuse escapees with a labyrinth of rooms and corridors. A knot of Soul Drinkers defended the dark-stained mortuary slabs of an autopsy room against Howling Griffons trying to force their way in. An altar became an aiming rest for a Howling Griffon covering his brothers as they charged into a room like a meat locker, with rails and hooks along the ceiling to hang prisoners from. Around Sarpedon several Soul Drinkers were holding the prayer room from the Howling Griffons whose armoured forms could just be seen through the smoke at every doorway.

'Back!' called Sarpedon to the Soul Drinkers around him. He led the way down the restraint-frame gallery to a security point at the far end. The security point was a miniature fortification embedded in the asylum, the only entrances a single door and firing slit windows. Sarpedon had to fold his many legs under him as he entered the room, more Soul Drinkers following him. Slit windows looked out in many directions, each one covering the corridors and rooms beyond. Immediately there were bolters at the windows firing out, forming crossfires through which the Howling Griffons would have to advance.

This place needed no help from Sarpedon to conjure horrors in his mind. Torn souls writhed in pain. Manic prayers, no more than wordless cries of desperation, blared all around him. Through Sarpedon, through the Hell, the lost souls found form, clawing out through the walls and up through the floors. Tormented faces seemed to bulge from the walls. Cracks opened in the floor and blood welled up. Everywhere they came, the dead of the *Herald of Desolation*, finally giving form to their terror.

It was working. The Howling Griffons were broken up by the labyrinth within the *Herald*, and distracted by the horrors assailing them. This was the Soul Drinkers' home ground and they had trained with Sarpedon before so they would not be so gravely affected by the Hell.

The Soul Drinkers could hold out. The plan was working. Incredibly, impossibly, the Griffon's wings were clipped and the *Herald of Desolation* was drawing them into the Hell to be swallowed up by the blazing crossfires of the Soul Drinkers.

In a shower of sparks the door was torn off the security room. Bolters turned to fire on the intruder but the coruscating blade of a force axe hacked left and right and Soul Drinkers fell, bodies sundered, gore pumping through rents in their armour.

The weight of the attacker slammed into Sarpedon before he could bring his force staff up. The rockrete wall behind him gave way under the tremendous force and Sarpedon and the attacker fell through into the room beyond. Sarpedon hit the floor, rolled and just avoided the axe slicing down to cut him in two. He was on his feet, sight obscured by the dust from the collapsed wall.

He was in a large room that had been arrayed as a torture chamber. Rusted, sinister devices of metal frames and blades were arranged down the middle of the room like an assembly line, as if the people tormented in there had gone through an industrial process, cold-blooded and detached. The iron floor had grates to drain away the blood and there were gouge marks on the walls where fingers worn to the bone had clawed hopelessly for escape. The apparitions conjured by Sarpedon's powers were writhing amid the torture devices, broken limbs reaching from between bars, blades slick with black spectral blood.

'Interesting,' said Lord Mercaeno, walking through the ragged hole in the wall through which he had barged Sarpedon, 'that you still believe you can win.' Mercaeno hefted his force axe, ready to strike if Sarpedon gave him the slightest opportunity.

Sarpedon had his force staff held ready, flickers of psychic power sparking off the gilded eagle that formed the head. 'You don't know what we believe, Mercaeno,' he said. 'You don't even understand what you're fighting.'

'And nor shall I, Sarpedon,' said Mercaeno. 'Who would want to understand the corruption of the Black Chalice?'

'There is no Black Chalice.'

'So your ally Thaddeus told me. Just before I killed him.'

The two men circled carefully, looking for an opening to strike. With the screaming of the *Herald*'s ghosts and the torture equipment around them, they could have been fighting a duel in one of the hells of the Imperial Creed, damned men for whom fighting was the only thing left.

'And this,' Mercaeno said, waving a dismissive hand at the faces that writhed in the walls. 'These tricks. These illusions. Did you believe they would stop us, Sarpedon? We, for whom the Emperor's will is our own?'

'Mercaeno, this is your last chance,' said Sarpedon. 'There is no Black Chalice. It was a creation of someone from our Chapter, from the Soul Drinkers, a long time ago. We are renegades now but before that one of our number did something here, in the Obsidian system, which left behind the legend of the Black Chalice. We have both been brought here by lies.'

'The oath we swore is no lie. And your corruption is as plain as could be, mutant. You and your kind die here.'

'Then let it be finished.'

The battle around them was fierce, every asylum ward and charnel house being fought over furiously. But the real battle was in the torture chamber, as Sarpedon and Mercaeno charged for one another.

Sarpedon just had time to see Mercaeno's aegis circuit glowing brightly, light burning up through his armour. Sarpedon could feel Mercaeno's psychic power, hot and sharp like steel in his blood. Then blood roared in his ears and the torture chamber dissolved around him.

Soaring columns of skulls reached up towards a distant ceiling like a sky of bleeding rust. The smell of cooking flesh hung stifling in the air. Blood-filled channels cut into the black marble floor spelled out giant runes that refused to be read. Through pits in the floor could be seen thousands of daemons writhing obscenely far below. Their gibbering and screaming filled the air, a million flavours of madness saturating the place.

Sarpedon fought to stay conscious as his senses were assaulted. He couldn't even look at the abomination in the centre of the enormous temple that had roared obscenely into life around him. Many men would have been broken by insanity in a few moments but Sarpedon held on, desperately forcing the madness from his mind.

Sarpedon looked up. The *Herald of Desolation* was gone. He was standing in the Throne Temple of the daemon prince Periclitor.

MEN HAD DIED to drive the 901st back.

Eumenes understood something that only true leaders could accept. To gain power, he had to risk lives. If he wanted to command the Soul Drinkers, he had to pay for that power in the blood of those same Soul Drinkers. Most men could not accept risking those lives. But Eumenes was not most men.

It had taken volleys of bolter fire and furious counter-charges to force the 901st back along the gun deck of the *Macharia Victrix*. The 901st still outnumbered Eumenes's Soul Drinkers by perhaps ten to one, even with so many of them forming a long trail of blood and sundered bodies, and every backwards step the 901st took was accompanied by fierce hand-to-hand butchery and the endless exultations of the 901st's preacher.

Eumenes threw the nearest trooper away from him, opening up enough range to blast a great smouldering hole in the man's chest with his storm bolter. He ducked down into the shadow of the last gun on the deck. Ahead of him an archway rose, leading to the next section of the gun deck where titanic orbital lasers rose, huge as buildings in the dusty gloom.

The 901st were reeling, but in a few moments they would regroup around the ferocious bald-headed killer who led them, and they would surge forwards like a pack of starving dogs. They were taking cover behind the archway, keeping up smatterings of fire to keep the Soul Drinkers at bay. Many of them had expended the power packs of their lasguns and fought on with bayonets, and Eumenes could see that more than a few were sporting captured orkish guns, unsubtle massive-calibre weapons perfect for close quarters where accuracy counted for little.

'Scamander!' shouted Eumenes as more Soul Drinkers took cover around the gun. 'Now! Wall of fire, everything you have! Keep them back!'

'Yes, commander!' replied Scamander, standing up clear of the cover of the gun. Las-fire whipped around him, one or two shots pinging off his power armour. The gauntlets of Scamander's armour were scorched and glowing faintly from the fire he had poured through them, while his face and the armour around his neck glistened with fragments of ice and freezing vapour hissed from between his teeth. He drew the heat from inside him, and around him, spidery fingers of frost spiralling across the dull metal of the orbital gun. His hands glowed again, cherry-red then orange, the ceramite of his gauntlets' fingertips beginning to melt and scatter in glowing drops.

A wall of fire, like a shining curtain of flame, sheared up in front of the archway. A couple of Penal Legion troopers, those who hadn't got into the cover of the arch in time, were caught up in it, sent flaming towards the ceiling. One fell to the ground in front of the flames, legs ablaze, and writhed as the fire ate through the muscles of his legs and up into his abdomen.

'Tydeus!' voxed Eumenes through the gunfire. 'Blow the doors! Now!'

For an agonising moment, there was only Scamander's wall of fire holding the 901st back from attacking again. The preacher's voice was raised, crying out that this was the last chance for the Imperium's murderers and scum to claw back a worthwhile life from decades of sin, by dying for their God-Emperor.

Finally the moment was gone. Explosive bolts along the inside of the archway blew, spewing shards of corroded metal. From either side of the arch, twin blast doors were forced across the breadth of the gun deck, carving up centuries of corrosion from the floor, metal shrieking against metal as they cut the gun deck in two.

Scamander gasped, coughed out a spray of frozen saliva, and slumped back down behind the gun. Ice flaked off his armour as he landed, hissing against the white-hot tips of his gauntlets. The wall of fire flickered and died.

The 901st ran forwards. A few of them made it. The preacher was among them, holding his lasgun in the air like a holy icon in the midst of the crush. The doors closed and trapped many of the troopers between their metal jaws – the preacher was one of them, and with his last breaths he tried to spit out a prayer. But only blood came, spattering down his chin as the blast doors crushed him to death. Men died around him, others had limbs crushed and torn off. A few made it all the way through but bolter shots picked them off as they turned to pull their fellow troopers free. The doors boomed shut, shedding bisected bodies as their locking mechanisms slammed home.

The decks were vulnerable, being so close to the hull. The *Macharia Victrix* had been designed to minimise the risk posed by a breach of the hull along the gun decks, with blast doors primed to slam shut and isolate sections of the gun decks. The vacuum created by a hull breach would therefore be contained. Tydeus had managed to isolate the emergency controls on the *Victrix*, and slammed the doors in the face of the 901st.

The doors had thick, age-smoked windows set into them. Eumenes jogged up to them to see the 901st clamouring on the other side of the huge doors. Unshaven, hate-filled faces, mad with frustration.

Eumenes smiled. 'Purge it,' he voxed.

Along the outer hull of the *Macharia Victrix*, open to the merciless emptiness of space, purging valves opened. Another emergency system, in case of fire or contamination. Air boomed from the sealed section of the gun deck in which the 901st were now trapped. It shrieked out in a terrible gale, and even from the other side of the blast doors Eumenes could hear the men shouting out in fear and anger. He heard curses spat at him, even as troopers were lifted off their feet and thrown around the deck by the force of the decompression, battered against the huge dark shapes of the orbital lasers.

A few of the 901st were running for the far end of the gun deck, where their assault boats had bored into the hull. But many were dying even as Eumenes watched – blood running from their eyes, spitting ropes of gore from ruptured lungs, crawling along the deck or being dragged towards the purging vents.

'Tydeus?'

'Commander?'

'It's done. Stand by.'

Sergeant Hecular finished off the last of the 901st on the survivable side of the blast doors. The battle for the *Macharia Victrix*, the Howling Griffons' feint, was done with. 'What next, Eumenes?'

'Next,' replied Eumenes, 'we win my ship back.'

## CHAPTER SEVENTEEN

'How do we overcome an enemy who
fights with lies?'

'Confront him with the truth of
destruction.'

– Daenyathos, *Catechisms Martial*

THE THRONE TEMPLE of Periclitor was hewn from the
living rock of a mighty granite crag, the very peak of
a vast mountain that was all but drowned in a sea of
heaving daemonic flesh. As far as the horizon, the
valleys of the mountain range were brimming over
with daemons, cavorting and writhing obscenely.
Armies of daemons, creatures wrought from the very
stuff of Chaos, formed a pulsating layer of wanton
corruption that flooded the world like a foul ocean.

The Throne Temple formed a great cavity in the peak of the mountain, surrounded by a web of black granite spurs like the bars of an ornate cage. The throne itself was like a dark parody of the Golden Throne on which the Emperor himself was said to sit – it was hewn from an enormous skull, taken from some vast warp predator, the ivory of its gigantic teeth carved into intricate scenes of violence and debauchery, its eye sockets set with braziers that roared with a baleful multi-coloured fire.

On the throne sat Periclitor. Titanic, winged, with dark grey flesh that oozed droplets of raw power such was the warp-spawned sorcery that fuelled him. His face was a wet maw surrounded by mandibles, dozens of eyes blinking in his hideous head, each one plucked from the socket of a different foe. One of those eyes had once belonged to Chapter Master Orlando Furioso of the Howling Griffons, and all of them rolled in pain even as they gazed out on the temple and the daemonic landscape beyond with an expression that reeked of arrogance and malice.

Once, Periclitor had been a Space Marine of the accursed Traitor Legions, a mortal champion of the Dark Gods. But the blood he shed in the name of Chaos formed a great lake in the warp, and so pleased were the gods that they granted him daemonhood. An enormous cannon, an engorged and twisted bolt gun, was leaned against the throne – it dripped with tears from the captive daemons that screamed from inside its ammunition magazine.

One shoulder pad remained of Periclitor's power armour, fused with his skin, and it was impossible to tell to which of the Traitor Legions he had once belonged.

Periclitor's many eyes fell on Sarpedon. The Soul Drinker was dwarfed by the daemon prince, and it took all a Space Marine's resolve to keep him from fleeing, or collapsing on the floor in a mad stupor. Sarpedon held his ground, pushing himself up off the floor of the Throne Temple. He reminded himself that as appalling as Periclitor was, Sarpedon himself was hideous, and men had balked in horror just to see him.

'You…' said Sarpedon, barely able to hear his own voice over the gales of gibbering and screaming from the hordes of daemons writhing below the temple. 'You're not… whatever you are.'

Perliclitor's maw opened and the revolting, wet, guttural sound that issued had to be laughter. 'You look upon Periclitor,' it said with a voice like an earthquake. 'Beloved of the warp.'

'No,' said Sarpedon, holding his ground even as Periclitor began to rise from his terrible throne. 'You're not here. I'm not here, it's not real.'

'You, who are as corrupt as the black heart of the warp – you defy me?' Periclitor's voice was as angry as it was amused. 'You wretch! You filth! I am Periclitor, abomination of the Alcmena Nebula, slayer of Furioso! Kneel before your master! Bow down before the warp incarnate!' Periclitor was on his feet now, raw power raining down from his glowing dark skin.

'I defy the warp!' yelled Sarpedon. 'And its gods! They tried to make me one of their own and they failed! They tried to use me, and then to break me, and then to kill me, and my battle-brothers over-came them all!' He took a step forward, even though every nerve of his body was urging him to flee. 'You are no more Periclitor than I am the Black Chalice!'

Periclitor roared, a terrible sound like a black wind of knives. A sword of deepest black, like a shard of the night itself, coalesced in one of his claws and he brought it down towards Sarpedon. Sarpedon dived to one side. The sword carved down behind him into the marble of the temple. A chunk of marble was sliced free and tumbled down into the daemons writhing below.

The swords sliced low this time, like a scythe at waist height. Sarpedon brought up his force staff and met the liquid black blade, the force of it almost throwing him down off his feet. He dug his talons into the stone and held his ground, refusing to give anything, even a backwards step, to the titanic lie in front of him.

He looked up at Periclitor, into his hateful eyes. Periclitor returned his gaze, and in his stolen eyes the faintest trace of frustration flickered. Sarpedon should have been on his knees, begging to serve. But he was fighting back. For a fraction of a second, Per-iclitor did not know what to do.

Periclitor lashed out in rage. The back of his clawed hand caught Sarpedon in the chest with such force that Sarpedon was flung backwards. He turned head over talon as he flew through a gap in the outer wall of the Throne Temple and out of the mountain peak. The daemon world span around him – the sky with its spiral storms like wounds weeping blood and bile into the clouds, the distant mountains like great gore-encrusted fangs of stone.

Sarpedon plunged onto a sea of daemonic bodies. These were the pure spawn of the warp, hideous malformed creatures of mismatched limbs, mad rolling eyes and drooling mouths that cackled and screeched insanely. Sarpedon lashed about him frantically as the sickly light of the daemon world's sun was shut out by the bodies pressing around him. Daemons came apart under his talons and gauntleted fists but more pushed in, eager to devour this newcomer.

With a roar of defiance, Sarpedon planted his force staff into the rock below him and pushed all his psychic power into its nalwood shaft. With a final effort Sarpedon forced all his power out of the staff in a wave of crackling destruction.

Daemons disintegrated. Lopsided mouths lolled stupidly as the bodies around them were shredded to ash. Sarpedon slammed wave after wave of psychic anger into the sea of bodies around him, blasting a clearing amid the clawing limbs and writhing flesh.

Sarpedon gasped for breath, his psychic power momentarily spent. He was standing in a crater lined with charred, misshapen bodies on the black marble of the mountainside. Sarpedon pulled the staff out of the stone and looked back up at the temple.

'An enemy worthy of the Howling Griffons,' shouted Sarpedon indignantly, 'would never be defeated by a trick like this! You will have to do better than wearing the image of a daemon to have a Soul Drinker begging for mercy!'

Periclitor appeared above Sarpedon, clambering between the curving marble bars of his cage-like temple. The sword was gone and in his hand was an axe – Mercaeno's force axe, blue lightning spilling off its glowing blade.

'You,' said Sarpedon, 'are a lot like me, Mercaeno.'

'Wrong,' said Periclitor. Ghosted over him, much smaller but somehow more imposing, was the image of Lord Mercaeno. When Periclitor spoke, it was with Mercaeno's face. 'You are a crude and brutal weapon. Sarpedon. You are all power and no finesse. The horrors you daub are like the drawings of a child. I forge worlds.'

Sarpedon tried to gather his wits. There was no Periclitor, and there was no Throne Temple or sea of daemons. It was in his head. Lord Mercaeno had put it there. Mercaeno was telling the truth – he had a level of control over his psychic powers that Sarpedon couldn't approach, and he built this entire daemon world in Sarpedon's mind.

'You have failed then, Mercaeno,' said Sarpedon. 'You think I am a servant of the Dark Gods, so you placed this daemon-thing before me in the hope I would kneel before it!'

'All that proves is that your kind have enemies in the warp,' spat Mercaeno. His image was becoming strong and he jumped down from the temple, walking on the writhing daemons beneath him as if they were solid ground. Periclitor was fading out, becoming a pale ghost behind Mercaeno's image. 'For evil despises evil. And that is not why I brought you here. I came to this place, my battle-brothers and I, this nest of foulness in the Eye of Terror itself.' Mercaeno held up his axe. 'This is the weapon that took the head of the daemon Periclitor! For a day and a night we battled him on this peak until only I remained, and yet I did not falter! I fought on, and drew from the Emperor's own strength! And finally I took its head, and I held it up on this mountaintop and watched the daemons fleeing before me. A man would have died in moments. A Space Marine would have fallen to Periclitor. But not a Howling Griffon. I brought you here to show you why.'

Periclitor was gone and only Mercaeno remained. Sarpedon would rather have fought the daemon – he had vanquished daemons before, and he knew that no matter what they would try to deceive and destroy, for that was the reason the Chaos gods created them. But Mercaeno was a different type of enemy.

'Because you made a promise,' said Sarpedon.

Mercaeno smiled. 'Finally, you understand why you must die. We swore to avenge Chapter Master Orlando Furioso. We did not rest until it was done. Not even death could dissuade us. And we also made a promise to defend Vanqualis from the Black Chalice. We will fulfil that oath just as surely.' Mercaeno was close now, within a staff thrust or axe swing, looking down on Sarpedon from the raised bank of daemons – but the daemons weren't really there, and in truth it was the solid deck of the *Herald of Desolation* beneath Mercaeno's feet.

Mercaeno was at home in the *Herald of Desolation*, as Sarpedon was. The psychic force that drenched the place was something Mercaeno, too, could mould, forging it into whole worlds of illusion in the minds of his enemies. But Sarpedon was a psyker, too – Mercaeno himself had said just how powerful he was. Sarpedon didn't have any finesse to his power, but he didn't need it, not now that Mercaeno had done all the hard work of creating a world around them.

'Your fate is sealed, Sarpedon,' Mercaeno was saying. 'Nothing you can do will change that. Fight on if you must.'

'My pleasure,' said Sarpedon, as his mind took hold of the hellish landscape around him and warped it horribly.

The sky fell dark. The daemons melted away and a distant ocean lashed against knife-like rocks of a savage shore. Mercaeno lost his grip on his world and suddenly it was Sarpedon's.

Staff and axe clashed in the darkness, and this time Sarpedon wouldn't be fooled.


IT SEEMED A lifetime ago that the Soul Drinkers had come to the unknown world, a planet of foul, polluted oceans and swarms of pox-ridden insects, to battle the plague daemon Ve'Meth. Dark thunderheads of swarming flies darkened the skies and the churning oceans spat up sea monsters and subterranean horrors. The inhabitants of its scattered, barren islands were cave-dwelling creatures devolved from cannibalistic humans.

On a mighty fortress that rose from an archipelago of black coral, Ve'Meth ruled. Ve'Meth was a disease, a pure vessel of the Plague God's will, and his physical form was a host of diseased bodies that spoke with one voice. Space Marines of the Traitor Legions defended his fortress, bloated and corrupted creatures dedicated to the Plague God Nurgle. Cloven-hoofed, goat-headed men formed his foot soldiers, led by champions whose bodies glowed with the glorious corruptions of Nurgle.

And yet Sarpedon had led the Soul Drinkers here, and the Soul Drinkers had destroyed Ve'Meth.

Mercaeno stumbled in the surf, forced to throw the haft of his axe out to defend from Sarpedon's force staff. He glanced around him, trying to get a sense of his surroundings while Sarpedon bore down on him. He was on a beach, heavy waves thick with filth and scum washing over him, the great fortress overlooking the beach like an enormous pustule of stone. Baleful clouds boiled overhead, thick and foul, and all around was the overpowering stench of decay.

Mercaeno lashed out, battering back Sarpedon's attack and wading through the surf onto the beach itself. He was well beyond fear, but he was still rattled, his psychic power turned against him.

'More sorcery!' he spat.

'You are not the only one,' said Sarpedon, 'who has fought the slaves of the Dark Gods. I slew a daemon here, my battle-brothers and I. We were manipulated and lied to, but all the servants of the warp got out of us was death.' Sarpedon scuttled up out of the surf, psychic power crackling off his staff with the effort of maintaining the illusion of the unknown world. 'I left a part of myself behind on this beach,' said Sarpedon. 'A leg, to be precise.'

Mercaeno sneered. 'You had plenty more, mutant.'

'So I told the Chaos champion who took it,' replied Sarpedon swiftly. 'Before I cut him to pieces where you stand now.'

Mercaeno roared and lunged. Sarpedon caught Mercaeno's axe on his force staff and span, lashing out with the legs down his right side. Mercaeno was swept off his feet, hitting the black sand heavily. Sarpedon cracked the butt of his staff against Mercaeno's head and the Howling Griffon reeled, falling backwards as he tried to get back to his feet. Sarpedon reared up over him but instead of rolling away Mercaeno planted a hand on the ground and kicked up into Sarpedon's stomach, throwing Sarpedon onto his back legs.

Mercaeno was back on his feet, blood running down his face. 'The Emperor knows the truth,' he said grimly. 'And so do I. Do you think you can make me down arms and accept that you are not corrupt?'

'I can't change your mind, Mercaeno. But I can show you the truth, even if you won't believe it.'

'The truth,' said Mercaeno, 'is that to the spawn of the warp will come nothing but death! So spake Roboute Guilliman! So spake the Emperor! And so it shall be!'

Mercaeno charged, a flurry of blows striking so rapidly it was hard to believe he wielded a weapon as huge and murderous as his force axe. Sarpedon was at his limit, bringing the haft of his force staff up like a quarterstaff to defend himself. Bright psychic sparks flashed as each man was forced back in turn, one prevailing over the other before a skilful feint or a blow of raw strength put the other on top. As they fought more memories came unbidden from Sarpedon, monstrous beastmen marching slowly down from the fortress, a hideous silent army come to watch the spectacle of the two Librarians fighting to the death. Torrents of rot flowed down the fortress, waterfalls of putrescence in which danced foul, necrotic daemons of the Plague God. The champion that Sarpedon had killed on the shore was among them, standing silently among the ranks of beastmen watching the battle.

Sarpedon slipped and was rewarded with a deep gouge into one shoulder pad, cutting down to blood and muscle. Mercaeno committed himself to a wild swing, which let Sarpedon crack the eagle-tipped head of the force staff into his face, ripping up a deep slash from temple to jaw.

Even as they two men fought, another battle was taking place. Each one tried to wrest away control of the illusory world and the shore of Ve'Meth's fortress shimmered and warped as they tried to turn it into something else.

With a roar of triumph Sarpedon wrenched control away, psychic power burning in blue flames from his eyes, and suddenly the befouled sky was replaced with the high vault of the Temple of Dorn on the Soul Drinkers' old flagship, the *Glory*. An enormous stained-glass window of Rogal Dorn looked down on them and incense was thick in the air, like a stifling fog. The pews and columns of the temple were smashed, because this was where Sarpedon had fought Chapter Master Gorgoleon for control of the Soul Drinkers. Mercaeno reacted to the shift a moment too late and Sarpedon charged him, slamming a shoulder into Mercaeno's chest and barging him up the steps to the altar below the window. Mercaeno's body smashed into the altar and it splintered behind him, spilling candles and devotional texts everywhere.

Mercaeno grabbed Sarpedon by the collar and waist joint of his armour and lifted the Soul Drinker off him, hauling him into the air and swinging his body around to smash Sarpedon into the ornate pillar beside the altar. The pillar shattered under the force of the impact and collapsed, twenty metres of carved stone toppling like a felled tree onto Sarpedon.

Sarpedon's breath was knocked out of him and suddenly the chapel was gone. He was in a trench now, artillery fire booming all around him, gunfire chattering from all directions. It was night, and the darkness was torn by explosions that sent flashes like lightning bolts high into the sky. The weight on him was not a pillar from the Temple of Dorn, but a heap of bodies – Imperial Guardsmen, torn apart by an artillery blast that had ripped a crater out of the trench behind him. Their blood mingled with the reddish earth, their gore-spattered faces locked in expressions of surprise and panic.

Sarpedon threw the weight off him. He didn't know where he was – this was a world from Mercaeno's memory. He ducked down instinctively as gunfire raked above his head. The trench had been dug for Imperial Guardsmen who were all a good head and shoulders shorter than a Space Marine, and Sarpedon had to crouch down on his haunches to keep his head out of the gunfire.

An engine rumbled and a Rhino APC drove over the trench a short way in front of Sarpedon, las-fire and bullets ringing off its hull. It was painted in the livery of the Howling Griffons, the griffon rampant symbol etched in deep blue over red and gold quarters.

The rear hatch of the Rhino swung down and Lord Mercaeno stepped out, heedless of the gunfire raking all around him. 'Scelus,' he said. 'On the edge of the Eye of Terror. The forces of Chaos spewing from the Eye won it from the Imperium. The Howling Griffons won it back.'

Sarpedon tried to clamber from the trench but a deafening explosion and hot violent darkness thudded into him. The artillery shell blew Sarpedon clean off his feet and for a moment he was blind and deaf, spitting out the hot red earth, unable to tell which way was up.

It was instinct that forced Sarpedon to keep his guard up. He rolled onto his back, staff braced across his chest, as Mercaeno's axe fell down towards him in an executioner's stroke. The axe cracked into the haft of the staff and Sarpedon pushed all his strength into keeping the thrumming, hot blade away from his face. Scalding rivulets of power dripped off the blade onto Sarpedon's face and the energy flaring off the axe blade was reflected in Mercaeno's eyes, flickering with blue-white flame.

The smoke and dirt rolled away on the hot wind. Sarpedon could see around him now. The trench wound a jagged path through a blasted, barren battlefield. Once it had been a forest but the ground had been chewed up and levelled so much that only isolated clumps of shattered tree stumps remained.

From one horizon rolled an army, a million men, with tanks and Sentinel scout walkers, advancing through withering fire down the slopes of tortured red earth. The Howling Griffons formed the cutting edge, a hard point of power armoured warriors in the heart of the line. Artillery fire thundered everywhere, blowing men and tanks into the air. The opposite side of the battlefield was a vicious snarl of fortifications. Ugly lumpy rockcrete buildings, once bunkers for Imperial troops, were daubed with runes and symbols born of the warp. Tattered banners carried the emblems of the Dark Gods. Bodies were displayed as proudly as heraldry, hands and heads, whole gutted corpses, splayed above firing slits in the bunkers or staked out like scarecrows along the front.

Unceasing gunfire spat from the bunkers, and artillery pieces behind the lines thundered. Chanting carried on the hot wind, the praises of the Chaos

gods, the voices of hundreds of thousands of corrupted madmen.

The axe blade was forced closer to Sarpedon's face.
'We won,' snarled Mercaeno. 'We stormed this place
and killed them all. That is what you are fighting.
That is why you will die, too.'

Mercaeno was strong, but so was Sarpedon. With
agonising slowness Sarpedon forced the axe away
from him, teeth gritted, every muscle drum-tight.

The battlefield of Scelus shimmered as Mercaeno
fought Sarpedon with such an effort that his hold
on the illusory world around him slipped. Sarpedon
took advantage and wrapped his mind around the
world, tearing control of it away from Mercaeno
again. Now they were on the hull of the *Brokenback*,
the smoke-laden sky gone to be replaced with endless black space scattered with alien stars. In the
vacuum, edged by the hard light of the stars, the two
Space Marines wrestled. This was where Sarpedon
had faced the daemon Abraxes, the servant of the
Change God, who had manipulated the Soul
Drinkers to the edge of damnation, and been slain
for its troubles.

Battlefields came and went, drawn from the
memories of both men. An alien world choked in
toxic fog and disease, with immense Titan war
machines striding through the darkness. The
massive battlements of Quixian Obscura, with Soul
Drinkers battling the alien eldar high above the
ground. An ocean world lashed by nuclear storms,
with fleets of ships clashing beneath a sky the
colour of blood. Stratix Luminae, where hordes of

374                    *Ben Counter*

living dead shambled across the frozen tundra and
spaceship wreckage rained from the sky. A
multitude of hells, visions of battle from two
lifetimes of war, flashing past as each man tried to
get the upper hand.

Sarpedon drew deep from the well of psychic
power inside him, but he was almost exhausted.
Mercaeno's strength matched his own and he knew
he had only one chance to turn the tide. He dug his
talons into the floor and shifted his body to one
side as he let go of his force staff with one hand.
Mercaeno's blade hammered down a few centimetres from his face, buried deep in the ground – the
ancient stone of a tomb-world where the Howling
Griffons must have fought long ago, haunted by
skeletal metallic creatures as old as the stars. Titanic
ruins rose all around, but Sarpedon ignored his surroundings as he scrabbled to get back on his feet.

Mercaeno had buried the axe in the ground with
such force that he had to pause to pull it out. This
was the opening Sarpedon needed.

He held his force staff in both hands, and twisted.
The nalwood was iron-hard, carved and treated to
resist the sternest punishment. But Sarpedon's
strength was too much for it. With a thunderclap,
the staff broke in two.

All Sarpedon's remaining psychic force flooded
out. Like an image painted on glass, the ruins from
Mercaeno's memory shattered and fell in great
glowing shards. Time seemed to slow down as the
senses of both men were assaulted by the collapse of
the reality around them. Mercaeno reeled,

bellowing in anger and pain as his mind was filled with feedback. Sarpedon stumbled, psychic power flooding out of him undammed.

They were in the domed room of the *Herald of Desolation*, with the ankle-deep water and the curved ceiling covered in carved statues, where Sarpedon had duelled Eumenes before the rebellion. Gunfire thudded dimly nearby as the Howling Griffons and Soul Drinkers continued to battle through the *Herald*'s cell blocks and galleries, but that fighting felt very far away. A hole in the wall and several shattered statues in the water showed where Sarpedon and Mercaeno had fought their way in, pinkish puddles of blood in the water a testament to the fury of their battle. Now for a few seconds they were quiet, the only sound the distant gunfire and the heavy breathing as they tried to pull some strength back into their limbs. The spectres of the Hell were gone from the *Herald* now, because Sarpedon had no energy left to conjure them.

Blood still ran down Mercaeno's face and his breastplate had deep rents torn into it by Sarpedon's talons. Sarpedon's legs bled, the exoskeleton battered and cracked, and blood seeped from one shoulder pad that was cut almost in two.

Mercaeno loped towards Sarpedon, force axe in hand – he looked ready to drop, bleeding and exhausted, animated only by the hatred in his eyes. Sarpedon dropped the broken halves of his force staff and grabbed Mercaeno's axe arm as the Howling Griffon charged onto him with the last of his strength. Sarpedon fell back against the torso of a statue fallen from above, wrestling with Mercaeno now, the men's movements sluggish and heavy. Sarpedon forced Mercaeno's axe away but Mercaeno kneed him hard enough in the midriff to dent the ceramite and knock the air out of his lungs. Sarpedon smashed the heel of his hand into Mercaeno's jaw and threw Mercaeno off him. Mercaeno dropped the axe and reached out to grab Sarpedon's throat, teeth bared and bestial. Sarpedon fended him off as best he could, Mercaeno ducking in and head- butting him hard enough to throw Sarpedon onto his back legs.

The two men traded blows like brawlers, their training and warrior instincts overcome by the exhaustion of their psychic combat. Blood stained the knuckles of their gauntlets and ran down their faces. Sarpedon reared up for one desperate lunge, stabbing his front talons down at Mercaeno, but Mercaeno grabbed a leg and twisted, throwing Sarpedon down onto his back. Mercaeno hauled Sarpedon to his feet and slammed a fist into the side of his head over and over again.

Sarpedon's head rang with a wordless white noise and his vision greyed out, the sinister contorted statues on the domed ceiling seeming to congeal into a landscape of writhing daemons. Sarpedon could hear the voice of the daemon Abraxes, promising him limitless power if he gave his Chapter over to the Dark Gods. He heard the words of the Inquisitorial pronouncement that had excommunicated the Soul Drinkers and damned them in the eyes of the Emperor's servants. He heard laughter, too, laughter from the warp.

Sarpedon lashed out and an elbow caught Mercaeno in the throat. Mercaeno stumbled back and Sarpedon dived forward, hoping to smother him to the ground and punch him until the Howling Griffon stopped moving.

With a roar, Mercaeno slammed an uppercut up into Sarpedon's jaw, Sarpedon's own weight added to Mercaeno's strength. Sarpedon's head snapped back and he spat a long plume of blood from a split lip. His many legs buckled underneath him and he slid into the shallow water, mouth lolling.

Redness tinged everything. The dome seemed as far away as the stars in the void, as did the sound of Mercaeno's footsteps splashing in the water as the Howling Griffon stepped over him.

Sarpedon's head lolled to one side. He couldn't move. Part of him felt almost relieved as he saw Mercaeno stoop painfully to pick up his force axe. Mercaeno's power was spent, too, so the blade no longer glowed with channelled psychic force – but an axe was an axe, and the edge of the blade was so sharp it shone in the pale light reflected by the blood-filmed water.

Mercaeno stood over Sarpedon. He raised the axe like an executioner, eyes fixed on Sarpedon as he wound up to cut off Sarpedon's head and destroy, in his mind, the leader of the Bearers of the Black Chalice.

A blade of purest blackness flickered behind Mercaeno. Recognition flared dimly in Sarpedon's mind.

Mercaeno sensed it, too, and tried to turn around. But he was completely spent, his reactions slow, his limbs too leaden to bring himself round to face the intruder who had crept up behind him.

Eumenes stood behind Lord Mercaeno. In his hands was the Soulspear, the most revered relic of the Chapter, a weapon with twin blades of glowing black vortex. In Eumenes's hands, and compared to Mercaeno's exhausted movements, it flicked as fast as a snake's tongue as Eumenes lunged forwards.

The blade of the Soulspear passed through the back of Mercaeno's head and came out through his mouth. Flesh and blood hissed as the vortex field annihilated the matter it touched. Sarpedon looked up, almost mesmerised, as Eumenes slowly brought the blade up, bit by bit bisecting Lord Mercaeno's head.

Sarpedon searched inside himself for some relief. Mercaeno was dead, the Howling Griffons were leaderless, and Sarpedon was alive. But he could find none. There was no triumph, no joy, nothing good or victorious in the way Eumenes smirked as the life shuddered out of Lord Mercaeno.

There was only horror, a cold horror that filled Sarpedon as he realised that somehow, with Mercaeno dead and his own battle over, he was watching the death of his Chapter.

The blade came free. For a few seconds Mercaeno stood, his eyes rolled back and blank. He took a step back, and the axe dropped from his hand. Blood sprayed suddenly from the dark red line that cut his face in two, and he toppled backwards to land with a crash in the water at Eumenes's feet.

Sarpedon pushed himself onto his front and brought his legs back beneath him. He didn't know if he had the energy left to stand. Eumenes stood watching him, the Soulspear at his side. Eumenes thumbed the gene-locked activation stud on the haft and the twin blades retracted, leaving the short cylinder of the haft, which Eumenes holstered like a pistol at his hip.

'Eumenes,' said Sarpedon. He looked down at Mercaeno's body. His blood felt like it had frozen, but some old proud instinct forbade him from showing the dismay that had swallowed him up. 'Did… is Luko still alive? Have we held the Howling Griffons at the archive?'

'As far as I know,' said Eumenes.

'Then it's over.'

'Maybe. If you were right.'

'I was,' said Sarpedon.

'He would have killed you, Sarpedon.'

'I know.'

'Then you do not deny it?'

'No. He had beaten me. I cannot deny that. You saw it.'

Eumenes smiled. 'Then I saved your life. I am your greatest enemy, Sarpedon. I brought you low when all the gods of the warp couldn't do it. And yet I saved you. You live on because of me. Is that not right?'

Sarpedon looked up at him. Through the blood in his eyes, he could see the look of shameless triumph on Eumenes's face. 'Yes,' he said.

'Yes, *my lord*,' said Eumenes.

# CHAPTER EIGHTEEN

'What do our enemies see when they
look upon the Astartes?'

'They see their gods and the heroes of
their corrupted myths, gathered before
them and heralding the end of their
world.'

– Daenyathos, *Catechisms Martial*

THE BROKENBACK'S ARCHIVE was wreathed in a fog of
gunsmoke. Between the bookcases and stacks of
data medium lay the battered bodies of Howling
Griffons and Soul Drinkers who had fallen during
the struggle over the archive, most of them struck
down by bolter fire, a few bearing the hideous
wounds of chainblades and combat knives.

The guns were silent now. The order to cease fire had been called out by Captain Luko of the Soul Drinkers, and mirrored by Captain Darion of the Howling Griffons.

Darion stepped out into the open first. His gun was in his hand but it was lowered. 'Is this true?' he asked, the question called out to the Soul Drinkers in position at the opposite end of the archive.

Captain Luko stepped out from behind the pillar he had been using for shelter. His armour was pocked with smouldering scars where bolter rounds had hit home. 'Every word,' he said.

Darion looked behind him. Amid the bodies and wreckage was a Howling Griffons Techmarine, dat-aprobes hooked into one of the black crystal stacks. The Techmarine's eyes flickered as he rapidly scanned the information held in the black crystal data medium.

'Your leader is dead,' said Luko. 'Lord Mercaeno has fallen. Does that leave you in charge?'

'Captain Borganor is wounded,' said Darion. 'So yes.'

'Then it's your decision. You know there is no Black Chalice. Do you fight on?'

'You are still renegades,' said Darion. 'Even assuming the information in this archive is correct. You might not be the Bearers of the Black Chalice but you turned your back on the Imperium. The Inquisition declared you excommunicate traitoris.'

'Maybe so, captain,' replied Luko. 'But there never was a Black Chalice, so the oath to destroy it is void. There is one oath that is not yet fulfilled, and unless I am mistaken about your Chapter, you all take that kind of thing very seriously.'

'Vanqualis,' said Darion.

'Vanqualis and the greenskins. Last time I checked they were about to land on Herograve and kill the people you swore to defend. I'd say that leaves you with a choice to make, captain.'

Darion glanced back at the Techmarine scanning the history of the Soul Drinkers. He only knew sketchy details about what had happened to the Soul Drinkers, but it was enough to suggest that whatever had happened to them the Black Chalice was not involved.

'If this is over, your guns fall silent too.'

'We won't shoot you in the back. We're not so far gone we don't honour a truce.'

'This is no truce,' said Darion bitterly. 'We will find you, renegade. We will bring you to justice.'

'You'll have to get in line,' replied Luko.

Darion cast a final look at Luko, then spoke into his vox-unit. 'Howling Griffons, this is Captain Darion. Lord Mercaeno is lost. Fall back to the boarding units. Repeat, disengage and fall back, all units.'

The Howling Griffons broke cover warily, covering their retreat with their bolt guns as they retreated from the archive back in the direction of the *Cerulean Claw*'s assault torpedoes. Captain Luko watched them go, holding out a hand towards the Soul Drinkers to indicate they should hold their fire.

Slowly, the gunfire from the *Herald of Desolation* began to fall quiet.

FAR BELOW, ON Vanqualis, thousands upon thousands of greenskins made up the first wave crashing onto the shore of Herograve. There were so many of them that the defenders didn't believe it, and some of them went into fits of fear and madness as they realised for the first time just what kind of threat was setting foot on the soil of their homeland.

The shore was barren and rocky, ill-suited for construction. The coastal settlements, less dense than the multi-layered hive cities further inland, formed a wall of tenement blocks and factorium warehouses to be held by the defenders.

Crouched in tenement windows or among the tarnished metal hulks of industrial equipment, the defenders consisted of House Falken household troops scrounged from the small garrisons trying to keep the peace in Herograve's cities, along with hundreds of militia taken from the coastal districts themselves, armed with anything from ex-Warder autoguns to hunting rifles. They were defending their homeland and in many cases settlements where their families and loved ones lived. Some of them carried weapons and wore body armour that their fathers had handed to them, with a stern warning that one day Vanqualis would have to be defended from enemies fated to return there. Thousands of men and women formed the line that had to hold before the greenskins.

Lord Sovelin Falken had gone to the coast to do his part and earn back some of the honour he had lost in failing to die like a man at Palatium. But he was the only member of House Falken there and he found himself in command without intending anything of the sort. Militia leaders, hard-bitten old men who had often served in the Warders before retirement, saluted him like a general and made their fatalistic reports. The household troops, almost unable to decide anything without noble consent, flocked to Sovelin to ask about the minutiae of their deployment.

Sovelin had done everything he could. He set up his command post in a waste treatment plant, a hideous lump of corroded rockcrete and steel that still pumped industrial effluent out into the sea, but which formed a bastion anchoring the coastal line. He placed the most competent-sounding militia leaders on the ends of the line, and as they left for their posts they had commented about how they had once served under a grandfather or great-uncle of Sovelin's, and how it was an honour to take an order from a Falken once more.

The household troops stayed close, guarding the plant and the areas around it, not because they were necessarily better troops but because Falken didn't want to leave them alone, cut off from the nobles they were sworn to serve, surrounded by militiamen from cities they had only recently been subjugating with brutality.

Lord Sovelin Falken begged the Emperor to show him something else he should do, some detail of the defence that he could see to, so that he could do his duty properly. But the Emperor did not answer, and Sovelin realised he was out of time when the first ork ships appeared among the churning waves. There were hundreds of craft, barely seaworthy, built from the trees of Nevermourn's jungles and crammed with uncountable numbers of greenskins. Their chanting mixed with the crashing of the waves on the rocks into a relentless rhythm of bloodlust and hate. Defenders quailed as they heard it, like a black wind whipping around the battlefield, like a song bellowed down from the orkish gods themselves. For a terrible age, perhaps an hour that felt like days, Sovelin listened to the war-chants getting louder and closer, and he wondered if he would simply turn tail and run at the first sight of a greenskin's hateful, bestial face.

The first ship, an enormous splintering hulk, rode up high on the crest of a wave and crashed onto the cruel rocks before the line. Its hull broke apart, sodden wood tearing with the impact, and the ship disgorged ten thousand screaming greenskin slaves onto the shore.

THE BATTLE WAS already well under way when the warlord set foot on the shore of Herograve. The holy shore that promised so much slaughter, the object of his destructive devotion for so long. Once, this land had belonged to the orks, just like Nevermourn – and like Nevermourn, it now belonged to the orks once more.

Ahead of him the pink blood-laden surf threw a tide of bodies onto the rocks. Slave-creatures littered the shoreline, heaped up where they had fallen in their hundreds. Gunfire streaked from buildings that stood over the shore, tiny dark human figures crouched in windows or on rooftops. The blocky, squat shape of the treatment plant rose in the centre of the battlefield, hundreds of slaves clamouring at its blood-streaked walls. The slave-creatures had served their purpose. They had absorbed the ammunition from the defenders' guns and given them something to shoot at so the real meat of the horde could make it ashore and begin the battle for real.

Thousands upon thousands of orks were storming ashore, charging past the warlord, blades high and guns spraying bullets at the shoreline more in celebration than to kill. They bayed and screamed with joy. Boats made of lashed timbers cut from Nevermourn's jungles crashed into the rocks, orks leaping from their prows – many of the vessels had sunk on the journey and left countless greenskins sinking to the sea floor, but three-quarters of the horde had made it and that was more than enough.

The warlord pointed his huge mechanical claw at the treatment works. It was the anchor of the line, the point where any breakthrough would end the defence of Herograve before it had begun. The orks barely needed the warlord's prompting and they surged past him, clambering over their own fallen, kicking wounded slaves out of the way.

Stray shots from the defenders fell among them, felling a few, and then the humans realised the

green tide was powering towards them and concentrated fire thudded into the orks. Autogun shots
blasted wet red holes in orkish chests and a few
long-las shots from snipers picked off the larger
leaders of the horde, tribal chieftains and greenskins
who had won renown in the thick of battle. But the
horde didn't need leaders now – it just needed a target, and soon the rampart of the dead was high
enough for the first orks to make it to the first vent
openings of the plant. They threw bundles of explo-
sives into the treatment plant – most died as the
ensuing explosions ripped chunks out of the grime-
streaked walls but each one had hundreds behind
him, fighting among themselves for the honour of
being the first into the enemy's den.

Deep within the warlord something new burned.
For as long as his orkish mind could remember he
had known nothing but hate, and an awful, gnaw-
ing lust to bring destruction to his enemies and win
vengeance for the orks. But now, there was more, a
bright flame that banished a corner of the darkness
inside him. Hope. Joy. Pride. At last, at long, long
last, victory was his.

A roar of engines overhead wrenched his attention
away. He looked up to see a host of gunships,
painted in red and gold, swooping down low over
the battlefield. Imperial aquilas shone brightly on
their prows.

'FALL BACK AND blow the stairways!' ordered Lord
Sovelin. 'Blow everything! Hold them back!' He was
on an upper floor that covered half the floorspace of

the treatment plant, suspended above the enormous treatment tanks that dominated the lower floor. The treatment plant was old and ill-maintained, stained rockcrete walls enclosing a vast floor dominated by treatment vats.

From Sovelin's position he could see the warren of walkways between the vats, held by the household troopers in their emerald greatcoats and peaked caps embroidered with the serpent symbol of House Falken. Many of the troops were holding the windows, pouring autogun fire out at the greenskins clamouring outside the treatment plant. Runners scurried around the plant trying to bring more ammunition to the men at the windows, others dragging the wounded back towards Sovelin's end of the plant where a triage station had sprung up with hollow-eyed medics trying to stem the bleeding. Men were dying there, men were blinded and paralysed. Sovelin's own command post on the mezzanine overlooking the plant was a few sandbags and a field vox.

The sound was the worst. Seeing men mutilated and dying was bad enough, but somehow the chanting of the greenskins chilled even more. Tens of thousands of orkish voices raised as one, a brutal chorus of hatred as deep as an earthquake. It shuddered through the treatment plant as if its walls were parchment-thin.

'Fall back, damn it!' ordered Sovelin over the field vox. 'They'll breach the walls! Get off the ground floor and blow the stairs, keep them penned in!'

The household troops began to abandon the windows and head towards the stairways leading to the gantries and command cradles that spanned the treatment plant. Had the order been given a minute earlier, a lot of them would have made it.

A series of explosions erupted and threw the far end of the treatment plant into a boiling mass of flame and dust. Treatment tanks ruptured and spewed hissing industrial waste, which flashed into white cauls of toxic steam. The building shook and Sovelin fell – he saw one trooper going over the edge of the platform and another tumbling from the gantries above. The sound was appalling.

The far wall collapsed. Even with his ears ringing, Sovelin could hear the chanting of the greenskins as they surged forward, as inevitable as the tides of the sea they had crossed. They roared with a savage joy as they poured into the plant. Hundreds of them. Thousands.

Sovelin just stared for a moment as the torrent of greenskin bodies forcing their way between the treatment tanks. Within a handful of seconds they were at the stairways. Some household troops brought fire to bear on them and they fell, but more followed, clambering over the dead and wounded. A man died under ork gunfire just a few paces from Sovelin, and another under the blows of a crude cleaver on the stairway in front of him.

Sovelin thought frantically. How many of the greenskins could the household troops kill here? How long could they hold the treatment plant, and buy extra vital minutes for the rest of the line? Not many, and not long. It wasn't worth the sacrifice of the household troops.

'Fall back!' yelled Sovelin. 'Blow the charges and fall back! All units retreat!' The trooper next to him relayed the order over the field vox but he needn't have bothered. The tide of greenskins pouring into the plant was such that any man with any sense was already running. A few had formed squads of two or three covering one another's retreat, but most has simply turned tail as ork gunfire raked through the building.

Sovelin vaulted over the sandbags, autogun on hand. In front of him rose a dark green shape, stinking of sweat and blood. He tried to bring the gun up but a massive force thudded into him and he was on the floor, feet and fists pummelling him. All around were the wordless jeers and whooping of the orks, the thud of gunfire and screams of men dragged down and killed.

All was noise and darkness. Sovelin was carried off his feet, snatches of the chaotic battlefield flitting by him as he was dragged along on the green tide. He had fleeting impressions of smoke and screaming, ork battle-howls, explosions, gunfire and defiant war-cries from the militiamen holding the rest of the line.

He was outside. The greenskins had realised he was an officer of some kind and they were carrying him aloft like a banner, clawed hands tearing at him as he was hauled along on a sea of charging orks, the open salt-tinged air tainted by the stink of greenskin sweat.

The shore whirled around him. Gnarled, clawed green hands were pulling him apart. Pain was everywhere. Sovelin looked up to the sky, the only thought in his mind now a wordless prayer to the God-Emperor to make the end quick.

Dashes of darkness moved across the clouded sky. Imperial gunships, Thunderhawks, in the colours of the Howling Griffons. The faintest spark of hope glimmered through the pain.

Then Lord Sovelin Falken was dragged down into the darkness beneath dozens of greenskin bodies. A blade fell and his arm came off at the shoulder, shocking ice-cold pain hammering through him. His ribs collapsed beneath a hobnailed boot. His skull fractured.

Pain drowned out the hope as Lord Sovelin Falken died.

THE WARLORD SAW the treatment plant fall, and the tremendous cry that went up from the orks around him should have filled his heart with triumph as hot and powerful and the fires stoked in his mechanical body. Thousands of greenskins raised their guns to the sky, celebratory fire erupting like fireworks all among the greenskin horde smothering the shoreline.

But the warlord had seen the gunships swooping in. They dived now, looping down for a long pass over the orks, and fire stuttered down from guns mounted on their prows and swinging on mounts from their doors. Explosive rounds stitched long curving lines of bursting blood through the masses of orks. Many of the orks turned their eyes to the sky as those around them fell, blasted open like wet red flowers spraying gore.

The warlord bellowed. He recognised the design of these gunships, blocky and powerful, gunfire streaming off them. In this moment of greatest triumph, the culmination of the crusade he had founded long ago in the Garon Nebula, his nemesis had come to face him. For any other species, the warlord would have been filled with despair, to see his victory jeopardised by the human elites of the kind who had wounded the horde so deeply at the Wraithspire Palace. But an ork did not think like that. For an ork, fighting was an end in itself, and even the driven warlord recognised the best kind of enemy when he saw it.

The armoured elites would make this victory complete, when they lay battered and bloody on the rocks, at the mercy of orkish blades. He could not hoped for a finer enemy to crown this greatest of victories. Steam sprayed from the joints of his mechanical torso and arm as the fires within him raged higher.

The gunships dived low again, coming in for another pass. But they were not just strafing the greenskins now. Doors swung open revealed armoured bodies crammed inside, in a spectacular livery of quartered red and gold. Like orks, they were not cowards. They wanted their enemies to see them. Hatred and respect in equal measure mixed in the warlord's mind, an emotion peculiar to greenskins that meant only they understood war in its purest, joyous form.

The humans jumped. They leapt from their gunships right into the centre of the ork horde, bolters firing even as they fell, chainswords raised to spear down like lightning bolts. Where they landed, a shockwave ran through the greenskins as if a bomb had hit. Orks were caught unawares and shot through the head or spitted on screeching chain-blades, or simply crushed by the weight of the armoured humans crashing down on top of them. The gunships kept firing, spraying fire through the orks who tried to surge towards the human attackers.

Dozens of greenskins died in a few moments. Dozens more followed as the humans found their feet and laid into the orks around them with bolters and blades.

More humans were dropping now, reinforcing the foothold their fellow elites had won. One of them was a leader in highly ornate armour and carrying a glowing sword, a jump pack on his back slowing his descent so he could chatter fire into the orks from his bolt pistol.

There were hundreds of the humans, landing directly in the heart of the army. The whole horde was reeling, orks being trampled underfoot as the horde tried to turn to face this new threat.

The warlord grabbed the nearest ork and threw him out off the way. He stamped towards the battle, his eyes on the human leader as he dropped into the midst of the carnage. No one would stop his horde, not here on enemy ground and now when victory was literally within sight. The human leader was his. All the humans were his to kill, his to rend apart and display as trophies.

Another gunship screeched low overhead, close enough for the downwash of its powerful engines to batter around the warlord like a burning gale. The warlord forged onwards towards the armoured human, crushing fellow orks underfoot in his determination to kill.

War-whoops and screamed prayers filtered down through the din of the gunship's engines. Dark shapes were falling around the warlord. Human shapes, unarmoured this time, unshaven and ragged. The same soldiers who had fought at the Wraithspire Palace – no, not the same, the very toughest of them, the hardest-bitten killers.

The warlord struck all about him. A filthy human who came at him with a bayonet was sliced in two by the warlord's claw. He grabbed another by the head with his normal hand, and crushed the human's skull. He flung the body so hard it smacked another human to the ground. These were no elites – they were ordinary humans, elevated to something more by sheer determination.

The humans were all over him, eager to die, trying to pull him down. The warlord was huge, but the gunship had disgorged many humans right on top of him. The warlord threw them aside, cut them in two, stamped on them and pressed forwards. But they were slowing him down. There were too many to kill all at once. They clung on like biting insects, snapping their bayonet blades off in his gnarled skin and spraying glittering fans of crimson las-fire into him. It wouldn't kill him, it barely even hurt, but he was swamped in fragile human bodies as if these ragged vermin were competing to die first.

The warlord stumbled. A human, big for his kind with a shaven head and an almost orkishly bestial face, rammed a combat knife deep between the warlord's ribs. The warlord wrestled him to the ground, punching. The human rolled to the side and kicked out with a heel so hard he broke a bone in the warlord's face. The warlord screamed. More humans were piling on, jumping on his back as if they were hunters bringing down a great kill.

In front of him the warlord could see the armoured humans. They were fighting atop a heap of dead greenskins. Their leader's armour was dark with orkish blood. The leader saw the warlord and directed the fire of his fellow elites. In a storm of bolter fire the orks between the leader and the warlord were shredded.

The warlord tried to force his way back to his feet to face the human leader. The big human beneath him was still alive, refusing to give in and die. With a roar the warlord picked up the human with his claw and threw him, but he was still on his knees, human hands trying to pull him down.

The human leader activated the jump pack on his back. The twin jets roared with flame but the human did not fly up into the air – he hurtled straight forwards, towards the warlord, glowing sword held out in front of him like the tip of a lance.

The warlord tried to bring his claw down to snatch the armoured human out of the air, but the humans on his back slowed him down a half-second too long. The armoured human crashed into the warlord, the tip of his sword punching through the warlord's metallic torso and slicing through the machinery that churned in his chest. The raging forge that served as his heart was punctured, raw flame spurting from the wound. The sword passed right through him and out through the gnarled flesh of his back.

The warlord reared up, finally throwing the humans off his back. The sword was still stuck through him. The armoured human let go, stepping back in the face of the white fire spurting from the warlord's sundered body. The warlord was bellowing, howling his anger, and it seemed the horde around him shrunk back in shock at seeing their leader wounded.

The armoured human yelled something and scrambled across the blood-slick rocks away from the warlord. The few surviving humans were trying to do the same, fighting to get through the orks still battling around the warlord. The pressure inside the warlord was growing, the unbearable searing heat building up to a crescendo.

The armoured human dived away from the warlord. The warlord stumbled forwards, determined to get to the human and avenge himself. But he was a few moments too late. His armoured torso finally gave way and the fires of the furnace inside him broke free.

In a great searing ball of white flame, the warlord exploded.

* * *

THE BRIDGE WAS kept dark, as Eumenes preferred it. On the seating around the edge of the spherical room were assembled the whole remaining Soul Drinkers Chapter. At first glance the gathering looked much the same as the one some time before when Sarpedon had stood before them and explained the Chapter's new destination, but on closer inspection the differences were profound. For one, there were far fewer Soul Drinkers now, as a result of the losses against the orks, in the second Chapter War, and in the stand against the Howling Griffons. Perhaps three hundred remained. There was also an undercurrent, unspoken but powerful, which ran through the assembled Space Marines. Half of them had sided with Eumenes, and the other half had stayed with Sarpedon. There was nothing that could be done to disguise the hatred that boiled just beneath the surface. The battle-brothers seated side by side would kill one another if they had the chance.

The most profound difference was that it was not Sarpedon who addressed the assembled Chapter. It was Eumenes.

'My brothers,' began Eumenes. His armour was now ornate, with chalice symbols on his chestplate and shoulder pad plated in gold, and he carried Lord Mercaeno's axe as a trophy. 'We have gone through the worst of our battles. What we have survived these last few days is the equal of anything the galaxy can throw at us. But we have prevailed. The Soul Drinkers have shed the final shackles that bound them to the past and now I can lead us all on a new path. This is not a path that I have plucked out of nowhere. It began with the death of Gorgoleon and continued with the harvest of new recruits. Finally I can show you that path.'

Young but brilliant, dynamic and convincing, it was easy to see how Eumenes had turned fully half the Chapter to his side before the second Chapter War had begun. Every eye, from the impassive sockets of Chaplain Iktinos's skull-helm to the haunted eyes of Apothecary Pallas, was fixed on Eumenes.

'The Imperium,' said Eumenes, 'is corrupt. It is an evil creation, a breeding ground for everything we hate. And it will be destroyed. It is the Soul Drinkers who will bring it down. We are free from its influences, we are strong and determined, and we have come through such tribulations that the Imperium itself holds no fear for us.

'For too long we have treated the people of the Imperium as if they were victims like us, as if we had some obligation to save them. Now we understand that those same people are the enemy. At best they are weapons, unthinking tools of the Imperium's rulers. At worst they are so utterly corrupt that death for them will be a blessing. Those of you who have sworn to destroy Chaos have also sworn to destroy the Imperium, for it is among the ignorant masses of the Imperium that the seeds of Chaos are sown. We shall burn it all, my battle-brothers. The liars and the butchers, the ignorant and the corrupt, we shall burn them all…'

Eumenes's voice trailed off as he caught movement at the edge of the auditorium. Eyes followed his own to see Sergeant Tydeus stumble onto the upper row of seating. His face was streaked with blood, one eye a red ruin, and panting as if every breath could be his last. With one arm he was supporting Scout Nisryus, the young psychic who had started out as part of Eumenes's scout squad.

'Tydeus!' barked Eumenes. 'What is the meaning of this? You are supposed to be standing guard!'

Tydeus's remaining eye was wide with fear. Fear, in a Space Marine. Tydeus had been taught, like all the Soul Drinkers, to control his fear, to strangle it as it formed in his mind and crush it with duty and discipline. But in Tydeus it had surged to the surface.

'He's... he killed Scamander...'

Eumenes's eyes narrowed. 'You let him loose?'

'He used the Hell...' Tydeus let Nisryus slither to the floor, unconscious. Nisryus's young, pale face was covered in blood.

'You idiot!' yelled Eumenes. 'You broken-minded fools! He is just one man! Can I not trust my battle-brothers to keep a single unarmed man in a cell?' He turned to Sergeant Hecular, who was in the front row of the assembled Soul Drinkers. 'Hecular, get your squad together. Take everyone you need. Hunt him down, leave him no...'

It was pure instinct that cut off Eumenes's words. Slowly, he looked upwards, to the ceiling of the bridge.

Sarpedon clung to the curved ceiling, surrounded by the captured banners and war-trophies, spidery legs splayed out above him. His humanoid upper half hung down and he was watching the proceedings with the faintest amusement in his face.

'You,' said Eumenes, coldly furious. 'You are under arrest. And now you have killed my battle-brothers to escape, your sentence is death!'

Sarpedon dropped with impossible grace, landing on his talons in front of Eumenes.

'I sentenced you to death,' said Sarpedon, 'some time ago.'

'No,' said Eumenes, brandishing Mercaeno's force axe. 'You relinquished command of this Chapter to me and submitted yourself to my authority. That was the deal, Sarpedon. You gave your word! Damn it, Sarpedon, you promised!'

The auditorium was silent now apart from Eumenes's voice, the tension wound up even tighter. Every Soul Drinker there knew how this would end. But none of them could intervene, because they also knew that if this conflict spread to the watching battle-brothers then an all-out battle would break out and would not stop until one side was entirely wiped out. The Soul Drinkers would annihilate themselves. So they just watched intently.

'You betrayed us,' said Sarpedon. 'You had Karraidin killed in front of my eyes. You betrayed every duty you ever had to this Chapter. You betrayed your very Emperor.' He pointed a gauntleted finger at Eumenes. 'You promised first.'

'No! We had a deal! Where is your honour, Sarpedon?'

'When a Soul Drinker speaks of honour, he speaks of the whole Chapter's honour. You say this is your Chapter now, Eumenes, so why do your brothers not gun me down where I stand? If they believe the

Soul Drinkers can be traded to you like chattels, why am I still alive?'

Eumenes looked around him. The Soul Drinkers were on their feet now, watching. The tension that had boiled beneath earlier was closer to the surface now, hands on the hilts of combat knives or the grips of bolt pistols. But no one moved.

'If you continue like this, Eumenes, this Chapter will tear itself apart. You know that. You cannot mould Space Marines to your will. You can only lead them as best you can, and pray that they find in you a man worth following. That is what I have learned as your Chapter Master. End this now, and the Chapter War will be over.'

'If you will not obey me,' said Eumenes levelly, 'if my brothers still need a display of my will, then we will settle this the old-fashioned way.'

Eumenes glanced at Hecular, who promptly threw a small dark cylinder towards him. Eumenes caught it deftly in his off-hand and the twin vortex blades of the Soulspear slid out from the haft. With Mercaeno's axe in one hand and the Soulspear in the other, Eumenes squared up to Sarpedon.

'Last chance, Eumenes,' said Sarpedon. 'Every Soul Drinker here knows you will lead us to destroy ourselves. That is why they have let me stand here and challenge you. You lost the soul of this Chapter the moment you began the Chapter War. Do not die for nothing more than pride.'

Eumenes did not reply. Instead he lunged forward, bringing Mercaeno's axe and the Soulspear down in a twin arc to cut Sarpedon apart.

The duel lasted a handful of seconds. The superior reactions and battlefield conditioning of the assembled Soul Drinkers meant they could pick out every movement, every nuance. Fast as it was, it seemed to go on forever.

Sarpedon dropped onto his back legs as Eumenes powered towards him. The twin blades arced past him, close enough for the Soulspear's blade of harnessed vortex to score a furrow down his breastplate. He could feel the whispers of the warp as the weapon passed by him, for the Soulspear's blades were gateways to the warp, caged wounds in realspace. The axe swung in a wide, loping crescent towards Sarpedon's face and it passed just under his chin, whistling as it went.

Eumenes barrelled forward, his full weight bearing down on Sarpedon. But he was off-balance now. Sarpedon shifted his weight, his rear legs forcing him forward to meet Eumenes in a way that only his mutations would allow. The two Space Marines collided.

Sarpedon's front legs were up like the horns of a charging animal. The talons punched into Eumenes's abdomen, the blade of Sarpedon's one bionic leg penetrating Eumenes's armour alongside the chitin and bone of his natural front talon.

Sarpedon pushed himself up by his back legs and lifted Eumenes into the air, his front talons breaking through the back of Eumenes's armour. Eumenes roared in frustration and anger, and Mercaeno's axe fell from his hand as he tried to fight back, wrest himself away from Sarpedon and start the duel anew.

Sarpedon angled his front legs downwards and Eumenes slid off them, clutching at Sarpedon as he fell. Eumenes hit the floor hard, and there was nothing but hatred written across his features. He tried to bring the Soulspear up to defend himself, but gravity and Sarpedon's reactions were faster.

Sarpedon crashed down on Eumenes, his front four legs arrowing downwards with all the force he could muster. Four talons tore through Eumenes's chest, pinning him to the floor, slicing through lungs and hearts, through Eumenes's spine and into the floor of the bridge.

Sarpedon's full weight settled on Eumenes, the talons sinking deep into his chest. Eumenes tried to speak but he could only splutter blood from his lips. One arm flailed upwards, trying to slash with the Soulspear, but Sarpedon grabbed Eumenes's wrist and wrenched his hand back, forcing Eumenes to drop the weapon. The spear's black blades retracted into the haft as it clattered to the floor.

Sarpedon leaned backwards and pulled his talons out of Eumenes's chest. Crimson fountains of blood followed them, Eumenes gasping out his last breaths as the life flowed out of him. The twisted bionic came out last, and by the time Eumenes flopped back to the ground, he was dead.

Sarpedon stood over Eumenes's body. Every one of his battle-brothers, those who had followed him and those who had chosen Eumenes, watched him in silence.

'I have brought us here,' said Sarpedon. 'I chose Eumenes for this Chapter and granted him the armour of a full battle-brother. I failed to see what he was planning and I failed to stop the Chapter War from breaking out. In all these things I have failed you, my brothers. If you will accept my command then I will be your Chapter Master again, not as a spoil won from Eumenes but as a burden of duty as heavy as any I might place on you. If you can no longer trust me to lead you, then I will step down and hand the position of Chapter Master to whoever believes they can lead the Soul Drinkers. No deals, no conflicts, just step forward.'

The bridge was silent. Sarpedon cast his eyes in particular over those who might believe they had earned the right to command the Chapter – Chaplain Iktinos, Luko, Sergeant Hecular – but none of them moved. Sarpedon gave them a long, tense moment to stand up and make their claim. But none of them did.

'Then if you do not accept me as your Chapter Master,' said Sarpedon at last, 'You may leave the *Brokenback*. Take a shuttle and go. There are worlds within a shuttle flight and we will not stop you. The Chapter War has claimed enough of us already. Captain Luko, take the Soulspear and lock it back up in the armoury. And Chaplain?' Sarpedon indicated the body at his feet. 'Bury my battle-brother.'

FROM THE SPIRE the whole of the city was laid out. In the daylight, filtered through the polluted sky, it seemed calmer than at night because the flames were less vivid and the blackouts less obvious. It was an illusion. The city still groaned, its billions of people locked in fear.

On the roof of the spire the wind was cold and it whipped the banners that hung around the spire-top, each one bearing a variation on the serpent heraldry of House Falken. The wind brought the taste of smoke with it, from burning buildings and autoguns.

Anchored to the top of the spire was the count-ess's yacht, its sleek form perching on the edge of the spire as docking-servitors attached fuel hoses to it and changed the air filters. The countess walked slowly down the yacht's embarkation ramp, her children in tow. In the cold wind she felt every one of her many, many years, as if the wind was blowing through her right to her very bones.

The countess looked down at the city. It stretched as far as she could see, merging with the horizon in a smog-choked band of grey. This was her city, and she felt a tinge of the real sorrow implied by her mourning-wear. The people down there were so frightened. They no could no longer rely on House Falken to keep them safe. They did not know when or how the end would come. Countess Ismenissa allowed herself a moment of weakness to feel sorry for them all. Many of them had lost people they loved. The countess had lost her family, who repre-sented the order and tradition that she loved. She had something in common with her people, a rare thing indeed.

The countess's chamberlain emerged from the doorway leading into the spire. The spire itself was a sky-scraping creation of columns and archways, home to one of the city's administrative departments. It was evacuated now because of the possibility of rioting in the streets where it was rooted into the hive, and the countess intended only to stop there as briefly as possible.

'There is news,' said the chamberlain, struggling to make himself heard above the whistling wind. 'From the front.'

'What news?' For the shore of Herograve to be called a 'front' at all suggested that the greenskins had not simply blown past the defences there, as the countess had expected.

'The Howling Griffons have returned to the fray,' said the chamberlain. 'It is said that they have abandoned the pursuit of the Black Chalice.'

'The Howling Griffons?' In spite of herself, the countess felt hope. 'How do we know this?'

'A Captain Darion was in communication with the hive authorities, but only briefly, and he has now returned to battle. Do you know of him?'

'Yes. He was subordinate to Lord Mercaeno.'

'It seems that Lord Mercaeno has fallen, my lady.'

The countess looked at the pitted metal floor of the spiretop. 'Then a great hero of the Imperium has been lost. The Emperor shall weep a tear for him. What of the greenskins?'

'The Howling Griffons fell upon them in force. The ork leader was killed. Orks are a fractious species, much given to conflict among themselves, according to the librarium records. Captain Darion reports that with their leader dead the greenskin force will lose direction. It has yet to break out significantly from the beachhead on the shore. The

Howling Griffons are organising the defence. They
have with them the troopers of the 901st Penal
Legion, though few of them remain. I have taken
the liberty of authorising the reinforcement of the
defenders there from all hives. Subject to your
approval, of course.'

The countess waved a hand. 'Of course. You have
it.' She looked the chamberlain in the eye. 'Can we
win?'

'Perhaps, my lady.'

The countess sighed. For an instant years of warfare
flashed through her mind, the struggle to rebuild
House Falken and the terrible wound it would leave
on the history of Vanqualis. Even with the Howling
Griffons, even victorious, Vanqualis would suffer. But
suffering was the nature of the galaxy. The countess
had to be strong. She was all her people had.

'Is there any news of Sovelin?' she asked at length.

'His part of the line fell. It is likely that he is dead.'

'I see. And the Black Chalice?'

'Captain Darion was not entirely forthcoming on
the matter. It seems that the Bearers of the Black
Chalice were never here and that we were somehow
mistakenly alerted to their presence. It seems that
there has been a great deal of confusion following
the invasion.'

The countess shook her head sadly. 'Poor young
Sovelin. I feared for him when he was young. He
didn't seem Falken material.'

'With Lord Sovelin dead, my lady, it would seem
that if any mistake was made regarding the presence
of the Black Chalice, it would not...'

'Do you suggest I use Sovelin as a scapegoat for this mistake?' asked the countess.

'Far be it from my station to suggest such a thing,' said the chamberlain, unruffled. 'But given the evident confusion, it behoves us all to ensure that the people and the Lay Parliament are given answers that will satisfy them, until the whole truth can be uncovered.'

The countess looked carefully at her chamberlain. Small, unassuming, his eyes screwed up against the cold wind, he did not seem like much and yet he had served her for a long time and offered her counsel through many crises. With the loss of so many of her peers at Palatium, it was perhaps best that she have someone so shrewd and dedicated to help her in her duties. 'I shall leave such things to you to deal with, chamberlain,' she said. 'I must concern myself with leadership. A new phase of this war is opening up on Herograve and the Vanqualians fighting there will need a figurehead to rally behind. It seems I am the only suitable candidate left.'

'Very well, my lady,' said the chamberlain with a humble nod.

'This war will be a long one. The greenskins might never leave. I only hope I am up to the task.'

'I have faith, my lady.'

'As must we all.' The countess turned to re-enter the yacht and leave the spiretop. 'I shall go to the coast. Even if we throw the orks back into the sea it will be years before we can cleanse the jungles of them, if ever. Perhaps I will not see the end of it, but do what I must for my planet. See to my cities while I am gone, chamberlain. Heal the wounds the orks have already dealt us, now there is hope on Herograve as well as fear.'

'It shall be done, my lady,' said the chamberlain as the countess walked up the ramp back into her yacht.

Years. Decades. The countess knew she would be a fool to think the greenskins were beaten. But if this Captain Darion was fit to take over from Lord Mercaeno, and if the people of Herograve took up arms against the greenskins to re-found the Vanqualian Warders, perhaps Vanqualis might be delivered from destruction after all.

She idly stroked the head of one of House Falken's dear children as the ramp closed behind her and the yacht took off, turning elegantly towards the distant coast.

MANY HOURS AFTER Sarpedon had asserted his position as Chapter Master of the Soul Drinkers, Chaplain Iktinos held funeral rites on the arena flight deck. He jettisoned the body of Eumenes, along with the Soul Drinkers who had fallen on the *Brokenback* against the Howling Griffons, into space. As their coffins spiralled away from the *Brokenback*, Iktinos offered a prayer to Rogal Dorn and the Emperor to accept them into the ranks of humanity. In the battle at the end of time, when Mankind finally faced Chaos in the ultimate conflict, the Soul Drinkers would fight side by side with all humanity's honoured dead.

The Chapter was in attendance. Sarpedon said nothing, observing the prayers said for each fallen brother. With the Soulspear locked in the armoury and his force staff broken Sarpedon now carried Mercaeno's axe, and with it saluted the coffins as they were fired off into space. Only those who had chosen to leave the Chapter – mostly scouts, including Hecular's squad – were not there to see Eumenes and the Chapter's other fallen brothers committed to the void.

When the rites were done, Iktinos asked leave to pray for the fallen and meditate on the events of the battle for Vanqualis and the second Chapter War. Sarpedon granted it, and Iktinos left his brothers to their mourning.

Iktinos did not return to his cell, or to the small seminary where he instructed his flock in the spiritual principles by which he guided the Chapter. Instead he headed deep into the *Brokenback*, to the half-flooded sanctum he kept secret from the rest of the Chapter.

THE SANCTUM TO a long-forgotten god had lain undisturbed since Iktinos had been there last. He made his way to the altar and read the printouts from the monitoring equipment there. He noted without emotion the point where the irregular scribbles of lifesigns had become straight lines.

Iktinos hauled the stone sarcophagus from the water. Inside lay the bloated, blackened body of Croivas Vel Scannien. The astropath had served his purpose, and Iktinos ignored his corpse. He turned instead to the piles of books and scrolls he had placed there after returning from the library orbiting Tyrancos, before he had descended to Nevermourn to fight alongside Sarpedon. Dozens of books lay stacked up on the altar, along with scroll cases and even a couple of carved tablets.

The Chaplain picked up one of the books. It had lain interred in the temple for thousands of years, its woven crystal pages loaded with such intensity of meaning that Iktinos hesitated slightly before opening it. The script flowing across the first page told him that it had indeed been touched by the hand of his master. It was almost too much for Iktinos to properly comprehend, the weight of that meaning, reaching out across thousands of years to touch his soul.

In the silence of his sanctum, Iktinos read. He learned more of the path along which he was to lead the Soul Drinkers, and the Chapter's ultimate goal.

Sarpedon did not know, of course. He was incidental to the true history of the Soul Drinkers. The Chapter's rejection of the Imperium had been prophesied a long time ago – Sarpedon was just another actor in the great play of the Soul Drinkers, and his part had been written out at the beginning. Iktinos rejoiced inside that he had been a Chaplain when those blessed events had occurred, and that he had been in a position to play his own role in his master's plan.

He read further. The next stage became clear. Iktinos would have to bring the Soul Drinkers to a place his master had prepared for them long ago. It was not far for a warp-capable craft like the *Broken-back* – deep in the Veiled Region, a slice of the galaxy notoriously difficult to navigate, and hence survive. Astropathic messages within the Veil tended to arrive at their destinations distorted, if at all. Iktinos allowed himself a rare smile. It was perfect. The next stage of the plan would be all the more certain if it were enacted within the Veil.

Iktinos memorised the location, and the first tasks he would need to complete once the Chapter arrived there. Iktinos would have to convince Sarpedon to take the Chapter there, of course, but he had needed little prompting to begin the journey to the Obsidian system. Sarpedon's principles and sense of duty made him predictable enough. Iktinos foresaw little difficulty in manipulating him again. Eumenes had been a complication, of course, but he had been dealt with. There would be no such distractions in the future.

Iktinos put the book down. He had much to do. He had to lead his followers in their prayers and counsel the rest of the battle-brothers to heal the rifts that still existed between them. Some, like Apothecary Pallas, would need much guidance before they felt a part of the Chapter again. And, of course, Iktinos would have to work out how to direct Sarpedon towards the Veiled Region.

The will of Iktinos's master would be done, there could be no doubt about that. But first, there was much work to do.

## ABOUT THE AUTHOR

*Ben Counter* is fast becoming one of the Black Library's most popular authors. An Ancient History graduate and avid miniature painter, he lives near Portsmouth, England.